THE GAME OF PAWNS

Predators of Darkness Series: Book Three

LEONARD D. HILLEY II

DeimosWeb Publishing

✿ Created with Vellum

For my wife, Christal, who reignited my desire to write. Without her this book would not have been written. And you? You would not be reading this.

Chapter 1

New Jersey: Winter 2076
   Mech Cybernetics Laboratories

MIKE GUNTER LOCKED GenTech's genetically altered tissue cultures inside a refrigerated chamber. Nervously, he shoved his hands into his lab coat pockets and sighed. His tired eyes glanced at the wall clock.

5:55 P.M.

With a swift swipe of his hand, he crudely combed back his brown hair before glancing around the room. The other scientists paid him no attention. They busied themselves by wrapping up their projects for the night. He was thankful for the weekend ahead.

Mike wanted nothing else than to drink a few beers and forget about the stale laboratory atmosphere. Watching football playoffs on ESPN allowed his mind drift to something other than the strange scientific experiments in their laboratory. He didn't want to concentrate on his current work assignment. The mutated cells growing in the culture dishes troubled him, and the less he was around them, the better. More disturbing was what GenTech's new owner—Mech Cybernetics—planned to do with them.

The cell cultures, however, were the least of his problems. Had he known that this was the last day he'd be alive, he might have opted to work a bit later or take a longer route home. Because tonight, two armed men waited in his apartment with orders to kill him.

By 7:09 p.m., Mike Gunter would be dead.

DOWNTOWN NEWARK, New Jersey
5:57 p.m.

LUCIAN DROVE along a quiet street with the car windows down. He welcomed the cold winter air that flowed around him. With his unique metabolism, his body radiated constant heat. While the outside chill made others shudder and wear heavier coats, he welcomed the icy weather. It soothed him, kept his thoughts sharper, and prevented him from burning excessive calories.

The radio station DJ warned people to be wary of staying outdoors past midnight. During the past week, more than a half dozen unexplained murders had occurred. These murders were connected, but no suspect had been named. A serial killer prowled the night like a silent shadow tethered to Death's robe.

Puzzled city police worried they'd never find the guilty party that mysteriously eluded them. An implemented curfew made the possibility of finding the criminal easier, but the ordinance had not come up for a vote by the city council. The majority of Newark residents disputed the idea.

Lucian's cell phone rang, so he turned down the radio.

He answered the call while parked at a red light.

"You have a lead?" he asked.

"No," Kat replied. "Kyle still believes the next victim will be in New Jersey."

"Why is he so certain?"

"Fits the protocol. The last three Red Pawn murders occurred here. All were scientists from GenTech, before their rival, Mech Cybernetics bought out the company."

Lucian sighed and turned left at the intersection. "Have you located Mech Cybernetics' address?"

"No. We believe they've hidden their operation inside a fake business front. Kyle has managed to trace an email from one of the dead scientists to a newly renovated hospital."

"A hospital?"

"It's not one anymore. We're not certain *what* they're manufacturing. It's possible they're working on far more dangerous experiments than the shifters and genetic soldiers Idris had created."

Lucian laughed. "Worse than me?"

"Nothing's *that* bad," she said.

"Damn, I was hoping for some excitement tonight. It's been six months since Lucas destroyed TransGenCorp. We've had nothing but dead leads ever since. I want to help you find the people responsible for Tyler's death."

Kat remained silent for a moment. "I want them stopped, too. We have to find their location first."

"Idris kept GenTech's location secret because he knew TransGenCorp was targeted to be shut down by the government. That's why Brockton and I were never allowed to visit their headquarters. Idris always demanded GenTech's scientists to come to us. Apparently, the only tie the scientists had to GenTech was their work I.D. badges. Even the media can't find a physical address."

"So, somewhere in all the files Lucas destroyed at TransGenCorp was GenTech's location?"

"Probably, but New Jersey is the last place I'd think to look."

"Major industries have always flocked to New Jersey," Kat said. "No difference for biotech companies to do the same."

"Maybe so, but with TGC staying in the media's scrutiny for years, you'd think anyone following similar genetic manufacturing would seek a smaller, less populated area."

"True. You're in the area where the last three murders occurred. Let's see what further information Kyle traces, if he doesn't get caught. He's tapping into the FBI's database. Carpenter is probably in New Jersey."

"So? He won't recognize me."

"No, but he'll be looking for anyone suspicious."

Lucian smiled. He watched the sidewalks for activity. No pedestrians. "He'd suspect me?"

"He suspects anyone that seems out of place. Since you're looking for the next possible victim and not familiar with New Jersey, he'll sense you don't belong there."

"I'll keep as low a profile as I can." He drove slowly, watching the empty street ahead of him. No headlights appeared in his rearview mirror, either. "The streets are strangely dead tonight."

"People are frightened."

Lucas shrugged. With the empty street and sidewalks, he was the only one outdoors, which made him easily seen by police and the serial killer. "Yes, let's hope it makes finding the murderer easier."

"It makes you a quicker suspect should the FBI or city police see you."

"I know," he replied.

"Hopefully, we find GenTech soon, shut it down, and get you out of New Jersey before Carpenter discovers you."

"Keep me posted. I'm watching for any unusual activity. So far I've not seen anything."

"We're working on it."

KAT DISCONNECTED the call and sighed. She placed her hand upon Kyle's shoulder. Kyle didn't seem to notice her touch. His mind was distant, and his eyes were hypnotically focused Newark's street grid map on the computer screen. From time to time, seated in his wheelchair, he uttered short muddled sentences.

She glanced at Brockton. He sat at the small circular table, reading a scientific journal on his laptop.

"I'll make some coffee," she said. "It's going to be a long night."

He nodded, never glancing up from his reading.

Chapter 2

5:59 p.m.

Violet, a slender brunette, walked toward Mike's workstation. Her soft, silk-like hair was tied in a ponytail. The lab coat she wore didn't diminish her beauty or her fit figure. Her eyes were her most flattering feature. They seemed to sparkle whenever she smiled, which was often.

Even if Mech Cybergenics permitted Mike the opportunity to spend time talking to her, he'd never brave the words. One look into her eyes, and his world vanished. He was lost. Her radiant eyes possessed a depth of mystery that overpowered him. Although he was handsome, he viewed her as someone out of his league.

Other eyes studied all of their activities and interactions.

Overhead surveillance cameras watched their activities. In recent days, security within Mech Cybergenics had heightened. Strange things had happened. Other scientists had been killed and four of these had transferred with Gunter from GenTech. They all had worked on the experimental cell cultures that he continued researching.

New orders from his former GenTech supervisors restricted interaction between coworkers. Each scientist received their mandated work orders through their computers and answered only to an assigned supervisor via email transmission. Even though this lack of privacy seemed severe, Mike didn't mind. He hadn't been at Mech Cybernetics long enough to make friends with his new coworkers. They had as little interest in him as he did them.

Violet passed his workstation and flashed a bold friendly smile. Flustered, his face reddened and his throat tightened. He pretended to look at the data sheets on his desk. He didn't want to appear rude, but with the cameras trained on them, he wished to avoid the company's repercussions if they detected he had returned the slightest hint of a smile. From the corner of his eye, he watched her pass his station to clock out.

An armed elevator guard instructed Violet to scan her thumb on a computerized clipboard. Mike waited until the elevator doors closed before leaving his station. If he followed too closely, the guard and surveillance supervisors might suspect the two of them were divulging information to one another. Suspicions could terminate his job or worse—end his life. He didn't dare risk the possibility, so he kept a safe distance between their departures.

When he placed his thumb on the identification scanner, his nervous face reflected on the guard's mirror-tinted helmet. The imposing guards intimidated him. However, not knowing what the person behind the visor looked like or his facial expression frightened Mike even more, which was what he figured the company intended all along. There was less risk of insubordination, if the workers never viewed the guards in a personable light.

Once the computer cleared Mike for the evening, the elevator doors opened and he stepped inside, alone. He released a deep sigh of relief after the doors hissed shut. For some unexplained reason, his heart hammered inside his chest. He held no guilt to feel fear, but his unwarranted anxiety intensified.

Three floors down, the doors opened to the dimly lit parking garage. Before he exited, the security camera caught his attention. Its deadlocked gaze froze him for an instant. Forcing himself forward, he tried to ignore the eeriness that a higher power projected through the electronic device. The camera followed his movement like a dark entity, like a predator studying its prey.

He walked past a newspaper stand. The main headline read: "**12ᵗʰ Red Pawn Murder in Two Weeks: No Suspects Named**."

Wisps of white fog escaped his mouth as he hurried to his white company car. Cold air forced him to tug his lab coat tighter. He pressed his thumb against the car door panel and it unlocked. He climbed in and slammed the door.

Pressing his thumb to the ignition switch, the engine roared to life. For reasons unknown, Mike felt uncomfortable driving to the security post. Sweat beaded his brow. He kept glancing at each mirror, looking for movement among the other cars. Shadows. Anything. But nothing ever presented itself. The gate arm lifted, and he drove into the darkening streets of New Jersey.

6:15 P.M.

Mike's computer screen at his workstation kicked on. The screen glowed to life. An image materialized. A red pawn lay tipped onto its side. The number 13 was etched into the round base and it blazed like smoldering embers breathing a strong wind. Blood oozed from the pawn and formed a thick, crimson pool beneath the chess piece.

6:17 P.M.

"Lucian, we've detected some strange digital activity," Kat said.

"What?"

"Kyle traced a message to a computer in your vicinity. It's an image of a red pawn. The computer is assigned to Mike Gunter."

"Which building?"

"The renovated hospital."

Lucian requested his map link on his dashboard console. After he commanded information for the building's location, a mini map popped up, showing the building and his proximity to it.

"I'm only a few blocks away."

"Don't go there," Kat said. "Mr. Gunter isn't there. He's gone home for the night."

"Where should I go?"

"Hold on. We're pulling up his home address."

Lucian pulled his car to the curb. While he waited for an answer, he checked the clip in his gun and slapped it back into place.

Kat said, "He lives at the Suncastle Highland complex, apartment 212."

"On my way."

KAT MOTIONED Brockton to come to the computer. Kyle remained quiet, almost spellbound. She pointed at the computer screen map when Brockton stood beside her.

"What is it?" Brockton asked.

She shook her head. "Follow me," she said, and led him to the other side of the room.

Brockton frowned.

"I sent Lucian to Suncastle apartments."

"So? Isn't that where Kyle directed?"

Kat nodded. "Yes, but he hasn't typed anything new into the computer. He keeps staring at the city map. Nothing else. I hadn't noticed that the screen was the same until after I told Lucian where to go."

Brockton looked over her shoulder at Kyle.

"You not find that odd?" she asked.

"It's different, I agree."

Kat placed her hands on her hips. "How do we *know* he's correct?"

"Give it a few minutes."

"On a hunch?"

"This is difficult to explain, but it's more than a hunch. He *knows* things. Well, perhaps I should say that he senses things. I've noticed it a lot over the past few months. Something in his mind has altered from all the different genetic enhancing drugs I've used to help repair the damage Idris did to him. His new abilities are getting stronger."

Kat muffled a small laugh. "Like a sixth sense?"

Brockton smiled. "Oh no. It's far more than that."

Chapter 3

6:22 p.m.

The streets had never been so empty. Even the homeless hid in any available crevice to stay out of sight. No one walked the sidewalks. No one huddled around burning trashcans to warm themselves. Shadows of the night darkened the already dismal buildings and aged pavement. Death and fear taunted the city and the same uneasiness squeezed Mike's chest, too. He chose not to make any unnecessary stops for reasons he didn't understand. He never suffered from paranoia, but after the rest of his GenTech research team had been killed, he felt isolated and marked for death.

Mike drove into the Suncastle Highland parking lot. He found an empty slot at the far end and parked. Getting out of his car, he cursed about the long distance he needed to walk through the frosty air before he reached the front entrance. The night was colder than he expected, or he'd have worn a heavier coat instead of his thin lab coat.

He hurried across the parking lot and placed his hand against the apartment security panel. The glass doors opened. The cheerful front desk attendant was absent.

Mike couldn't shake the menacing sensation that he was being watched. When the doors sealed shut, he immediately noticed the wall camera. Its cold stare sent harsher chills through his body than the night had. He hesitated before proceeding into the lobby. For a moment, he truly believed a dark entity watched him through the lens and plotted to destroy him should he make any unacceptable move.

Mike contemplated whether to use the elevator to the second floor but decided instead to use the stairs. Since the elevator possessed another camera, and as far as he knew, the stairs didn't, he chose to walk up the one flight instead.

The carpeted stairs silenced his steps while he headed up the stairwell. He pushed the second floor door outward, and the quiet hall greeted him with a deceptive kiss. A sense of comfort eased the paranoia that had crept inside him. This place was his home. His sanctuary. He reached into his pocket for the key to his door.

The cracked and peeling green wallpaper beneath the faint glow of sconce lights reminded him of the chaos that tore at his soul with his ongoing GenTech experiments at Mech Cybernetics. The disorder within his residency was the opposite of the pristine lab and why he enjoyed living in the rundown apartment complex.

However, what he perceived to be normal was everything except.

6:26 P.M.

Two gunmen sat in silence on Mike's couch. Their eyes were frozen in a dead stare at the door. Cool patience was their strong suit. The dark apartment shrouded them. Their hearts beat even, ruthlessly cold paces. No second thoughts. No remorse. Orders were obeyed, never questioned.

Both wore black Armani suits and tight, black ski caps that covered their ears and cropped along their eyebrows. Seated within this absence of light, they sat invisible to anyone who entered the room.

One man rubbed a red pawn piece between his thumb and forefinger of his left hand. His right hand rested on his holstered 9mm.

In the hall came the faint approach of footsteps, muffled slightly by thin carpet. Their hands instinctively tightened on their guns. Keys jangled in the hallway, only inches away from the door. Both men stood and commenced firing.

6:26 P.M.

Mike fumbled with the keys in his hand. Near the door, they slipped through his fingers and dropped to the floor. He stooped to pick them up and gunfire ripped through the door and into the plaster wall across the hallway. The faint zip of silent bullets buzzed past him. Chunks of splintered wood burst into the air and rained down. Bullets ripped plugs of plaster from the wall. As the silencer effect eroded from firing too many bullets in succession, the explosive, crescendo of popping sounds rattled the realization that *he* was being shot at. He grabbed the key ring and rolled, but the violent blasts of gunfire didn't lessen. The echoes grew closer, nearer.

6:28 P.M.

The gunmen methodically holstered their weapons. White plaster-dust and splintered door remnants settled. Without emotion, they approached the cratered door. The frame crashed into the hallway when one of the gunmen turned the knob. Expecting to see a dead, bullet-ridden body, they were alarmed to find no victim. Mike Gunter was gone. The stairwell door at the end of the hall tapped shut.

"The stairs, Simon," The taller man said with a nod. He pulled his gun and slammed a fresh clip into the grip. A long, jet-black ponytail hung down his back and stopped a couple inches above his belt. His black pupils swallowed any hint of irises.

Simon didn't hesitate to reload his weapon and run in fast strides toward the stairwell door. His long, wolf-gray hair flowed like waves of thick silk while he ran. His eyes resembled small, obsidian stones.

"Dammit, Trey, how'd he know?" His muscled jaws tightened. He hissed through parted lips that revealed his sharp wolf-like teeth.

Simon thrust a muscled shoulder into the stairwell door. The impact cracked harshly against the wall. He waited for Trey to run past and then followed his brother downstairs.

"Not sure," Trey replied. "We need to stop him before he contacts anyone."

Chapter 4

6:30 p.m.

Mike rammed his keys into his pocket and sprinted down the stairs. His panic consumed him. Too busy looking over his shoulder and not for obstacles in front of him, he hit the wall at the bottom turn of the stairs. The collision knocked him off balance and he stumbled, falling forward. Catching himself on the long, metal door handle, he clung and fought to regain his footing.

The above stairwell door crashed open.

They were pursuing him. His frantic mind searched for a reason why anyone wanted him dead. He had been a resident of New Jersey for less than two weeks. During that two-week period, four of his GenTech associates had been killed without explanation. His premonition that he was next was a nightmare that came true. No one at Mech Cybernetics spoke about the transferred GenTech workers or their deaths. Nor had any evidence ever been disclosed about their deaths. It didn't appear they had violated any company rules. If they had, company officials weren't releasing the information. But what had he done? How had these men gotten inside the building? The apartment complex security wasn't the greatest, but they did have some measures to prevent nonresidents from entering the building.

He pushed his weight against the door handle, pivoted, and spun himself around, running into the lounge. The vacant front desk ended his hope to yell for someone to call the police.

Mike reached over the desk to grab the phone. The attendant lay dead behind the desk. A pool of dark blood soaked into the carpet around the man's head. Fear froze the dead man's facial muscles. His wide eyes held his last moment of surprise before he died. Mike was certain his face mirrored this man's.

He rushed through the front door; grateful that exiting didn't require a palm scan. Outside, on the sidewalk, he paused, uncertain which direction to run, or where to hide, before his adversaries caught him.

The cold night air enveloped him. Running toward his company car, he believed it was his fastest escape. Halfway across the parking lot, a gunshot echoed. The round from a 9mm ricocheted off the pavement ahead of him. He bolted between a van and a pickup truck. Another burst of gunfire popped. Too scared to run farther, too scared to breath, he leaned his back against the van and tried to calm himself. He fished through his lab coat pocket for his cell phone. When his hand wrapped around it, their clicking footsteps approached on the pavement.

Mike took a deep gulp of air, lowered his head, and darted from his hiding place. He sprinted down the side alley of the apartment complex. This decision offered him no refuge and placed his life into direct jeopardy. The narrow alley allowed his enemies a better opportunity to shoot him, but he didn't have another alternative.

He typed 9-1-1 as he ran, but the call never went through. His phone was dead, deader than his lingering hope to stay alive. Someone had disabled his phone service.

He paused in the darkest recess of the alley and crouched beside a dumpster. He dialed again.

Nothing.

The light of his phone died.

Unbelievable.

He had inserted a new battery the day before. He tapped the back of the phone several times, hoping the jarring might reconnect a possible loose connection. Nothing.

"Damn," he sighed, wiping away tears of frustration from his eyes.

Rough scraping shoes stopped across the alley from him. Mike held his breath and winced. He hoped they couldn't see him in the darkness.

The shorter man pointed and raised his 9mm. Mike spun, rolled, and forced himself from crawling to running. A bullet missed him, striking the brick wall above his head. Flakes of metal and mortar showered in a tiny cloud near his face. He closed his eyes and shielded his face behind his elbow and continued running blindly.

He dared a glance back over his shoulder. Were the men this bad a shot? Or was this a game? The broad, hungry smiles on both men's faces gave him his answer. They holstered their guns and sniffed the air. They weren't running, but instead, they were walking at a steady pace. Mike ran faster after witnessing a splash of silver ripple across their eyes. They weren't human. What they were exactly, he didn't know, but the one thing he knew—he was in grave danger. His feet moved quickly, but he feared they'd never move fast enough to escape.

6:35 P.M.

"How far are you from Suncastle apartments?" Kat asked.

"One block," Lucian replied.

"You'd best hurry."

"Why?"

"Police scanner reported gunfire inside the apartment complex and it continued into the parking lot. You have to find Gunter before they kill him. It's the only way to find who's behind GenTech."

Lucian sped through a yellow light and took a sharp left. The tires squealed as he straightened out of the turn. When he came into view of the apartment complex, blue and red lights flashed in the parking lot.

"Dammit," Lucian said. He drove a half block further, killed the lights, and parked at the curb.

Without hesitating, Lucian got out of the car and tucked his gun behind his belt.

"Kat," Lucian said. "I'm outside my car. There are several police cruisers in the parking lot. A black Lincoln just entered behind them. I will try to find Mike Gunter before his assassins do."

"Be careful."

Lucian laughed. "I'm bulletproof, remember?"

"Yeah, but not Carpenter proof. Don't let him see you."

Lucian watched Carpenter get out of the car and head toward the offi-cers. "Well, your assumption's correct. He's here."

"I told you he was in the city."

"I know. I'll call you when I find Gunter."

Lucian disconnected the call and headed into the apartment parking lot. Wherever Mike Gunter was, Lucian needed to find him quickly, and preferably, alive.

Chapter 5

6:39 p.m.

Mike tried to hide in the shadows of parked cars and leafless trees along the next street, but the two men found him, even in the darkest places.

He felt like a rat in a maze, but the goal wasn't finding the cheese. The goal was avoiding the large snake tracking his scent.

Barely able to breathe from fear and running, he pushed himself to move, to run, ducking from vehicle to vehicle, and staying low. Several toying gunshots had come within inches of claiming his life, shattering the side windows of cars that he ran past. More gunfire followed and he kept moving, hoping to stay alive.

These two men didn't even run to keep up with him, but they had no problem finding him. They fed on his fear, like predators feast on the blood of hunted animals. They allowed him time to stop and catch his breath. Once he had regained some stamina, they suddenly appeared and flushed him from hiding by shooting near him. He didn't wonder when it would be over. He understood this game ended with his death.

6:40 P.M.

Mike ran three more blocks and finally stopped at a fenced-in business. Exhausted, he fought to climb over the chain-linked fence and then he dropped hard to the concrete. His cold, numb feet stung from the sharp fall. Loose, scattered bits of gravel slid between his shoes and the concrete. He wobbled and flung his arms over his head to steady himself but fell to one knee.

He stood and limped several paces before ignoring the pain enough to run again. Looking around, he realized that he was inside an auto repair lot. The concrete wall towering behind a line of junked vehicles was too high to climb. A locked chain secured the entrance gate. Once they discovered that he was trapped, they'd kill him. Their demented game ended here.

Mike crept into the cascading shadows created by the splash of security lights above the parked cars and trucks. Even in the darkness, he felt more exposed than hidden. They'd find him. He had nowhere else to run and no one he trusted could help him.

His white lab coat damned him from hiding. The bright reflection beamed off the black pickup door in the gloomy dusk. He peeled the coat from his shoulders, wadded it, and tossed it beneath the truck. He huddled his back against the rear tire and hugged his knees.

The chill of the night air bit his bare arms. His teeth chattered, and he vigorously rubbed his arms to warm them. He regretted wearing a short sleeve shirt under the lab coat. Faced with the possibility of his unexplained murder, other things gnawed at him as well.

He thought about his ex-wife and his eight-year-old son in Dallas. Nothing remedied their broken marriage or her spiteful hatred of him, but he wished he could apologize for his mistakes before he died. He wished he had one last chance to tell his son how proud he was of him and how much he wanted to spend time with him, but the distance between them robbed him of the quality time that he craved.

6:42 P.M.

The fence rattled. Scratching soles scraped against the rough pavement and gravel. Even though Mike's eyes had adjusted to the darkness, he was unable to locate which area of the fence they had crossed. Ignoring the cold, he crawled from the truck tire to the next car and peered over the trunk.

Enough light flooded the yard for him to see two shadows moving toward the garage. Their eyes glowed silver like a wild dog's at dusk. He feared they were somehow blessed with night vision. He also worried that they were something created by his lab through genetic manipulation. With the experiments he administered, he wondered if part of his research contributed to their strange nature.

The men stood outside the ominous garage. Perhaps if they entered the garage, he'd gain enough time to dart to the lower part of the fence and clear it before they shot him in the back. It was worth a try, he reasoned. The longer he waited, the more likely they'd find and kill him.

He lifted his hands from the trunk and the lid wobbled. Closer inspection revealed the trunk wasn't locked but tied down with a twisted piece of galvanized wire. While the men checked the locked garage doors, Mike unwound the wire. When the trunk door rose, he gently guided it upward as silently as possible.

The smell of mildewed, oily carpet permeated the air.

He patted the carpeted bottom until he located a cold piece of metal. He slid the tire tool into his hand and gripped it tightly. Easing back into the shadows, he waited.

6:48 P.M.

Lucian watched the paramedics push the dead desk attendant into the parking lot on a gurney. Concerned apartment residents huddled in small groups outside the apartment complex, which gave Lucian the opportunity to meander through the crowd with less suspicion.

Carpenter talked to one of the paramedics. Lucian eased closer to hear their conversation.

"Did you find a red pawn piece near the body?" Carpenter asked.

The paramedic shook his head. "No, sir."

"The desk attendant is our only body?" Carpenter then asked an officer standing by.

"Best we can tell. There was more shooting on the second floor. A lot of gunfire, but no blood. No one reported hearing a gun near the desk."

Carpenter nodded and weighed the information. "Probably used a silencer on entry."

Lucian worked his way through the crowd. No red pawn. The dead man wasn't Mike Gunter. So *where* was Gunter?

More shooting had occurred in the parking lot. He scanned the lot, hoping to find broken car windows, which might indicate the direction Gunter had fled.

Nothing.

He followed the sidewalk and noticed the dark alley. Without a lot of speculation, he assumed the alley was Gunter's choice for escape. Shadows were intimidating, but when hiding, they offered the best cover. Peering over his shoulder, he watched Carpenter and two police officers head through the front door of the apartment complex. Once Carpenter was out of sight, Lucian disappeared into the alley with his gun in hand.

Through the alley, Lucian sensed the team pursuing Gunter. He didn't fully understand how he felt their presence, but he knew they were near. A few blocks from where he stood.

In part, the injections of shifter DNA he had given himself had heightened some of his sensory awareness. Even these modifications didn't mean he could prevent Gunter's death, but it increased the odds in his favor to succeed in finding him before they killed him.

Another reason his mind sensed these two assassins were because they were like him—not fully human. Certain brainwave frequencies matched his ability to receive radio waves. Since their minds were similarly attuned, Lucian realized how close they were. Perhaps the shelter of his car or use of his cell phone had blocked his ability to locate them before now. But for whatever reason, the interference was gone. He honed in on them and started running toward their location.

An abrupt revelation dawned on him. He sought to kill men like himself. He thought about if the situation was reversed, and they were hunting him. Self-defense gave him reason to kill them. But did he have the right to kill because of *what* they were?

They were all lab-created minorities. Unnatural humans. Yet, humans, just the same.

Lucian slowed his pace. The thought burned through his mind. Did it make sense to destroy them when they weren't all that different from him?

"Yes," he whispered. "I'm free and these men are controlled and assigned to kill innocent people."

Not only were they to be eliminated to save society, their creators must be stopped as well. If the creators were stopped first, perhaps there was hope for others like himself.

A gunshot echoed. Lucian ran faster, pulled his 9mm and clicked off the safety. The closer he came to these genetically mutated men, the more he realized these men held no hope for redemption. Darkness leapt from their minds, their souls, and gravitated toward him, taunting him with a coldness he'd never felt before. They were far more dangerous than he had ever imagined.

Chapter 6

7:00 p.m.

Mike held his breath when the two sets of silver-glazed eyes turned from the garage and in his general direction. He pushed himself tighter against the cold concrete wall. The two men stood silent. Their eyes searched for him. The growing lump in his throat hurt. Swallowing didn't lessen the pain. He stopped breathing, and for a moment, he wished he could silence his heartbeat. He believed they could hear the slightest sound his body emitted.

The men walked opposite directions toward the fence line. They stopped and sniffed the air. Not only did they have keener sight, their sense of smell was beyond comprehension. The two men would probably walk the perimeter and work their way inward through the parked cars until they found him. Although he couldn't see their guns, he knew they held them.

Mike stepped between the car and pickup again and tightened his grip on the tire iron. He lay flat on the ground and crawled under the truck and waited.

The steady approach of hard soled shoes eased near the pickup. Loose gravel crunched with each step the man took. Closer. He closed his eyes. When he opened them, the man's feet had stopped right beside his face. His whole body vibrated with surging fear. One foot stepped back. The man dropped to one knee. In seconds, the man's silvery eyes peered into his own.

Although Mike had no premeditated action, just instinct, he swung the tire iron and hit the man directly in the forehead. The harsh shock of the blow sprayed a stream of warm blood across Mike's face and the grimy pavement. The man collapsed instantly, without uttering a sound. His eyes closed, and blood pooled from his mouth. A large bruise spread across his forehead while a thin stream of blood flowed from the contusion.

Mike dropped the tire iron and wiped the blood from his face. His hands trembled. He wanted to scream but didn't dare. Instead, he pried the gun from the assassin's tight fingers and took it. He pulled himself across the cold, rough stones and pavement and rolled out the opposite side of the truck. The other man walked along the opposite fence line, his back to Gunter, and apparently unaware that his partner was down.

Mike hurried along the fence toward the garage and hoped to find somewhere safe to hide.

Chapter 7

7:01 p.m.

Lucian sprinted through the alley, across a street, and down another alley. Darkness welcomed him. The thought of his freedom from Trans-GenCorp was a liberation he couldn't compare to any other emotion he possessed. Lucian had promised Lucas that he would keep his face reconstructed so he didn't look like his genetic prototype and that was a promise he had kept. Instead, Lucian rather enjoyed the random facial changes he'd made during the past six months. With his desire to help those in distressing situations, he used different disguises as tools to gain a person's trust, or as a counterfeit mask to gain access to places otherwise off-limits.

Kat had befriended him, in spite of his past, and for the most part, he understood that she was using him to fulfill her own revenge. Tyler's death had crushed a part of her that he believed had been pure, but now was tarnished. He wondered if she could find redemption like he had.

Lucian had killed people, some by accident, when TransGenCorp had fenced off the tip of Pittsburgh. Since Lucian was Lucas', Idris had plotted to use him to kill Helmsby, Daniel, and the other occupants residing inside Helmsby's Research Center. Others, during that same time, he had killed to protect Daniel because, for unexplained reasons, the deep friendship between Lucas and Daniel had somehow been transposed into Lucian's memories. This bond of loyalty was something Idris had detested, and later, the reason why Lucian turned against Idris and killed him. For freedom, yes, but also to protect Lucas and Lydia. Without Idris in the picture, Lucian had a life, or at least a chance to discover what potential the world held for him.

But he had no idea how much corruption remained in the New Age of Biotechnology. Cloning, breeding super humans, and creating stranger creatures than the shifters continued. The ultimate goal was to make something stronger than Lydia's prototype. Something indestructible that didn't possess a conscience. Someone who could infiltrate an organization undetected until after it was too late for anyone to stop her.

7:07 P.M.

Simon had found Trey's body. He huddled over his brother. Blood congealed on Trey's forehead. Simon sat down and rested his brother's head on his lap. Anger rushed through him. He felt for a pulse. Faint, but steady.

The muscles in Simon's face tightened and then strangely contorted. His fingers grew two phalanges longer. Sharp thick claws lengthened. His eyes blazed yellow, like a dog, and his teeth grew sharper points. He exhaled, and the sound carried a slight growl. He sniffed the air, detecting the nervous scent of Gunter's fear lingering on the night air.

"Brother," Simon whispered. "He's near. I'll be back. He will suffer for this."

Simon eased his brother's head gently onto the pavement. He stood and slinked around the truck. Gunter had discovered an open door to get inside the garage. Simon smiled. Gunter was trapped and had nowhere to run.

7:08 P.M.

Mike felt his way along a greasy table in the garage. One car rested atop a hydraulic lift. He stood in absolute darkness with the gun shaking in his hand. He hoped to discover a rear exit, provided one even existed. And if it did, he doubted he'd find it.

His ears rang from the silence. The stillness soon faded. Several rodents scurried from their hiding places. The faint ticking of tiny feet across paper scraps frightened him. Though the animals were small and harmless, the darkness magnified their size inside his mind. His fear and anxiety grew as well.

Near the door where he had entered, a piece of metal clanged against the concrete floor. Gunter took a step backward but not quickly enough. From the other side of the room, yellow eyes glowed. He raised the gun and tried to squeeze the trigger, but it seemed jammed. It didn't fire. He'd never used a gun before, and now, not understanding how to fix this problem, he realized how useless the weapon was for him.

Fierce eyes stared at him, vanishing beneath a slow blink. When the eyes reopened and turned silver, the man rushed Mike.

Chapter 8

7:09 p.m.

Lucian stopped running when the bloodcurdling scream broke the calm night. The second, muffled scream alerted him which direction to head. He sprinted and headed for the garage. With an agility he'd not used in months, he cleared the fence without touching it, rolled upon landing, and loaded the gun's chamber with a click. The garage door stood ajar.

Inside the garage, Gunter shrieked. Lucian hurried through the door and followed the snarling sounds that ripped into Gunter. Lucian's eyes adjusted to the darkness. Gunter's limp body dropped to the grimy floor. Silver eyes turned and faced Lucian.

"Try me," Lucian said with a smile while tucking his gun behind his belt.

A sharp breath of surprise expelled from Simon's mouth. Blood dripped from his teeth. Before Simon prepared a defense, Lucian flung him into the metal garage door. The metal buckled, rattled, and Lucian slammed Simon a second time before his opponent regained his footing.

Lucian's fingers lengthened, his muscles swelled, and he discovered an animal's hunger for blood. The craving startled him and he loosened his grip. Simon extended both hands forward with crushing blows that brought Lucian off the ground and sent him reeling backwards.

Simon growled and hunkered into a grappling position as he lunged for Lucian. Lucian countered with a sharp, upward kick into the man's abdominals, expelling the air from his lungs and tossing him further into the dark garage.

Silver eyes glowed.

None of the genetic soldiers at TGC had eyes like this, nor did he. He wasn't familiar with this genetic alteration.

Simon paced back and forth.

Lucian understood his adversary wasn't certain how to fight someone near his equal. He pulled his gun and fired. Simon recoiled in pain with an angered hiss.

Simon placed a hand against the heated wound and the warmth of blood gushed between his fingers. Cloth ripped in the darkness. A low growl rumbled in his throat. Hate-filled eyes glared at him.

"Damn," Lucian whispered.

"Who are you?" Simon asked, clasping his chest, slowing the blood flow.

"You really don't want to know."

Lucian slid his hand against the wall, found the light switch, and flipped it upward. The overhead fluorescent bulbs hummed with sudden harsh brightness. Simon blocked the light from his eyes with his free hand, wincing to see. He yanked the snowcap from his head and tossed it aside. His shirt was ripped open where he had inspected his bullet wound in the dark. The bullet wound was closing, which didn't surprise Lucian, but other characteristics about this man did.

TGC had tried unsuccessfully for two years to combine canine DNA with human, and somehow, GenTech had succeeded where TGC had failed. This man's squared jaws were layered with sharp, doglike teeth. His eyes pierced with the gaze of a hungry wolf. His ears pointed back, which explained why he'd wear a ridiculous snowcap with an expensive Armani suit. He was similar to the soldier that had tried to kill Morton and Daniel's family. The ears had been the only canine feature TGC had succeeded with, and only once. The shape of the ears enabled acute hearing. The disadvantage came when they were subjected to extreme noises. The oversensitivity of their eardrums, when exposed to higher decibels, paralyzed their central nervous systems, dropping them like a Taser neutralizes and incapacitates the muscles of an enraged man. Although the debilitation was only momentary, sometimes all an enemy needed was a few seconds to gain the advantage.

Even though Simon held a remarkable resemblance to a wolfish creature, his skin remained smooth, and not overgrown with sparse patches of fur. Not a flaw by any means. At least these soldiers could blend into society without drawing too much attention to them. Extreme facial hair spread rumors of wolf-men and such alarming news guaranteed that government agencies would track them down and stop their operations. With the worldwide knowledge of TransGenCorp's demise, future biotech companies worked harder to conceal themselves within a dark underworld society.

Mike Gunter lay dead in a spreading pool of blood. His throat was ripped out and his closed eyes were silent in death. A gun rested in the grime and grease several feet away. On Gunter's chest rested a red pawn piece.

"What crime had he done?" Lucian asked.

Simon gnashed his teeth with a powerful snap. His narrowed eyes studied Lucian, looking for an opportunity to attack. "Mind your business."

"*This* is my business. The thirteenth red pawn? The last four have been here in New Jersey. Why the murders? Why the red pawns? *Whom* do you work for?"

Simon arched his back and popped his neck. Another inevitable fight was coming, which is what Lucian wanted, but prolonging their clash for any gleaned information about GenTech and Mech Cybernetics proved to be more valuable. Killing this mutant didn't end the string of murders. Someone higher up had assigned and ordered the killings. More murders were guaranteed to follow regardless if this wolfish man lived or died.

"Just walk away," Simon said. He spat bloody spittle on the floor and rubbed his jaw. "I have no red pawn for you. There's no need for you to die."

Lucian frowned and his eyes shimmered green. "You humor me. I'll walk away. But you won't."

The change in Lucian's eyes drew curiosity from Simon. A tinge of fear reflected in his eyes. "*What* are you?"

Lucian didn't answer. Instead, he charged forward, grasped the man's wrists and twisted outward. Simon howled in pain. Lucian snapped the man's forearms and dislocated at his elbows. The severity of the injury brought new transformations in his enemy. Simon snarled with sharper teeth, reared his head back, and struck forward like a cobra, trying to bite Lucian's throat.

Lucian kicked Simon's left knee. The crushing blow buckled him. He fell to the ground screaming. Unlike Lydia, he felt pain. Lucian swung his foot into the man's canine mouth. His head twisted, followed by another series of cracking noises in his neck, and then came sudden silence. After several moments, the wolfish mutant gasped.

Lucian shook his head and looked down at Simon. The man's body slowly reverted into human form. The excessive damage reduced the mutated man into a near comatose state to allow healing. His ribcage expanded and contracted in slow, rhythmic breaths.

Lucian stood over his body and fired three rounds into the back of the man's head. Simon's body jerked with each shot. Holstering the 9mm, his shoulders slumped. He shook his head and sighed. Killing other genetic soldiers to protect society was grisly, but doing so possibly protected innocent people like Gunter in the future.

He walked to Gunter's body and knelt beside him. Taking the red pawn into his hand, he studied the crudely carved number 13 on its base. He clenched a tight fist around the chess piece and looked at Gunter's face.

Muscles in Lucian's face contorted, narrowed in certain places, lengthened in others. His eye color changed to match Gunter's. In less than five minutes, he appeared identical to Mike Gunter.

Lucian stood and considered the chess piece again. "Thirteen's always been my lucky number," he said with a grim smile.

He rummaged through Simon's suit pockets, retrieved a wallet that didn't yield any personal information, and then he took the man's gun and cell phone.

Lucian's cell phone rang inside his pocket.

"Yes?" he asked, still looking through the wallet.

"Have you found Mr. Gunter?" Kat asked.

"I was too late."

"Damn. He's dead?"

"Yeah. Three minutes sooner and it'd have been a different outcome."

Kat remained quiet for a few seconds. "At least we were closer this time. You get a good look at the attackers?"

"Our problems are much worse than we anticipated."

"Why?"

"The genetic soldier I just killed is more advanced than anything TransGenCorp ever produced. Much more advanced than even I am."

"And you still killed him?" Kat sounded amused.

"Chalk it up to my experience and wisdom. Otherwise, he'd have easily killed me. He has canine genes. It was like fighting a man with the strength of a bear. If his fighting skills were more seasoned, you'd be finding yourself a new recruit."

"With Gunter dead, I don't know if this means the trail is cold now, or what."

"Oh, it's red hot."

"You discovered something else?"

"No. I am Mike Gunter."

"You've assumed his appearance?"

"I will until we stop whoever was assigned the man to kill Gunter. When we do, we've found the people responsible for Tyler's death."

Lucian winced the moment he mentioned Tyler's name. Kat became silent.

She changed the subject, but her voice didn't hide her sadness. "To be certain we had the right address to where Mr. Gunter worked, I had Kyle retrace the email again. It is the renovated hospital."

"I'll report to GenTech as Gunter tomorrow."

"Kyle wants you to bring Mr. Gunter's body to the hotel with you."

"Why?"

"So he can meld Gunter's memories into yours. Otherwise, Gunter's GenTech supervisors and the Mech Cybernetic guards will recognize that you're not him."

"Kyle can do that?"

Kat whispered. "He seems to think he can."

"The body's a bloody mess. His throat was ripped out."

"We can try not to soil the carpet. Just bring his body back."

Lucian sighed. "Damn, I'm nearly five blocks away from my car. At least the streets are empty. Not many ways to explain a dead body slung over your shoulder."

"I know."

"I'll be there as soon as possible."

He placed the cell phone in his pocket and stripped Simon of his Armani jacket. If Gunter's blood was going to stain someone's clothes, Lucian preferred it not be his own.

After pulling the Armani jacket over his, he heaved Gunter's stiffening body over his shoulder and walked to the locked gate. He pulled his 9mm and shot the lock. He yanked the gate open and disappeared down a dark alley.

IN THE SHADOWS, Trey pulled himself through the dusty gravels in the direction of the garage. His head wound had ceased bleeding. The bluish-black bruise on his forehead was fading. His head throbbed but at least his blurred vision had cleared. Light spilled from the open garage door.

He lay still when Lucian carried Gunter out. He blinked hard several more times, trying to make sense of what he saw. Trey wondered how severe Gunter's injuries were, or if Gunter had a twin because the man carrying Gunter *was* Gunter. He shook his head. How hard had he been hit to give him such delusions?

After Lucian vanished down the alley, Trey pulled himself across the pavement on his elbows until he reached the door.

Using the door for leverage, he rose to his feet and shielded his eyes from the light. He staggered into the garage. When he found Simon's body, he dropped to his knees and felt for a pulse in spite of the loss of blood and the bullet holes through his brother's head.

He wailed and vowed his vengeance.

Chapter 9

Kyle sat in his wheelchair, staring at the computer screen. His mind was clearer than ever after Helmsby had injected shifter DNA into the lobotomized sections of his brain, but some motor skills had not yet completely repaired. His transformations over the past six months were far better than Brockton had expected, though Brockton had no knowledge of Helmsby's experiment.

Helmsby had not revealed to anyone the forced lobotomy he had performed. Yvonne, his fiancée, knew but kept her silence. Under different circumstances, she understood Helmsby would never have done such a procedure. Since they never associated with Brockton, Kat, and Lucian, they had no knowledge of Kyle's improvements. But Kyle also progressed in ways that Brockton didn't know about.

Kyle's mind remained brilliant, but his ability to verbally communicate limited lengthy sentences. His slow speech frustrated him at times. Brockton gave him a computer as an easier means to communicate.

Brockton also had a special prosthetic hand constructed for Kyle. The hand functioned remarkably similarly to a human's. The synthetic material that imitated flesh was frighteningly realistic. From a distance, no one knew otherwise. Electronic sensors in the hand communicated with Kyle's neurons immediately, without complication.

The wheelchair was necessary but Brockton held the hope that the daily physical therapy Kyle underwent would soon eliminate the need for one.

Kat placed a hand on Kyle's shoulder. "Lucian's on his way."

Kyle nodded and stared at the monitor. Kat poured herself a cup of coffee.

Brockton sat at a table, studying files of Kyle's mental progress over the past month and wrote updated notes into a lab journal.

"He's getting stronger," Brockton said.

Kat smiled and took the seat across from him. "I've seen drastic improvements."

Brockton nodded, meeting her tired gaze. "Yes. I believe we'll see even more positive results."

"Giving him the computer has helped."

"I agree," Brockton said. "He spends hours each day reading scientific journals. He's rebuilding his mind, and with the new medicines, he's progressing well."

Kat sipped her coffee. "Lucian informed me that the man who killed Gunter wasn't fully human."

"Oh?"

"Yes. The man has canine genes."

Brockton chuckled. "Interesting. If Idris were still alive, I'd love to see his reaction. He never succeeded with such experimentation. He'd be pissed to know someone else has."

"Lucian believes the genetic soldier might've been stronger than he is."

Brockton shrugged. "I really doubt that. Lucian has expanded his genetic boundaries by progressively updating himself. He's lived nearly four years longer than he should have."

"Will he always need his enhancer injections?"

"I'm afraid there's no way around that. His telomeres are too short. Without the injections, his cellular components shrink beyond repair. He'd age fifty years in a matter of days."

Kat bit her lower lip. "So there isn't any research you could do to lengthen them?"

"No. He's free from TransGenCorp, but still a prisoner to the enhancers."

"That's a shame."

"Yes, it is," Brockton smiled. "You've grown to like him, haven't you?"

Kat blushed and looked away. "We're friends."

"But you've also grown fond of him. You no longer view him as an animal and a murderer."

"I never thought of him as an animal."

"You held a gun on him. You shot him. But now, you look the other direction."

Kat nodded. "I guess I have to in order to avenge Tyler's death. Lucian's able to do things others can't. I believe I can trust his promise."

"But you're fond of his company."

Her eyes narrowed. "What point are you driving after?"

"My point being that you don't view him as an experiment anymore. You see him as a person."

"Of course he's a person, but it doesn't mean I have feelings for him, other than friendship. And if I did, what does it matter?"

He shrugged. "There's nothing wrong with it. In spite of his alterations, he's still human. So are you."

"I know. People need people."

Brockton closed his folder and stood. "And people *need* more than friendship, too."

She nodded. Her eyes brimmed with tears.

He smiled. "He's never known love. Did you know that?"

"No," she said. A tear escaped her left eye and meandered down her cheek. "I knew love once. But . . . I don't know that I ever can again."

"Love isn't necessarily elusive."

"It hurts too much to pursue."

Brockton smiled. "Sometimes, and sometimes you have to surrender to it."

Kat wiped her eyes and turned away.

"If you need me when Lucian returns," Brockton said. "I'll be in the next room getting Kyle ready for bed. It's been a long day."

"Kyle needs to be here when Lucian brings Gunter's body."

"Just knock."

Kat watched Brockton push Kyle's wheelchair through the adjoining door, leaving her to sit and think.

She thought of Tyler, his brutal death, and Lucian's promise to help find those responsible. She trusted Lucian to fulfill his end of the bargain, but what then? She had never given much thought about what happened between them afterwards. Did Lucian leave to pursue other goals and interests? And if so, how would she feel if he wasn't around?

True, they were friends. His absence might bring a new void she had not anticipated. Running on vengeance fueled reasons to ignore her need for a man in her life. Once justice came, that fire was gone. She hadn't really thought about anything more. Now, new questions bore through her mind. Tyler was gone, regardless of how this all ended, and the conclusion was the possibility of being alone. She never thought about other outcomes. She knew exactly what Brockton hinted at.

Time would tell, she thought.

Chapter 10

Lucian set Gunter's body between a dumpster and a brick wall, shed the bloody Armani suit, and hurried through channels of alleys until he was in the apartment parking lot again. The police cars, ambulance, and Carpenter were gone, so he did a quick walk up the street to his car.

He drove cautiously through the intersections, hoping to avoid any police cruisers lingering in the area. After a few minutes, he parked near the dumpster, opened the trunk, and lugged Gunter's body to the car. Looking around, he listened for any approaching cars or vagrants. Silence assured him that no one else was around. He placed Gunter's body inside and lowered the trunk lid.

KAT PEERED through the door's peephole when Lucian knocked. With her hand on the door, she hesitated opening it. Gunter's smiling face stared back at her. Having seen Gunter's photo on the computer, she knew it was Lucian. She opened the door and a sense of relief rushed through her.

Lucian brushed through the door with Gunter slung over his shoulder. The situation was eerie.

Kat closed the door.

"Where should I put his body?" he asked.

A thick drop of blood fell and glistened on the carpet.

"Put him in the bathtub. I'll get Kyle."

Brockton rolled Kyle to the edge of the tub while Kat and Lucian stepped aside.

Gunter's flesh was a blend of blue and death white. Dried blood caked on his shirt. The torn strands of tissue surrounding the gaping throat wound were stiff.

"The assassin did this?" Kat whispered.

"Yep. With his claws."

She swallowed hard.

"Bring me . . . closer," Kyle said.

"That's as close as you can get," Brockton said, resting the right side wheel against the tub.

"No," Kyle said. "I need to touch him with my hand."

Lucian gave Kat an odd glance.

She shrugged. "I don't know."

Brockton eased Kyle forward in the chair and placed his hands on Kyle's shoulders to prevent Kyle from falling on top of Gunter. Kyle placed his real hand and the prosthetic one on Gunter's blue-tinted temples. He closed his eyes and his hands shook.

"Place your hands on his head," Kyle whispered.

"Me?" Lucian asked.

Kyle nodded.

Lucian glanced at Kat. She shrugged. Lucian stepped to the edge of the tub and put his hands on Gunter's head.

Kyle's face flushed red. Veins swelled in his thin forearms and in his neck. Whatever he was doing pulsed through him with great force.

"What the hell?" Lucian asked. His knees buckled. Kat grabbed his arm to hold him upright.

"What's wrong?" she asked.

"What are you doing, Kyle?" Lucian asked, leaning against the wall. Though lacking balance, he kept his hands on Gunter's forehead.

"Accept his memories," Kyle said.

Images rushed through Lucian's mind. He closed his eyes and his eyelids fluttered. He whispered, "What the hell?"

Vivid thoughts came to Lucian faster than he could translate, and a powerful surge of energy flooded through him. He held the memories in his mind, but the one that stayed the longest after Kyle finished was that of a woman. He clearly read the name stamped on her lab coat tag.

Violet.

Whatever Kyle had done to capture this man's memories and transpose them into Lucian's mind had worked. Gunter's most recent memories were the strongest and most important. Lucian couldn't get the young woman out of his head. Her face. Her eyes.

Violet.

Lucian realized she was a person of interest. They needed to find her. She could provide answers to help them.

"Did it work?" Brockton asked.

Lucian nodded. "I think so. I don't know how, but I have vivid memories of his past few weeks. What happened today has an even stronger visualization."

Brockton wheeled Kyle out of the room.

"What did you see?" Kat asked.

"I have a clear view of what the laboratory looks like, and a woman."

Kat frowned. "A woman?"

"A coworker, I think. Her name's Violet. At least that's the name on her work badge."

"Is she pretty?" she teased.

"Gorgeous."

"Oh."

"Something tells me that if I can talk to her tomorrow, we'll discover new information about GenTech that can help us."

Lucian took Gunter's right pale hand and placed the fingertips against his.

"What are you doing?" Kat asked.

Lucian shrugged. "I don't know if this will work, but I'm trying to match his fingerprints to mine. It will take deep meditation, but still, this may not work."

"Why would it matter?"

"To get into GenTech, or to even start Gunter's car, I'd have to use his finger prints, and in some situations, possibly his palm print as well."

Kat shook her head. "It won't work that way, anyway. His right hand is your left's mirror."

"I just noticed that, too."

Lucian pressed his right index finger against Gunter's right index finger. "Damn, the computer won't read that either. It's backwards."

Brockton smiled. "Wait one minute. I have something that might work."

Brockton returned with a paper bag and emptied the contents. Three plastic eggs of Silly Putty landed on the floor beside the bathtub.

"I bought these for Kyle. His motor skills improve the more he works the putty between his fingers. But, you can get great fingerprint impressions by pressing your hand firmly against it. Is that all you need? A good impression."

Lucian shrugged. "Like I said, I'm not certain this will work. If it's possible for me to mimic the prints as my own, I'd need a perfect mold."

"Okay. Hold his hand and I'll see how well I can spread the putty without contaminating it with my prints."

Fifteen frustrating minutes passed before they finally got a clear set of prints without smudging them. Brockton put the putty mold on the sink counter. Lucian lined his hand above Gunter's handprint and carefully lowered it and pressed hard. He waited another fifteen minutes and peeled off the putty.

Brockton studied Lucian's hand against Gunter's palm and shrugged. "I honestly cannot tell if it's a match."

"Tomorrow's the test. If it works, I can infiltrate Mech Cybernetics. If not? We'll find another solution."

"Very well. I need to get Kyle to bed."

Kat and Lucian followed Brockton into the adjoining room. He was pulling back the blankets on Kyle's bed.

"Let me help you with him," Kat said.

She and Lucian lifted Kyle from the chair and eased him over to the edge of the bed. She lowered Kyle's head onto the pillow, and her heart ached. Although she had not known Kyle prior to his present condition, it troubled her to see him less than how Daniel had described him being years ago, before the nuclear strike in Pittsburgh.

Kyle had regained his intelligence at a remarkable, if not miraculous, rate; but he rarely overcame his frustration when trying to talk clearly. His physical abilities improved week to week, but he didn't seem capable of gaining weight, no matter how much they fed him. She wondered what kind of person he would have been had Idris not disrupted the lives of thousands of people in Pittsburgh.

More reasons, she thought, to stop Mech Cybernetics during its elementary stages before the scientists graduated to more advanced technologies that rendered them unstoppable. She couldn't stop until she was certain there'd be no more Kyle or Tyler-like tragedies.

Knowing Mech Cybernetics had merged GenTech's top scientists and experimentations with their own, and that they were more advanced than TransGenCorp had ever been with combining canine DNA with human DNA, she knew their technology was far beyond TGC's. What dangers were to be birthed and released, if they failed to stop them?

"Lucian?" Kat asked, as she tucked the blankets around Kyle. "What did you do with the body of Gunter's killer?"

"Still in the garage."

Brockton shook his head. "That's not good."

Kat smiled. "No, but what I'd like to do is take the corpse and have an autopsy performed."

Lucian shrugged. "Not a bad idea, but it will lead to a lot of media attention."

She shook her head. "Not if I get Todd to do the forensics analysis for us."

"He does most of the work for Carpenter, doesn't he?" Lucian asked.

"He'll keep this quiet for me, if I ask."

Lucian nodded and looked at Brockton. "Want to go with me?"

Brockton glanced at his watch. "Sure. I'd like to see what this canine-like man looks like."

"I'm afraid he's uglier dead than alive."

THE DRIVE to the garage took less than a half hour. The garage gate was wide open, and nothing but a pool of blood remained on the concrete floor. Simon's body was gone.

"It's not possible that he walked out of here," Lucian said. "I fired three rounds into his forehead. I have no doubt that he was dead when I left."

Brockton kneeled by the coagulating blood pool. "I agree. He lost too much blood to have even survived without a bullet to his head."

"Dammit!" Lucian stuffed his hands into his pockets and kicked the floor.

Brockton smiled and filled a glass vial with blood. "Not all is lost, Lucian. We can learn a great deal from this sample."

"Maybe, but not as much as we could have learned from his body."

"Perhaps he wasn't alone?"

Lucian's jaw tightened. "When I first looked for Gunter, I sensed more than one person chasing him. Once I got here, that feeling vanished. If he had an accomplice, why would he let me kill his partner? He'd fight me, too, don't you think?"

"I don't know. The best thing we can do right now is make certain the owners of this garage don't discover that a murder took place here. It will get the police involved and with the police, this *will* have full media coverage. The Red Pawn Murders have enough attention right now. Whoever sent the men to kill Gunter will learn that he died. We cannot have that if you're planning to go to Mech Cybernetics posing as him."

"True," Lucian nodded. A sensation of memory jolted him, and he staggered to catch himself.

"Are you okay?"

Lucian nodded. "Yes. Whenever Gunter was hiding, he apparently knocked one attacker unconscious with a tire iron. Smacked him dead center in the forehead. It wasn't enough to kill him, so I'd say that's how this body disappeared. He carried his partner away."

"Sounds reasonable to me."

"We still need to cover the blood, so no one knows."

"What's in the barrel by the tool table?" Brockton pointed.

Lucian lifted the lid off the large barrel. "Looks like cat litter," he said, somewhat surprised.

"They use that to soak up grease and oil spills. It will work on blood, too. Cover the blood spill with a thick layer."

Lucian took a scoop of litter and headed to the pool of blood. Before he dumped it, he noticed bloody handprints all around the area where the body had been.

"Someone else was here," he said. "He carried the corpse out."

Brockton sighed. He placed a rubber stopper plug the top of the vial. "Can't worry about that now. The person or persons are long gone."

Brockton helped Lucian bury the blood beneath layers of dusty cat litter.

"You have everything you need?" Lucian asked.

Brockton gave a solemn nod.

Chapter 11

The following morning, Kat sat at the small hotel table and watched Kyle sitting at his computer.

She found it difficult to believe the corpse in the garage was gone. From what Brockton and Lucian described, the man couldn't have recovered. Gunter's memory clued Lucian to a second genetic soldier, but was that memory reliable? If the memory was false, they were dealing with stronger genetic soldiers than before. If true, another assassin remained on the loose. By taking the body to erase their tracks, they prevented the genetic knowledge from being evaluated by other scientists. For now, they had succeeded.

Kat agreed to watch Kyle while Brockton and Lucian found a place to leave Gunter's body. Once Lucian succeeded in posing as Gunter in Mech Cybernetics to retrieve needed information, they'd report to the police where Gunter's body was *accidentally* found.

Kyle groaned softly with his head tilted backwards. His eyes were closed. Kat walked across the room and gently placed her hand on his shoulder. His lips moved in silence, uttering inaudible words. Often, his mind drifted to places she wished she could see.

"Are you okay, dear?" she asked. A map of Nevada was on his computer monitor.

Kyle ignored her. He continued his silent chat. Lately, he had done this more, and she feared the action was a side effect of the vast medications Brockton had administered. Kyle's health improved, but his mental state changed daily.

The computer Brockton had given him was something she really didn't think Kyle would have had any interest using. But he did research scientific discoveries and memorized vast amounts of detailed geographic data of various regions in the U.S. and Canada. She didn't know the specific reason for this new interest, and on several unsuccessful attempts, she had asked Kyle why.

His sporadic mood swings occasionally led to brief fits of rage, only for him to quietly venture back into a tranquil state at the mention of Daniel's name. Kat placed a framed picture of Daniel and Morton from a book jacket beside his computer. This photo lessened the dramatic behavior whenever he worried about his friend.

All the genetic technology to radically alter human genomes wasn't a topic Kat would have considered valid until she played a key role in TGC's shutdown. Meeting and befriending Lucian brought her closer to what gene manipulation could achieve, and yet, she understood how deadly this technological knowledge was in the wrong hands.

Kyle's strange ability to meld Gunter's memories into Lucian was beyond her comprehension. What bridges had connected inside Kyle's brain that allowed him the power to pass through another's memories or speak thoughts into someone's mind? Did everyone possess such capabilities if unlinked neurological pathways connected?

Kat also wondered if Kyle had somehow linked to Gunter before his death because he knew exactly where Gunter was running without having a New Jersey map on the monitor screen. She feared Kyle may have witnessed Gunter's demise, and if so, she didn't know how his mind processed it.

ONE HOUR later

KAT ENTERED Starbucks with her purse slung over her shoulder. She had taken time to put on makeup and fixed her bobbed brown hair. The coffee shop brimmed with people busy with their thoughts and goals. She walked to the counter and studied the beverage plaque on the wall and ordered.

"Café latte with a double espresso shot," she said, digging through her purse for her billfold.

"Make that two," Carpenter said behind her. He stepped up and slid a twenty-dollar bill across the counter to the cashier. "Charge hers to me, too."

"That's not necessary," Kat sighed.

The cashier held the twenty with a questioning look, gazing at Kat and then back to Carpenter. Carpenter nodded with a wink. The cashier charged both coffees to him.

He smiled at Kat, but she refused to face him. She studied his reflection on the silver espresso machine. Fatigue hung in dark circles beneath his eyes. He looked older than she remembered. The Red Pawn Case was under his skin and inwardly gnawing through him. He was a hostage to his need to find the truth.

"You're looking well," he said with a genuine smile.

"Less stress does that for a woman."

"It doesn't surprise me that you'd be in New Jersey," Carpenter said.

"Really?" Kat never moved. "You're following me?"

"No, just in the area."

"How convenient," she said without smiling or glancing in his direction.

"I can assume you're here about the Red Pawn Murders?"

She gave him a confused stare, slightly cocking her left eyebrow. "*What* are you talking about?"

"We need to talk, Kat."

"Why?"

"It's been awhile. Let's get everything out into the open. The situation has had plenty of time to air out. We can make a fresh start."

Kat took her coffee and headed for a table near the window. Carpenter followed.

"On what?"

"Our friendship, and I want you to come back to the agency."

She laughed softly and stared out the window. Pigeons huddled on the cold sidewalk, sulking for handouts.

Carpenter sat at Kat's table. He blew steam off his coffee and smiled.

"Many in the agency view you as a rogue agent. They consider you to be dangerous."

Kat smiled evenly. "Perhaps I am. Or maybe they're jealous that I'm doing the job they're unable to do."

"Kat," Carpenter shook his head. "I understand your bitterness."

"Do you?"

"Tyler was my friend, too. In fact, I knew him years longer than you did."

She looked out the window, her eyes distant in thought. "He was more than just a friend to me."

Carpenter's brow rose. In a hushed tone, he said, "Meaning? You two *dated*?"

Kat swallowed hard, her face reddened, and she fought back tears. "Once, but it could've been a lot more if I'd have been bold enough to allow it. Now, I'll never know."

"I'm sorry, Kat. I never realized . . ."

Carpenter reached across the table and put his hand on top of hers. She pulled away.

"His death is why I take what happened at TransGenCorp personally, Carpenter. That's why I'll find those responsible. No matter the cost. I'll get justice for Tyler."

"Kat, come back to the agency and we'll work on this together."

"I can't."

"You cannot go after them like this. You don't have the law behind you."

"Tyler did and see what that got him?"

Carpenter's jaw tightened. "Kat, be realistic. We can help you, but only if you work with us."

"This is my battle now."

Carpenter sighed. "If you pursue them with this anger and hostility, you'll do something you'll regret."

"Like?"

"Kill someone or maybe end up killing the *wrong* person. That shit happens. I'd hate to be the one that has to arrest you."

"I'll do whatever's necessary for justice."

"Being a vigilante is still a capital crime, no matter what your reasons are."

Kat shrugged, blew her coffee, and then took a sip. "You were at Tyler's funeral?"

"Yes, of course."

"Did you happen to notice the two men who were watching us?"

Carpenter's eyes revealed he had not. "No. What men?"

"The problems with TransGenCorp may be over, but they were just one faction of what's still out there."

"So there are other renegade biotech companies?"

Kat smiled. "Several."

"Whom have you been talking to?" Carpenter folded his hands in a prayer-like manner while he studied her face.

She knew he worked interrogations for years. He was excellent at reading a person's reaction to questions, but she maintained a stone cold gaze.

"I cannot reveal my sources," she said.

"I can subpoena your records."

Kat shrugged. "You could, but my records don't list my sources."

"Very well, Kat. Since you brought it up, what exactly are you implying? TransGenCorp has been shut down. The front doors are welded shut. No one is allowed access into the building anymore. Hell, for all we know some of the creatures still roam inside freely, but there's no possible way they'd ever get out."

Kat studied his aged eyes. In spite of her resentment, she still felt the warmth of Carpenter's friendship. He was genuinely interested in helping her. His honesty outweighed any thought that he'd ever betray her.

"You ever hear of GenTech?"

He shook his head. "No, I haven't. Why?"

"Recently, GenTech was bought out by Mech Cybernetics."

Carpenter shrugged. "So? What do you know? Do you think they're involved with the Red Pawn Murders?"

"Yes."

"Why?"

"That's what we're trying to figure out. The last five murders occurred in New Jersey. We believe . . ."

"Five?" Carpenter frowned. "Only four have been reported with a red pawn."

"Four, right. Sorry," Kat said, pretending to correct herself. "That's what I meant. But those four murders were people we believe worked for GenTech."

"What does this GenTech Corporation do?"

"Mech Cybernetics possesses their scientific research, but they both do the same type of research as TransGenCorp."

"Shit. So they're connected?"

"Not directly, no."

"And you know this, how?"

Kat shook her head. "I'm unable to give you that information right now."

"Kat," Carpenter said softly.

"I can't, but I will soon. I promise. You're right though. I'll need your help on this, but not right yet."

"Why not?"

"Let's just say, I have someone on the inside trying to get some answers."

"Okay." He still looked agitated, but sat back against the cushioned booth seat and sighed.

"Long night?" she asked.

He nodded and rubbed his eyes. "Yeah. Too long, and no new clues."

"No red pawn last night?"

Carpenter took a coffee stirrer and mixed his espresso. "A murder, but no pawn. There wasn't a reason for the murder. No robbery. Someone just killed an apartment manager. On the second floor, a failed ambush took place for Mike Gunter, but apparently, he escaped. A couple blocks away we found two pools of blood in a garage but no bodies. Someone had attempted to cover the blood with cat litter but one of the workers had scrubbed the floor the night before. Otherwise, it probably would have gone unnoticed."

Kat swallowed a gulp of coffee too fast and coughed to keep from choking.

"You okay?" he asked.

She patted her chest. "I'm fine."

"It was a strange night. The only reason I'm even telling you the details is because we need your help."

"I'll offer my help to *you*, but not to the agency."

Carpenter sighed. "Right now, I'll settle for that."

"DNA results come back on those blood samples in the garage?"

"Not yet."

"Care to fax me the results when they do come in?"

"Sure."

"Thanks."

Carpenter offered a tired smile. "Answer one question for me."

"Depends on the question."

"The clone. What ever happened to him? Did you not cross paths with him in the bunker? His body was never found."

"If I recall correctly, you never found him after the Pittsburgh incident, either."

"No. We didn't."

Kat shrugged. "Perhaps he's a master at quick escapes?"

"Or he has connections with Mech Cybernetics."

"That's always possible."

Carpenter studied her face. "You really don't know?"

"I have nothing I can offer you about him. Honest."

He nodded. He looked at her and his eyes softened. "I wish we still worked together. I never meant to make you believe you couldn't trust me."

"That's not it. I don't trust how the agency works."

Carpenter's cell phone rang. "Hello? Okay, I'll be right there."

Kat finished her coffee and when he finished his call, he leaned closer and whispered, "Keep me posted on any useful information you get. I'll give you some leeway for now. But if it starts to get too dangerous, please call me."

She smiled. "I will. I promise."

"When I get the DNA results, I will send them to you."

"Thanks."

Chapter 12

Felicia sat at her tea table and poured grape Kool-aid into her cup. She looked across the table at Morton, her cat, who wore a doll bonnet with an attached yellow, curly wig.

"More for you?" she asked.

Morton gave a small nod. "Of course, my dear."

Felicia carefully poured the Kool-aid, and Morton extended his paw digits to hold the tiny teacup. He took a sip, swirled it in his mouth, and managed not to spit the purple liquid out.

"To your taste?" she asked.

Morton nodded and wiped his liquid moustache with the back of his forepaw.

Felicia placed two gingersnaps on Morton's plate. He smiled. When he reached to take one, a voice entered his mind.

"Morton," the voice whispered.

Morton's paw hovered above the cookie. His furry eyebrows rose, and he struggled to hear more.

"Morton?"

The cat tilted his head, deep in thought. The voice held a familiar tone. He listened once more and with his mind, Morton thrust his reply. "Kyle?"

"Yes."

"How?"

"I'm not certain. We need your help."

"Who?"

"Kat and Lucian."

Morton frowned.

Felicia's eyes widened. "You not like the cookies?"

Morton shook his head, realizing his paw remained two inches above the cookie. With a quick slide of his paw, he took the cookie and smiled. "Oh, yes," he said. "Thank you. These are my favorite."

After they finished the cookies and Kool-aid, Julia called for Felicia to take her bath. Morton untied the bonnet and wig and pranced into Daniel's office. Daniel sat at his desk, working on his next novel.

"Tea party is over so soon?" Daniel asked.

"Bath time. One brave kid you have there."

"You take baths. Unlike most cats, you never seem bothered by them."

"I'm not referring to water, Dan. You ever drink her Kool-aid? I think she used salt, not sugar."

"That bad?"

"Are my eyes still crossed?"

"I think you've recovered."

Morton sighed. "Glad I had the cookies to wash down that Kool-aid. But that isn't the reason I came to your office."

Daniel turned in his swivel chair. "Oh? What's up?"

"Kyle."

The mention of Kyle's name made Daniel suddenly uneasy. "What about him?"

Morton jumped to the desk, sat down, and shrugged. "This will sound weird, but he just spoke to me telepathically."

"You're sure?"

The cat huffed. "I don't think salty Kool-aid is hallucinogenic. However, I'm certain it's him."

"How?"

"I sensed his personality, not just words."

Daniel rested his nervous hands on the desk. "No, how is it possible for Kyle to communicate like that?"

"When Helmsby had Kyle at TransGenCorp, and we came to visit, do you remember Kyle sensed your presence outside his door, even though the window was mirror-tinted on his side?"

"Yes, that was eerie."

Morton stared directly into Daniel's eyes. "On our first meeting, I spoke to your mind. Remember?"

"Even eerier. I thought I was delirious."

Morton cocked a brow. "You understand the pattern, then?"

"No."

"Helmsby created my mind with such abilities. I don't have any reason to use my psionics. Well, I didn't until *now*. If Kyle now has that capability, do you believe Helmsby made that possible?"

Daniel's eyes narrowed. "With Helmsby, anything's possible. But what purpose did he have to conduct such an experiment?"

Morton lifted a forepaw forward. "One sec. Call coming in."

"Kyle?"

Morton nodded while placing a single paw digit to his mouth. He sat in silence for several minutes. Even though Morton never spoke aloud, Daniel understood the cat was telepathically speaking to Kyle.

Morton nodded. "The Red Pawn Murders. You know about them?"

"Just bits off the news. Why?"

"Kat's investigating it. They need my help."

Daniel straightened in his chair. "Why?"

Morton smiled. "Cats can get into places people cannot."

"Usually leads to trouble."

"Hasn't killed me yet."

"Every time is different."

"Thousands of cat lives left, Dan."

Daniel sighed. "Came a bit too close last time."

"Life goes on."

"I guess they'll need me, too?"

"Kyle didn't request *you*. Just me."

"Oh."

"Safer for Julia and Felicia if you're here anyway. This isn't the same as TransGenCorp."

"Why?"

"No one's bent on killing *us*. The only similarity is that it deals with genetics, but under a smaller operation."

"Too bad Helmsby's still in Europe, he'd leap at this situation."

"I'm certain. I'll leave you to writing while I ask Kyle more questions."

"Where is Kat's operation?"

"Virginia, but they're in New Jersey right now."

"Let me know what else Kyle needs. Tell him I said, 'Hi.'"

Morton smiled. "I'm sure you can do that in person. You'll have to drive me. Of course, if Helmsby had given me wings . . ."

Daniel changed the subject. "What will you tell Felicia?"

"I don't know." Morton pursed his furry lips and looked at the floor. "I don't know."

"You'll never fully understand just how much we really need you, Morton."

Morton frowned with a side-glance. "Don't get mushy."

"You're more than what any cat could be. You're family."

"Getting squishy."

Daniel rubbed the back of Morton's ears. "Yep, but you know, that's where true love is. In the squishy stuff."

Morton purred softly and closed his eyes. "And then life zaps you with salty Kool-aid. Sucks the life right out of you."

"But love is there, all the same."

Morton nodded. "Always."

Chapter 13

Hamburg, Germany

DR. HELMSBY HELD Yvonne's hand while they walked through the airport terminal. He draped his other arm across Nancy's shoulders.

Helmsby sighed and shook his head. "This trip has been phenomenal. I wish I had taken the time to do this years ago."

Nancy smiled. "At least we did this together, Dad, as a family."

Yvonne squeezed Helmsby's hand. "I enjoyed the castle tours the most."

"Those were nice," Helmsby said. "But I think visiting the new space facility captivated me. You really believe you'll enjoy working there, Nancy?"

"For a few years, yes. It will be a great opportunity."

They neared the gate to present their tickets, and two men in dark suits stopped at the far end of the terminal. Both men held briefcases. Helmsby took a sharp glance in their direction, and Yvonne immediately sensed his uneasiness.

"What's wrong?" she asked.

"It's probably nothing," he replied.

Yvonne looked back. "Those men were in the museum earlier, weren't they?"

Helmsby nodded. "Yes, and in the church before that."

"So you believe they're following us?"

"It would appear so."

"I'm not so sure about that," Nancy said.

"Why?" Helmsby replied.

"The couple in front of us," she said, pointing. "They were also in each of those places. Perhaps they're following them?"

Yvonne placed a gentle hand on Nancy's arm and lowered it. "Pointing draws attention to us."

"Sorry."

Helmsby studied the man and woman ahead of them in the terminal. They appeared to be an ordinary married couple, possibly in their early thirties, and touring Germany, as were they. But Helmsby held his reservations about the situation because he had always been a scientist that seldom interacted with others outside of laboratories. Having been isolated from the outside world culture, he didn't know whether the couple should be anyone's concern. And after enduring all his ordeals with TransGenCorp over the years and his brief imprisonment by his only true enemy, Idris, Helmsby clung to a deep paranoia that prevented him from ever trusting anyone outside his small circle of friends, which had grown even smaller since their escape from Pittsburgh.

"If these men are following anyone, it's probably us," Helmsby said.

Yvonne patted his arm and shook her head. "Hon, you need to stop thinking everyone is out to kill you."

Helmsby offered a small nod. "I know, but it's been difficult. I've done well during these past six months in Europe. Well, until today."

"Your paranoia was fading," she said. "Maybe you're overly nervous about returning to the States. You feel safer here."

"That's possible, I suppose. I do feel safer."

"You've allowed yourself to relax. Don't let that freedom be robbed by fear."

Helmsby sighed. "I'll try."

They showed their tickets to two security officers and passed through the gate to board the plane. Helmsby sat beside the window, but his apprehension didn't lessen. The married couple sat in the middle seats, five rows ahead of them. For a few minutes, he thought the two suits had boarded a different flight. Then the men approached the stairs and boarded the plane.

The two men walked down the aisle toward them and Yvonne entwined her fingers with Helmsby's. Helmsby's tightened grip forced her to yank her hand free. The men walked past and took their seats near the back of the plane.

"Bob," she whispered, massaging her fingers. "Calm down."

Helmsby straightened his glasses, folded his hands in his lap, and looked out the window. The runway appeared before them and the plane gained speed. In a few seconds, they'd be in the air, leaving Germany behind, and he wondered what would happen once they reached New York, hours from now. He couldn't picture any positive outcome, no matter how hard he tried.

Chapter 14

Lucian returned to Suncastle Apartments, placed his thumb against Gunter's car door, and closed his eyes. He didn't expect the cloned fingerprints to work. To his surprise, the door unlocked. He started the engine and drove to Mech Cybernetics' parking garage. He chuckled, thinking about the surprise Gunter's superiors would experience once they discovered he wasn't dead and had returned to work. Lucian realized that assuming Gunter's identity put his own life in danger. He prepared himself to expect the worst. There was a good possibility that they might make a bolder attempt to kill him inside the lab.

TREY HID with his brother's body near their company car. Since the morning traffic had picked up, getting to his car without being seen by pedestrians was impossible. His strength and energy had waned. He barely had enough strength to carry his brother away from the garage before Gunter and another man returned. Three more hours passed before he regained sufficient energy to carry Simon an additional ten yards. Afterwards, he stopped for a half hour before continuing. He needed food, sustenance.

Simon's corpse was stiff and cold. Although he had killed others, Trey had never held or touched a dead body before. The chill of icy flesh disturbed him. Through the night he whispered to his brother, hoping Simon would awaken, but the bullet holes in his head never healed. The eyes he once regarded with genuine brotherly compassion were glazed white and lifeless. In the strange world he had only known for a few months, he was alone. Not only was his brother dead, a part of him had died as well.

For the first time, he experienced the confusion of remorse and tears. And for the first time, he had failed to carry out his assignment.

If he had had his gun when Gunter returned, he'd have shot his brother's killer. He didn't understand how Gunter had become two people, twins. Until he managed to kill the second one, he was concerned about reporting the failure to his superiors. Failure meant death.

With his brother in his arms, he struggled to his feet. Staggering forward, he reached the car and propped Simon against the back door while opening the front. He placed him in the passenger seat and shut the door. Placing his hands on his knees, he leaned over and vomited onto the sidewalk.

Too many emotions assailed his mind too quickly. He didn't know how to react and his sensory perceptions overloaded. He hoped his superiors could explain why it felt like his insides were being torn out.

NEW JERSEY HIGH TOWER

"TYPHIS, YOU HAVE TO SEE THIS," Steph Franks said, sitting at her computer.

Typhis Black turned his tall, slender body toward her. His olive skin glistened with sweat. His dark eyes pierced into hers like a hungry raven. The dark circles beneath his fatigued eyes mocked death.

"What is it?" he asked in an agitated whisper.

"We just received a report that indicates Gunter started his car."

"Impossible. His assassination occurred last night. He's Pawn 13."

"I understand that was the mission. However, Trey and Simon have never reported in either."

Typhis flinched at her remark. His hands shook. A puzzled expression showed on his face.

"We had no complications with the first twelve pawns. Trey and Simon killed them quickly and quietly. What happened?"

"I have no idea. No reports have been filed nor has any updated progress."

"Review the video footage from the Mech Cybernetics cameras. Tap into the street cameras and view what occurred during his route home. I want the full report with pictures on my desk in no less than two hours."

She smiled. "Not a problem."

"If he survived, *why'd* he come back? What does he want? Let's see what he came for. I'll inform my infiltrated guards that he's arriving. He can come inside without confrontation, but he leaves in a body bag."

MECH CYBERNETICS

LUCIAN PARKED Gunter's car near the elevator in the parking garage. He left his 9mm under the driver's seat but wished he didn't have to leave it behind. Flash memories informed him that Mech Cybernetics had a metal detector that couldn't be avoided once he stepped from the elevator. If he found the materials Gunter had been working on quickly, he'd have no reason for a gun anyway.

The elevator opened on the second floor and a guard presented an electronic scan board. The guard's face was hidden behind a bronze-tinted glass helmet. A wave of intimidation flooded through Lucian. Several moments passed before he realized this fear was Gunter's trepidation and was imprinted into Lucian's mind as it sought to override Lucian's instincts. Involuntarily, Lucian swallowed hard and his chest tightened. These emotions he'd never known before attempted to control his own.

"You're clear," the guard said. "Go to your station."

Lucian nodded, and the phone at the guard's station rang.

Across the room, Lucian identified Gunter's workstation and headed to it. Midway, he passed Violet. She looked up with a broad, almost seductive smile, and he couldn't resist a bold smile in return, which flattered her even more. Excitement rushed through him. He realized Gunter had possessed a deep crush on this young, beautiful lady. He easily understood the desire.

Lucian wondered, though, why Gunter hadn't expressed his feelings to her. One look in her eyes revealed her obvious interest in him. Men with low self-esteem were clueless to recognize a beautiful woman's vivid interest in them, and too often, they missed out on the opportunity for such a relationship due to their blindness.

He sat at a high-back chair and watched her. Although the crush was Gunter's, Lucian's personal interest intensified. His nervous stomach ached. He wasn't certain what Kyle had done. More than Gunter's memories had melded into his brain. Unfamiliar emotions were bombarding Lucian as well.

Nervousness and intimidation weren't part of Lucian's nature. Copied from Lucas' genetic template, Lucian would have asserted himself to make an introduction and ask the woman out. He wasn't here for such reasons, but he had to find a way to talk to her about Gunter, GenTech, and Mech Cybernetics soon. He wanted to transfer his outer appearance back to normal and wash Gunter's memories and emotions from his mind. With two sets of battling emotions flooding Lucian's mind, his own reflexes weren't responsive, and these possible hesitations were dangerous delays that could get him killed during a violent confrontation.

Staring at Violet, a sense of dread and apprehension rose when he thought about approaching her. He didn't understand the reason.

For a room filled with ten scientists, the laboratory was overly quiet. When he gazed into the eyes of any coworker, they immediately broke eye contact and busied themselves with other tasks. Most never glanced up from their projects.

Violet stood from her station and made her way toward the vending machine room. Lucian followed. She took a Styrofoam cup and poured herself a cup of coffee. She set the cup beside a microwave, ripped open a couple of creamer packets and sweetener, and then she stirred them with a plastic stick. Her back was to him when he entered the room.

Sensing her attraction to Gunter, Lucian wanted to play on their possible romance. He figured that would be the easiest way to ask her more questions about the workplace and the experiments Mech Cybernetics conducted.

Lucian cleared his throat and said, "You're Violet, correct?"

She stiffened. The coffee stirrer dropped into the cup. She turned, wide-eyed, and extremely nervous. The attraction he had noticed was replaced by fear.

"Sorry. I didn't mean to alarm you," he said.

She shook her head and placed a finger to her lips. She eased closer and whispered in his ear. "Are you trying to get us killed?"

"I'm sorry? I thought you were attracted to me."

She offered a slight smile. "I am, but you know that after the murders within our company, we're not allowed to speak. Even in *here*. Dammit, they've probably already picked up our voices."

Her attention turned toward the door.

"It's best that we get back to our workstations," she said. "If we're fortunate, they didn't detect our conversation."

She grabbed her coffee and headed to the door. He turned her toward him. She yanked away.

She scowled. "I know you're new here, but you're going to get us killed."

Lucian sighed. "I need to talk to you. Not here, but maybe after our shift?"

"I can't."

"Can we meet *somewhere*? Anywhere? Your life may be in jeopardy."

With narrowed eyes, Violet returned an even smile. "Any danger for my life started three minutes ago when you first spoke to me."

"I'm serious."

"So am I," she hissed and bolted away.

"Can we, please?"

She placed her hand on the doorknob and paused before opening it. "Sure. I'll wait near the elevator in the parking garage, but I won't wait long."

"Thanks."

Violet pushed the door outward and was yanked through the door with extreme force.

TYPHIS SPOKE into the elevator guard's helmet mike. "Gunter's here for Violet. I'm not sure why, but kill them both."

"Yes sir."

Chapter 15

Violet screamed when the guard grabbed the back of her hair and forced her to the floor. Her hot coffee splashed across the man's boot. Placing his foot against her neck, he aimed the rifle at her face. Her horrified eyes glanced toward Lucian. She pleaded wordlessly for help. Before he squeezed the trigger, Lucian was across the room and flung him off her.

Unarmed, the last thing Lucian needed was a confrontation with a militant guard. The guard, in full body armor, shuffled back to his feet and rushed forward. Lucian thrust his fist through the glass visor, impacting glass shards into the man's face. He blinked and shook his head. Blood streamed from the lacerations and his broken nose. His eyes shimmered silver, like the man in the garage, and his rage ensued.

Lucian wondered what genetic component made these men's eyes different from all of Idris' genetic soldiers. The silver shimmering occurred just seconds before their appearances altered.

Violet crawled across the floor and huddled near the counter and vending machines. Though frightened, she couldn't take her eyes off the guard.

The guard ripped the helmet from his head and reached for his 9mm. Lucian kicked the man's knee and snatched the gun from its holster. He slammed the butt of the gun across the man's face and dropped him. Pinning the guard with a knee to the back, he cuffed the guard.

He motioned for Violet. "Come on," he said.

She looked around the room, expecting more guards. After the better part of a minute, she finally stood and walked to him.

Growling stopped them from leaving the room. Lucian turned. The guard snapped the cuffs and scurried across the floor for the rifle.

Lucian fired two rounds into the side of the man's head. He collapsed with his hand outstretched, only inches from the weapon. Had he been a few seconds faster he would have reached it.

Lucian took Violet's hand and walked to the door. "If they didn't detect our voices, there's no mistaking gunfire. Let's get out of here."

"I can't."

"Why not?"

"They'll kill me if I leave with you."

"They certainly will if you don't."

She pulled back. "I didn't break company policy. *You* did."

"You really think that matters? He was going to shoot you without question."

"I can negotiate for myself," she said.

"He didn't seem too inviting to hear anything you had to say."

"I didn't do anything wrong."

Lucas nodded. "I know. The others who were killed didn't violate company code, either. Nor did Gunter."

Violet looked confused. "What are you talking about? You *are* Gunter."

Lucian smiled. "I *look* like Gunter. Gunter was murdered last night."

Angered, she shook her head. Her beautiful eyes glared a death stare. She said, "I'm a scientist, and you're treating me like a fool. I don't know what your game is, but I'm not playing."

"Whatever the game is, we're both players in it now. Like it or not. We don't make the rules, and we cannot change them. To win, we must survive. They don't allow any timeouts here." He pulled the red pawn from his pocket. "This was left on Gunter's body after he was killed."

She gasped. "The news stated that red pawns were left on the bodies of the other members in Gunter's team when they were killed, too."

Lucian nodded. Gunter's memories informed him the other four were his coworkers. "Why his particular station?"

"I don't know. They transferred here with you. Surely, you have some knowledge as to why they'd want you dead."

"I told you that I'm not Gunter. My name's Lucian."

Violet's face reddened. "This is bullshit! I'm going to my workstation. God help you when they come for you."

She turned to leave, and he yanked her arm. "Maybe this will clarify things."

Shaping facial muscles and shifting bones and flesh, he returned to the face he had worn the night before. Her arm shook in his grip. She pried at his fingers to be released, but he didn't lessen his grasp.

Horror filled her voice. "*What* the hell are you?"

"I haven't time to explain, but if you want to get out of here alive, I need your help. Other guards will be coming soon."

Staring into his eyes, she tried to hide her desperation and surrendered a slight nod. Closing his eyes, he concentrated on Gunter's facial image in his mind and replaced his face with Gunter's.

"What do you need?"

"I need to retrieve whatever experiments Gunter and his team worked on. I believe we'll find clues to discover who's responsible for the murders. Then we get the hell out of here."

"I can show you where they store their research samples, but it is print locked. You'd need his thumbprint to unlock it."

"Not a problem."

She glanced at his hands. "His handprints, too? You have to explain how you're able to do that."

Lucian nodded. "For today, I am Gunter. I tried to rescue him before they killed him, but I failed. I won't fail in finding the people responsible for killing him and all the other Red Pawn Murder victims."

The other eight scientists huddled in the floor behind their tables when Lucian stepped into the room with the 9mm in hand. Violet led him to the refrigerated cabinets.

Lucian pressed his palm against the scanner and the sealed door popped open. A cloud of frosty air spilled from the chamber. He pulled the door open. Stacked rows of labeled Petri dishes rested on metal grid shelves.

"Get me a cooler," he said.

Violet started hunting through the lower cabinet doors. She finally found an insulated transport cooler used to move tissue samples from one laboratory to another to prevent degradation to outside temperature changes.

"Here."

"Open it, so I can place these inside."

After she slid the top open, he placed the petri dishes into neat stacks inside the cooler. He emptied all the cultures from the refrigerator and filled the cooler, closed it, and placed his hands tightly upon hers where she held it.

"You carry it," he said. "Whatever you do, whatever happens, *don't* drop the cooler. You keep it protect, and I'll protect you."

"TYPHIS," Steph said. "Mike Gunter killed the guard."

She pointed to live video surveillance feed inside the GenTech lab. "Now he's taking the tissue samples your men were supposed to steal."

"Dammit."

"Does he know what they're for?"

Typhis rubbed his fatigue eyes. "He must."

"What are you going to do?"

A smiled formed on his thin, cracked lips. "He has to be eliminated."

Typhis walked from the room and stood in a hallway with large windows that featured a panoramic view of Newark. Placing his hands against the cold glass, he spoke into his head mike. "Mr. Gunter will be exiting the elevator in less than three minutes. He has Violet Prater with him. Kill them and take possession of the cooler he possesses. I want them dead. Do not allow the contents to be harmed in any way."

The garage guards gave him affirmation they'd carry out the orders.

Chapter 16

Lucian stood at the elevator and aimed the 9mm at the sliding doors. She placed her hand over the print scanner. "You want me to open it?"

He nodded. "Yes, I'm ready."

She pressed her hand against the scanner. His hand tightened on the gun. The doors slid open but no one was inside. Sweat crept along his brow. His breathing increased. The gun shook in his hand. He swallowed and expelled a long sigh. Gunter's emotions were trying to control him again.

"You okay?" she asked.

Lucian nodded. "Yeah. You go first."

Violet eased into the elevator. He backed his way in, watching for anyone approaching. A scientist in the room gasped when a side stairwell door opened.

"Close the doors!" Lucian said.

She pressed the button. Right as the door sealed shut, three soldiers dropped to their knees, aimed, and fired at the elevator.

The elevator descended. Lucian lowered his gun and leaned against the wall. Bullets dented the outer door. He shook his head. "Getting in was easy. Getting out won't be."

TYPHIS RETURNED to Steph's desk and watched the elevator camera footage. He studied the man he thought to be Gunter. Amused, Typhis said, "He's scared to death. In a few minutes he won't have anything to ever fear again."

THE COOLER SHOOK in Violet's hand.

"You okay?" Lucian asked.

"If you get me out of this alive, I will be."

"Getting out of the parking garage is only the beginning. They'll send more men after us."

Lucian closed his eyes and leaned back against the elevator wall. His stomach sickened. When he opened his eyes, he looked directly at the surveillance camera and winced. Using the 9mm like a hammer, he jumped up and smashed the camera lens with the gun butt.

Violet studied him with curiosity. "What is this all about?"

He shrugged. "I was hoping you could tell me."

"I work with gene splicing. I have no idea about anything else."

"Do you have any idea what Gunter worked on?"

"No. His team came here from GenTech after the merger. Whatever they worked on was secretive and never disclosed to the rest of us."

"Does Mech Cybergenics sound familiar?"

She nodded. "Of course. That's our company."

Lucian frowned. "Strange that Gunter and his team were the ones killed."

She nodded. "I know. We weren't ever allowed to associate with them or even introduce ourselves."

"Before the murders started?"

"Yes, we were warned a week before they came not to speak to them at all."

"But you were attracted to Gunter?"

Violet blushed. "Maybe that's why. The forbidden are always more desirable."

OUTSIDE THE ELEVATOR, the guards took their positions behind parked cars and concrete supports. They watched the light above the elevator doors as it detailed each floor the elevator passed. Like S.W.A.T. snipers, they held their guns and patiently waited.

Typhis also watched the doors via a garage surveillance camera.

THE ELEVATOR STOPPED at the basement floor. Lucian stared into Violet's catlike eyes. She hit the emergency lock button on the panel.

Lucian wiped sweat from his brow. "That won't keep them out long."

"How do you plan to get past the guards?"

He shrugged. "Kill them. There isn't another option."

Her eyes narrowed with concern. "But they have the same body armor as the guard upstairs, right?"

"Yes, and they probably better weapons."

"How do you expect to stand a chance?"

He smiled. "Fast, accurate shots. When the doors open, press yourself into that corner out of the line of fire."

Violet stepped to where he indicated. He leaned against the corner beside the control panel. He reached for the button to open the doors, but he hesitated.

Gunter's memories of two men pursuing him through dark streets and alleys froze his hand. Uncertainty gripped him. He fought to push the button.

"What's wrong?"

Lucian shoved his determined survival instinct and consumed Gunter's timid, lingering fears. He slammed the button, and when the doors slid open, he raised the 9mm and fired.

The first two guards were crouched twenty feet away from the elevator doors. Lucian fired direct shots to their heads. Their visors shattered and the men fell. Watching the two guards drop, Lucian stepped forward to exit the elevator. A rifle fired. The round struck Lucian's shoulder and the impact slung him back. He dropped to the floor.

Violet screamed. She set the cooler down and took a step toward him.

"No!" Lucian yelled. "Stay there. I'll be okay."

Blood soaked his shirt and seeped into a small pool. He rolled into the safety of the corner out of the line of fire.

"You're losing a lot of blood," she said.

"I'll be fine. Just don't move from that spot."

Lucian rolled to his stomach, noticed a brave guard stepping out from the protection of a concrete support. He fired a headshot and dropped him.

WATCHING the garage surveillance footage of guards dropping to the concrete dead, Typhis frowned. "There's no way in hell that's Mike Gunter."

"What?" Steph asked. "Who could it be? All the facial scanners indicate it is him."

Typhis shook his head. "No, it cannot possibly be him. The real Gunter has no experience with guns, and he's too much of a coward to act so boldly."

"I can do a facial scan through the surveillance camera to make certain."

"That won't be necessary. Once he's dead, it won't matter."

LUCIAN WATCHED for movement among the parked vehicles, but no one else moved. It was possible that no more guards remained, but doubtful.

Glancing at Violet, he said, "Any idea how many guards are posted inside the garage?"

"No. But I've seldom seen more than two and those are usually at the gate."

Lucian rose to his feet and pressed his back against the wall panel. The shoulder wound had stopped bleeding.

"Stay where you are," he said. "I'm going out to see how many more are out there."

"Do you have a death wish? You don't seem afraid to die."

"We're both dead if we stay in this elevator."

Lucian ran to the nearest line of parked cars and ducked. No guns fired, so he stood and scanned the dim garage. Nothing. He walked back to the elevator. He expected far more soldiers.

Placing a hand on her shoulder, he said, "Let's get out of here before they send reinforcements."

Violet grabbed the cooler and followed Lucian to Gunter's car.

STEPH MOTIONED TO TYPHIS. "Gunter is in his car."

Typhis smiled. "Have the GPS keep track his location. He won't get far."

She nodded and typed commands into the computer.

Chapter 17

New York City

DENNIS SCHRADER WALKED down Franklin Street. Being an attorney, he liked wearing the best suits available and wasn't ashamed to flaunt his wealth. Wearing a black trench coat that waved like a cape behind him while he walked along the cold, windy street. He paused to check the time on his platinum Rolex.

Having earned a black belt in Aikido, he occasionally liked to lure muggers into attacking him so he could enact his own type of justice outside the courthouse.

Two men had followed him for three blocks. He pretended to window shop and noticed their reflections on the storefront windows each time he stopped. They didn't attempt to hide their presence from him.

His stalking shadows were dressed in ostentatious suits like his. Not all thugs wore leather rags. The worst possibility was that these men were possibly members of various mobs that he had helped convict and sent to prison over the few years. His relentless reputation to shut down Mafia family members had brought numerous, anonymous threats, but Dennis paid little attention to them.

To venture his own amusement, Dennis stepped into a side alley, knowing they'd pursue. The men didn't hesitate. He smiled. He had a few surprises he wanted to share with them. What he didn't expect was that they had some surprises of their own.

NEW YORK
JFK International Airport

HELMSBY REMAINED SEATED until the two men he believed were following him had exited the plane. Then he followed Nancy and Yvonne to the exit and descended the stairs. After retrieving their luggage, he felt a sense of relief in not seeing the men anywhere inside the terminal.

Once they stepped to the curb to hail a cab, the two men approached. Both were wearing mirrored shades and visible earpieces. Neither revealed a federal badge, but they acted as professionally as federal agents would.

"Dr. Helmsby," the man said, extending his hand. "I'm Donald Beck."

Helmsby placed his handbag on the curb and cautiously shook the man's hand.

Beck said, "We understand that you've retired from your genetic research? Is this true?"

Helmsby nodded. "I have."

"Would you consider entering the field of biotechnology again, if the price was acceptable?"

Helmsby smiled. "I don't need money. My investments over the years will adequately support me for the remainder of my life."

"Money's not an interest?" Beck smiled. "I can understand that. But, what if I told you . . . you'd be working with alien DNA."

His eyes widened. "Alien DNA? Meaning extraterrestrial? "

"Yes, sir. Alien DNA is what has allowed our cryogenics program to become possible."

"How did you come across this?"

Beck smiled. "Ah. Now, we can only discuss this more if you agree to return to our laboratories with us."

Surprise and a sudden thirst for new genetic discoveries glowed in Helmsby's eyes. He looked at Yvonne and then to Nancy.

Yvonne smiled. "You'll never rid yourself of the genetics bug, will you, Hon?"

"But Yvonne," he said, scratching his goatee. "This is an opportunity of a lifetime. Think of what discoveries such science holds—what we could learn, newer advancements in biotechnology. The progress and knowledge is never ending."

"I know," she replied. "We've had a great six months. I imagine you're eager to get back to the lab."

A glance toward Nancy and his eagerness faded. He sighed. "I made a promise."

Nancy embraced him. "As far as I'm concerned, you've kept it. You've given me a lifetime of father and daughter memories during these past few months. This project's important to you. There's no denying that. I couldn't live with myself if I stood in your way. Besides, I'm scheduled to return to Germany and start working for their space program."

"I should postpone this until then."

"No, it's perfectly fine."

Helmsby returned his attention to Beck. "I suppose that settles it. Where do I report?"

He replied, "You ride with us."

"And Yvonne and Nancy?"

"We'll drop them off wherever they want to go."

"I stay with Bob," Yvonne said, folding her arms.

"Very well." Beck dialed a number on his cell.

A few minutes later, an almond-colored limo with mirrored windows pulled alongside the curb. Helmsby and Yvonne exchanged glances.

"This is a government operation?" he asked.

Beck smiled again. "Closely associated."

A sense of apprehension filled Helmsby when Beck opened the rear door of the limo. He wondered if his lust for biotechnology had ensnared him into a world more sinister than TransGenCorp had been.

Yvonne placed a hand on his shoulder. "Bob, are you sure about this?"

He leaned closer to her ear and whispered, "I think it's too late to back out now."

She squeezed his arm.

Another car with tinted windows parked behind the limo. More muscle, Helmsby thought. What discoveries waited at the end of this rabbit's tunnel? What dangers?

Beck held the door open, unsmiling, and with a stern face, he gave an insistent nod. Helmsby seated himself between Yvonne and Nancy on the back leather seat. Across from them sat the man who wished to hire him.

The man was broad shouldered with a thick chest. The bulge of his biceps strained the arm stitches of his charcoal Armani suit. His face was stern, muscled, and young, an obvious contrast with his grayish-silver hair. No blemishes or wrinkles cursed his confident face.

"Welcome to Grayson Enterprises," the man said, extending his huge muscled hand. "I'm Boyd Grayson, the owner."

Helmsby accepted his hand with a forced smile. "Thank you. This is Yvonne, my fiancée, and my daughter, Nancy."

Grayson shook their hands graciously and said, "I'd offer you champagne, Dr. Helmsby, but I understand that you won't drink anything with alcohol in it."

Helmsby studied Grayson's face. "I don't understand. Have we met before?"

Grayson smiled, revealing perfect white rows of teeth. "No, Dr. Helmsby, we've never met, but I've been an avid follower of your work for years. Your dedication to genetics impresses the Hell out of me. Few people in this world hold my admiration."

"I see."

"However," Grayson said, pointing to the cabinet beside Helmsby. "There's a thermos of hot, green tea in there. Help yourself."

Helmsby opened the cabinet. "You do know my favorite beverage."

Grayson nodded. "We're alike in many ways, Dr. Helmsby."

"How?"

"Research is the central focus of our lives. Yours is based in genetics. Mine is with people, technology, and financial gain."

Helmsby sipped the tea. "Money's never been a high priority for me. Science is though."

Grayson smiled. "That's why I need you."

"I see."

"I'm afraid you don't. Not yet, anyway, but you will. I'm offering you a very lucrative position with my company in the newest field of biotechnology."

"Your assistant mentioned your field of cryogenics and the use of extraterrestrial DNA."

Grayson folded his thick hands and rested them on his lap. "That's just scratching the surface of what we've obtained. Our field of technology will expand far beyond that, with you working for me, of course."

Yvonne cleared her throat. "Not intending to belittle your hospitality, Mr. Grayson, but I have something I'd like to ask."

"Sure. Anything."

"Do you make it a practice to follow potential employees several days before you offer them employment? Overseas is a bit extreme."

Helmsby's eyes widened. "Yvonne!"

Grayson laughed. "It's okay, Dr. Helmsby. That's a legitimate question. I see where she may have concerns as to my integrity."

Yvonne smiled. "I wasn't head of security at TransGenCorp for any other reason."

"Let's just say I have some very competitive rivals in my business. We had to recently adjust to modifications we didn't expect."

"Like what?" she asked.

"Expansions and some drastic cutbacks, but the situations will balance out soon. As far as my men following you, that was mere coincidence. They happened upon you."

Yvonne frowned. "In Germany? How is that coincidence?"

"Germany is rapidly advancing their space program, but they are still a few years behind my technological advancements. We placed an offer on the table to work together. They declined. Their loss, of course."

Helmsby rested the thermos between his legs. "So you're working with space technology, too?"

"We're scheduled to launch our first expedition to Mars next year, Dr. Helmsby. I have a small base camp on the Deimos moon. I understand Nancy is interested in the space technology field?"

Nancy nodded. "Yes."

"Would you consider working at Grayson Enterprises? It'd be nice to have another Helmsby working for me. You could have an office in the same suite as your father."

She looked at Helmsby and a smile spread across her face. "That would be nice. But what job are you offering me?"

Grayson smiled. "Where do your interests lie? What job did you hope to obtain in Germany?"

"Nuclear physics engineer in propulsion engines."

Grayson chuckled and glanced to Helmsby. "Quite a daughter you have."

"Indeed."

"I'd say you taught her well?"

Helmsby smiled. "I did what I could, but her desire to study and learn is something I didn't instill in her."

"I'm sure you set a prime example of being a hardcore scientist."

"I tried," Helmsby said with a slight shrug. "If I may change the subject, how'd you get alien DNA?"

Grayson popped open a briefcase on the seat beside him. He handed Helmsby a yellow folder. "Confidentiality forms first, Dr. Helmsby, and you, too, Nancy and Yvonne. I had a feeling you'd be eager to learn more about it. But you've not given me a definite yes or no."

Helmsby looked for a supportive answer from Yvonne. Both she and Nancy nodded.

"A definite yes," he said.

Helmsby signed his name with bold pen strokes and handed the folder to Yvonne. She signed her form and passed the folder to Nancy. She didn't hesitate to place her signature on another form.

Grayson shook hands with Helmsby. "Glad to have all of you aboard. I believe having the Helmsbys work for me will expand Grayson Enterprises beyond even my imagination."

The thought of having access to studying alien DNA thrilled Helmsby, but part of him believed he had just signed his soul over to the devil. Everything had progressed too quickly. He wished he had talked to Daniel before making this hasty decision.

Chapter 18

The dark alley Dennis entered was quiet except for the two sets of footsteps advancing behind him. A large mural of half-dressed, pole-dancing women covered a large section of the wall. La Vida Erotica was painted in bold, red letters above the women. He stood in the alley behind this club.

To the right of the sign was a rusted ladder that led to rooms above where these dancers earned extra money from patrons after hours. The thought of the sideline jobs these women did disgusted him. Although he had not represented any of the women in this establishment in court, he had represented abused women from other such clubs. Some women accepted the abuse as what came with the job, but not him. He wished to protect such women from the sleaze balls, which he could only do once they pressed charges. Not before. Thus, this was one reason why he chose to inflict justice outside of the courtroom. Sadly, courts frowned on such vigilante activities.

But La Vida Erotica was different from the other gentlemen's clubs, if truly that was what they should be called. The irony sickened him.

No complaints had come from any women who worked at La Vida Erotica, but several of the male customers had actually filed abuse charges against the club. These suits were settled out of court and records were sealed from the media, but he often wondered how severe and what the abuse had been. What injuries had these men sustained? Had the women assaulted the men, or had the bouncers overextended their duties to protect them? He had no way to know exactly what had happened.

Dennis led the two men midway through the vandalized, graffiti-painted walls and stopped where dumpsters lined both sides of the narrow alley. This area was far enough from the main street to lessen the chance that the police or other passersby might see him. Reaching into his pockets, a smile eased across his lips. He slid brass knuckles onto his left hand and released the safety on the gun in his right.

He had expected these men to make their demands known well before now. Their unexpected silence puzzled him. He loved the thrill of mugging muggers, of tipping the justice scales in favor of good. It gave an additional excitement to his otherwise mundane life. Of course, presenting his arguments in court brought some satisfaction, but whenever inadequate juries or pantywaist judges incorrectly concluded their decisions, many culprits returned to the streets to keep doing whatever wrongful deeds they wished. Citizens were their prey.

Dennis turned quickly with his gun drawn. The smile on his face quickly drained.

These men's motives and suits suddenly no longer held his interest. Their strange faces and eyes did. Without realizing it, warm urine trickled down his left leg and dripped into his shoe. His hand lost grip on the gun. When he tried to steady it, one of the strange men rushed him, snapped his right wrist in an instant, and picked up his gun.

Dennis sobbed. The shock of seeing their pallid complexions, blue-tinted lips and glazed eyes brought a rush of bile to the back of his throat. His useless hand hung limply. He was too stunned to feel the pain. The only thing he offered was pathetic whimpering. A few seconds later, he died by his own gun. His whining ceased.

Blood seeped from the side of his head. His killer dropped a chess piece on his chest.

A black pawn.

A smooth, laser-carved number was printed on the bottom.

Number 1.

VANESSA POWELL SQUEEZED her back against the cold bricks and swallowed hard. She held her breath. She had never seen a man die or witnessed a murder before. In the shadows between two dumpsters, she bit her lower lip to prevent herself from screaming.

When the chess piece dropped on the man's bloody chest, she peered with wide eyes. Though quiet, she thought the one man might have heard her. After he released the black pawn, he turned in her direction. His strange eyes stared at the wall above the dumpsters, but from their strange frozen appearance, she wasn't certain he could actually see. She had seen the same glazed sheen covering the eyes of a dead rat or cat, but these two men appeared to be very much alive.

After two endless minutes, the man finally turned away. Fifteen minutes later, she was still uncertain of her safety, but she crawled into the alley anyway. She couldn't hide there forever. La Vida Erotica would send one of their protectors to find her. Her john had paid handsomely and left, but she couldn't leave the club. They owned her. She had no freedom.

Rodents peered at her from beneath the dumpsters and from the vent in the wall. They crinkled their noses in the air, smelling the sex scent her body still possessed since she had yet to shower.

Vanessa tucked her skirt tightly between her legs and kneeled forward into a crawling position. Nervous sweat mingled with her sweaty pheromones. She dared to look around the dumpster in the direction where the two men had left. Other than her and the dead man, no one else lingered in the alley.

She rose to her feet and wiped the grime and filth from her knees. With timid grace, she crept to Dennis Schrader's dead body with the curiosity of a child. His face was pale. His eyes were empty. She touched his warm face and shook him. He didn't respond.

The black pawn lay in a small blood pocket. She knelt and patted his jacket pockets and found his cell phone. Being isolated inside La Vida Erotica, she knew no one she could call. But she remembered a female bartender telling her about 9-1-1.

"If you ever get into trouble, dial those three numbers," she had said. "And the police will come."

She did have enough knowledge to know which numbers to type into the cell phone, but La Vida Erotica had deliberately limited the dancers' education and trained them as pets for high paying men and women executives. "Living, Virtual Sex Toys," was what they advertised.

Vanessa didn't know why, but she felt remorse for the dead man. She found his wallet and opened it. His driver's license informed her of his name. Several hundred-dollar bills and a fifty were stashed inside. She left the money because she had not earned it, but she found a plastic foldout that held numerous pictures. These fascinated her.

Dennis Schrader was in most of the pictures with a very attractive woman. She didn't realize this was his wife, but in each picture, he held a broad, genuine smile. On the flipside of the photos were more pictures. She frowned while she studying these. They were of a baby. Dumbfounded, she didn't have a clue what to make of them. She had never seen an infant before. In fact, she didn't remember anything about her childhood or have any idea *what* existed earlier in her life. Uneasiness settled upon her. She folded the wallet and tucked it back inside his vest.

Overhead, on the balcony, the doorknob to her assigned room rattled. Before her assigned protector opened the door to step out onto the fire escape, she hurried between the dumpsters and dialed 9-1-1.

The police might not be able to help Dennis Schrader, but she hoped they rescued her. Maybe she'd discover who she really was and where she had come from.

Chapter 19

Lucian drove Violet away from the parking garage. The gate arm guard had been one of the casualties, so he stopped the car and pressed the lift button himself. The cooler containing the genetic tissues rested on the floor between her feet. After he pulled onto the city street, he looked at his beautiful passenger and smiled.

She placed her hand beneath his shoulder strap and inspected his shoulder with a confused expression on her face.

"You should be dead," she said.

"Some would say."

Violet frowned. "How did you do all of this? The loss of blood should have killed you."

"I know. I have to get food soon or I'll be very sick."

"How the hell did you change your face like that?"

"You work with gene splicing?"

She nodded. "Yes."

"Let's just say I'm a more advanced scientific experiment than you've ever work on."

Cocking her head to the side, she tried to look into his eyes. "What are you saying? You're a manufactured human?"

Lucian's eyes narrowed. "Something like that."

"You have my attention. I'm curious. What exactly are you?"

"Knowing what I am might get you killed."

"Top secret shit?"

"Exactly."

"My life's already in jeopardy. I cannot return to my job and probably not to my apartment."

Lucian nodded. "I strongly recommend that you do neither."

"So, I've nothing else to lose."

He sighed and looked into his rearview mirror. She turned and stared over her shoulder. A black BMW with mirror-tinted windows sped up from behind. Lucian turned left at the next intersection. The car followed. He turned right. The car kept a close pace behind them.

"Are they following us?" she asked.

"It appears so." Lucian pulled his 9mm from under the seat and rested it between his legs.

"Oh, God," she whispered. "Not again."

He smiled. "You didn't think it would be *that* easy, did you?"

Her eyes widened. "Easy? Shit, we almost died once."

"As I said, that was only the beginning."

KAT'S CELL PHONE RANG.

She answered and Carpenter said, "Kat, are you certain you won't come work for us?"

"Why?"

"It seems the Game of Pawns has taken a new slant."

"What do you mean by game?"

"A second player has emerged. Someone killed Dennis Schrader in New York today. They left a calling card. A *black* pawn with the number one cut into it."

Kat frowned. "Was Mr. Schrader a scientist?"

"No. An attorney."

"Damn."

"What?"

"That complicates things."

"Why?"

"If he had been a scientist, we'd have a solid pattern, possibly even a revenge motive. But big city attorneys make a lot of enemies."

Carpenter sighed. "I know. So, will you help us?"

"I'd have to talk it over with my associates."

"How long will that take?"

"I'll let you know within the hour."

"Make it quicker than that, and I can give you the identities of the first nine red pawns."

"I'll get right back to you."

<hr>

CARPENTER RAN a hand through his gelled black hair and put his cell phone inside his inner vest pocket. He knelt beside Dennis Schrader's body.

"Damn," he whispered.

"What is it?" Denton asked.

Carpenter looked up and half-smiled. "He was wearing brass knuckles. An attorney with brass knuckles?"

Denton nodded. "That's a bit odd."

Carpenter tugged a latex glove over his hand, lifted Schrader's left hand and inspected the brass knuckles. "There's no blood on them. He never landed a punch. And his right hand appears broken at the wrist."

"That eliminates suicide," Denton said.

"Yes. Ballistics will tell us for certain if his own gun was used on him."

Denton shoved his hands into his pockets and looked up at the rusty fire escape. A man wearing dark shades stood with his hands on the railing, watching them.

Denton nodded and pointed with his eyes. "We have an onlooker."

Carpenter remained crouched and glanced up. The man pushed off the railing and entered the door at the side of the fire escape.

"Find out who he is and if he witnessed anything," Carpenter said.

"Sure."

Two police officers brought Vanessa to Carpenter. Carpenter rose to his feet.

"She's the one who called 9-1-1," Officer Johnston said.

"Thanks," Carpenter replied. "Leave her with me. I have some questions to ask her."

Johnston nodded and helped other officers secure the area.

Vanessa's face held the haunting expression that plagued anyone who had witnessed a traumatic event. Her thin clothes concerned him. She wore much less than someone should wear outside in the cold. Her knees were scuffed and soiled with sticky grime.

Carpenter tried to ease her tension with a gentle smile. "Did you see who murdered this man?" he asked.

She took in a sharp breath and nodded.

"Can you give me a description?"

Vanessa looked away, scared.

"It's okay . . . what's your name?" he asked.

She glanced back and replied, "They call me Vanessa."

"Okay, Vanessa, tell me what happened? *Who* did this?"

Vanessa looked down at Schrader's body and wrung her hands.

"I assure you," he said. "They won't harm you. We will protect you. Tell me what you saw."

"The man was dressed in a nice suit, like him. But his face, his eyes, they were so odd."

"What do you mean?"

"They both had pale faces. Pasty white."

"So . . . two men?"

Vanessa nodded and stared at the ground, recalling what she had seen. "Yes. Their eyes were white, or gray, like a dead man."

Carpenter frowned. "I'm not certain I understand what you mean."

"They weren't . . . *normal*. Their eyes were glazed over. They didn't have any color."

"So you're saying their eyes looked dead?"

"Yes."

"Okay. I want you to come back to headquarters. We need to ask you more questions. You'll be safe there. Is there anyone you want us to contact before you go with us?"

She stared at the unopened door near the fire escape and shook her head. "No, there's no one to call."

Carpenter followed her eyes and noticed that she watched the door where the man had entered. She hugged herself, partly from the cold breeze that howled through the alleyway, and partly from fear.

"You work there? In La Vida Erotica?" he asked.

Vanessa replied with a hesitant nod. Carpenter sensed her apprehension and quickly led her back to his car.

"You'll be safe with us," he said.

She climbed into the passenger seat, and in a near whisper, "Thank you."

Chapter 20

The dim lights inside La Vida Erotica made Denton pause right inside the door to allow his eyes to adjust before he walked to the bar.

Rock music played from large wall speakers. Mirrors lined the sides of the stage to mimic a trio of dancers when one fit model stripped her clothing while dancing around a metal pole. Several cages loomed overhead near the smoky lights.

A redhead dressed in leather swayed around the pole while a few lustful patrons sat at the front tables. In the shadow of the stage, two men stood with their arms folded. Denton identified them as bouncers, but the men seemed too small for such positions. Most bars and clubs had thick, muscled men to keep people in check.

While Denton watched the young redhead unbutton her top, the barkeep looked up and noticed him.

"What da you have?" he asked.

The question shook Denton's attention from the dancer. He turned toward the barkeep with an inquisitive stare, not quite certain what the keep had asked.

"Can I help you?" the bartender asked.

"You have a name?" Denton replied.

The barkeep smiled. "If you're buying drinks, you can call me Mick. If not, buzz off."

Denton flashed his badge.

Mick nodded. "Ahh, I see. We run a clean operation here."

"I'm here concerning something else. Not much we can do about you hiring out women since the city now taxes the profession." Denton leaned across the bar and whispered. "There was a murder in the alley behind this establishment. I think one of your workers may have seen something that could help our investigation."

"Male or female?" he asked.

"Male. He was outside on the fire escape earlier."

"Which of our dancers was with him?"

"No one was with him. One of your dancers made the 9-1-1 call, though."

Mick stopped wiping the bar with his towel. His eyes grew narrow, cold. "Which dancer? What's her name?"

"Vanessa."

"You probably saw Vincent then. He's her bodyguard. He went to find her earlier. She's not checked in for some time now."

"Well, she's in safe hands."

Mick folded his arms. "She's supposed to be on stage right now. So you can inform her she needs to get back to work."

Denton shook his head. "That's not going to happen."

"What do you mean? She's our most requested dancer. If she's not on stage, we lose money."

"She witnessed the murder. She's at headquarters."

"How long before she can report?"

"Could be hours."

"Damn."

"Where can I find Vincent?" Denton asked.

Mick waved a topless waitress over. She flashed a smile at Denton. He was glad the dim lights hid his embarrassment.

"Hana," Mick said. "Find Vincent and bring him here."

After Hana left, Denton said, "Mind if I look around?"

"You have a warrant?"

"I need one?"

"Enjoy the stage show, but if you want to see more than that, you'll need a warrant."

"I can get one."

Mick smiled evenly and wiped a beer mug with his towel. "Do so, and you can browse all you want."

Denton yanked out his cell phone and called Carpenter.

CARPENTER ANSWERED on the first ring. "Yes?"

"I need a warrant. How soon can you bring one in?"

"With today's technology? In less than a half hour. You having problems?"

"Bartender's being a smartass."

"I'll be there in a bit."

"Thanks."

Chapter 21

Denton sat on the barstool and watched the redhead swivel her hips while she danced around the pole. She seemed oblivious of the leering men seated in front of her. Her hypnotic movements made him wonder if she was somehow bound in a trance. She trampled their money underfoot without any thought she'd been given tips.

Club dancers he had seen before had routines and knew how to ignore the audience, pretending they didn't exist, but this was a lot different. She appeared to be focused inside a virtual reality game where nothing else existed. The cage dancers overhead acted the same way.

By the time Carpenter arrived with the warrant in hand, Vincent still had not been found. Hana returned to tell the bartender that he was gone. Denton assumed Hana's search was to warn Vincent to hide. With a warrant, they probably didn't need him to find the answers they wanted.

Carpenter smiled as he slapped the warrant on the bar. He stared at the liquor bottles shelved beneath the bar mirror, rubbed his tired eyes and spun around to sit on the stool next to Denton. His face flushed red and he loosened his tie. Perspiration beaded across his forehead.

"Keeping you entertained?" he asked Denton.

Denton sighed. "Hardly. The only reason I know that girl's alive is because she's moving, but not enough to excite me."

"She does appear rather zoned out."

Denton motioned to the cage dancers with a nod. "They all do."

"Drugs?"

"I don't know. That's why I want to look around."

Mick shrugged. "Help yourselves."

Carpenter headed to the side stage door and one of the bouncers stepped in front of him.

Carpenter said. "We have a warrant."

The bouncer didn't move. His dark eyes pierced into Carpenter's. The glare was more intimidating than the man's size. The man couldn't weigh more than a hundred and seventy pounds. Carpenter tried to step around. The thin man shoved him.

Denton went for his gun.

"Whoa!" Mick yelled. "Easy. Let them through!"

The bouncer shook his head in response to Mick's voice and stepped aside. In an instant, his eyes shifted back. His attention returned to the redhead on stage.

"Some crazy shit," Denton said as they went through the door.

"It's odd, but not as strange as what Vanessa said about the two men who killed the attorney in the alley."

"What'd she say?"

Carpenter chuckled. "If we took her for exactly what she's telling us, we're looking for zombies."

Denton shook his head. "That's absurd."

"I know. I've asked a psychiatrist to evaluate her. The trauma of seeing the murder has probably stressed her and played havoc with her memories."

"The bartender is pissed we have her."

"That doesn't surprise me. She's scared to death to return here."

Denton gave him a confused stare. "No pun intended?"

Carpenter shook his head. "No pun intended. The mentioning of this place frightens her."

Denton nodded. "Not all women are happy with how they have to earn money. You think maybe she's being *forced* to work here?"

Carpenter looked down the dark hall behind the stage. Several half dressed women walked in and out of dressing rooms without any concern that two strange men were headed in their direction.

"That's a possibility. It's harder to protect women now that prostitution is legal, provided they have a license to do so. If a woman owes a debt to a person or a corporation like this, and they might pimp her to make her pay back the debt."

"Did she act like that was happening to her?"

"Vanessa?"

Denton nodded.

"I don't know. She acts much younger than she looks. Mentally, she's at a disadvantage. It's like she's not educated at all. Amnesia might explain it though."

"Why?"

"I asked where she was born. She has no knowledge of her birthplace, her parents, or anything outside of La Vida Erotica."

Carpenter glanced into the dressing room. None of the women even acknowledged his presence. He and Denton headed further down the hall to three storage rooms. The first two were unlocked and were used to store kegs of beer and boxes of various liquors. The third door was locked.

Denton slid his lock pick pouch from his back pocket and gave Carpenter a questioning glance. Carpenter nodded.

In less than three minutes, he unlocked the door.

Carpenter pushed the door inward. No light switch was on the wall. He pulled a small flashlight from his pocket.

"What do you suppose this room is for?" Denton asked.

"Not sure. It doesn't look like anyone's been inside it in years."

Dusty cobwebs hung from the ceiling and a tug chain dropped from a single light bulb. Carpenter pulled the chain and the light glowed. A dozen large crates lined the far wall. After a brief inspection, they found them all empty.

Carpenter's light washed across the side of one crate.

"Oh hell," Carpenter said.

In bold black letters was, "Property of TransGenCorp."

"What now?"

"We scour this place," Carpenter said.

Denton unsnapped his 9mm but didn't remove it from its holster.

They searched through the storage rooms, moving boxes of liquor and beer kegs, but didn't find anything else that tied La Vida Erotica to Trans-GenCorp. There didn't appear to be any hidden panels that unlocked possible, concealed doors. The upstairs apartments didn't have anything other than paying patrons with their hired dancers.

Carpenter sighed. "Why would those crates be here?"

Denton shrugged. "No idea. You think maybe these women are like the clones? Creations by Idris?"

"It's possible, but I thought we had closed off TGC."

"Perhaps he sent out his projects before Lucas set Operation Meltdown into place. I don't think we're going to get any answers here."

Carpenter smiled. "You're right, we won't, but we do have one advantage."

"What?"

"Vanessa. If it turns out that she was manufactured, that explains her amnesia-like state. She may not have had a childhood at all. They probably didn't bother to program one for her."

"Manufactured prostitutes? Damn, that's sick."

"Extremely, but there's only one way we'll ever find out."

"Question her?"

Carpenter nodded. "The psychiatric examination might reveal her limited knowledge of her past, but that's not necessarily the proof we need. We need to have a geneticist examine her DNA composition."

"That's all the evidence we'd need. But if she's like the clones, can we close this place down?"

"I don't think any judge would continue to let them operate. These women, if manufactured, aren't here by their own choices. They are no more than sex slaves, even if they have no understanding of what they're doing."

Denton sighed. "No sign of Vincent."

"Did you really think we'd find him?"

"No."

"I figure he's long gone."

Two topless dancers walked past and headed for the stage. Their feet held a steady pace but their eyes didn't seem to notice Carpenter or Denton.

"Ladies," Carpenter said, but they gave no answer.

Denton shook his head. "Let's hurry and stop this."

"I'm for that."

Chapter 22

Lucian sped through a yellow light a second before it changed to red, but the BMW kept pace with him.

"They keep coming," Violet said.

"Yes. They don't plan to back off. Fortunately, there are too many witnesses for them to make a violent attack yet. If it were past curfew, they'd have already attacked."

"So you think they'll try to kill us?"

He nodded. "It's how they operate."

His phone rang. "Yes?"

"Lucian, we have a problem," Kat said.

"How'd you know?"

"You're in trouble?"

"They're in pursuit."

"Did you get the tissue cultures?"

"Of course, and I have a passenger."

"Violet is with you?" Kat's voice hinted disappointment.

"I couldn't leave her," he said.

"I don't see why we need her."

"They tried to kill her, too."

"Oh?"

"Yep. What's this new problem we have, other than the people following behind me?"

"The Game of Pawns is bigger than we thought."

Lucian frowned. "Game of Pawns? We've named this?"

"That's what the FBI is calling it."

"I see. Carpenter's been in touch again?"

"He wants our help."

Lucian cut a hard right, leaving the busier street for one with less traffic.

"I imagine he does."

The BMW slammed his rear bumper.

"Gunter . . . Lucian, watch out!" Violet said.

Kat sighed. "I told him I'd confer with you."

"What do you think we should do? Is it risky?"

The BMW pulled alongside Lucian. The side window lowered, and a man aimed his gun with a silencer at him. Lucian slammed the brakes, brought up his gun, and fired two shots through the back glass of the BMW. Shards of glass dropped like shattered bits of ice. The BMW swerved.

Kat said, "I don't want anything to do with the agency, but he believes we can end this game quicker. It will be dangerous for all of us though."

"Why does he think it's a game?"

"A black pawn was found on an attorney's body today with the number one carved on it. So there's another team of assassins, apparently seeking revenge for their recent losses. Besides, he says that if we work with him on this, he'll tell us who the first nine pawns were."

"That's a huge bargaining chip."

"It is. Should we do this?"

"You know me, Kat," he said, ramming Gunter's little car into the side of the BMW. Metal crunched. "If there's danger, I'm in."

Violet gave Lucian a perplexed stare. "How can you talk so calmly while they're trying to kill us?"

Lucian smiled at her.

Kat said, "I'll inform Carpenter that we're working with him. Please be careful."

Lucian fired at the BMW's passenger side tire. The front of the car dropped and spun to the right. After he disconnected the call, he turned Gunter's car around and parked it.

He glanced at Violet. "Drop your seat to the floor and stay down."

She did so without hesitation.

Lucian opened his door and got out.

"What the hell are you doing?" she asked.

"Ending this."

Both men in the BMW flung open their doors and used them as shields. With inhuman speed, Lucian rushed the passenger side door with his shoulder and pinned the man. The man's shinbones cracked from the impact and his gun fell to the pavement. Lucian pulled the door open and jerked the man from the side of the car, using him for a body shield.

The driver aimed but didn't have a clear shot around his partner. His partner struggled to stand on broken legs, Lucian backed around the car, keeping his gun on the driver.

"Drop the gun," Lucian demanded.

The driver shook his head. His eyes didn't alter, but they widened slightly with fear. These men were hired to kill Gunter and Violet and retrieve the cooler. But Lucian had a feeling these men weren't associated with GenTech or Mech Cybernetics at all.

Lucian fired a round, striking the man's hand. The gun dropped from his hand. The man grabbed his bleeding palm and clutched it against his chest. The driver lost all courage, which clued Lucian that his newfound enemies weren't genetic soldiers.

Lucian pulled his body shield back ten feet and threw him to the ground. The driver knelt for his weapon, but before the driver retrieved the gun, Lucian tackled him. Lucian slammed the man's face into the ground several times until the driver lost consciousness.

"Violet," Lucian said. "Come pop the trunk open for me."

She raised her seat and peered through the open car door. The radiator in Gunter's car hissed. Steam rose from the hood. The BMW passenger writhed in pain. Lucian dragged the driver's limp body toward the trunk of the car.

Cautiously, she stepped from the car and headed to the BMW, reached beneath the steering wheel, and pushed the trunk button. The trunk popped and rose. Lucian heaved the driver and dropped him beside the spare tire. Then he carried the struggling passenger and placed him beside his partner. He slammed the trunk lid shut.

Lucian grabbed the cooler and started walking down the sidewalk. Violet ran after him.

"Where are you going?"

"Gunter's car is tracked by the owner. It's best we leave it here."

"We can't just walk."

"The radiator is busted. We won't get far in that."

"We're easier targets on foot."

"I suppose so," Lucian said, pointing at the 9mm on the pavement. "Take that. We may need it."

She leaned down to get the gun and said, "I don't know *how* to use this."

He shrugged. "Let's hope you don't have to learn."

A black Mercedes turned onto the street and sped toward them. Lucian grabbed her hand. "More company."

He led her down a narrow alley. A back door to a business was propped open while a custodian emptied trash into a dumpster. After throwing the garbage bag into the bin, the worker stood with his back to them and smoked a cigarette. Lucian motioned her to go through the door and he followed. Tires squealed in the alley.

Lucian peered around to see two men exit the Mercedes. He pulled the door shut. The worker shouted and beat on the door.

"Circle back to the front of the store," Lucian said.

Violet left the clothing storage room and ran through the shop clothes racks toward the front glass door. She paused at the door when the cashier shouted. Lucian showed his gun, and the lady crouched behind the counter, fearful they were robbing the place.

"Hurry," he said. "Run to the Mercedes."

"Why?"

"It's our only way to get away quickly."

"Not if they shut off the engine. You'll need a thumbprint to start it."

Lucian shook his head. "It's still running. But the longer we wait, the shorter our window of opportunity to take it becomes."

Violet started to push the door open when Lucian stopped her. "Lose the lab coat and let your hair down."

She removed the coat, and he helped undo her hair. He ruffled her hair. He looked into her eyes, and she smiled. Gunter's memories of desire no longer controlled him. However, his own attraction toward her burned deep into his soul.

"I see why Gunter was attracted to you," Lucian said.

Her eyes widened. "He was?"

"Of course. Why *wouldn't* he have been?"

She blushed and turned away, afraid to see his face.

Lucas focused his attention on his face and brought back the familiar face he had presented for the past several months. He took a ball cap off a shelf and put it on her head.

"This slight change in appearance should buy us enough time to get to the car unnoticed."

They exited the shop, and the two men brushed past them on the sidewalk. Lucian took her hand and ran to the Mercedes. She got into the passenger side before they turned around and noticed the cooler.

Lucian opened the door and climbed in, passing the cooler to her. The men pulled their weapons, and Lucian pressed the accelerator to the floor. Even if these men tried to take their comrades' BMW, they'd have to change the front flat, and that gave Lucian and Violet at least a good fifteen-minute head start.

Violet smiled. "You do this kind of stuff a lot?"

"More lately than before, it seems."

"Is this what you really look like?"

"For a few months, yes."

"You're handsome," she said, putting her hand to his cheek. "But what does your real face look like?"

Lucian sighed. "I've not worn it in six months."

"Why not?"

"It's complicated."

Regardless of the promise he had made to Lucas, Lucian longed to return to his original face. After all, it was his true appearance. He found that he missed seeing the familiar features he had grown to recognize as his outer shell. But he had promised, and somehow, he *owed* Lucas that much to amend at least *some* of the wrongs he had exposed his prototype to.

"Why?"

"I'm a clone. I wear this face to protect my prototype. I swore an oath not to look like him anymore."

"I see. Why not pretend to be twins?"

Lucian forced a smile. "The fact I'm alive haunts him. He's not fond of my existence."

"I don't understand."

"I told you it's complicated. I'd rather not discuss it further."

She nodded. "Okay. Thanks."

"For?"

"Saving my life."

"We aren't out of this yet. We still have something they value enough to kill for. They'll keep hunting us."

"You were right. The guard at Mech Cybernetics was going to kill me without question. I just don't understand why."

"The orders came from higher-ups. Whoever wants these experiments to remain secret will kill anyone who has knowledge of them."

"They're just tissue cultures."

"They're much more than that. The biotech companies want to advance their horizons to make soldiers that can help them rule the world. This isn't a small thing. An individual who was like-minded created me. I was forced to murder for him or die if I didn't."

Violet studied his face. "How did you get away?"

"I killed him," Lucian said with an icy tone.

She looked away. "Where are you taking me?"

"As soon as Kat calls back, we find where to meet her."

"We'll be safe?"

"She works with the FBI."

"Not sure that clarifies it for me."

"It never has for me. Nothing's guaranteed."

"You trust her?" she asked.

"I trust few people. But her, yes, I do."

Violet sighed. "That's good enough for me."

Chapter 23

Trey sat in a metal chair. His arms were clamped inside metal sleeves. I.V. drips fed his body to help repair the damage Gunter had caused. Across from him was a two-way mirror. Subliminal programming had ceased a half hour before and his eyes focused on his reflection.

"Where's your brother?" a voice he recognized as Father said through an intercom.

Tears streamed down his cheeks. "Mike Gunter killed him."

"Incorrect. Simon killed Mr. Gunter."

"Yes, but Gunter's twin killed Simon."

"I have no evidence of a twin."

"Father, I saw him. He came later. He took his brother's body and left Simon dead."

"Why didn't you kill him? Why didn't you help Simon?"

Trey closed his eyes and his body convulsed with heavy sobs. "I tried. I was unable to get to him."

"Why, Trey?"

"Gunter nearly killed me. I was injured."

"Your brother needed you, and *you* failed him."

Emotions rushed through Trey. His fragile mind turned against him. Unless he began to understand these strange inner feelings and get a grasp on his self-control, he'd kill himself before they destroyed him. Swollen veins surfaced along his temples and the I.V. dripped faster. After several minutes, he took a deep breath and calmness settled over him.

"Help me, Father," Trey cried. "What's happening to me? My mind's splitting apart."

"Easy, son. Everything will be okay. Just sleep. When you awaken, you'll be better. I promise."

The I.V. dripped. Trey's eyes closed. Two nurses entered the room while a guard unlocked Trey's metal cuffs. Another man pushed a gurney to the chair. They placed Trey's body on the gurney, pushed him to an operating room, and the nurses organized the dissecting scalpels, a circular saw, and other stainless steel tools.

***

IN THE NEIGHBORING ROOM, Simon's body lay on a gurney. Blue swollen tissue surrounded the bullet holes in his head. A coroner and his assistant examined the corpse.

"Beyond repair?" Trey's Father asked via intercom.

The coroner nodded. "Yes. The bullet wounds prevented healing regeneration. Whoever did this knew it, too. The shots to the head were deliberate."

"We're looking for his murderer. When we find him, I have experiments I want you to undertake on him."

"Gladly. What do you want me to do with Simon's body?"

"His brain's destroyed?"

"Yes."

"Drain his blood, Dr. Owen, and then cremate him. We have nothing else we can do for him."

"And Trey?" Owen asked, looking at the mirrored wall.

"The surgeons are removing his head now. Cryogenics techs will begin the second phase of his life."

Dr. Owen scratched his forehead, evaluating the decision. "You think this will work?"

"It's what the twins were created for. We only needed to test their prowess in the field for a short period. Thirteen murders proved them successful."

"Before their failure."

"No. Nothing could have prepared them for what they encountered that night. They succeeded in killing Gunter as they were assigned. However, an imposter, someone who took on the appearance of Gunter, caught Simon by surprise and killed him."

"Any idea how he accomplished this?"

"No. That's why I want him found and brought to me. It's a trait I want to know more about."

Dr. Owen smiled. "It has my interest as well."

Chapter 24

Nevada Extreme Motocross Dirt Pit Finals

LUCAS STOOD TALKING with his Navajo friend, Joseph Shadow-talker, while Lydia strapped on her protective gear for the upcoming dirt bike competition.

Rex stood between Lucas and Joseph. His tongue panted and his tail wagged.

The fading golden sunset swirled with silky layers of pink, red, and orange stratus clouds and was more spectacular than an artist could ever hope to capture on a canvas. The towering stadium lights flickered on and steadily glowed into harsher brightness.

"Are you ready?" Lucas asked Lydia. He removed his sunglasses and hung them on his shirt collar.

"Yes," she said, carrying her helmet in hand.

The three of them walked toward the pit. Joseph nodded toward the motorcycles. "Luke. What's that kid doing at Lydia's bike?"

A young man knelt beside her motorcycle. The teenager was running his hand along the side of the bike. He glanced around nervously and when he noticed Lucas and Joseph approaching, he turned to run.

Lucas frowned. "I have no idea, but he best get the hell away from it."

Joseph sprinted ahead of Lucas, grabbed the teen by his jacket, and slung him around. The young man, probably no older than seventeen, waved his hands in surrender. Rex bared his teeth and growled. The teen's face paled, and his haunted eyes moistened.

Lucas caught up and placed his hand on Rex's head. "Easy, Rex."

Rex sat but kept his teeth snarled. A low growl rumbled in the half-grown dog's throat.

"I didn't do anything," the kid protested.

"It looked like you were messing around with her bike?" Lucas asked, leaning into the teenager's face. "What'd you do?"

Terror seized the young man. He shook his head and waved his hands. "Nothing. I was just looking. I swear."

Joseph kept a tight grip on the teen's jacket and rested his right hand on the gun tucked behind his belt.

"Lydia?" Lucas said, looking back. "Did he bother anything?"

Lydia searched the bike over and shook her head. "Nothing seems to have been tampered with."

Lucas leaned closer and clutched the teenager's jacket collar. Joe took a step back. "What's your name and *why* are you in the pit?" Lucas asked.

The teen swallowed hard. Sweat glistened on his face. "Wes Larson. I work here. I was just making my rounds before the race. Sorry to have upset you."

"Well, Wes," Lucas said, shoving him back a few feet. The teenager shuffled his feet to keep his balance on the dusty gravels. "We manage our own affairs, especially when it comes to our bikes."

"Sorry," Wes said, trying to make himself taller while composing himself. "I meant no harm. It's just—"

Lucas raised an eyebrow. "What?"

Wes sighed. "There were two men at her bike before me. I was making sure they hadn't done anything."

"Who?" Joseph asked, looking around.

"I don't know. Two men. They didn't look like they were from around here."

"What do you mean?" Lydia asked.

Wes shrugged. "They were wearing fancy suits."

Joe said, "Suits at a dirt bike competition? That is definitely out of place."

"Which direction did they go?" Lucas asked.

"Up in the stands, I think. They should be easy to find. No one dresses like that around here."

"If you see them," Lucas said. "Point them out to me."

"Yes, sir," Wes replied. "I will."

Joseph followed Wes through the pit while Lucas walked with Lydia. She pushed her bike to the starting line. Thunderous roars of motorbikes echoed and rumbled.

"I wish I was in this competition with you," Lucas said. "I'd feel more comfortable."

Lydia smiled. "Me, too. But until the doctor gives you a clear report on your ribs, I don't think it's a good idea."

"I know. The last jump would've been the longest one I'd ever cleared, had I stuck the landing. It's a shame I don't heal like you."

"You can't win them all."

Lucas laughed. "Easy for you to say. You've not lost a contest during the past two months."

"What can I say? You taught me well." Although she smiled, her eyes stared straight ahead, deep in concentration, like she always did before a competition. She had more focus and determination than anyone he had ever known.

Lucas looked down, shaking his head. "Riiight. There's nothing I could teach you that you can't learn without me."

"Modesty . . . I love that about you."

"It's true. You know it. Any sport competition we train for, you've mastered it better than I ever have."

Spike Watson, wearing number sixteen, pushed his bike alongside Lydia's. In his early twenties, sporting a green Mohawk and five rings tacked through each eyebrow, he was already known for his dangerous maneuvers on the track and had caused several near fatal accidents. His attitude and reputation made him one of the most hated bikers in the Motocross circuit.

"Trophy's mine today, sweetie," he said.

"Winner's flag hasn't dropped yet," she replied, not bothering to glance in his direction.

"I see your man isn't listed to compete today. Time you got yourself a *real* man."

Lucas stepped around and Lydia placed a hand on his arm, shaking her head. She leveled a sharp glare at Watson. "Spike, you can't match Lucas in anything manly. When you grow a pair and *become* a man, I doubt even then you'd come close to being compared to him. Hell, I'm a woman, and you can't beat me on the track. But maybe that's it? I've beaten you so many times at these meets that I've given you a neuter complex. The Vatican can use more choirboys. Apply there."

Watson's jaw tightened, and his face flushed red. "I wager that you won't even cross the finish line."

Lucas placed his hands on Watson's handlebars and stopped him. "Is that a threat?"

Watson sneered. "No. It's a promise."

"If anything happens to Lydia because of your recklessness on the course, you'll learn how much damage a real man can do to you."

Lucas stared into Watson's eyes until Watson lowered his gaze and mumbled words under his breath.

Lucas stepped aside, and Watson pushed his bike to the starting line.

"That's what I thought," Lucas said.

Chapter 25

The loud speakers announced: "Two minutes until the competition begins. Riders take your positions."

The roar of motorcycles and screaming fans made hearing one another nearly impossible.

Lydia smiled. "That's my cue."

Lucas kissed her. "Even though you don't need me to say it, good luck."

"Thanks." She pulled her helmet down over her head.

Lucas hurried off the track while Lydia secured her helmet and fired up the engine. The crude track had steep, single-lane, forty-five degree, angled ramps along the course. Smaller mounds of earth for landing were constructed between the ramps and used to gain speed for the next jump.

When the beginning flag waved, she revved the motor. Her rear tire spun side to side as she tore from the starting line. Ten other racers fought to shove their bikes ahead of her, but she kept a tight push forward.

Lucas watched from the pit. Lydia gunned her bike straight up the ramp, did a quick handstand on the handlebars, and swung her legs back down. Upon landing, Watson bumped her rear tire, causing her to tailspin slightly. She straightened out and pulled further ahead. He back tire slung dirt all over the visor of his helmet.

He sped beside her and swerved toward her. She accelerated and bumped his front tire with her rear tire. He weaved sharply to bump her again, but she sped ahead to the ramp and jumped. He followed and tried to drop his bike on top of hers. She threw her weight to the left and cut the steering wheel sharp, missing the collision by inches. If she wouldn't be disqualified, she'd have taken that opportunity to shove him off his bike.

TOWARD THE MIDDLE of the infield, Lucas watched an ambulance flip its emergency lights on and pull away from its parked position. No bikers had lost control or crashed. He wondered if they were testing their lights or perhaps someone in the stands had suffered cardiac arrest.

SITTING in the front of the ambulance, a man wearing a blue paramedic jumper opened a remote control device and watched Lydia make her first jump. Another man sat in the rear of ambulance, removed his suit, and pulled on paramedic clothes. The man in the passenger side watched Lydia, removed his 9mm, and checked the clip.

"It's show time. Get ready," the driver said, flipping on the emergency lights. He put the ambulance into drive and headed across the green.

On the second jump, with Watson dangerously close to Lydia's rear tire, the man pressed the remote control button. The screaming crowd grew silent. A thunderous explosive blasted and echoed through the arena.

Chapter 26

The ambulance moved across the infield slowly. When Lydia's bike left the second ramp, her gas tank exploded. Lucas watched in disbelief. He ran without realizing he had taken a single step. Joe ran beside him.

"What the hell just happened?" Lucas said.

"Doesn't look good, my friend," Joe replied.

Lydia's body was blown clear of the crumpled wreckage. Watson wasn't as lucky. Metal spokes from Lydia's rear tire had pierced through his chest protector. Blood streamed from the wounds.

Joe looked at Lucas. "I don't think Spike had anything to do with it."

"No. You're right. He'd never risk harming himself."

Caution flags waved and the announcer declared a temporary postponement of the race until the area was cleared. Spectators watched in stunned horror. The ambulance sped to the accident with its siren wailing.

Lucian ran to Lydia. She lay on her side, trying to remove her helmet. He eased her back against the dirt mound and helped her pull off the helmet. She blinked several times and closed her eyes with a heavy sigh.

"I'm okay," she said. "Just give me a minute to collect myself."

"An ambulance is headed this direction, dear. Just relax."

"I'm fine, Luke," she said. Rex licked her cheek, and she rubbed the dog's neck.

He shook his head. "Without pain receptors, there's no way you can be absolutely certain."

She smiled and narrowed a cold stare at him. "I heal fast. Remember?"

"I know, but not in front of a crowd of thirty-five thousand people. Just stay down. The media will suspect something unusual if you simply walk away from this. We cannot afford any added attention to ourselves."

"I don't give a damn. I don't want to go to the hospital. Any blood tests will damn us, too."

Lucas nodded. "I know. We won't allow that, but we have to ride the ambulance out."

Lydia exhaled a frustrated sigh.

Several news reporters and Motocross magazine photographers snapped photos of her, and an ESPN cameraman tried to make his way closer to get a report on her and Watson's conditions.

"What happened up there?" Lucas whispered.

"Not sure. Something exploded beneath the seat."

Wes approached warily. "Are you okay?" he asked.

Lucas yanked the teen to the ground by his collar, ignoring the flashing cameras catching his obvious rage. "You have anything to do with this?"

"No, I told you what I know."

Lucas studied the young man's eyes. Although scared, the boy didn't look guilty. "What part of the motorcycle did you see the men bothering?"

He swallowed hard. "Looked like they might have been tampering with the gas tank, but when I checked, I didn't see anything out of the ordinary."

Lydia glanced from Wes to Lucas.

"I didn't either," she whispered.

Lucas gave a sharp nod toward Spike and asked Wes, "Was he near her bike or with those men?"

Wes shook his head. "No."

The rear ambulance doors opened. Joe knelt beside Watson and tried to slow the bleeding with a handkerchief until the ambulance arrived. More cameras flashed and reporters noted Spike's obvious anguish.

The paramedics rolled a gurney from the back of the ambulance and stopped beside Lydia.

Lucas waved them off. "Take Spike first. His condition is much worse. He's bleeding badly."

They ignored him and lifted Lydia onto the gurney and strapped her down.

"What the hell are you doing?" Lucas demanded. "Spike's clearly in worse shape. He needs medical attention immediately."

"Out of our way." The paramedic pushed Lucas back.

Lucas rushed to strike the man, but stopped. From inside the rear of the ambulance a man dressed in a suit stood with a 9mm pointed at him. He held a vantage point, out of view of the photographers, and a silencer was attached to the end of the gun. He could shoot Lucas without drawing any attention to himself.

"Don't," the man with the gun warned. "Step away."

"Like hell."

Wes saw the man in the rear of the ambulance. "That's one of the men."

Lucas started to move, but Joe thrust his arm in front of Lucas' chest.

"Move, Joe."

"Easy, bro."

Lydia struggled against the restraints. "Let me go, you bastards."

A paramedic, wearing black, injected a needle into her arm. Lucas shoved Joe's arm out of the way and ran toward the gurney. Joe tackled him as the man from the ambulance fired. The bullet missed Lucas by inches and flicked dirt into the air. The bullet probably would have killed Lucas if Joe hadn't tackled him.

Lydia's eyes closed and she faded from consciousness.

Lucas rolled, tried to get to his feet, but Joe wrapped his arms tightly around his ankles. He pushed up, but was unable to break Joe's hold. Pain from his broken ribs shot through his chest and into his arm. He winced and dropped face first into the loose dirt.

The paramedic climbed into the ambulance's driver seat, and an emblem caught Luke's attention. A sharp pang of icy fear seized his heart. A blazing red, triple helix was patched to the man's jacket sleeve.

The suited man helped the paramedic load Lydia's gurney into the ambulance, jumped inside, and slammed the rear doors shut. With lights and siren activated, it sped for the stadium exit but had to slow dramatically to the swelling crowd that spilled from the stands to see what was happening.

Lucas glanced at the black tag on the ambulance. No numbers or letters were visible. For a moment, he thought this man worked for Trans-GenCorp, but the lower part of the helix symbol was different. Strangely, it resembled a three-fingered hand. The tips of each finger broke off into a separate helix branch.

Finally, after the ambulance drove away, Joe released Lucas.

"What the hell did you do that for? You let them take her," Lucas said, pushing himself to his feet.

"You can't save her if you're dead," Joe replied softly.

"Where are they taking her?"

"More importantly," Joe said. "Who are they, and *why* do they want her?"

A second ambulance pulled alongside Watson and the paramedics unloaded a gurney. Watson was pale and fading. The front of his suit was slick crimson. This ambulance was probably too late. Lucas looked at this ambulance's tag. It had Nevada plates and a hospital name painted on the sides. This one was clearly different from the ambulance that had taken Lydia.

Lucas grabbed the arm of a paramedic tending to Watson. "Where's the other ambulance headed?"

He shrugged. "No idea. They're not with our hospital."

"What? Then what right do they have taking her?"

"I don't know. Different hospitals and rescue squads attend these races. They're probably from another hospital."

Lucas glanced at Joe.

"Doubtful," Joe said.

Lucas ran for the nearest motorcycle, fired the engine, and headed for the exit. The rear tire tore a gulley of dirt and gravel as he sped away.

Joe found state policemen and explained what had just happened. He hoped they'd help Lucas pursue the kidnappers. Rex held his ears back and sniffed the air, trying to find Lucas.

Lucas didn't know who had taken Lydia, but he understood why and for what purpose. He may have destroyed TransGenCorp, but he hadn't stopped others from pursuing the same biotechnological advancements. Lydia was still a prototype that any corrupt band of scientists would kill others to possess.

Speeding down the highway, Lucas looked for the ambulance's flashing lights, but the men weren't fools. They had probably turned off the emergency lights and even the headlights. The rising full moon in the clear desert sky provided ample lighting for anyone to see the highway.

Away from the bright lights of the stadium, the darkness of night swallowed Lucas. The single beam of the bike headlight barely cut through the blackness.

A sick, churning knotted his stomach and made him want to stop and vomit. But every minute he wasted was another minute more that these men had to hide Lydia. His heart ached, and fear crippled his mind. He needed to find her, but desperation clouded his judgments.

Tears flooded his eyes. With each passing minute, his frustration consumed him. All that lay before him was desert and highway. He wasn't even certain he was headed in the right direction. If they had gone the opposite direction, he was getting farther away from the one he loved. Without her, he knew he couldn't survive. He loved and needed her that much. He knew without a doubt that she loved him.

Where had they taken her? Where had they gone?

Lucas pulled the bike to the edge of the road and wiped tears from his eyes with the back of his hand. His cell phone rang.

"Luke?" Joe said. "Do you see them?"

Lucas cleared his throat. "I lost them, Joe. They have her, and I don't know where they went."

"Head back, bro. We'll find her together."

He pictured her helpless, unconscious form on the gurney. His throat tightened. He rubbed his eyes. With a broken, choked sob in his voice, he said, "What will they do to her?"

"We'll find her, bro. I promise. Just remain focused."

Lucas took a deep breath and released it. "I'm on my way back to the stadium. Give me a few minutes."

"I'll be here."

He turned off the motorcycle and listened to the night. His body shook. In spite of the warm air rising from the black asphalt, a chill swept through him. He worried that Lydia was gone forever. He didn't want to consider what life would be like without her.

And for some odd reason, he recalled what Idris had told him the day Lucas had destroyed TGC. "Are you certain, Lucas, that what you're doing is in your best interests? By destroying one thing, you will be unleashing numerous other dangers you're not aware of."

"Shit!" Lucas said and started the bike. He revved the engine and spun around on the highway.

He had thought what Idris had meant was within TransGenCorp, but apparently, it included far more than other shifters. Other corporations and scientists were bent on utilizing superior humans and beasts. In a roaring hum above the sound of his motorcycle came what he understood to be Idris laughing hysterically.

As badly as Idris had wanted to repossess Lydia, there was a good chance that he had informed other corporations about her and her uniqueness. Should that hypothesis be accurate, he was surprised that no one had tried to take Lydia before now.

Lucas drove faster. When he finally turned off the highway and into the arena parking lot, Joe and Rex stood at the entrance. With Joe were three more Navajos.

He shut off the bike.

"The police aren't exactly buying my story," Joe said.

"Why not?"

Joe shrugged. "They seem to think that we're overreacting. We should check the area hospitals."

Rex nuzzled Lucas' hand.

"None of the public hospitals will have her."

"I know," Joe said, clasping Lucas on the shoulder. "But my brothers have bikes, too, and they are going to scout the highway both directions. We'll find her, Luke."

Through clenched teeth, Lucas replied, "I hope so."

Joe offered a reassuring smile. "They've not been gone more than fifteen minutes. We know the area better than they do."

"You informed your brothers that these men are armed?"

Joe's three brothers eased open their denim jackets and revealed their 9mms. They smiled.

Lucas grinned. "Let's find her."

Chapter 27

Phil Silvas, the passenger in Lydia's ambulance, punched a series of numbers on his cell phone.

"We have her," Phil said. "Yes, she's secured and sedated. No one has followed us."

After he disconnected the call, he turned to the driver. "Desert Field Laboratories want us to deliver her tonight, R.J."

R.J. checked the rearview mirror. "You should've killed her husband."

"Lucas?"

R.J. nodded. "He'll keep looking for her. He won't ever stop hunting us."

Phil laughed. "By the time he has a hint where she's at, it'll be too late."

"Sedating her seemed a bit severe."

"According to the people at the laboratories, she's very dangerous."

R.J. gave Phil a side-glance. "How dangerous could she be? I'll admit that she's probably tough since she does stunt races. But be serious. It's the three of us against her."

"The scientist there cautioned me to have her knocked unconscious and strapped down. He didn't elaborate but implied she's very dangerous."

"I thought Mech Cybernetics wanted her."

"Desert Field Laboratory is a part of Mech Cybernetics."

"They have our money, Phil?"

Phil smiled and lit a cigarette. "High six figures, R.J."

"Quickest money we've ever made."

"True, so true."

"After we deliver her to the laboratory, we fly to New York."

"Why?"

"New assignments."

"Ahh."

"Yep, even more money."

LYDIA REMAINED unconscious but aware of what was happening around her.

Tight restraints fastened her arms to the gurney and a stinging prick withdrew blood from her right arm. If she truly desired, she could force herself awake, but she understood this wasn't the best time to act. Not while bound, and not inside the ambulance. She wasn't certain why, but she needed to know where they were taking her.

The ambulance moved along a rough, bumpy surface. The driver had left the main highway and seemed to be driving across the desert terrain. The vehicle wasn't from an area hospital, either.

While the paramedics weren't posers, but actual paramedics, she wasn't certain whom they worked for.

She was keenly aware that the man who shot at Lucas wasn't directly tied to the paramedics. She saw the twisted determination of a trained assassin reflect in his dark eyes. Had everything not transpired so quickly after her bike had exploded, this man would have seen the same exact glare projecting from her eyes to his. He'd have flinched, and she'd have taken him out.

Although she struggled inside over the three men she had killed at her farm, she never discussed those feelings with Lucas. Lucas loved her, and the best she could do for him was allow him to think she had buried that night. She hadn't. But, she determined that her nature to kill another human occurred only when she was pushed outside her inner sanctuary. She controlled *when* she killed, but never *if*. She never doubted that she'd kill again. After all, a predatory prowess was programmed into her genome and her mind through subliminal projections. She couldn't erase them. She couldn't turn off the switch. Her need to hunt remained, and she had no way to expunge that desire. Self-control of her inner demon demanded a great deal of energy and suppression. One push the wrong direction unleashed her rage.

They had pushed.

Her rage surged.

Chapter 28

Joe Shadow-talker pulled his pickup truck beside Lucas' bike.

"Climb in, bro," Joe said.

"We can cover more ground if we each drive," Lucas replied.

Joe shook his head. "Climb in. We need to talk while I drive. My brothers will cover the highways while we journey after her together."

Lucas shook his head and set the kickstand. He climbed into the passenger side, shut the door, and rolled down the window.

"Tell me, Luke. Who would want to take Lydia from you? Who is your enemy?"

"I don't know who did this. If I did, they'd be dead."

Joe nodded, stared through the windshield, and pulled the truck into gear. "I don't doubt that, my friend. But there's more that you're not telling me."

A slight smile spread across Lucas' face. "I can't hide anything from you."

Joe shook his head. "We've been friends for years. Your aura screams even when your mouth remains silent."

"You remember the problems I've had with TransGenCorp and my frame for murder earlier this year?" Lucas asked.

"Of course."

"Three years before that I was trapped inside Pittsburgh."

"I remember. If I had not sensed your troubled spirit, I'd have thought you dead. So, you think someone within TransGenCorp is responsible?"

"No, but people like them."

"Revenge?"

"No."

"What possesses someone to do this, if not for revenge?"

Lucas looked out the window and chewed his lower lip. "I told you that I met Lydia in Pittsburgh when we were trapped there."

"Yes."

"Well, that was half true."

Joe faced Lucas with a sad expression, as though he thought Lucas hadn't fully trusted him. "And what other half did you not trust to tell me?"

Lucas sighed. "It wasn't that I didn't trust you. I wanted to protect her."

Joe smiled. "From me?"

"No. From them. From the people who have her now."

"You've just run me full circle without telling me anything. We're back to square one. *Why* do these people want her?"

"Lydia wasn't in our group at Helmsby's Research Center. She was a project created inside TransGenCorp."

Joe looked surprised. "They made her?"

Lucas nodded.

"Damn. You should have grabbed an extra woman for me while you were there. Save me from the added trouble of all those barroom rejections."

"But she's far more than just a beautiful woman, Joe."

"I know. She has a wonderful personality, which is even rarer to find. But, you know, I've always had a hard time reading her. There's a part of her that I've never understood. A wild darkness. Perhaps, this is why."

Lucas nodded. "Perhaps."

Stars hung over the horizon as Joe drove. The outside air grew cooler, and Lucas rolled the window back up.

"Her beauty and personality are not what I'm referring to, though. She was genetically created to be an assassin," Lucas said.

"Lydia?" he asked with an amused smile. "She's as delicate as a dove."

"As my lover and spouse, she is, yes. As your friend, yes. But, I've seen what she can do when pressed against a wall or into a tight corner. She has fighting skills that I wish I had half the ability to perform. And marksmanship? Hell, I can't match her. I'm nowhere near her equal."

"And they want her because of these abilities?"

"That and more. She heals from major injuries within minutes. She also doesn't have pain receptors, which is dangerous because she doesn't know when to stop fighting. They will clone her to make new genetic soldiers."

Joe nodded. "That explains how she survived the explosion. An ordinary person might have died. They certainly wouldn't have been moving around."

"Yes, but now they have her."

"Tell me, do you think TransGenCorp is behind this?"

"I destroyed TransGenCorp by corrupting all their hard drive files. The operation was closed down. I don't think they're the ones who took her. Idris is dead."

"Even so, these people may have ties to TransGenCorp?"

"Possibly."

"So a laboratory might be responsible?"

Lucas nodded.

Joe smiled. "Why didn't you say so in the first place?"

Joe stopped the truck and called one of his brothers. "We may know where they took Lydia. You know the laboratory that keeps polluting our gulch? We look there first."

Chapter 29

Lydia thought about Lucas. The fear in his eyes after he watched the paramedics strapped her to the gurney had shattered him. She had known him long enough to know he'd never stop searching for her. Her spirit smiled.

Without him, she understood she'd have never known a deeper love had he not rescued her from TransGenCorp. Love wasn't an emotion Idris would have implanted in her mind. Without Lucas, love didn't exist. But she wondered if his love was enough to prevent her from being what she was created to be. Her mental struggles to not relinquish her self-control were wearing her down. Sometimes she believed it would be easier to give in, to become the assassin Idris had created.

The ambulance slowed and stopped. The driver spoke to a guard through his lowered window. After several minutes of identification checks, chains rattled at the front of the vehicle. The crude scrape of a metal fence gate against the rocky ground grated the still night air.

The ambulance moved forward again.

"We're here," R.J. said.

Phil pointed. "Drive to the rear entrance. That's where the cloning labs are."

Lydia flexed her arms and tugged tension between the restraints and the metal gurney rails. Her strength could eventually stretch the material enough to free her hands, but not fast enough. Once they discovered she had awakened, they'd sedate her with more powerful drugs to keep her into a coma.

Bright lights blared through the ambulance windows. The ambulance made a sharp turn under the lights and she dared a peek.

The paramedic nearest her looked out the rear doors and prepared to open them when they came to a complete stop.

The assassin in the passenger seat extinguished his cigarette in a cold cup of coffee. He pulled his blazer over his holstered 9mm.

In a few minutes, the element of surprise smiled in her favor.

Chapter 30

Morton listened to Julia read Felicia her bedtime story. When she kissed Felicia and tucked her in, she turned and scratched Morton's head. The cat allowed gentle purrs and nuzzled his head against her hand.

Julia smiled. "You're staying to talk to her?"

"Yes. She has to know."

She leaned down and kissed his head. "We'll miss you. Please be careful."

"I will," Morton replied.

Julia stood with tear-moistened eyes. "Good night."

"Good night. You needn't worry."

After Julia headed down the hall, Morton pattered to Felicia's pillow and curled beside her.

"Best tea party we've had," he beamed.

Felicia frowned and puckered her lips. "Kool-aid tasted a bit strange."

"You noticed that, too?"

"Bleck!" she said, sticking out her tongue.

"Maybe it was a bad packet. Next time I'll *help* you make it."

"Thank you," she said, rubbing his ears.

Morton studied her bright blue eyes and her chubby, radiant smile. His little heart ached. He cleared his throat with a small cough.

"I have to leave for a few days," he said.

"Why?"

Morton thought for a few minutes before giving an answer. He didn't want to lie to her, but he couldn't exactly divulge the truth, either. She wouldn't understand the dynamics anyway.

"Cat business," he replied. "We cats have reunions from time to time. It's been a while since I attended one."

Felicia ran her hand down Morton's back and gave gentle strokes that smoothed his fur."

"Kinda like a tea party for cats?"

Morton nodded. "Huge party."

"When will you come back?"

The cat looked away. "I'm not certain how long it'll take, but I'll call you and let you know how I am in a few days."

Felicia puckered her lips. "I don't want you to go."

"I know. But I have to."

"When will you leave?"

"Tomorrow morning. Your father will drive me."

"I'll miss you," she said, wrapping her arms around him.

"I'll miss you, too."

"Will you sleep beside me tonight?"

"Of course, dear."

Morton curled closer to her head and watched her eyes grow heavy, close, and sleep claimed her. He licked the tip of her nose.

"I love you, Felicia," he said. He curled into a ball on her pillow and watched her sleep.

Chapter 31

Lydia waited for the paramedics to unload the gurney before she escaped. In their process of securing the wheeled legs, she yanked the tight leather restraints that strapped her arms down. For some reason, they hadn't bound her legs, which gave her one less obstacle to worry about in her escape.

Her fierce strength didn't tear the straps, but the force popped the metal rivets that held the buckles to the leather. Her freed hands grabbed the closest paramedic by the collar. R.J. was stitched on his vest. She heaved herself to her feet and spun a sharp roundhouse kick to the other paramedic's head. He fell back against the sidewall and lost balance. He dropped to the floor, and then she kneed R.J.'s groin. His eyes bulged and air escaped his mouth.

She dropped him and turned her attention to the man rising to his feet beside the gurney. He placed his hands on the metal bars to steady himself, and she thrust the palm of her hand into his throat. Tumbling backwards, wide-eyed, he clutched his throat and tried to breath.

Phil pulled his 9mm and emerged through the passenger door. By the time he rounded the rear doors Lydia had disappeared. Both paramedics lay on the ambulance floor.

R.J. lay with his hands clutched between his legs. Tears rolled down his cheeks and his face was turning blue. If R.J. survived, it would be a miracle.

Phil grimaced, looking down at R.J. *"That's* why they wanted her sedated."

He searched the ambulance for Lydia but couldn't find her. With locked arms outstretched before him, he pivoted the corner, ready to fire. Leaning over, he peered under the ambulance, but still no sign of her. He turned to check the inside of the ambulance again and the rear door slammed against his jaw. Several teeth spewed into the air with a wad of blood and spittle. He staggered but didn't drop to the ground. His gun spun and scratched across the smooth sidewalk.

Before Phil had a chance to clear his vision, Lydia punched his mouth several times, kicked his groin, and side-swept his feet.

He collapsed to the pavement and pivoted onto his back. She picked up his gun. When he opened his eyes, the gun was aimed at his forehead.

"Who sent you to take me?" she asked.

He wiped blood from his mouth and stared at it. He shook his head. "You might as well kill me. I don't know."

Lydia fired a round into his knee. He screamed and pulled himself into a fetal position with his hands wrapped around the wound. She aimed at the other knee. An amused smile spread across her face.

"Depending on how many bullets you have left in the clip, this can last a while."

Growling to stop the pain from carrying in his voice, he said through clenched teeth, "I don't know."

She fired a second round. The bullet ripped through his right shoulder.

"Dammit! I don't know!"

Lydia knelt and studied his wounds to see if they were healing. The blood flow didn't lessen. Skin tissue wasn't mending. He wasn't a genetic soldier, and he definitely experienced pain.

"I heard you tell your partner about the amount of money you were getting for delivering me. Now, whom do you work for?"

His eyes stared at the gun. His lips trembled. "Look, I don't know the man's name. We never met in person. After I dropped you off here, he is to wire the money to my account. I received a code name, nothing more. I've never seen his face. Honest."

"His code name?"

Phil swallowed hard. "He calls himself, 'Alpha.'"

"Is he here?"

"I don't know."

"What place is this?"

"Desert Field Laboratories."

Lydia tightened her finger on the trigger and pointed at his head. "I suppose I have all the information I need."

"Don't," he said.

From behind her, a man said, "Lady, put down your gun."

Phil glanced from her gun to see the night guard standing at the entrance door with his gun aimed at her. He smiled.

"Kill her," Phil said. "Or she'll kill you."

"Ma'am," the guard said. "Place your gun on the ground and step back. I don't want to hurt you."

"She's dangerous," Phil said. "She killed the two men with me. Shoot her. It's your only chance."

Lydia's arm stiffened. She contemplated squeezing off the final round to end Phil's life. He flinched and closed his eyes. The shoulder wound had lacerated an artery, and he was bleeding out. Another shot was mercy because it only stopped the inevitable. He was going to die before a new team of EMTs could arrive to help him.

"Don't!" the guard said.

She thought about Lucas. He'd be disappointed when he learned about how she had reacted to this situation. Killing Phil while he was unarmed wasn't ethical, but this man had delivered her here to endure torturous experimentations for his own financial gain. She had no problem justifying her reactions.

The guard fired a warning shot into the air. Lydia swung around and fired. The bullet tore through the guard's heart. He toppled backwards and crashed through the glass door. He didn't move again.

Her shoulders slumped. She thought he had tried to shoot her and, in turn, she killed him out of instinct. Although she was immune to physical pain, nothing excluded her from the psychological remorse that ate at her.

Lydia placed the gun behind her belt and headed toward the dead guard.

"Wait," Phil said. "Don't leave me here."

She ignored him.

"Are you heartless?" he asked.

Lydia stopped walking. Without looking back, she said, "No more than you bringing me here for whatever purposes they planned to do to me. Treat me like an animal, and I react like one."

She took the guard's gun and headed into the facility. The aroma of disinfectant greeted her. She expected other guards to approach, but the hallway was empty. No one sat at the reception desk. She wondered if the guard was the one she was to be delivered to.

This medical facility didn't appear to have been opened long. Fluorescent lights lit the hall. Before going further into the laboratories to see what awaited her, she stopped at the desk and studied the surveillance screens of the cameras throughout the operation. No one seemed to be stationed here, and she wondered why.

Beside the phone were different office numbers of the doctors or scientists that resided there. She scanned through them, but didn't recognize any of the names. She had no doubt Dr. Helmsby probably knew most of them through scientific conventions or research articles they published in journals.

Lydia found the CEO's number, but no name appeared beside it. She wrote the number down on Desert Field Laboratory stationery, folded it, and stuffed the paper into her pocket. Although she had memorized the number, she wanted to send the slip of paper to Helmsby for his analysis of the facility. She was certain that he had no knowledge of Desert Field Laboratory.

A floor map of the building was posted on the wall behind the desk. She stood on the top floor and three more floors descended underground. The third floor had an extremely large room. She wondered what discoveries she'd find there.

Carrying two 9mms, she headed down the silent hall. If her destination was meant to be here, others must be inside the building, waiting. Somewhere. But where? Flushing those people out for questioning might take some time, but she needed to rid any future threats on her life by eliminating anyone tied to this operation. In doing so, she feared she'd never be able to face Lucas again. She thought it strange that her need for self-preservation inflicted her with immense shame.

The elevator doors were protected by a palm scanner, as was the stairwell door, but it had not sealed shut. She pushed the door inward and a cool draft flowed from the metal stairs. The walls were carved, polished stone. The temperature was cave-like. Down the stairs circling bats chirped.

The second floor entrance didn't have any security locks on the door, so Lydia entered and was shocked by what she witnessed. Large, empty chambers filled an entire room. These were like the incubation chamber Lucas had found her in at TransGenCorp. She was thankful no people were inside them. She wasn't sure what she'd have done to rescue them.

She pulled her gun and looked both directions down the hall. No guards, scientists, or personnel of any kind. Apparently, the facility was still under construction.

The faint glow of panel lights reflected from the one chamber near the row of computers and electrical boxes. Lowering the gun she stepped closer to read the brass plate fastened to the front of the incubation chamber.

Lydia Ridale Prototype was engraved on the plate.

She swallowed hard and peered around the room. She no longer believed she was alone in the laboratories. They wanted her alive, so she needed to make certain she located them *before* they spotted her. They'd use tranquilizer darts to take her down. Her only defense was to kill them before they captured her.

The laboratories wouldn't be filled with workers until after they secured her in the incubation chamber and began making genetic clones from her.

Lydia eased back to the door and listened for footsteps. When she didn't hear any movement, she headed for the stairwell and went down to the next floor.

A military helicopter rested silently near large bay doors. A smaller, octagon-shaped room filled the center of the bay. Computer stations, file cabinets, and surveillance screens glowed from within. She headed toward the room. If she needed information, this room probably held access to the records.

Midway across the bay, a man said, "Lydia, thank you for saving us the money we paid to retrieve you. Phil was an expense we no longer needed."

She squinted into the darkness, and located the man behind a glass wall. The darkness concealed his appearance. Raising her gun, the man laughed.

"Your gun's useless."

"Who are you? Are you Alpha?"

"Does it matter? In a few minutes, you belong to us. You will generate an invincible army. Quite a lovely army at that."

Lydia squeezed the trigger. The bullet ricocheted off the bulletproof glass. The man shrugged.

"See?"

She had no questions she didn't already know the answers to except *who* they were. She knew why they wanted her. She knew what they'd do to her, and if they succeeded, she was trapped forever.

Lydia pushed her gun firmly under her chin. "Dead, I'm useless to you."

He shook his head. "Don't be foolish."

Her finger tightened on the trigger. "I'll be no one's project."

Shadows hid her adversary's face. "You always have been. Did you not know that?"

She frowned. "I've made a life for myself."

"Yes. Yes, you have. And every step of your life has been studied and evaluated. You've adapted, but you cannot kill what you truly are inside."

"What do you mean?"

"Idris placed a tracer chip inside you. When TransGenCorp collapsed, I received access data to trace your every move. I've known where you were at any given time. It's all recorded."

"I saw the incubation chamber with my name on it. I refuse to become what I once was."

"Lydia," the man said. "I witnessed what you did outside to escape. You exhibited a phenomenal display of militaristic tactics. You kill so gracefully and without conscience."

She shook her head. "That's where you're wrong. The guard was an accident. I didn't mean to kill him."

He laughed. "And the attack on your farm earlier in the year?"

"I have remorse for those people."

"Do you? From what I understand, your remorse came from not having more people to kill. I will credit you for your self-restraint. You've been able to sustain your need to kill. Perhaps that's just a flaw within Idris' programming? I'm not certain, but I think I can weed that out."

"Who are you? Are you Alpha?"

The man turned on an inside panel of lights within the octagon room where he stood. The light let her see his face, but she didn't recognize him.

She kept her gun pressed tightly to her throat.

"Alpha? No," He shrugged. "I know I have the advantage on you, but what's in a name, really? You don't seem to know me by appearance, so a name won't clarify your ignorance, will it?"

"I'd like to know your name so I can notify your next of kin after I dispose of your body."

His laughter echoed through the bay speakers. "I like that. Though it does you no good, I'm Dr. Wilks. It will be my pleasure to become your permanent guardian."

Lydia's peripheral vision caught sight of a man slinking through the shadows near the helicopter. He wore night vision goggles and carried a sniper rifle. He slowed at the front of the helicopter. She spun and fired. The bullet sliced through his throat. He fell to his knees with his hands clutched around the blood-gushing wound.

"How many more?" she asked.

Air swooshed. Another soldier fired a tranquilizer dart and it struck the back of her neck. She yanked out the dart and seconds later, and her arms fell limp to her sides.

"Damn," she whispered, falling to her knees.

"Sir," a soldier behind the computers said. "We have more company outside."

"Load her into the chopper. We cannot keep her here yet."

"The sedative won't last long."

"Bind her with titanium cuffs. Keep an I.V. in her with more drugs to keep her under. We must move her from here. Fast."

Chapter 32

Joe Shadow-talker put his truck in park near the ambulance outside Desert Labs. Lucas opened his door and cautiously examined the small parking lot, looking for armed men.

"What is this place?" Lucas asked.

"These are laboratories that were constructed inside an old, abandoned silver mine."

"How did you learn of them?"

Joe smiled. "My brothers and I do archaeological digs in the gulch beyond this site. Maybe a quarter of a mile away. Recently, we've discovered a lot of pollution they've dumped in the dry creek bed near the site. Some of it is very toxic."

"And you think this is where they took Lydia?"

Joe shrugged. "It's the most likely place."

Lucas noticed Phil sprawled out near the ambulance. Blood slowly congealed around his body. The distant look in his eyes indicated he'd be dead within minutes.

Lucas leaned down and said, "Where is she?"

Phil's eyes searched until they finally located Lucas.

Phil whispered, "She's inside."

Lucas pulled his gun and pointed it at Phil's forehead. He couldn't forget the face of the man who had threatened to kill him and helped the paramedics to abduct Lydia. He clicked off the safety. His arm grew rigid.

Joe shook his head and put his hand on Lucas' shoulder. "Easy, Luke. He's almost dead anyway. Even if we choose to spare him, he'd never reach a hospital in time."

Lucas' hand shook. After several seconds, he clicked the safety on his gun. Joe's brothers rode in on their motorcycles and shut off the engines.

Joe looked at the three bodies on the ground and the dead guard near the shattered glass door. Joe shook his head and said, "I see what you mean about her darker side."

Lucas sighed and tears burned his eyes. "I understand why she killed the men who kidnapped her, but why did she kill the guard?"

"It's something you'll need to ask when we find her."

"I'm not sure I want to know."

The churning of helicopter blades thundered over the bluff behind Desert Field Laboratories. The blinking lights rose higher and turned to the east, slowly disappearing over the horizon.

"Shit!" Lucas said. "They're leaving with her."

Joe shook his head. "We don't know that yet. Let's look the place over to make certain that's not a decoy."

Lucas' heart sank in despair. He had failed to save her. He was too late. Scanning the rear of the ambulance, he found a vial of blood a paramedic must have taken from her.

"She's no longer here," Lucas said.

Joe nodded. "You sense it, too?"

"Yeah."

"Just the same, we can find clues here. We must check out the laboratories. We might discover where they're taking her."

Tightness gripped Lucas' chest. He grabbed the rear door of the ambulance to prevent himself from falling. Joe helped seat Lucas in the back of the ambulance.

"You need medical help?" Joe asked.

"No, I'll be okay."

"My brothers have already entered the laboratories. Do you want to stay here?"

Lucas shook his head. "No. I need to know what's in there."

"When you're ready," Joe said.

Lucas winced and stood. "No time like the present."

"You're in pain?"

"My ribs ache. I'll be okay."

"No, bro, it's more than that."

Sharp pain ran down Lucas' left arm. He grabbed his chest. Sweat beaded his brow. His face paled. The world grew black and Lucas lost consciousness. He collapsed on the ground.

Chapter 33

Felicia patted Morton's head. The cat purred and brushed his face against her tiny fingers.

"Tell the other cats 'Hello,' for me," she said.

"Certainly," Morton said.

Julia wiped a tear from her eye and scratched behind his ears. "You be careful."

"Not to worry."

"Are you ready?" Daniel asked.

Felicia hugged Morton tightly.

Morton nodded. "If I don't go now, I'll never leave."

"Here," Felicia said, handing him a cookie.

"Thank you," he said, taking it between his teeth.

Daniel opened the door that led to the garage. "The drive to the airport will take about an hour."

Morton grimaced. "I'm not flying in a pet carrier. No way, no how. It's just not my style."

"You won't have to. I have a friend who has his own private plane. He's agreed to fly us to Jersey."

"That's more like it. Just because Helmsby didn't bother giving me wings doesn't mean I can't have some luxury."

Daniel opened the front car door. Morton hopped in and took his place in the passenger seat. After Daniel backed out of the garage, Morton turned the heat on and aimed a vent full blast at his face.

"What are you doing?"

"Nothing like a fluffy cat face to break women's hearts."

"I doubt we'll see any women on this trip."

"All the same, I have to look my best."

Daniel shook his head. "And what's that about Felicia wanting you to tell other cats, 'Hello?'"

"I had to tell her something, so I told her I had a cat party to go to."

"Ahh, I see."

"I have dreams too, you know? A world filled with talking cats would make my existence less awkward."

"How's that?"

"How would you feel if you were the only human that could talk? It gets a bit lonely from a cat's perspective."

"That makes sense."

"I usually do."

"I wasn't trying to undermine you."

"I know, but I'm logical. I'm the Spock of cats."

Daniel gave Morton a side-glance. "Watching *Star Trek* again?"

Morton shrugged. "Marathon on cable. What can I say?"

"You watch too much television."

The cat made a Vulcan hand sign with his altered paw. "Live long and prosper."

Daniel sighed. "This is going to be a long trip."

Chapter 34

Kat answered her cell phone. "Hey, Kat woman."

"Hi, Todd. You find out anything on the blood samples yet?"

"This stuff you sent. It's a joke, right? You're trying to get back at me for sending you a dozen black roses on your thirtieth birthday?"

Kat frowned. "No, why?"

Todd chuckled. "Whatever blood you sent me is all screwed up."

"What do you mean?"

"Well, the RBCs and WBCs, they're all okay. They appear normal. But the other shit floating around in the plasma . . . I ain't ever seen anything like that. You wouldn't by chance have access to the body where I could get some tissue samples for analysis?"

"Unfortunately, no."

"See? See? I knew *that's* what you'd say."

"Todd, I'm serious. This isn't a prank."

"So where's the body?"

"We don't know."

"Well, don't keep me in suspense. Otherwise, I'll remain suspicious."

"The Red Pawn Murder investigation. You're familiar with that?"

"Yes, of course."

"The blood is from someone we believe is involved with the killings."

"And he gave this blood sample freely?"

"Not exactly. We took it from his fresh corpse."

"That just doesn't sound right."

"Why?"

"Besides the strange cellular components floating around in the sample, necrobiotic activity shows this body should have been buried long ago."

"I'm afraid I don't understand."

"DNA fragmentation shows signs of someone that has been dead a long time. A very long time."

"The corpse was fresh, I assure you."

"Wait a minute. You just said that you don't have the corpse."

"That's true, Todd. We don't."

"So why do you no longer possess it?"

"My colleague returned to the garage to retrieve the body. It wasn't there."

"May have gotten up and walked away."

"I don't think so. When he left it, there were three bullet holes in its head. Besides, you just mentioned that the blood shows the man should have been dead for a long time."

"Yeah, that's what confuses me, but the necrotic tissue in the plasma isn't exactly dead. That's why I'd like to find the body. These strange fragments have the capability to regenerate by swallowing RBCs."

"It consumes its own red blood cells?"

"Exactly. Almost a symbiotic relationship. That's why I said that it might have gotten up on its own. There's the chance the body healed itself."

"Is this similar to the cat blood at the Hutchinson apartment?"

"No. Much more advanced. Totally different. The cat's DNA possessed shifter markers like the animals found in TransGenCorp. This is something I've not seen before."

Kat sighed. "Keep me posted if you discover anything new."

"Will do. So how do you like working with Carpenter again?"

"You can't ignore a toothache."

"Come on, Kat. He's not that bad."

"Maybe not."

"He has grieved for months over your leaving the agency."

"Is that so?"

"Would I lie to you?"

"On occasion."

Todd chuckled. "Well . . . not this one. He took it hard when you left. I think he started drinking again. He seldom sleeps, and he's a real pain in the ass whenever he comes around. He doesn't have your tact."

Kat was horrified. "I never knew he had a drinking problem."

"He did years before you came to the agency. Some thought he rolled the death dice on purpose. He put himself into dangerous situations. Sometimes he was half drunk."

She thought of the fatigue that consumed Carpenter's face at the coffee shop. "What made him drink like that?"

"I don't know if I should tell you. It's personal."

"I'll keep it between us."

Todd sighed. "His wife was killed in a car accident. She was six months pregnant."

Kat swallowed hard. The news was like a harsh kick in her gut.

"And what stung even more was that the accident was probably staged by someone he had been investigating at the time. A major drug trafficker. Slayton Arton. I think that's the dude's name."

"Did he catch him?"

"Yeah, but he could never link the man to the accident. Carpenter almost lost his job. He lost control and beat the man into a coma. He was suspended for three months. The man regained consciousness but strangely refused to press any charges, so the agency brought Carpenter back under probation."

"At least they captured the man."

"Slayton escaped. He's still on the run."

"Strange, I've never heard about this."

"Nah, Kat woman, it's a cold case. Slayton is another phantom that haunts Carpenter."

"Was Carpenter a field director then?"

"No, but he maintained an impeccable record and was eventually promoted. Anyways, I'm glad you're back with us. I'm afraid he was veering the wrong direction. Maybe you can help him get back on track and re-board the wagon."

"My working with the agency isn't a long term thing, Todd. I promised to help Carpenter with the Red Pawn Murders. Nothing more. I have my own investigative office now."

"Sorry to get my hopes up, but please consider what I told you."

"I know. I will."

"I'm not trying to guilt you into staying, but if Carpenter's a friend to you at all, he needs your help."

"Thanks, Todd. I'll think about it."

Chapter 35

"Typhis," Steph said. "You're right. That wasn't Gunter. Police just found Gunter's body in an alley three blocks from where Simon was killed."

Typhis interlocked his long fingers and popped his knuckles. "I knew it couldn't be him. I'm curious, though, as to whom we're dealing with, why he posed as Gunter to get my tissue samples, and whom he's working for. Who knew about the cultures other than GenTech? Why do they want them? When we catch this man, I'll have the answers tortured out of him."

Steph flipped her hair from her face and then nodded. "I don't think finding him will be too difficult. He's taken one of the hit man's cars."

Typhis appeared stunned. He said, "I thought he'd be smarter than that."

She typed in commands. A few minutes later, she had images from inside the car on the computer screen. Her eyes widened with surprise.

"You're not going to believe this."

"What?"

"His face is different."

Typhis frowned. "You're sure this is the same man?"

She brought up a side view camera image. Violet sat in the passenger side.

"It has to be. Violet is with him."

"Bring up the surveillance video from the block where he took the car. Backtrack every step until you see him as Gunter. I want to know how he's able to do this."

"I'll send the video footage to your office."

Typhis' narrow lips formed a tight smile. "I have a meeting to attend. I'll be gone for a couple hours. Make certain you find what I need by then."

Steph nodded. "Consider it done."

LUCIAN ABANDONED the car six blocks away and hailed a cab. He and Violet climbed into the backseat. He stared at Violet. Color slowly came back to her face, but her beautiful eyes still contained undying terror.

"It gets better," he said to her.

Violet forced a smile. "I don't know. No one has ever tried to kill me before."

"I've faced the threat more times than I can remember."

She wiped a tear from her eye. "I haven't. I don't know how to handle it."

He squeezed her knee. She placed her hand atop his and slowly their fingers entwined together. A lump rose in his throat when the warmth of her hand greeted his. He looked at her, and she smiled.

Lucian tried to think of the last time he had felt this way for a woman. Only one person came to mind.

Lydia.

No, he shook his head. No. Those were subliminal memories Idris had tried to implant so Lucian would destroy Lucas. Those weren't his true feelings.

Dwelling on the thought, he realized that he had never truly found a woman that he desired above all the others. He had never allowed the time to explore his long-term dream of what he wanted in a woman. With Gunter's memories still fighting against his emotions, he wondered if this was Gunter's rising desire for Violet and not his own. When he looked at her again, her eyes gazed at his lips. In moments, if he didn't turn away, they'd be locked in a passionate kiss.

Too early for that, he reasoned. Too many dangers lurked. He looked away.

Her hand squeezed tightly around his thick fingers. "I never thought I worked under such dangerous people."

"You might be surprised to know most people do."

Violet shook her head. "They'll find us eventually."

"They'll find the car, but not us."

Lucian dialed Kat's phone number.

Kat answered. "Are you okay?"

"Yes. I heal fast."

"Were you shot?"

"Well over an hour ago, but it's nothing my metabolism cannot cure."

She sighed. "I've worried about you."

"Why?" Lucian laughed.

"It's been a while since we talked."

"I lost track of time while dodging bullets."

"Do you still have the materials Gunter was working on?"

"Yes."

"So where are you?"

"We're on our way to the hotel."

"You're bringing her with you?" she asked. Her voice hinted slight disappointment.

"You have a better idea?"

Kat was silent.

"She helped me. Now she needs us," Lucian said.

"I know." Kat sighed. "I'm just trying to figure out what we should do with her."

"She'll have to stay with us for a while. They will be looking for her. She won't be safe."

"You plan to protect her?"

"I have to. It's my fault they want her dead. And since she left with me after I stole the tissue cultures, they'll kill her on sight. She cannot safely return to the life she knew before."

"How long before you get here?"

"Ten minutes."

"Okay. I have a meeting with Carpenter in an hour. I'll need you and Kyle to help."

"Not a problem."

Kat disconnected the call and Lucian clipped his phone shut.

"So you really think they'll keep looking for me?" Violet asked.

Lucian nodded. "For a few weeks, I'd say."

She looked out the window and sighed.

Lucian took her hand. "We'll keep you safe. You may have to change your name and relocate."

Her eyes met his and she smiled. "I trust you. Can I trust her?"

"Kat?"

Violet shrugged.

"Yes. You can trust her with your life."

"Doesn't sound like I have any other choices."

Lucian smiled. "Actually you don't. Unless we protect you, they'll kill you. I don't want that to happen."

"I don't either."

Chapter 36

Brockton noticed Kat seated on the edge of the bed. She appeared upset. "Is everything okay?" he asked.

She replied with a slight nod.

"Was that Lucian?"

"Yes. He's on his way here."

"So he got Gunter's cell cultures?"

"Yes. He's bringing one of the workers, too."

Brockton shrugged. "That's not necessarily a bad thing. He could . . ."

"*She*," Kat inserted.

Brockton bit his lower lip to keep from smiling. "She can give us information we cannot retrieve any other way."

Kat stood and glared at him before turning to go to the restroom.

"Something wrong?" he asked.

She stopped walking but didn't face him. "Your insinuated assumption of how he feels about me was wrong. After this assignment, I think he'll be able to move on fine without me."

"Wait," he said. "You mean he's already taken interest in her?"

Kat shrugged. "Does it matter? She's just one more interference I have to deal with."

She closed the door.

"So I did read you correctly, then?" he asked.

"Shut up and go away."

"Kat?"

"I entertained the idea for a few hours, but I shouldn't have since he works with me. It went bad with Tyler. It's a good thing this has happened."

"Be patient."

"I'm fine. Attend to Kyle. I need a few minutes of privacy here. This *is* the bathroom."

"Sorry."

DR. HELMSBY STARED through the microscope ocular at a slide of the alien tissue. He shook his head in disbelief.

Grayson smiled. "Worth signing on for?"

Helmsby nodded. "This is unbelievable. How did you manage to get this?"

"I'd rather not go into full detail about that at this particular moment." Grayson shoved his thick hands into his jacket pockets. "You signed confidentiality forms because this is top secret. No one outside my company knows I even possess this. Competition between the other biotech companies is too rigid to let news of this discovery leak out yet. Those cutthroats will go to extremes to take this from me. Only a handful in my employ has knowledge of it."

"I understand. So, what do you want me to do with this?"

Grayson smiled. "You're the scientist. Analyze it and give me a detailed report about everything you discover."

"Glad to, sir. This is an opportunity too great to resist. Thanks for having me aboard."

Grayson chuckled. "There's no other scientist I'd have work on this. Your reputation in the scientific world has no equal."

"Just curious. What do you hope to gain through this?"

"To rule the world, my friend," Grayson said, placing a hand firmly on Helmsby's shoulder. "World dominance comes to the one who possesses the greatest technology, and currently I do. Who knows what else this discover will add?"

An icy chill ran down Helmsby's spine. The confidentiality contracts he had signed essentially sold his soul to Grayson's lustful devil. Death was his only way out. No one ever walked away from such an organization that held secrets like the one he was researching. What sickened him most was he had placed his fiancée and daughter as a part of the offering as well.

"I have some errands to attend to, Dr. Helmsby. Enjoy yourself."

Helmsby nodded. "I will."

After Grayson left the room, Helmsby wiped sweat from his brow. He wasn't certain where Yvonne was or where they had stationed Nancy, but he hoped to see one of them soon. Being isolated to this lab brought back the uneasiness that had possessed him when he resided in TransGenCorp under Idris' control.

Chapter 37

Brockton was helping Kyle eat when Lucian knocked on the hotel door. Kat peered through the peephole before she unlocked it. She stood behind the door and pulled it open.

Violet released Lucian's hand and stepped ahead of him. She cautiously scanned the room. Lucian pushed the door closed, locked it, and as Violet reached to hold Lucian's hand, Kat intercepted and shook hands.

"I'm Kat."

"Violet," she replied with a nervous smile.

Kat forced a smile. "Would you like some coffee?"

Violet nodded. "Please."

Brockton left Kyle and greeted them. Lucian handed him the cooler.

"Ahh," he said. "Let's see what you have in here."

"They're really pissed that we have it," Lucian said.

"I don't doubt that." Brockton put the cooler on the bed and opened it. "Quite a bit of tissue to evaluate. If you and your friend don't mind, I need you to fill the tub with a layer of ice. These require refrigeration."

"Not a problem," Lucian said. "But what we need is a laboratory."

"I know, but we haven't time. Kat is scheduled to meet Carpenter soon. Kyle might be able to find us a temporary lab by this evening."

Kat couldn't stop staring at Violet. The young lady's beauty was graceful, regal, and almost too perfect. Although Lucian didn't portray any attraction for Violet, she knew there was no way he'd deny the exquisiteness she possessed.

"Lucian said that you're someone I can trust," Violet said with a slight smile.

Kat smiled and nodded. "Yes, of course."

"I don't think I've ever been as afraid as I was today."

"How long have you worked for Mech Cybernetics?"

"Nearly four years."

Kat responded with a skeptical frown. "You barely look nineteen."

"Thanks. I'm twenty-six, actually."

"Make yourself comfortable," Kat said, walking away. "I need to talk to Brockton."

Lucian grabbed the ice bucket and motioned to Violet. "Come with me," he said.

Outside on the balcony, Violet hugged herself as a brisk wind funneled up the stairs and down the open corridor. "She doesn't like me, does she?"

"Why do you say that?"

Violet shrugged. "She just seemed too short with me."

"A lot of stuff is going on. She's trying to find the people behind the Red Pawn Murders. At a normal pace, she would have sat and chatted with you for an hour."

"You think so?"

Lucian nodded. "Yes. Sometimes, you can't get her to *stop* talking."

"She acted uncomfortable with me in the room."

"Kat's fine with you." He laughed. "Hell, you should have seen how she acted the first time we met."

"Really? What happened?"

Lucian thought about Kat shooting him in the bunker and perhaps it wasn't the best information to give Violet. He shook his head. "Never mind. I'll tell you later."

Lucian led her down the concrete stairs, rounded a corner, and headed to the back vendor room on the ground floor. He opened the icemaker and filled the bucket with ice.

"We're going to need a lot more than this," he said. "Take out that garbage bag and bring the trash container to me. It should be big enough."

He heaved the full trashcan of ice up the stairs and back to the hotel room. When they entered, Kat was whispering to Brockton.

Brockton stepped away from her and opened the bathroom door. "Here, let me help you," he said nervously.

Lucian gave him a strange glance as he stepped past, but didn't say anything. He dumped the ice into the tub. Brockton brought the Petri culture dishes and started setting them atop the layer of ice.

Brockton said, "This should hold them for a few hours until we can find a better place to store them. Go help Kat with the camera."

Chapter 38

New Jersey FBI Office

KAT ADJUSTED her blouse and tapped the earpiece hidden beneath her hair. She walked through the front door.

"Can you hear me?" she asked.

"Loud and clear," Lucian replied from their van parked on the curb.

She straightened the center button camera on her low-cut blouse. "How's the visual?"

"Any clearer a shot of your breasts, and we'll have to file this under triple X."

Kat's face reddened. She quickly adjusted the camera's angle.

"Is that better?" she asked.

Lucian cleared his throat. "Not for me, but it's now set for a straight ahead shot. Just be certain not to accidentally place your hand over the camera."

"I'll try. I've not ever done this before."

"I still don't understand why you won't just introduce me to Carpenter as one of your associates."

Kat sighed. "He's too suspicious. He's certain I had a hand in your escape from the TGC bunker."

"Well, you did," Lucian said.

"Yes, but it's not something he ever needs to discover."

Lucas said, "I've made an excellent facial disguise. He'd be none the wiser."

"We'll get more information if our relationship remains discreet. Besides, he'd run a full background check on any name we give him."

"How long do you think this meeting will take?" Lucian asked.

"Not sure. Why?"

"We have to pick Morton up at the airport in about an hour."

"It shouldn't take too long," Kat said, glancing at her watch. "To solve this case, I'll need to get all the information I can."

"I know," Lucian said. "I'm worried about leaving Violet unprotected at the hotel."

Kat closed her eyes and stopped walking. "I shouldn't ask, but do you have feelings for her?"

"I'm not sure. Why?"

"Don't let your emotions interfere with your duties."

"I haven't, Kat. And I won't."

Kat sighed. "I think you already have."

"How could you say that?"

"It's true. You're acting like a lovesick pup."

"And you're acting like a jealous lover."

Kat bit her lower lip. "Be honest. Have you ever really been in love before?"

Lucian was quiet for a long minute. "No, Kat, I can't say that I have known what it is to truly love someone. It wasn't something instilled into my existence. After all, Idris created me to kill, not to love."

"I'm sorry, Lucian. I have overstepped my bounds."

"No, Kat, you didn't. You made a valid point."

"No, I shouldn't have . . ."

"Easy Kat. You don't owe me an apology. You wanted honesty, and I'll always give you that."

"Lucian . . ."

"I don't know what my feelings for Violet are. I'm still struggling with Gunter's emotions from Kyle's mind meld. I can't really explain what my true feelings are for her because I don't know how much of Gunter's infatuation still exists. I hope it fades soon. Maybe being away from her will allow me to sort through this."

Kat fought tears of her haste. Lucian had become such a close friend that she failed to realize that his origin had merely been a twisted experiment. She took several deep breaths to calm herself before she met Carpenter. If she lost composure, she'd have a hard time explaining why she was upset. She fanned her face and focused on being as happy as possible.

"Lucian, I'm sorry I sounded callous. I tend to speak without thinking sometimes."

"Let's forget about it, okay?"

"I can't imagine living without ever feeling loved."

He laughed. "I didn't say I had never *felt* it. I said I didn't know if I have loved someone."

"How can you feel it but not know if you love?"

"Even I can sense when someone loves or cares about me. I have friends. You are one."

Kat smiled. "I'm proud to be."

"I know. Okay. Are you ready to talk to Carpenter?"

"Yes. Is Kyle alert?"

"He and Brockton are at the computers in the rear of the van. Everything seen and said will be recorded by them."

"Good. Then here we go."

Kat waited at the reception desk until Carpenter stepped from the elevator and greeted her. Part of her apprehension faded when she saw his broad smile. He seemed as relieved to see her as she was in seeing him.

They entered the elevator and exited on the third floor. He motioned her to head to his office.

"I have the files waiting, so we can get started immediately."

Carpenter sat at a small table in the corner of his office. Kat sat across from him. He opened a manila file and slid a paper across to her.

"I'm glad you've decided to help in this," he said.

Kat looked over the paper and said, "Pawn number one was a housewife in Freehold, New Jersey?"

Carpenter nodded. "Yes. Francis Teeks, a diabetic. She was a test subject in gene replacement therapy."

"Let me guess? GenTech sponsored her therapy?"

"Yes."

"Pawns two through four were just random killings?"

Carpenter replied, "Street bums. Gutter trash people. Killed assassin style. No motive. What money and valuables the victims had weren't taken."

Kat glanced from the paper to Carpenter. "So, maybe these were killed to hone their tactic training?"

"That's my guess, but I'm open for your opinions."

"What about pawn number five?" Kat asked with a frown. "You have a cross reference number beside it."

Carpenter rubbed his tired eyes and sighed. "Yes. Bizarre murder."

"Why?"

"The woman's son and daughter were abducted."

Kat's chest tightened. "Any reason why?"

Carpenter fished through another stack of papers and handed her a profile sheet. "Her children were test tube babies."

"So?"

"Genetic selection technology."

"Meaning she chose the hair color, eye color, and sex of each child and they manipulated the genetic makeup inside her embryos?"

"Exactly. The practice is becoming more common nowadays; especially by any woman who doesn't want a husband or a father in her child's life."

Kat flipped the piece of paper for more information and said, "Where are the children? Please tell me they've been found."

"I wish I could, but we're still hunting for them."

Kat offered a slight smile. "I think the deeper we get into this game, the closer we'll get to finding them."

"I hope so."

"Well," she said, looking at the list of pawns. "If this game continues, the perpetrator will eventually leave us a trail that leads back to him."

Carpenter stood and stretched. "Coffee?" he asked.

Kat nodded. "Yes, thanks."

He walked to the coffee pot and poured coffee into Styrofoam cups. He brought her a cup and placed sweetener and cream packets on the table in front of her.

"The rest are somehow associated with GenTech?"

Carpenter pulled his chair around the table beside hers. "Number six drove a limo for GenTech's former CEO."

"Why kill the driver and not the CEO?"

"Not sure. Perhaps they thought he was in the limo, and he wasn't. The CEO vanished after the attack."

"Who is the CEO?"

"Steven Matthews." He slid a photo and Matthew's profile information to her.

"I recognize him."

Carpenter nodded. "Most people certainly would. He had been on the news a lot before the attempt on his life. He wanted to bring the age of embryonic gene selection to the forefront of genetic research."

"Why?"

"He believes that genetic selection in embryos could rid future generations of flaws and end disease, possibly allowing humans to live another forty years past the current longevity span. By gene selection, he believes all genetic diseases can be annihilated."

Kat shook her head. "Another demented Frankenstein like General Idris. When will the scientific world understand that we're not supposed to live forever?"

Carpenter chuckled. "When you have millions of dollars, you want the dream of immortality to become a reality because you cannot spend money after you die."

"Matthews is definitely a person of interest. We need to question him."

"There's a search for him as we speak."

Agent Denton entered the office and waved at Kat. "How've you been, Kat?"

Kat smiled. "Quite well. You?"

He sighed. "All tied up with the Game of Pawns case lately."

Carpenter smiled. "That's why she's here."

"You're helping?" Denton asked.

"I'm scouring through the information. Maybe we'll make some headway of it soon."

"That'd be great. I could finally get some rest if we find out what's going on." He placed a hand on Carpenter's shoulder and said, "Have you told her the news yet?"

Carpenter shook his head. "No, not yet."

Denton gave a slight nod and headed toward the door. "Nice to see you again, Kat," he said.

"And you," she replied. After Denton left, she said, "Tell me what news?"

"I'll bring that up after we've gone through the files here."

"Fair enough. Who was Pawn number seven?"

"Number seven was a stock broker who sold stocks for GenTech. Number eight drove a delivery truck for GenTech before they merged with Mech Cybergenics."

"I see. I recently learned of Mech Cybergenics. Do you know who owns it?"

Carpenter sipped his coffee and nodded. "Yes. Mr. Boyd Grayson owns it. He also owns Grayson Enterprises."

"So Boyd Grayson bought out GenTech and merged it with his company?"

"Yes. Grayson's space enterprise division in L.A. is almost finished, too."

"I see. The next four Pawns were scientists that worked with GenTech."

"Five," Carpenter corrected. "We found Gunter's body, so now he's accounted for. However, all five of these scientists were killed *after* the merger."

"So someone within Mech Cybergenics wanted to eliminate the former GenTech employees?"

"It seems like what's happening, but why?"

"Maybe they knew too much? Or maybe it was a hostile takeover?"

"Could be," Carpenter said. "Or perhaps the former owner of GenTech is killing them to prevent Grayson from possessing his scientific knowledge."

Kat nodded. "That makes sense, too. Who sold GenTech to Grayson?"

Carpenter flipped through more file papers. "Typhis Black."

The name jolted Kat.

"What's wrong?"

"Isn't he the mayor of Newark, New Jersey?"

Carpenter smiled. "Yes, just recently he was elected to the seat."

"And he owned a biotech company?"

He shrugged. "It's not a crime to make radical career changes."

"No, but it's odd."

"I agree."

"Perhaps he has a hand in it?"

"Why would he?"

"Maybe he doesn't want Grayson to succeed. Corruption runs deep, even in some political circles."

Carpenter shook his head.

"Don't be so quick to rule him out," Kat said.

"I still think Matthews and Grayson are our best bets."

"I agree that Matthews has motive. He lost his CEO position when Grayson bought GenTech. Since he was on the brink of new major discoveries within gene selection techniques, it stands to reason that he might want to kill those who had worked for him. Maybe he wants to start a new biotech lab and develop his techniques before Grayson succeeds."

"Grayson has motive if Matthews is behind the murders. Stock prices for Grayson Enterprises dipped soon after the Game of Pawns began."

Kat shook her head. "It's not a hostile takeover then. It's a damn war."

"The casualties are piling up."

Kat glanced at her watch and looked at Gunter's file. "Wasn't the attempt to kill Gunter in his apartment done in an executioner manner?"

"As best we can tell, that's probably the correct assumption. Although the initial attack at his apartment wouldn't have ended that way. It was more violent than any of the previous attacks. However, his death would have been more merciful had they killed him at his apartment."

Kat acted surprised. "What do you mean?"

"His throat was ripped out."

"God."

Carpenter nodded in sympathy. "It wasn't a pleasant way to find his body."

"How were the other scientists in his group killed?" she asked.

"Each was at home or just arriving home when they were shot to death."

"Ballistics?"

"All bullets came from the same two 9mms."

She nodded, still reading through the names. "So we have a two man assassin team."

"Until Black Pawn number one showed up, we did. Dennis Schrader died from his own gun. It wasn't suicide. His right wrist was broken. No powder residue was found on his hands. Someone attacked and killed him at point blank range. However, all thirteen red pawn murders seemed to have been done by two people."

"They never changed guns. That indicates they never feared getting caught."

"True. Keeping the same weapons does show cockiness."

"That and they wanted their game to be known as a game with only two players."

Carpenter nodded. "Yes, but now someone's retaliating and settling the score. Gunter was the last red pawn and the last GenTech worker at Mech Cybernetics. Schrader's murder gave us something else that we didn't have before, too."

"What?"

"A witness."

"Of his murder?"

Carpenter smiled and nodded.

"Who?"

"Vanessa Powell, a dancer at La Vida Erotica."

"Was this what Denton hinted about?"

"Yes, but there's a lot more. We found TGC crates locked inside one of the storage rooms at La Vida Erotica."

"Damn," she said.

"Yes, each lead opens into more bizarre situations."

"Do you mind if I speak with Vanessa?"

Carpenter shrugged. "For whatever good it will do you."

"Why?"

He laughed. "I've sent her to be evaluated by a shrink."

Kat's eyes widened. "For what reason?"

"Her story is too unbelievable, even after all the stuff we've discovered about TGC."

"Care to elaborate?"

"You talk to her. Maybe you can make some sense of it. Right now, let's see what else is involved with the pawns." He glanced at his watch. "She should be back in about twenty minutes."

"So we only have one black pawn and with that, we now have a witness?"

"Yes."

"That doesn't help us find out who left the red pawns."

"I know. Gunter's body is the last red pawn so far. There will probably be more."

"I'm not so sure about that," Kat replied. "Something went wrong when they tried to kill Gunter. They made mistakes."

"And tried to cover them up. But, we still don't have one of the assassin's bodies."

"No, but my team recovered evidence that will help us get closer to solving this."

"What?"

"We took blood samples from the garage where Gunter was probably killed. The blood belongs to one of the assassins."

"How did you get this?"

"We were searching the area around the same time you were there."

Carpenter's face flushed red. "Kat, I warned you *not* to withhold evidence."

She shook her head, and innocence beamed in her eyes. "I'm not. If I was, I wouldn't be telling you this, nor would I have sent the blood to Todd's lab for analysis."

He loosened his tie and released a long sigh. "Okay, what did you discover?"

"Have Todd fax you the blood analysis report. He contacted me with shocking news about the blood components. Read his report, and we'll bounce off more theories later."

"Okay, I appreciate you bringing this to my attention."

"How can I not? You've helped me gather a better understanding of the murders by sharing death accounts with me."

"Although in the future I'd like to get this kind of information up front."

"I understand."

Carpenter stood, refilled his coffee cup, and motioned her to the door. "Let's see if Vanessa Powell is back."

"I can't wait to speak to her."

"It's a conversation you won't soon forget. I assure you."

Chapter 39

Kat sat across the table from Vanessa Powell. Carpenter stood in the next room on the other side of the mirrored glass. He hoped Kat divulged better information from this dancer than he and the psychiatrist had.

Vanessa folded her hands on the metal table and gave Kat a blank stare. Kat studied her several minutes. Childlike innocence creased Vanessa's smile, and yet, in spite of her age, the young lady's actions exhibited that of an adolescent girl.

"Vanessa, I'm Kat."

She responded with a slight nod, but offered no words.

Kat smiled. "I was told that you saw what happened to Dennis Schrader."

"Who?"

"The man in the alley near where you work."

Dread filled her eyes. Her pupils narrowed. She nodded nervously. "Yes, they were horrible."

"What did they look like?"

"Dead men. Their faces were pale. Their eyes dead, empty."

Kat turned toward the mirror and gave Carpenter a puzzled stare, even though she couldn't see him.

"These dead men," Kat said. "How were they dressed?"

Vanessa thought for a moment. "Very nice suits. If not for their faces, they could have been business patrons where I dance. But no amount of money they offered could tempt me to . . . pleasure them."

"Think for a minute, dear. Describe their faces in better detail."

She closed her eyes. Visible chill bumps rose up the girl's arms. "Their skin was ashen white. Some skin was flaked in places. Their hollow eyes were black, empty."

"How long have you worked for La Vida Erotica?"

Confusion molded her brow with deep furrows. "I don't know."

"You don't know how long you've been there?"

"No."

"Do you remember your parents?"

Vanessa shook her head. "No."

"Nothing outside of La Vida Erotica?"

"No."

"Excuse me, Vanessa. I'll be right back, hon."

She stood and headed out the door. Carpenter met outside the adjoining room.

Carpenter smiled. "I told you that she has some delusional problems."

Kat shook her head. "No, Carpenter. You need to call Todd. Get his blood analysis sheets."

"Why?"

"The blood samples from the assassin. He mentioned something like this. Something about how the body should have been dead a long time ago, but the blood components were regenerating themselves. Strange as she sounds, it's not the first time I've heard about a zombie-like person."

"So you believe there's some validity to what she said?"

Kat shrugged. "Possibly. We need to talk to Todd."

Lucian spoke to Kat via her earpiece. "The man I fought in the garage looked nothing like what she's saying. He could walk into a crowd of people undetected. Well, except for having doglike ears. I'm not certain *what* she thinks she saw."

Kat fought not to reply because she wanted to find out exactly what was going on. An open response, even by accident to Lucian, let Carpenter know she wasn't entirely alone and that she didn't fully trust him. Even though she was growing fond of working with Carpenter again, she could never gain back his trust if he knew Lucian was eavesdropping on the investigation.

"We need that body," Carpenter said, shoving his hands into his pockets.

"That would help," she replied. "Let me see what else Vanessa might know."

"How do you perceive her?"

"She doesn't act like a woman in her twenties. She's more like a child. At least, mentally."

"I noticed that, too. It's why Denton and I refused to leave her in the alley at La Vida Erotica. The last thing she needs is for her handlers to get their hands on her again."

"So there are other women like her?"

He nodded. "Yes. About twenty more."

"Dancers?"

"And prostitutes."

"That's beyond immoral."

"Exactly. If we prove they are laboratory creations, we can shut them down for good and press charges. Prostitution may be legal, but creating women solely for that kind of entertainment *isn't*."

Kat placed a hand on his arm. "Let me see what I can learn. There may be nothing more, though, but I'll try."

Carpenter smiled. "It's better than nothing. The longer we keep her here, the longer we can protect her."

Chapter 40

Violet sat at the computer and maximized different windows Kyle had been looking through. She reflected over the way things had unfolded from the time she had reported to work. She was thankful to still be alive. Never had she expected to find someone like Lucian—part savior, part nightmare. She had no doubt he'd protect her, but they had left her alone. They had important matters to examine in order to stop those who had tried to kill her.

The isolation strangled her with fear. She worried that whoever had attempted to eliminate her was closing in. She had seen how easily they could find her. Lucian had said they wouldn't stop. Again, she wondered why he had left her alone. Not completely alone. He had left the 9mm with her and quickly explained how to use it.

Violet went to the bathroom and splashed cold water on her face. When she patted her face with the plush towel, she stared at her reflection in the wall length mirror. For the best part of a minute, she no longer recognized herself. Her eyes resembled those of a frightened rabbit running for its life. The beauty of her self-confidence was gone.

Ice shifted in the bathtub and startled her. She turned and realized the melting ice was settling. A dark line on the outside of the tub caught her attention. She knelt and discovered dried blood that someone had attempted to wipe away with a towel.

Violet lowered the toilet lid and seated herself. Her mind drifted back to Lucian being shot while protecting her. He had genuine concern to keep her alive and risked his life to do so. Had he been less than human, she understood her life would have ended inside that elevator. She couldn't forget the amount of blood he had lost and yet, he lived. She had never seen so much blood. Or death. Guards had died for her to survive and so Lucian could keep the Gunter's cultures.

After several minutes, she stood and returned to Kyle's desk. She had no idea how long Lucian expected her to wait. She hated being alone. Her nervousness prevented her from wanting to wait by herself for any extended period. She fished in her back pocket for her cell phone.

Violet scrolled down the list of phone numbers on her phone screen and stopped at the one person she still trusted, even though she'd not heard from him since GenTech's merger. She dialed the number and after the third ring, the man answered.

"Hello? Violet?"

"Yes."

"Where are you?"

"I'm safe," she replied.

"Are you okay? I saw the GenTech murders on the news."

Violet took a deep breath. "I'm fine. Just scared and lonely. I needed a friendly voice to talk to."

"Tell me where you are. I'll drop by and keep you company."

Violet paced the floor and thought. She ran a hand through her brown hair. She sighed and went to the hotel window, pulled back the edge of the curtain and stared at the parking lot. Although she didn't see any threat waiting, she didn't want to be alone.

"Violet? Are you still there?"

She nodded, pulled her hair from her eyes, and said, "Yes. I'm here."

"Where are you?"

"At the Borden Hotel in Jersey."

"I know where that is. Stay there and I'll see you soon."

"Don't bother. I'll be fine."

"But you're alone?"

"Yes."

"I'll come ease your loneliness. I assume you left with Gunter's lookalike?"

"Lucian, yes. He left me here where I'd be safe."

"I see. What did he do with the tissue cultures he stole?"

Violet swallowed hard. "How did you know about those? The news didn't mention that."

The phone went dead. A greater fear resurrected inside her. She had said too much. Lucian had warned her of the hidden dangers. Like a fool, she ignored his cautions.

"Damn," she whispered.

She grabbed the cooler and ran to the bathroom. Shoving her hands into the ice, she grabbed the stacks of Petri dishes and carefully packed them into the cooler. She didn't know where she'd hide, but she didn't want Lucian pissed at her either.

Coldness stung her hands each time she rammed them under the ice until eventually the cold numbed them. She didn't care. Lucian had risked his life to save her and for whatever reason, these cultures were important to him. If he had sacrificed so much, she couldn't do any less. She'd take the tissues and wait somewhere else. When Lucian returned, she'd bring them to him.

She picked up the final stack, and the hotel door crashed open. Seconds later, a shadow loomed in the doorway behind her.

"Thanks. I'll be taking those," he said, leveling his gun at her beautiful face.

Violet opened her mouth to scream, but the man shook his head. She looked at the gun, closed her eyes, and hot tears spilled down her cheeks. She had survived so many perils earlier in the day, but for some reason, Death continued seeking her and refused to let her escape. But this time, Lucian wasn't near. He couldn't save her.

Chapter 41

Kat returned to the table where Vanessa sat. "You don't remember anything before you began working at La Vida Erotica?"

She shook her head. "No."

"What do you remember?"

"Tanks filled with liquid. The water drained, and I fought to take my first breath."

Kat took the seat across the table. She placed a gentle hand on top of the girl's folded ones. "What else do you remember?"

"Freezing cold air. A man unhooked cords and wires from my shivering, nude body."

Lucian whispered in Kat's ear. "Incubation chamber."

"Yes," she whispered back. "Go on."

"Another dancer wrapped a heated robe around me. A heavy man took me to dark room with a bed." Vanessa looked away. Shame overshadowed her.

"What did he do?"

"He examined me." She swallowed hard. "Down there."

Kat's stomach knotted. "He had sex with you?"

"Yes." Tears ran down her cheeks. "The pain of his thrusting movements burned through me and it is the first thing I remember. While he did this, he explained that this was my duty, my job. He told me how to please a man and that I would be rewarded. When he finished, I was taken to a room where they placed a visor over my eyes and a headset over my ears. I don't remember much after that."

"He subliminally programmed her *after* he raped her," Lucian said to Kat.

Kat placed her hand over her mouth and whispered, "Why is she remembering this?"

"If she has a program chip implant, it's possible that it has malfunctioned. Find out who this man is. I'll punish him. Severely."

"What did this man look like?"

"Big and heavy. Smelled like smoke. Cigar smoke. He was an older man."

Kat squeezed Vanessa's hand. "You're safe. Don't worry. We'll find him. He'll pay."

Involuntary tears leaked from the girl's eyes. Kat released her hand and left the room before she shed tears of her own.

Carpenter shook his head when she entered the room. He said, "I'll make certain that she's put under constant protection and gets physical and mental medical attention. Not much more than that can we do."

"Can you imagine?"

He frowned. "We'll find the son of a bitch, Kat."

"He manufactured women to do such unspeakable things."

"It's sick. Popping their cherries for himself, and then training them to be dancing prostitutes."

"We have enough to close them down, don't we?"

Carpenter nodded. "We have her testimony on film, so yes, we can shut them down. But closing La Vida Erotica will prevent us from discovering their tie to TGC. The crates are evidence of cloned humans."

"Yes, but how long have those crates been hidden there?"

"Good question. The girls may have all been purchased from TGC years before Lucas performed the Meltdown. I'll send Denton back and see if he can find a shipping date on any of the crates."

Kat patted the sides of her eyes dry with a tissue. "You and Denton have been inside La Vida Erotica. How did those girls act?"

"They're like beautiful, drug-controlled zombies. Nothing fazes them. In fact, your conversation with Vanessa was more information than we received from anyone else. None of the others seemed to notice us."

"Maybe she's stronger spirited than the others."

Carpenter shrugged. "It's possible."

Lucian whispered to Kat. "We need to leave. Kyle senses that Violet is in trouble."

Kat looked at Carpenter. "Let me know what Denton discovers."

"You're leaving?" he asked.

Glancing at her watch, she said, "I have another appointment that's urgent."

"Take a seat."

"Honestly, I can't."

"Two minutes is all I need," he said.

Kat sighed and sat down.

Carpenter's eyes narrowed when he stared at her. "This is something I need to know. Do you have any idea where Lucas' clone is?"

She shook her head. "No. Why?"

"I received disturbing news from the Nevada FBI office this morning. Lucas' wife, Lydia, was abducted last night at a Motocross competition. I have reason to believe the clone might be the one responsible for kidnapping her."

"That pompous son of a bitch," she heard Lucian say through the receiver in her ear.

"Lydia was abducted?"

Carpenter walked to his desk, retrieved the morning paper, and handed it to her.

"I doubt the clone has anything to do with this."

"Why?" Carpenter asked.

"What would he stand to gain?"

"He tried to kill her before."

"That's the theory. We have no proof. Besides, he killed Idris to help Lucas and Lydia escape from TransGenCorp."

"I'd like to know whatever became of the clone."

"I understand you want to wrap up any loose ends associated with TransGenCorp, but most all of the cases end without us knowing everything that transpired."

Carpenter shoved his hands into his pockets. "I suppose you're right."

"What's the word on Lucas?"

"He's in the hospital in Nevada."

"Is he okay?"

"We don't know."

Kat looked at her watch again and rose to her feet. "I really have to go, but once you get the report from Todd and read it, please contact me."

"I will, Kat," Carpenter said, leaning toward her and giving her a small hug. "And thanks."

Chapter 42

Lucas awoke in the hospital.

Joe sat in the chair beside the bed and smiled. "Good morning, bro."

"What happened?" He replied, rubbing his eyes. "Heart attack?"

"The doctor said that you suffered an angina. Not a heart attack, but it's a warning that unless you slow down and lower your stress, you may have one eventually."

"No shit?"

Joe shook his head. "No shit."

"Damn."

"Doctor says that you should be able to leave later today."

Lucas sat up and swung his feet over the side of the bed. "No, I need to go *now*. We have to find Lydia."

"Easy, bro," Joe said, putting a hand on Luke's shoulder. "This is exactly what put you in here."

Lucas sighed. "I know, but what the hell am I supposed to do? I can't live without her. If we wait too long, we'll never find her. There's no telling what they will do with her."

"We'll find her. You have my word."

"What did your brothers find out about the Desert Labs?"

"They reviewed the tapes. Lydia was there, and they used a tranquilizer dart to kidnap her."

Lucas closed his eyes and shook his head slowly. "What else? Did you see who the person was?"

"No, but we did find something of peculiar interest."

"What?"

"There is a room filled with rows of incubation chambers, like you mentioned that Lydia came from. Her name is stamped on one of them."

"I hope you busted them all to hell."

"No."

"Why not?"

Joe smiled. "Think about it, Luke. They wanted her *there*. By leaving everything intact, it's likely they will bring her back once things have cooled off."

"That's possible, I suppose."

"They have invested too much time and money in the facility to simply abandon it. I estimate they spent millions of dollars building it over the past three years. They won't rebuild. They might have plenty of money, but they don't have that kind of time."

"But if they know we've found their lab, they won't risk using the place."

"Even if they noticed our arrival, they won't have a way of knowing it was us."

Lucas frowned.

Joe shrugged. "We took all the surveillance tapes and replaced them with blank ones."

"I don't know what I'd do without you," Lucas said with a broad smile.

"What are blood brothers for?"

"I owe you greatly."

Joe shook his head. "Finding Lydia alive and in good health is reward enough."

"Thanks."

"Never a problem."

A doctor dressed in white and carrying a clipboard entered the room and stopped at the foot of Lucas' bed.

"How are you feeling, Mr. Ridale?"

"I feel fine. I have no pain."

"Glad to hear that."

Lucas gave a sly grin. "So when can I leave?"

"Not yet. We have a few more tests we need to run to make certain that you're okay. Although you didn't have a heart attack, the symptoms of angina are generally a warning sign. It's best we examine you a bit longer to be on the safe side."

"I feel fine."

"It shouldn't take long. Two more hours at the most."

Joe nodded. "Kick your feet back and relax."

"I really can't."

"Be patient," the doctor said. "I'll send a nurse in."

"Luke, if we have to travel fast, it's best we know that you're healthy enough to go."

Lucas lay back against the pillows and folded his arms across his chest. "Joe, I don't have enough patience to be patient."

"Stress put you here. You need to find a way to focus on the positive and relax."

"Bullshit. They have my wife. There's no telling what they will do to her or if I'll ever find her. That kind of stress doesn't lessen."

"I know. But realize that I always keep my promises. I promise we'll find her."

"How can you make such a guarantee? Where do we start looking?"

"All these years we've been friends, and you still haven't learned?"

Lucas gave Joe a puzzled expression. "Learned what?"

"You still haven't learned how to listen for a spirit on the wind. You know her better than anyone else, correct?"

"Of course. She's my soul mate."

"Then close your eyes and listen for her spirit. She's calling for you. She'll find a way to lead us to her."

"I'm not sure how. Can't you do this?"

"As I told you before, I've had a hard time reading her aura. But you know her and you sensed that she wasn't at the laboratory. You can find her. Just listen."

Lucas closed his eyes, pushed away his anxiety, relaxed, and listened. Several moments passed, but he allowed his mind to drift. Seeking. Searching. Floating. Suddenly, his heart leapt. Warmth greeted him as smoothly as a gentle kiss, but from a far distance and from a cold dark place. He hoped to hear her voice, but he understood why he couldn't. Sedatives held her captive, restraining her. Her mind slept. But he did feel her. He had hope. It was a new start.

Chapter 43

Lucian pulled the van to the curb when Kat stepped outside of the FBI office. She hurried into the passenger seat, and he pressed the accelerator.

"What kind of trouble is Violet in?" Kat asked.

"I don't know," Lucian said. "Kyle sensed trouble back at the hotel."

"But we weren't followed."

"I know, but it doesn't mean they don't have ways to find her. Her cell phone may have had a tracer."

She gave him a side-glance. "Or she was foolish enough to call someone."

"I doubt that."

Kat shook her head. "You've only known her for a few hours. Don't assume more than you know."

He sighed. "You're right."

Kat turned in her seat. "Brockton, how has Kyle been?"

The doctor smiled. "He's getting more physical reflexes, and his new mental abilities seem to be advancing."

KYLE SAT with his eyes closed. His mind retraced the premonitions he had experienced while Kat was discussing the case with Carpenter. In clear perception he sensed Violet at the hotel and the danger she was in.

"She," he said to Brockton. "She made a call."

Kat glanced at Lucian. "See?"

Lucian remained silent.

"To whom?" Brockton asked.

"That I don't know."

Kyle focused harder. The camera on his hotel computer opened into his mind. He had a clear sight of the entire room.

"The tissue cultures," he said.

"What about them?"

"They're gone."

Lucian glanced over his shoulder. "What?"

"They're gone."

"Shit." He glanced at Kat. "How does he know this for certain?"

She shrugged. "He's not been wrong yet."

"Dammit!"

Thinking aloud, Kat said, "So GenTech sent someone after them?"

Lucian shook his head. "We don't know that. Since there are two sides to this game, we really don't know whom she might have called. But we do know that both sides want those tissue cultures badly enough to kill for them."

Lucian sped through a yellow light, and weaved back and forth through the traffic lanes. Kat placed her hands on the dashboard to steady herself.

"Let's get there alive, Lucian."

"I plan on it."

"What if she purposely called someone to exchange those cultures for money? She'd know the value those tissues are worth as well as anyone on either side of this game."

Lucian's jaw tightened. "If that was the case, Kyle wouldn't have implied her life was in danger. He's never wrong, you said."

"Yet," she sighed.

"What do you have against her?" he asked, looking at her.

"Nothing. I just don't think it's safe to trust her so easily."

Lucian turned a sharp left, missed a pedestrian by a couple feet, and straightened the car out. "I guess I'm relying too much on Gunter's memories."

"Those were vague though, right? His crush fantasies?"

He nodded and sighed. "Yes, I suppose you could call it that. I don't see why *you're* so concerned over it."

Kat stared out her side window. "I don't want to see you get hurt."

"Ahh, I see."

She shook her head and thought, "I wish you did see."

"Whether Violet has a hand in it or not, we still need to retrieve those tissue cultures."

Kat faced Lucian. "I didn't mean that her life isn't important. If she's in trouble, I'll die to protect her. I just wanted you to understand that we don't know her."

Lucian smiled. "I appreciate your concern, and you're right. I'm still trying to drive out Gunter's memories."

He drove into the hotel parking lot. Pulling his gun, he rushed up the stairs and Kat followed. The door was ajar. Lucian shoved it open and leveled his gun straight ahead.

No one was present in the bedroom.

Lucian's chest hesitated. Then he slowly eased to the bathroom door, apprehensive of what he might find. He visualized Violet's dead body sprawled on the floor. He peered around the door's edge. She was there. Unfortunately, all the Petri dishes were gone, too.

Kat holstered her 9mm. "At least she's not dead."

Lucian knelt inside the bathroom door to inspect a small pool of fresh blood. "We don't know that. She's been injured. And the cultures are gone."

Brockton entered the hotel door, gasping. "Hurry. Kyle thinks her abductor has Violet a few blocks from here."

"How would he know that?" Kat asked.

"Traffic jam report was on the radio. The instant he heard it, he became anxious for us to get there. He believes they're stuck in traffic."

"Well, if she is, this is the first time I'll ever be thankful to see a traffic tie up." Lucian said. He tucked his gun behind his belt and nodded.

Kat said, "It doesn't look like they bothered anything other than the cultures."

"What else would they want?" Lucian asked.

Brockton hurried down the stairs. He never liked to leave Kyle unattended. Kat followed and Lucian pulled the door closed. He told a maid in the hall that someone had busted the door open and the door needed repaired.

Chapter 44

Violet held her hand over her swollen, bruised lip. The butt of the gun had cut her right jaw when he struck her in the hotel bathroom. The impact forced her lip to swell like a tiny balloon. The small laceration had stopped bleeding, but the cold air encouraged a constant fiery sting.

She tasted blood. As best she could tell, none of her teeth had been broken. She braved a glance at the driver. He didn't look familiar. He wore leather gloves, dark shades, and a black trench coat. His frustration built the longer they sat in the traffic jam.

"Who sent you?" she asked. "I didn't call you."

"He did."

"Why? He told me that he'd come."

The man's smile was broad, thin, and lizard-like. "You really think he'd risk the exposure, even for you?"

Violet looked through the dark, tinted window. "At one time he would've."

"You're not worth it anymore. I think he phrased it as "worthless."

Tears welled in her eyes. "Then where are you taking me?"

He shrugged. "Somewhere quiet."

A lump rose in her throat. "He ordered you to kill me?"

"You know too much for us to leave you alive."

"But I got the tissue samples he wants back for him."

He laughed. "I have them now. He no longer needs you."

Violet reached for the door handle. Cold metal pressed against her jaw in an instant. The clicking release of the safety froze her hand.

"It doesn't have to be a quiet place. You can die right here."

She lifted her shaking hands above her head. "I'm sorry. I won't try to escape again."

"You do," he said in a stern voice. "And I'll throw your dead body on the asphalt where you open the door."

Violet offered a surrendered nod. Tears trickled down her face. She stared at the unmoving lanes of traffic ahead of them. They hadn't moved one car length during the past fifteen minutes.

"You might as well get comfortable," he said. "Looks like we have a long wait."

LUCIAN DROVE down the alley Kyle had directed. Within minutes, they came to where the cars were stalled.

"We still don't know which car they're in," Lucian said.

Kyle stammered. "Just get closer."

Kyle closed his eyes and focused his attention on the cars packed in long lines. Darkness loomed, but he still wasn't close enough to pinpoint the exactness of the driver they pursued.

Having only met Violet for a few minutes, he didn't know her mind well enough to track her personality. But fear—he could sense her fear— and her enemy's anger.

Lucian looked over his shoulder. "This is as close as I can get. No one's going to let us cut into the line. Besides, if we get into this mess of traffic, we won't get back out. We cannot afford to get stuck in there. Once we get her and the cooler, we need a way to drive away. Fast."

Kyle ignored him. Advancing into deeper meditation, he suddenly found his spirit hovering above the van. Lightness consumed him, as if gravity possessed no hold on him. His body remained in the van. This was a new sensation. He had never experienced this before.

Somehow, he had expelled his spirit from his body. The only similarity of this phenomenal feat was astral projection, but he had no idea how he had done this or where this spectral ability had come from. He wondered what things Helmsby had done to him before Lucian rescued him from TransGenCorp. What more abilities had Helmsby enabled him to do that Kyle would later discover?

Kyle swept forward like a ghost over the street and scanned through dozens of cars. People no longer looked like people. Instead, the color of their auras illuminated like candle flames. In spite of the frustration of being trapped in the traffic jam, most aura colors streamed positive vibes, but what he needed to find were two extreme opposite colors from inside the same vehicle.

Drifting like he was being carried by the wind, he moved over the cars. His eyes searched. Finally, he came upon a black Jaguar. A black aura filled with evil contempt glowed above the driver's side. A yellow glow flickered softly in the passenger side. Violet.

In what seemed no less than a blink of the eye, Kyle awoke inside his body. "She's two blocks up the street to the right."

"What type of car?" Lucian asked.

"Black Jaguar with black tinted windows. It's stalled on the inside lane."

"Thanks," Lucian replied, stepping out onto the street.

Kat climbed from the van and released the safety on her gun.

Lucian glanced at her. "I don't think there's any way not to kill him in order to rescue her."

"Probably not," she replied. "Our guns will attract a lot of attention."

Lucian grinned. "This is one of those shoot first, ask questions later, situations."

"I hate those."

Lucian shrugged. "Less paperwork."

They stuck to the sidewalk, knowing the car with Violet wasn't close to the curb. The driver's attention would be on the cars ahead of him, but he'd also be focused on keeping Violet in the car. He probably also had enough egotism to believe no one would find him, so he probably wouldn't be looking over his shoulder. They might be able to ease closer without the chance of being spotted. If the driver saw them, Violet was as good as dead.

"WHO ARE YOU?" Violet asked.

The annoyed driver didn't look at her. "Consider me your final messenger."

"At least let me talk to him first."

He smiled. "He has nothing else to say. If he did, I wouldn't be here, now would I? He wants what was his. I have the cooler, so all I need to do is dispose of you."

Violet grabbed for the door handle and cringed. Cold metal pressed against her temple.

"I warned you," he hissed.

"Kill me here, and you'll have to explain my murder to the police."

He laughed. "Most of the police work for us."

Her hands shook when his finger tightened on the trigger. She shut her eyes tightly, releasing a stream of tears. The harsh crack of the gun caused her to jump. Glass shattered. A horn blared. She opened her eyes. The driver lay slumped sideways over the steering wheel.

Violet almost screamed when her car door suddenly opened.

"It's okay," Lucian said, putting a hand on her shoulder. "I see we got here just in time."

She rushed into his arms and embraced him fiercely. She pulled back and planted her lips against his.

"Ouch," she cried, placing her hand over her bruised face.

Lucian gently touched her cheek and shook his head. "He really worked you over."

She kissed his lips again, only softer. "But I'm alive."

Lucian nodded.

Kat glared at him.

People left their cars and circled around to see the dead driver. Kat flashed her badge while Lucian searched the man for identification but he found nothing.

Kat said, "FBI, everyone remain calm and back away. Clear the area. Police will be here shortly." To Lucian, she said, "Grab the cooler, and let's get the hell out of here."

Police sirens echoed in the distance. He grabbed the cooler. With cellphones, police were notified within seconds, which was a good thing during an actual emergency. The bad risk with cellphones was that someone had probably recorded everything they had just done. They ran back to the van and climbed in.

Lucian looked at his watch. "Damn."

"What?"

"We have to meet Daniel at the airport to get Morton. We're running late."

Brockton looked inside the cooler. "Head to the airport. There's enough ice to keep these safe until we get back to the hotel."

Chapter 45

The private jet landed and circled back to the terminal where Kat and Lucian stood waiting. Daniel came down the stairs with Morton in his arms.

Kat extended her hand to Daniel. "Thanks for bringing Morton."

Daniel shook her hand and smiled. He regarded Lucian with a curious stare. "He insisted. And you are?"

"Lucian."

"I half expected to see Lucas' twin."

Lucian looked away. "No. I promised I would assume a new face."

Daniel shrugged. "Perhaps that's a good thing."

Kat smiled at Morton. "Kyle believes you can help the investigation."

Morton replied, "Never send a human to do a cat's job."

"Where's Kyle?" Daniel asked, glancing around.

"In the van," Kat replied.

Daniel looked for the van. "I'd like to see him."

"About that," Kat said. "He's asked that you not see him in person yet."

"Why?" His eyes reflected shock and deep hurt at the remark.

"He's still sorting through past traumas. Besides, there's no time right now."

"I don't understand. How is he?"

Kat smiled. "He's doing great. His mind is remarkable. He's regained approximately ninety percent of his mental capacity and gained some new, *unexplained* abilities. We believe he'll excel even more over the next year."

"And seeing me might make him suffer a relapse?"

Kat put a hand on Daniel's arm. "I'm sorry, but it's something he requested."

Daniel nodded. "It's okay. But he's done more than simply recover lost motor skills. He contacted Morton telepathically. How?"

"We're not certain. Dr. Brockton is puzzled by it, too."

Morton licked his forepaw. "Maybe this is something that Helmsby did. After all, he programmed my genome to allow my mind to do the same thing."

"How would Kyle know you have that ability?" Kat asked.

"I don't know."

Lucian nodded toward the private jet. "Is that your route home, Daniel?"

"Yes. Why?"

He sighed. "We have troubling news."

"What?"

Kat handed Daniel the morning paper. "Lydia was kidnapped yesterday and Lucas is in the hospital."

"Kidnapped? By whom?"

"We thought you might want to visit him," Lucian said. "I'll cover the fuel costs."

Daniel nodded. "That's appreciated, but not necessary. I have plenty of money for that."

"Please allow me," Lucian said. "I owe Lucas so much. If I weren't needed here, I'd be on that plane to Nevada with you."

"I appreciate the gift."

Lucian smiled. "It's already been arranged. I paid for the jet to be fueled before you arrived. Just do what you can to help him find Lydia. Hard for me to explain, but I know how much she means to him."

"Here," Kat said, handing him a business card. "You can call my cell number if you need any help. And here's the name of the hospital where Lucas is staying."

"Thanks." Daniel knelt and rubbed Morton's head. "Come back to me safely, my little furry friend."

"Always. I promised Felicia and Julia that I would. I keep my word. Go help Lucas find Lydia. I'll do all I can on this end."

Daniel's eyes moistened. "I know you will. I just hate that we're not working together."

Morton nodded. "Me, too. You never know. Our paths might cross in these searches."

"Anything's possible," he replied.

Kat scooped Morton into her arms. Her eyes met Daniel's. "We'll watch out for him."

Daniel couldn't speak. He turned and headed toward the plane. Morton had become a major part of their lives over the past four years. During that time, they'd never been separated for more than a few hours at a time. With this assignment, he didn't have any idea how long it would be before they saw the orange fluff ball again.

The look on Julia's face when he and Morton had left indicated that her broken heart grieved for the cat as well. At least Felicia thought Morton was attending a cat convention. She didn't know he was venturing into dangerous territory.

Daniel would have stayed in New Jersey to keep a protective eye on Morton, but Lucas needed him. The fact someone had taken Lydia meant her life was in grave danger. He feared another underground biotech corporation had taken her and they'd never see her again.

He didn't mind helping Lucas, but not without Morton. The cat had keener wit and abilities to get them out of danger without having to try too much. He realized how much confidence he placed in Morton. He never paused to think how little confidence he held in himself. He laughed as he thought he'd have to wean himself from a cat.

Chapter 46

New Jersey: Typhis' Warehouse

A FLASH of metallic silver shimmered across two soldiers' eyes. Dusk settled and the salty spray of ocean waves lapped against the pier. The two men awaited orders to slink into the hidden labs inside the aged warehouse.

Dennis Schrader had been an easy target, one to make Typhis flinch; however, the task before them was a greater challenge to test the soldiers' prowess and tactical skills. They had to succeed. They had no second chance. Failure meant death.

To the outside world, Typhis' new laboratories were camouflaged as a warehouse full of storage crates. The reality concealed behind hidden walls contained areas where he had modified the research Mech Cybernetics thought they had purchased. Typhis' underhanded scam had not slipped past the radar undetected. Revenge was set to even the score. He had crossed the wrong man. Not only would his corruption be revealed, he would be dethroned to miserable failure.

These soldiers were prototypes, but in the eyes of science, many considered their mutated appearances flawed. Their faces radiated the morbid resemblance of aged corpses with strange eyes darkly similar to those of hungered ravens.

Harsh sunlight blinded them, but their pupils exhibited an increased ability to see in the darkness, absorbing minuscule fragments of available light from the surrounding area with much the same capacity as night-vision goggles. Thus, their assignments came during the darkness of night to draw less attention to them, utilizing the full use of their unnatural strengths.

The taller man, Xnith, aimed his rifle at the nearest surveillance camera and fired. A small magnet attached to the metal camera frame and blurred the surveillance screens with streaks of static.

They sprinted to the door beneath the camera. Xnith's partner, Apex, had less than forty seconds to pick the lock before the magnet demagnetized and dropped to the ground. By allowing the static to cease, they drew less attention from security personnel evaluating the inside monitors. Generally, when static occurred for a long time, someone was ordered to inspect the camera.

After fifteen seconds of fidgeting with a metal pick, the door unlocked. The deception of a dark, empty warehouse lay before them. The guise might fool anyone with lesser intentions, but they sensed each stationed guard's proximity. Their eyes sought body heat with colorful visuals, and their ears pinpointed heartbeats twenty yards away.

They pulled their 9mms with attached silencers and blended into the darkness. Each kept black marble pawns in their pockets. Tonight they came to even the score, and to raise the bar a couple of levels.

They never exchanged words. They responded only to the transitional command frequencies traveling through the airwaves.

Ahead, in the vast realms of shadows, a guard stood wearing night vision goggles. Without such external devices, Xnith and Apex saw him well before he noticed them advance. With pinpoint accuracy, Xnith's shot pierced through the man's heart. The man dropped with a solid thud. Apex placed Black Pawn number two on the dead man's chest.

Neither soldier bothered to check the victim for a pulse. They didn't need to. His absent heartbeat boasted their success.

In the same stalking manner as a praying mantis silently nabs its prey, Apex and Xnith killed six patrolling guards the moment they stepped within range, bringing the total of Black Pawn deaths to an alarming eight. Number nine died outside the laboratory door.

What appeared to be a fire alarm switch was actually a concealed thumb print scanner. Apex hefted the guard's arm and pressed his dead thumb against the print reader. The red light on the panel vanished, and was immediately replaced by a green light. Xnith eased the door open.

Apex dropped the man's limp arm and followed his partner inside. Due to the lack of activity in the lab, the lights were automatically reduced to their energy-saving phase. With only half of the available lights on, the assassins crept inside without having to shield their eyes.

Somewhere in the room a heartbeat tapped rapidly, indicating a woman was nearby. They scanned the room for body heat but were unable to locate her. She was farther in the room, possibly even a side room. The inner walls were cold stainless steel, which hid her body heat.

Xnith took one step forward and triggered a sensor that activated the unused, overhead lights. The room burst to blinding white and silver, forcing them to shield their faces with their free hands.

A female rushed out of her office. "Who the hell are you?" Her eyes widened when she saw their disgusting, decayed faces. "*What* the hell are you?"

Their acute hearing overrode the need for sight. The genetic soldiers fired simultaneously, not in reaction to her voice, but in response to her elevated heartbeat. Two bullets ripped through her heart in the same instance. She gasped, clutched her chest, and dropped to the floor, her eyes still wide. Blood seeped from her chest and soaked into her lab clothes. Her hand unsnapped her nametag from her coat and slid off her body.

Dr. Marissa Block was stamped on the tag with her photo.

Firing a barrage of bullets at the ceiling lights, they extinguished enough of the bulbs to dim the room comfortably and uncovered their eyes. They pulled a key ring off her belt. In exchange, they stood a chess piece in her gaping chest wound. QB was etched in its base, which meant: Queen's Bishop.

Apex found the light control panel and turned off the remaining overhead lights. Using one key on the dead scientist's key ring, they unlocked a refrigerated walk-in storage room. Plastic storage containers lined the shelves. They stopped in front of one, as if they had knowingly placed it there, and retrieved it.

Wiping frost from the front, frozen dead eyes peered back at them. Their mission was complete. They quickly escaped with their prize.

Trey's head.

With their trophy in hand, they entered Dr. Block's office and disarmed all the surveillance cameras. After sealing the laboratory door, they took their trophy to their car. From the trunk, they removed two five-gallon fuel cans and returned to the warehouse. After splashing fuel on dry crates and pallets, Apex dropped a match and the old sagging building roared into a fiery blaze.

They sped away to deliver the head to their commander before the blaze captured the attention of police and firefighters.

<hr>

KYLE SAT deep in thought at his computer. Although he didn't know Lydia personally, he knew Lucas. He sensed the grief consuming Lucas and projected his mind to see if he could find Lydia himself.

With his computer screen showing a GPS location of Desert Field Laboratories, he zoomed in on the picture and brought it to full view. The majority of these laboratories were constructed in an underground silver mine. Since rocks were nearly impossible to see through, Kyle hacked into several test spy-planes as they flew over the area. He tapped into their sonar scanners to produce a 3-D image map of the facility.

Kyle's frustration eased when he finally gained access to the surveillance cameras on each floor. The halls and labs were empty. The research equipment reminded him of the dark rooms inside TransGen-Corp. He had seen incubation chambers before. What emerged from them were callous, vicious men with the unquenchable need to kill.

Staring at a photo of Lydia, he tried to reach her mind.

Nothing.

He thought of Lucas and projected his thoughts to him.

"Who are you?" Lucas questioned within his mind.

"Kyle. Daniel's on his way. We're going to find Lydia."

Kyle detected Lucas' tears of gratitude.

"We'll find her," Kyle said again, and disconnected his mind link to Lucas.

KAT DROVE to meet Carpenter at the FBI headquarters, and Morton sat in the passenger seat. She wondered what was so urgent. She tried not to think about leaving Lucian with Violet at the hotel. She couldn't shake the memory of the young woman's passionate kiss after he had pulled her from the car. She never thought she'd get this jealous so easily. Inwardly, she chided herself.

There had been a slight surprised look on Lucian's face when Violet kissed him, so maybe she was giving the situation too much thought. She wanted to discuss her feelings with Lucian, but the investigation required their direct attention. She didn't have time to waste or sidetrack their minds with a situation that could wait. Since Brockton had detected her feelings for Lucian, she wondered if Lucian had noticed, too.

Kat sighed. Probably not, she reasoned. Even though he was the same physical age as Lucas, mentally he hadn't been exposed to the deeper emotional desires enough to read others. Then she thought of her conversation with him, and he had expressed that he knew when someone loved him. Had that been a hint? She smiled.

Morton turned his attention from the street and stared at her. "What's troubling you?"

Sudden embarrassment reddened her face. "It's nothing really. Just a woman thing."

"Oh. Well, when you get a *cat* thing, I'll be glad to help."

She patted his head. "Daniel thinks the world of you."

"Of course," Morton replied. "Cats own humans, you know?"

Kat smiled. "So I've heard."

"It's true. We get our way or else."

"I've never actually had a cat for a pet. But I've had several dogs."

Morton rolled his eyes. "So you're one of *those* kind of people?"

"What do you mean by that?"

Morton's eyes narrowed, and he hacked a nasty sounding gag in his throat. "Sorry. I need to hock this fur ball somewhere. This conversation sets badly on my stomach."

"You have something against dogs?" she asked.

"Why should I have anything against a creature that's far beneath me?"

Kat laughed.

"Seriously. Why do you think Egyptians worshipped us centuries ago?"

"Okay, you've made your point."

"I could go on. Witches favor us as familiars, but then I'm just bragging."

Kat drove the car into the FBI parking lot.

"Why do you think Kyle wants me here?" Morton asked.

She shut off the engine.

"I honestly don't know."

"So this game is pretty intense?"

Kat sighed and nodded. "Yes. Right now, we're not certain who all the players are. Victims have been showing up for days. No real tie to the killers."

"So you know there are two sides involved?"

"As best we can tell, yes."

"But there could be more than two?"

"We don't know. Possibly. When I get back to the hotel I can show you all the data."

"That would be good."

CARPENTER SMILED when she brought Morton into his office. "Morton? Why do you have him?"

"Kyle believes we can use him," she replied.

"How?"

"He hasn't told us yet."

Morton leapt to the desk, sat back on his haunches, and licked his forepaw. He eyed Carpenter. "So, where's my badge?"

Carpenter laughed. "Badge?"

The cat nodded. "If I'm working with the FBI, it has to be legit."

"I'll see what can be done."

Kat glanced at her watch. "What'd you need to see me about?"

Carpenter sighed and rubbed his tired eyes. "There was a fire on the docks last night. A large warehouse burned down."

"And you suspect it has something to do with our Red Pawn Case?"

He nodded. "Yes, but I think we should officially change the case name to 'The Game of Pawns.'"

"Why? What did you find?"

Carpenter slid a handful of Ziploc bags across the table. Eight bags contained black pawn pieces. One contained a black knight and the last, a black bishop.

He said, "As you suggested on a hunch, we have a war between biotech companies. Eight more black pawns and one black queen bishop. And the police found a dead city councilman in a black Lincoln near the fire with a black knight piece on him."

"Shit. This is retaliation," Kat said.

"Exactly, but the ranks are getting higher than just pawns."

"Queen Bishop?"

Carpenter slid a file across the desk to her. "Dr. Marissa Block was a genetics engineer."

"Why was she inside the warehouse?"

Carpenter smiled. "Apparently she was working in an underground genetic laboratory."

"And the Knight?"

"Councilman Jonathon Adams. He was a close friend of Typhis."

Morton sat in silence, taking in the information.

"GenTech and who else?" Kat asked.

"We don't know," Carpenter said. "However, I traced the warehouse deed to its owner. Typhis Reed."

Kat's eyes widened. "I told you he had a hand in this."

"Somewhere in this he is involved."

"No doubt his game opponent wanted him brought out into the open by revealing the hiding place of his new research facility."

"True."

"This game's larger than you might anticipate." Morton frowned. "Finding Lydia will answer a lot of your questions. Whoever took her, wishes to make more clones from her genome."

Carpenter looked at the cat. "Why?"

"I thought you knew?"

"What?" Carpenter asked.

"Lydia was Idris' prototype. Lucas stole her from his lab, fell in love with her, and married her."

Carpenter stared at Kat. "Did you know of this?"

"Not until now," she replied.

"I only tell you because our timeframe's limited. If we don't find her before they begin their experimentations, she'll possibly die. They don't really need her alive to do what they plan to do."

Carpenter and Kat were stunned.

Carpenter folded his hands on the table. "This information opens up a whole new avenue to explore."

"Why didn't Lucas ever mention this to us?" Kat asked.

Morton shrugged. "I guess he feared if he revealed who she really was, the government would have taken her and performed experimental tests on her, too. He wanted to protect her. She didn't even know she was a prototype until Idris told her in TransGenCorp during the Meltdown."

Kat crossed her arms across her chest. "Lucas kept that information hidden from her?"

"Yes."

"Who all knew?"

"Only our inner circle. Daniel, Julia, Lucas, and me."

"Helmsby didn't know?" Carpenter asked.

"Not fully. He suspects she was just another clone made from a prototype."

"So no one told him she was the prototype?" Kat asked.

Morton cocked an eyebrow. "Would you want Helmsby to know something like that? Look at the experiments he did on Kyle, trying to get Kyle back to normal. Helmsby's need for scientific research always outweighs his rationality. Lydia would have been someone he'd have wanted to study."

Kat nodded. "Lucas would have opposed that."

"Lucas would kill to prevent it," Morton said. "Even now."

Carpenter stood and walked to the coffee pot. "Our best chance to get information is by talking to Typhis, see who his enemies are, and where he stands."

"I agree," Kat said.

Carpenter handed coffee to Kat. "Do you think Helmsby was right about Idris being able to create super soldiers?"

Morton nodded. "He already had them when you attacked Trans-GenCorp."

"I know we killed some of them, but was Idris the only one who had them? Does GenTech possess the same technology?" he asked.

The cat sat forward on the desk. "He probably scattered his technology throughout different, smaller tech corporations. After TransGenCorp collapsed, it's possible information was traded between groups to access the lost technology. Idris would have set it up for revenge if something happened to him anyway."

Kat pursed her lips. "That sounds like Idris."

"Seems his ghost is as big a problem as he was alive," Carpenter said.

"The roots of twisted genetic research run deep," Morton said. "All we did with TransGenCorp was chop off the top of the tree. Poison the roots of this system before the branches emerge and we can end this."

"Helmsby decoded most of Idris' research," Carpenter said. "What hand does he hold in this?"

Morton narrowed angry eyes. "Are you implying he'd venture to do sinister research for monetary gain like Idris?"

Carpenter shrugged. "He has the know-how."

"He also has virtue."

"Maybe," Kat said. "But like you said, Morton, he did experiments on Kyle."

"For Kyle's benefit, not his own."

"We need to talk to Typhis, and then find Helmsby," Carpenter said. "Maybe he can tell us information that we haven't discovered yet."

Morton stretched out, yawned. "Helmsby retired the last we heard. He's been overseas for a while now. If he's returned to the states, he hasn't contacted us."

Carpenter nodded. "I know, but it doesn't mean he hasn't been approached by a member of the Game of Pawns."

"He doesn't play games," Morton replied. "Not even crossword puzzles based on genetics questions. He's rather bland and boring."

"Still, I think we should find him."

Kat looked at Morton. "It would be wise to see what he has to say."

Morton shrugged his little cat shoulders. "I'm here to help, but Kyle still hasn't given me the reason why I'm needed. The last thing I need is more people knowing I can talk. Typhis is one individual I should steer clear of."

Kat rubbed the back of his neck. "Agreed. You'll stay with Kyle and Brockton while we interview Typhis."

Chapter 47

Lydia's subconscious had felt Lucas' brief connection, but she also sensed that he was nowhere near. Emptiness shadowed her heart. Her mind was barraged by the constant churning of helicopter blades overhead. The even beat of a heart monitor tapped behind her, indicating she was alive but her mind was trapped without a voice.

She had no idea how long she'd been in the chopper, but it seemed an eternity. Although not completely certain, she believed the chopper had landed and refueled sometime during the night.

Between the medication and the voyage, she felt the sensation of floating. At times, it didn't seem she was still inside her body. She continually tried to open her eyes, but she couldn't. She understood they were using stronger drugs in her I.V. than what her kidnappers had used in the ambulance. With the I.V. drip pumping the sedatives into her system, she was helpless.

Lydia worried about how Lucas was handling the situation. He'd either lose it or erupt with a pure, endless rage until he found her.

Occasionally, she could hear the pilot talking into his headset. Her best interpretation was that he was requesting for checkpoints, but none of this information clarified where she was.

The chopper dipped slowly forward and hovered. After several minutes, the skids touched down on a landing pad. The blades slowed and stopped. Her gurney was unlocked from the helicopter and carefully placed on the landing pad. Through her closed eyes, bright blue and red landing lights danced a blurred harsh blend of colors that made her thankful her eyes were shut.

Cool air blew briskly across her blanketed body. The wheels of the gurney stopped outside an elevator. The doors opened, and she was pushed inside.

Lydia mentally commanded orders to her arms and legs, but they never responded. She was a living prisoner inside her body, a cocoon, and she wasn't able to emerge. Nothing was more horrifying than wanting to move and her body not obeying. She didn't know how or if Lucas could find her, but she hoped he did.

Soon.

HELMSBY STARED through the microscope at the alien skin tissue. He frowned. The cells appeared to be fresh. How Grayson had obtained these frustrated Helmsby. To obtain something that didn't technically exist troubled him as well. Who had made the initial discovery?

The door opened and Grayson stepped into the lab. "Making any progress?" he asked.

Helmsby stepped back from the microscope and rubbed his hands together. "Yes. I plan to run an electrophoresis of the DNA sample later today."

Grayson didn't smile. His solemn face was tired. His gray eyes held a hint of anger as he swept a glance around the room.

"Is something wrong?" Helmsby asked.

"Nothing I cannot handle."

"Well, sir, if there's anything I can do to help."

Grayson placed his muscled hand on Helmsby's shoulder and squeezed. "I like your nature, Bob. Actually, there's something I need you and your family to do."

Helmsby smiled. "Anything."

Grayson sighed. "We've prepared rooms for all of you to stay for the next few days. At the most, perhaps a few weeks."

"Inside this facility?"

"Yes. There have been problems lately. I fear your lives are in jeopardy outside my property."

Helmsby frowned and rubbed the stubble on his chin. After a minute, he said, "I don't understand. *Why* would we be in danger?"

Grayson unfolded a newspaper that he had tucked beneath his arm when he entered the lab. "Read this."

The headlines stated the murder of Dr. Marissa Block, the councilman, and the guards at the warehouse.

"What does this have to do with us?" Helmsby asked. "These people didn't work for you, did they?"

Grayson shook his head. "No. But haven't you heard of the Red Pawn Murders?"

"I'm sorry, but I seldom keep up with the news."

"The last five Red Pawn Murders were genetic scientists. *My* scientists. They had worked at my other tech laboratories. Dr. Marissa Block was a genetics engineer at another lab. A black pawn was left on her body."

"You think I might be a target, too?" Helmsby swallowed hard. He failed to hide his nervousness.

"Let's hope not," Grayson replied. "But for your safety, I can best protect you within my facility."

Helmsby thought about the situation and surrendered a nod. "Whatever you think is best, sir."

"Thanks, Bob," Grayson said with a narrow smile. "I have to protect my investment."

Helmsby frowned. "Meaning me?"

"Yes. My technology cannot advance without you."

"I'm flattered you believe so. I appreciate your hospitality and concern also."

"Anything you need, Bob, just let me know."

Grayson headed for the door.

"Have you seen Yvonne?" Helmsby asked.

"No. But I can page her to your lab if you'd like."

Helmsby smiled. "Thank you, yes."

"Remember to call me if you need anything."

"I will."

Grayson left the room. Helmsby picked up the newspaper, crossed the lab and looked outside the laboratory window. The security glass surrounding his lab was thick with crisscrossed wire fused inside. These recent events suddenly made him feel like a prisoner again.

Down the stainless steel hall, he stared, hoping to see Yvonne or Nancy. Across the hall behind the nurse station were more glassed-in rooms like his lab. Those stations were one of the few places where he wasn't allowed entrance. He wondered what they researched. Perhaps they were testing genetic drugs to cure diseases? It was an answer he didn't see the hope of retrieving anytime soon.

The elevator at the end of the hallway opened. A nurse and doctor pushed a gurney out and headed for the nurse station. The gurney neared his window, and he dropped the newspaper in horror. He shook his head. On the gurney lay Lydia, unconscious. A shower cap was tugged over her hair, but her face was clearly visible. It was Lydia. Why was she here?

The door opened again. "Grayson said you're looking for me?" Yvonne asked.

Helmsby nodded slowly.

She noticed his pale complexion. "Are you okay?"

"I was. Hurry, come here and look."

When she reached him, he pointed at the window. "That's Lydia, isn't it?"

Yvonne watched the two nurses pushing the gurney. She squinted to get a clearer view of the patient's face. Her eyes widened upon recognition and said, "I believe it is. Why would she be here?"

Helmsby faced Yvonne. "I have no idea."

The nurses pushed the gurney through swinging doors into the infirmary where Helmsby wasn't allowed access. His attention was drawn to the paramedics' jacket sleeves. The red triple helix symbol spiral caused his heart to skip. He gasped.

"Damn," he said.

"What?"

"The emblem on their sleeves. It's TransGenCorp all over again."

Yvonne shook her head. "Almost the same design but not quite."

Helmsby looked again. "There's a slight difference with what looks like an alien hand at the bottom. Other than that, it's too close for them not to have had some kind of association."

"I agree it appears very suspicious."

Helmsby told her what Grayson had said to him about not leaving the facility.

"What's going on?"

"I'm not certain."

"We're being locked in?" she asked.

"It appears that way."

Her jaw tightened. "I thought Grayson's offer sounded too good, but I didn't want to sound paranoid and have you turn down the opportunity of your lifetime."

Helmsby grabbed the telephone. "Working with alien cellular components is beyond anything I ever hoped to study. Until we know exactly what's happening though, we cannot make drastic assumptions. However, seeing Lydia on that gurney invigorates my doubts and paranoia."

He started to tap the numbers on the phone dial.

"Who are you calling?"

"Daniel."

She shook her head and took the receiver from his hand. With a gentle twist, she snapped off the back of the phone, pointed at a metal coil, and then she reattached the cover. On tiptoe, she whispered in his ear, "It's bugged."

"Oh, shit."

"Exactly. Any call coming or going is being monitored."

"We're not allowed to leave," Helmsby said, realizing how he had been beguiled. "We have to get a message to Daniel. He needs to know Lydia is here and warn Lucas."

"That feat will be nearly impossible."

"Why?"

She whispered, "I've been scouting around. Other phones are bugged, too."

"Your skepticism never lessens, either."

"We have Idris to thank for that."

"I'm not complaining, but damn me for being too hasty to discover new genetics links."

Yvonne patted his arm. "You wouldn't be who you are if your passion for genetic discoveries wasn't so strong."

"Maybe not, but I'd get myself in less trouble and have fewer enemies if I wasn't."

"Perhaps, but you'd be less exciting," she said. "Why do they have Lydia in the first place?"

"I really don't know. Idris had made a clone from her several years ago, but TransGenCorp is no more. Why would Grayson take her?"

"I don't know," she replied.

"What about using our cell phones?" Helmsby asked.

Yvonne shook her head. "No. I'd say that Grayson records and traces any calls within this building."

"I don't understand why they'd want Lydia, except to do more cloning or worse with her."

"Where's Lucas? That's a better question."

Helmsby shrugged.

"Wherever he is, he's probably insanely hunting for her."

"We should find a way to let him know," Helmsby said. "Daniel and Lucas might be the only chance we have of getting out of here."

She placed her hand to his cheek. "Hon, just act like you didn't see her."

"I'll try."

Yvonne shook her head. "No, you must. If Grayson discovers we know she's here, we're stuck here indefinitely."

"I can't let him take a friend and sit quietly," Helmsby said.

"You work on the alien DNA analysis. I'll figure out how to get a message outside without being traced."

"Please be careful."

"I will."

"Have you seen Nancy?" Helmsby asked.

"Yes. She's working upstairs in the space tech lab. She's fine. She's excited about her opportunity to work with space technology."

"She has a passion for it."

Yvonne nodded. "She did mention that they may transfer her to Grayson Enterprises in California."

Helmsby adjusted the microscope stand and his hand shook. "So soon? Tell her as indiscreetly as possible what's going on and to be alert."

"I will," she said. "In the meantime, relax. Idris was menacing, but Grayson hasn't made any verbal threats."

"No, he hasn't. He's been rather gentleman-like."

"The less we reveal about what we know, the better our chances are to find out what Grayson is up to. Being low on his radar will help us if the situation worsens and we do need to escape."

Helmsby sighed. "Maybe we're just overreacting? Since Lydia is a genetic creation, there's the chance that something on her molecular level has gone haywire, and she's here for medical help. Think about it. There's no other place that could help her."

"While that could be a possibility, I'd still not allow Grayson to know that we know about Lydia being here."

"I agree."

"I'll find Nancy and be back as soon as possible. Keep a grip on your emotions."

Helmsby nodded.

Yvonne eased out the door and down the hall. She paused outside the window where he stood and winked at him. Helmsby returned a feeble smile, but his insides quaked.

He wanted to give Grayson the benefit of the doubt and hoped that Lydia was here because she had chosen to be. Otherwise, they were dealing with another unstable scientist like Idris. However, the longer he dwelt on the scenario, the less he like their present situation.

The confidentiality forms meant no exiting this job. Grayson was overly protective of this top-secret project with the alien DNA. Helmsby couldn't simply quit. His job as well as his life might be terminated. That worried him even more.

Chapter 48

Newark, New Jersey

KAT AND CARPENTER arrived at Newark City Hall. They waited a half hour outside Typhis' office for the mayor to see them. Carpenter's lack of patience reflected in his tense facial expression.

"He certainly doesn't seem too worried about the FBI wanting to talk to him," Kat said.

"He's a pompous son-of-a-bitch, Kat. He always has been."

"We could barge right in," Kat said with a charming smile.

Carpenter shook his head. "That's probably what he's waiting for. Then he can call my superior and try to get us charged for harassment."

The secretary stepped to the outside hall. "Typhis will see you now."

"Finally," Carpenter sighed.

The secretary pushed the heavy panel door inward and motioned for them to enter. Typhis sat behind a large polished maple desk. The blinds were closed. A single lamp at the edge of the desk lighted the dark room. Even in the darkness, the sour expression on his wrinkled face indicated he didn't wish to be bothered, especially by them. He wrung his long, slender hands while they seated themselves across from him.

"What's so urgent for the FBI to pay me a visit?" he said.

Carpenter cleared his throat. "The warehouse that burned last night had several casualties all employed by you."

Typhis sneered. "I'm aware of my losses. It's a tragic situation."

"It is indeed," Kat said. "Where were you last night, sir, if you don't mind me being forward?"

Coldness settled in Typhis' eyes that wrought an unspoken threat of spiteful contempt. "If you bothered to read the newspapers or watched the evening news, you'd know that I was at a political banquet last night until midnight and nowhere near the warehouse. Are you insinuating I had something to do with this?"

"No, I wasn't implying that you're responsible," Kat said. "But it appears someone specifically targeted your property and your workers. They may not be able to get to you, but they are sending a strong message."

"Or perhaps they were thieves who came to vandalize and steal from me, only to find nothing of value and killed their way out."

Carpenter shook his head. "No, your guards were killed by trained assassins. Our investigation reveals that none of your men fired a single shot."

Kat opened a manila folder. "Dr. Marissa Block. She was a genetic engineer, correct?"

Typhis shrugged. "So?"

"She worked for you?"

"Yes."

Kat nodded. "You sold GenTech to Mech Cybernetics, which happens to be a subsidiary of Grayson Enterprises, sometime back, right?"

"Yes."

"Why hide a new biotech facility inside your warehouse?"

Typhis' thin lips formed a narrow smile. "It's no crime for me to start a new biotech company, is it?"

"No. But why hide it?"

"I have my reasons."

"Do you also have enemies?" Kat asked.

"Every person with great authority has enemies."

Carpenter straightened in his chair. "If you have enemies, we can offer you protection."

"I can protect myself."

Carpenter smiled. "You've been targeted. Nine people under your employ were murdered last night. In what way did you protect them?"

Typhis scowled. "I have ways. It won't be a repeated mistake."

"Could last night's attack be retaliation, Mayor Reed?" Kat asked.

"For what?"

"We're certain you're aware of the Red Pawn Murders," Kat said. "Perhaps you're the one responsible for those, and last night was simply your opponent's ruthless revenge?"

Thick veins pulsed in Typhis' forehead. He failed to hide his indignation. "That's ludicrous. How dare you make such an accusation against me?"

"You sold your biotech labs to Boyd Grayson," Kat said, staring into his dark pupils. "And the last five Red Pawn Murders were GenTech scientists who had worked for you. If you truly didn't want your research to continue under another company name, there's motive to destroy that knowledge by killing them."

"You realize you're grabbing at stardust and moonbeams, young lady?" Typhis said. "What proof do you have of such a thing?"

"None yet, but election year is near. Word of your possible conspiracy might hurt you in the polls."

"Careful," Typhis said. "I'm not one you should be hurling threats at."

"Neither are we, Mr. Reed," Carpenter said.

"When have I threatened you?"

"Seconds ago," Kat said.

"Nonsense."

"Do you remember Mr. Steven Matthews?" she asked.

Typhis nodded. "Brilliant young scientist. He used to be my CEO and the head of GenTech's research and development team before I sold the company."

"Red Pawn number six was his limo driver," Carpenter said. "We believe their intended target was Mr. Matthews."

"I haven't heard of that," Typhis said.

"Have you seen Steven Matthews?"

Typhis shook his head. "Not for several weeks."

"Have you had problems with Grayson since the transaction of GenTech?"

"I've not heard a word from him or any of his company execs."

Kat frowned and stared into Typhis' dark eyes. "So you're certain you've not heard anything from Matthews?"

"Nothing."

Carpenter slid a paper across the desk. "So you won't mind us looking through your files, your bank records, and your former GenTech office?"

Typhis turned the paper around and looked at it. "What's this?"

"Search warrants."

His eyes narrowed with pure resentment. His slender hands balled into fists. He set them into his lap. Through clenched teeth, he hissed, "You can look through my files, but you're won't find anything useful. Certainly nothing that ties me to this conspiracy bullshit that you're insinuating."

Carpenter stood. "Let us discern what's useful to our investigation. Someone is bent on destroying your new labs, maybe even trying to kill you, so maybe we'll find out who you've pissed off enough to attack you."

"If you find out, I'd definitely like to know," Typhis replied.

Kat smiled shrewdly. "I'm under the impression that you already know."

Typhis ignored the comment and paged his secretary. She stepped into his office, and he said, "Steph, show our guests to the records room."

Steph's eyebrows rose in question. Typhis gave a solemn nod.

"This way," she said, motioning to the darker side of the room where a massive beveled door hid within the paneled wall.

"And, Mr. Carpenter," Typhis said. "Steph will stay in the room with you at all times."

"Not a problem," he replied without glancing over his shoulder.

The door opened into a twelve by twenty foot library. Scanning the bookends as they passed, most of the book titles were either biology or law books.

A computer set atop a desk in the center of the room. Several polished reading tables were littered with open books and notepads.

Steph typed her password into the computer and waited for the access screen to pop up. "You can access any of the database files through here. It contains all our research experiments, employees' data sheets, payroll, etc. It's here."

Kat smiled. "Thanks."

Steph nodded and walked to one table and took a seat. She eased back into the chair and opened a book.

Carpenter whispered to Kat, "Where do we start?"

"Steven Matthews would be the best name to search first."

"Have at it," he said.

"Typhis seemed more than a bit agitated about the Red Pawn Murders, didn't he?" Kat asked.

"As with everything else. He's guilty of something. Finding out exactly what he's hiding might take some time."

She typed in Steven Matthews and the search engine brought up a long file.

"Damn," Carpenter sighed. "Imagine making that much money?"

"Over two million dollars a year. If Red Pawn number six was meant for him, he has enough money to go into hiding."

"True. Or enough reason to seek revenge."

Kat sent the file to be printed.

"Now what?" he asked.

"Dr. Marissa Block."

Dr. Block's file was shorter than but just as interesting as Matthews'.

"Do you know who's doing the autopsy on her?" Kat asked.

"No."

"Let's find out and have her body sent to Todd."

"Why?"

"Indulge me this favor, and I think we will gain new evidence."

Carpenter nodded and dialed a number on his cell phone. After a few minutes of negotiating, he disconnected the call and smiled. "Done."

"Thanks."

"Don't mention it. Just keep me posted on what details you find."

"Certainly."

After an hour of assessing dozens of different files and printing off information, they were ready to leave. Steph put her book down and led them to the door. Typhis had left his office by the time they left the records room, which didn't surprise either of them.

In the parking garage, Kat said, "I have to check in with my associates."

"That's fine, but I'd like to buy you dinner later, if that's okay."

"You getting sweet on me?" she teased.

Carpenter's face flushed red. "No. I just want to talk and see what other evidence you might find between now and then."

"Get a lady's hopes up."

He shook his head. "I'm glad you're back, Kat. Really I am."

"Don't forget that this is temporary."

"How can I? You insist on reminding me."

She opened her car door and sat down. "Call me later with a time and place and we'll eat."

A smile spread across Carpenter's tired face. "Deal."

Chapter 49

Typhis stood in the surveillance room and watched the camera footage from the parking garage monitor. He paused the screen when Kat smiled at Carpenter. He zoomed in on her face. Her broad smile infuriated him. The brightness of her eyes angered him more. He hated how she had stared into his eyes and never flinched. She had no respect for his authority, nor did she possess fear. Without possessing either, she became a problem.

Placing his cellphone to his ear, he said, "Kat Gaddis. I want her dead."

NANCY USED a computer program to test the agility of the proposed spacesuit Grayson Enterprises hoped to use on their first Mars exploration within the next six months. Alex Nestor watched over her shoulder.

"Damn, you're good with the simulator," he said, tightening the braid of his blonde ponytail to get his hair off his shoulders.

Nancy smiled. "Thanks, but the computer does most of the work once you plug in the proper formulas."

"I heard you're a genius, but I think that's an understatement. Your father's a legend. You should surpass him without any hurdles at all."

Nancy laughed. "No one surpasses him."

"You will."

She cocked an eyebrow. "You always flirt with new employees?"

He tried to keep his face from turning red, but it had already passed its dark pink tint a minute before. The shade of red creeping up his neck was seconds from claiming his face.

"Sorry," Alex said. "I've never met a woman who's intimidated and intrigued me like you do."

She gave a slightly crooked smile. "I intimidate you? Why?"

"Your credentials and I.Q. tower well above mine."

Nancy shook her head. "You didn't have a persistent father with an obsession to mold you into the equivalent of a human computer."

"No, I had a mother who harped and nagged me into Harvard. Failure wasn't an option. To be honest, I was more than ecstatic to move to the university than stay at home longer than my teenage sentence mandated."

"Sounds like we have a lot in common."

"As long as our parents never meet."

Nancy laughed. "Why's that?"

"They might fall for each other and make it awkward for us."

Nancy blushed and returned her attention to the computer monitor. "Meaning?"

Alex shrugged. "I should do it before they meet."

"What?"

"Ask you out."

"You *are* a flirt."

His face was burning red. "Honestly, I'm not. I've never behaved like this. But would you?"

"What? Behave like this?"

"No," Alex said, shaking his head and trying to regain his composure. Nervously, he loosened his shirt collar and cleared his throat. "Would you allow me to take you to a Broadway production or a musical."

"Of course. I'd love to go. I've always wanted to go to Broadway but never allowed myself the time."

"You're too much like your father."

Nancy nodded. "Yes, but not all of that is bad. I refuse to become obsessed with science to the point that I have no personal life. I do venture out into the real world."

"I'll get us tickets then. I'm not certain what's playing."
"It doesn't matter. Just going will make a pleasant evening."

TYPHIS BIT his lower lip until he tasted blood. Sitting in his dark office, he stared at the wall. Word from his investigators had informed him that the only thing missing from the refrigerated storage room was Trey's head. This baffled him. He wondered what sickness possessed his enemies to steal his dead son's head.

He rose from his desk and crossed the dark room to his liquor cabinet. He poured himself a glass of bourbon. He took a small sip, and the warmth of tears meandered down his cheeks.

Trey and Simon had been genetics experiments. Fraternal twins. In part, they were from his genome, composed of the best traits his imperfect body offered. New, enhanced traits were bridged into their genomes to make them stronger, faster, better. Though experiments, he sorely missed them. He grieved.

He hated to take Trey's life, but with the miracle of Cryogenics, he had planned to place his son's head on a genetically stronger body. The mental downtime Trey earned during his slumber should erase the breakdown he had suffered at the loss of Simon. The chance to resurrect Trey was gone.

With drink in hand, Typhis walked out onto the balcony. Tables turned, he reasoned to himself. Things were set in motion.

The sun disappeared behind the western horizon, and the Newark city sirens wailed. During the brief pause three minutes later, a computerized voice beckoned from loud speakers atop buildings throughout the city.

"Newark is under city curfew at six p.m. Please go to your homes and stay there. Repeat. Newark is under city curfew at six p.m. Return to your homes. This is for your own protection."

The sirens rose to full blast again and pierced the darkening sky. Crowds of people rushed along the sidewalks while others hurried to their cars. Police cruisers flashed their red and blue lights. Short horn bursts warned citizens to hurry.

Frantic paranoia loomed over the pedestrians of an impending, approaching doom. No greater fear tapped a heart like not knowing what was coming. The fear of the unknown.

Death.

Typhis placed his free hand on the cold, metal railing and sipped his bourbon. Cold air blew against his olive skin. He watched the panicked people. A smile spread across his thin face. The streets and sidewalks slowly emptied.

Police cruisers combed the city. Should Kat somehow get caught in the crossfire, no one could discern whether it was an accident or not.

"Come for me now," Typhis whispered with a narrow smile.

Chapter 50

Steven Matthews sat behind his new office desk and rummaged through the files inside a manila folder. His brown hair was cut short and neat. His brown eyes stirred a confidence few men possessed.

His office door opened. Matthews gazed from his notes to the man entering the room. He closed the file with a boyish grin.

"Good afternoon, Mr. Matthews. How do you like your new accommodations?"

Matthews stood and extended his hand. "I've not worked in a better facility."

Grayson shook his hand. "Please, call me Boyd."

"Checking up on me so soon, Boyd?"

Grayson laughed. "No. Just wanted to pass some news onto you."

"Such as?"

"I'm certain you're now aware of Typhis Reed's warehouse fire last night?"

Matthews nodded. "Yes. I saw that on the news."

Grayson straightened his tie and then shoved his hands into his pockets. "I believe the fire was arson. With the murders of five of my scientists at Mech Cybernetics, I cannot help but assume that more attacks are inevitable."

"It is an issue for concern."

"Yes. When your limo driver was killed, I think they were gunning for you."

"I've often wondered about that myself."

"With these brutal murders and Typhis Reed's top scientist, Dr. Marissa Block, getting killed last night, I've asked Helmsby and his family to remain here a few nights for their protection. I offer you the same."

"Here?"

"Yes. We've temporarily converted several suites into nice bedrooms."

Matthews' brow creased. "The threat's that high?"

Grayson sighed. "I believe so."

"I'll consider it. I generally work late into the night anyway."

"The majority of the Red Pawn Murders occurred late at night."

"I'd definitely accomplish more if I didn't have to commute. Which room will be mine?"

Grayson smiled. "My secretary will contact you."

"Thanks."

Grayson scanned the room. "Mind sharing what new experiment you're working on?"

"In time, sir. I don't like discussing new projects until I'm confident I'm headed the right direction."

"Sometimes bouncing ideas back and forth brings more clarity."

"For some, perhaps. Under the proper circumstances, maybe. However, I've never had much success with that method. I strive to make myself solve my own puzzles, no matter how cumbersome they are."

"I know. That's why I hired you. I admire analytical thinkers. It's difficult for me to find like-minded people."

Matthews grinned. "A burden to us both."

Grayson nodded and turned toward the door. "I'll let you continue with your research."

Matthews didn't reply. Grayson closed the door and headed down the hall.

"Bastard," Matthews whispered.

Steven rolled his chair back from the desk, grabbed a glass box, and set it on top of his desk. Trey's cold, dead eyes stared at him through the frosted glass.

He picked up his cellphone and pressed three on speed dial.

"Jensen," Matthews said. "How close are we to beginning?"

"Depends on which project you're referring to. If it's the cryogenic one, we can start in thirty minutes. Lydia, however, she's not prepped yet. She arrived less than an hour ago. We have some problems, too."

"What kind of problems?"

"Since Lydia was prematurely sent here instead of staying at Desert Labs, we're going to need some equipment to accommodate the experiment."

"Have whatever you need from Desert Labs flown here."

"I don't think we have that kind of time," Jensen replied. "Or the proper amount of concealed space."

Matthews sighed. "See what you can do."

"I'll evaluate her condition and our situation, but there's something else."

"I'm listening."

"Dr. Helmsby. I believe he recognized her when we exited the elevator."

"You tend to the other problems with Lydia and the cryogenics experiment. I'll take care of Helmsby."

Jensen lowered his voice and said, "Helmsby is working on Grayson's pet project. Grayson has safeguards on Helmsby at all times."

"Jensen, I'll take care of it. Helmsby's just another obstacle that needs to be removed. If Lydia hadn't created the problems she did at Desert Labs, we'd have her project up and running."

"If Grayson gets wind of what you're doing—"

"Stick to the plan. I'll take care of Mr. Grayson, too, even if I have to kill him."

Matthews placed the phone into its cradle. With a gentle rubbing motion, he wiped frost from the glass box. He studied Trey's dead eyes, his blue lips. In a half hour, he wanted to see the transformation. He wanted to know if his Cryo-Mech project succeeded.

The expression on Typhis' stunned face before Trey killed him was something Matthews longed to see. If this operation were successful, he'd capture the image on film to view time and time again.

If the Tyler project delivered positive results, Matthews gained an opportunity to obtain both Typhis and Grayson's empires.

Matthews carefully placed the glass box into a duffel bag, slung it over his shoulder, and made his way to the private lab Grayson had allotted him.

Before Matthews agreed to work for Grayson, he insisted that he be granted a laboratory that only he had access to. Matthews hired his own security team to install coded locks, cameras, and motion sensors. The codes could only be changed after a retina scan of Matthews' eyes. Any attempts to offset the codes triggered silent alarms that messaged Matthews via cell phone while temporarily blinded the perpetrator.

JENSEN STOOD near a large sleek machine that was about the size of a motorcycle. The silver machine had two propulsion hover jet engines attached to its base. A glassed-in compartment was centered between two laser rifles. Directional cameras on the front and back of the craft were wired to the main computer. Inside the glass globe, snaking wires weaved together, waiting for the final attachment.

"Impressive," Matthews said. "Quite a killing machine."

"Thanks," Jensen replied. "It's taken me years to get from my blueprint design to this machine before you."

"Time to see if it's worth your sweat and tears," Matthews said.

Matthews handed the frosted glass box that contained Trey's frozen head to Jensen. In places, melted frost dripped. The beading condensation meandered down the side of the glass. Through the glass, Trey's blue tinted face and dark lips were difficult to look upon. Jensen reluctantly accepted the box.

"Let me wire the connectors into his brain. In an hour or so we'll see if his reactivated brain accepts the cryo-transmission."

"What is the probability that this will work?" Matthews asked.

Jensen shrugged and slightly winced before he said, "This is the first time I've tried it. A lot of this is still theory and hypothesis. Depending upon how long this man was dead before they placed his head into the cryogenic refrigeration will determine the viability of reanimating his brain."

"Okay, but what percentage of success do you predict?"

"Mr. Matthews, this is purely speculation upon my part, but I'd say roughly sixty-five percent."

"That's all?"

Jensen stared into Matthews' hardened gaze. "The longer I wait answering questions, the less that percentage drops. Doing what is required is a delicate process."

Matthews waved his hands and nodded. "You're right. I'm hindering you. Get started with what you need to do. Where is Lydia?"

"Still in the nurse ward," Jensen replied, opening the box.

"I'll be back in a half hour."

Matthews took a side door and stepped into another research lab. One wall held a dozen rat cages. A female researcher, Becky, held a clipboard and checked off various boxes for each rat's evolutionary progress.

He stopped at the cages and watched the vermin. Several stood on their hind legs, wrinkling their noses, and sniffing the top of their cages, eagerly expecting food.

"Are the metabolic injections having any effect?" Matthews asked.

"None we've noticed yet."

Matthews shook his head. "Really? After two months of those injections, I'd have thought we'd see something."

"They appear stronger. They go through the mazes and figure out puzzles much more quickly than the placebo group."

He frowned. "But still no indication of speech patterns?"

"No."

"Damn. Give them another month of injections before we try something new. Otherwise we might have to scrape the project altogether."

"They are super intelligent, sir. So something's working."

"I need more than that."

Through the far door, Matthews exited, walked a short hall, and turned left at the nurses' station. He stepped into a small, dark enclosed room.

Lydia wore a thin gown and lay inside the CAT scan. Matthews walked into the neighboring glassed-in room. He watched the scan readings on the monitor as her body passed through the machine.

"Any abnormalities?" he asked the doctor.

"No," Dr. Wilks replied. "She's healthier than anyone I've passed through this machine."

"So we shouldn't have trouble placing her into an incubation chamber?"

"No. But there's no problem putting her inside one. But, once you do, you can never remove her."

Matthews looked concerned. "Why not?"

"If you do, she'll die. The electronic trauma to her brain will be too much for even her to recover. She won't survive."

"I understand."

Wilks nodded. "The only other question I have is whether you want to do this here, or wait until we can transport her to Desert Labs."

"I want the process done here. Afterwards, we can fly her to Desert Labs."

"Are you certain?"

"Yes. Why?" Matthews asked.

"Once she's hooked up, moving her incubation chamber across country is too risky. Should you have a power failure or a computer glitch, there's the possibility that we won't be able to keep her alive."

"I see."

"So prep her?"

Matthews sighed. "Let me think this over for a bit."

"It would be wise to evaluate the potential risk of failure."

"I know," Matthews said. "She was Idris' prototype. There's not another like her."

"Without her, you cannot start from square one. She's all you have."

"I'll give you an answer first thing tomorrow morning."

"I'll keep her sedated until then."

<hr>

Chapter 51

<hr>

Emptiness and tragic loss weighed down Lucas' facial expressions. He forced a smile when he saw Daniel. Daniel pulled him close and embraced him. Tears gripped Lucas' lashes like the morning dew glistens on grass.

"I'm so sorry," Daniel said. "What happened?"

Lucas took a seat at an airport table in the cafeteria. He introduced Joe to Daniel and then explained the circumstances of Lydia's abduction in careful detail.

"Have you returned to Desert Labs?"

"Not yet," Joe replied. "My brothers are watching the facility from a distance. They will call me if anyone arrives."

"We're going to find her," Daniel assured Lucas.

Lucas stared at the table. He seemed determined not to cry. "They took her in a helicopter, Dan. She could be anywhere."

"Kat and Lucian are working on this, too."

Lucas looked around Daniel's feet. "Where's Morton?"

"With them."

Lucas shook his head. "Wait. Did you say Lucian?"

Daniel nodded.

"That bastard."

"Easy, Luke," Daniel said. "He's sincere. He bought the fuel to get me here. And, he no longer looks like you."

219

"That's supposed to make up for what he's done?"

"No, but I've thought a lot about what Lucian has done over the years."

"And?" Lucas frowned.

"Some of the deaths, like Vicki's, weren't really his fault. Like he told you at TransGenCorp, his life depended on following orders. Once he realized killing Idris released him from assassination assignments, that's what he did. He killed Idris."

"It still doesn't cleanse his hands."

"I know, but anyone can be pushed to murder."

Lucas thought of Lydia and her captors. He nodded. "That's true. If I find the people who took Lydia, I know their outcome."

Joe cleared his throat. "There's a difference between revenge and protecting those you love. Nature teaches us that any creature will kill to protect its own, no matter how big or what its enemy is."

"True," Daniel said. His gaze met Lucas. "We're family. I'm in this fight with you."

Lucas rubbed his eyes. "I appreciate that. I just hope that she's okay."

"We can be certain she's alive, considering the type of people who have her. She's useless to them dead."

"I know. I'm more worried as to what they've done to her."

Joe's cell phone rang. "Yes? Good. We'll be right there."

"What is it?" Lucas asked.

Joe smiled broadly. "My brothers caught two men in a delivery truck outside Desert Labs. Seems they were sent to disassemble an incubation chamber and take it to the airport."

Lucas rose to his feet. "Let's go."

<hr>

MORTON NUZZLED Kyle's chin while Kyle typed commands into the computer. Kyle smiled at the feline's gentle touch.

Morton used their psionic connection to communicate because Kyle expressed himself more clearly if he didn't have to enunciate his words. With Violet in the other room, Morton also thought it best not to disclose his talking ability. Although Kyle somewhat trusted her, he had not been around her enough to get a positive vibe from her.

"Can you sense Lydia?" Morton mentally asked Kyle.

"Yes. She's close, but silent."

"Sedated?"

"I think she is."

"What should we do?"

"Wait for Kat and Carpenter. Typhis may have given them the information that can lead us to her."

Morton sat on his haunches. "Typhis has a hand in this?"

"A big hand. We just need proof."

"I hope we get evidence soon."

THIRTY MINUTES LATER.

KAT UNLOCKED THE DOOR. She and Carpenter walked into the hotel room. Lucian closed the door and Brockton came in from the adjoining room.

"Anything new?" Morton asked impatiently.

Kat smiled and looked at Brockton. "Get Kyle ready. We need to take a short trip."

"Sure," Brockton said. "Where are we going?"

"The city morgue."

Morton cocked a brow and grinned. "I'm not sure what you're thinking, but Kyle's intellectual state is on a major upward swing."

Kat patted his head. "Always silly, huh?"

Morton shrugged.

Violet stared at Morton and then glanced at Lucian. "What the hell?"

"Damn," Morton said and stared at the floor.

Lucian shook his head. "Long story, but he was created through similar scientific processes like those you were working with."

"Really?"

Lucian extended his open hand toward the cat.

Morton smiled and said, "You have any better guesses?"

Kat stepped to the open adjoining room and said, "Brockton, bring all the materials we used when Kyle viewed Gunter's memories. We need him to view Marissa Brock's last visualizations and find out who killed her."

Carpenter folded his arms and shook his head. "Kat, I don't understand what you plan to accomplish."

"Trust me. This will work."

Morton frowned and stared at Kyle. "So Kyle can speak to the dead?"

Kat shook her head. "Not exactly. He has the ability to process their recent memories and see what they last saw."

"Sounds cooler the way I described it." Morton grinned.

Carpenter's phone rang. He stepped outside and answered it. A few minutes passed before he came back inside.

"If we're going to do this, we'd best hurry," he said.

"Why?" Kat asked.

"Typhis has placed Newark under city-wide curfew."

"That shouldn't apply to us," she said.

"No, our authority won't be jeopardized, but it makes it easier for him to trace our whereabouts at all times."

"You think we're marked for death?"

Carpenter nodded. "If Typhis is involved in the Game of Pawns, we're targets, especially after our interrogation with him earlier today. Without any others wandering around outdoors, he can find us. My guess is this is exactly why he initiated the curfew."

Perturbed, Kat shook her head.

Morton sat upright. "Sounds like you need the use of a cat."

"Why?" Carpenter asked.

"No one suspects a cat, even as mischievous as we are."

Kat smiled. "That's true."

Brockton brought a duffle bag and set it on the edge of the bed. Kat pulled a toboggan onto Kyle's head.

"I have discovered reasons why they wanted the tissue cultures from GenTech," Brockton said.

"Why?" Carpenter asked.

"These tissues possess regeneration properties like those in the shifter creatures Idris created," Brockton replied. "However, they are far more advanced."

Morton narrowed his eyes. "In what way?"

"From my research inside TGC, I discovered what the shifters' biggest flaw was. If you killed the brain or the nerve reception from the brain to the injured tissue, the cells are unable to regenerate. They suffered major necrosis and died. But not these cells in the petri dishes. They successfully heal without any brain stimulation."

"They don't die?" Carpenter asked.

Brockton shook his head. "I've not found a way to kill them and they're in Petri dishes. Imagine what kind of creature you'd have if they're created solely from these cell tissues."

Kat closed her eyes and sighed. "I can't imagine what we'd face then."

Lucian nodded. "Idris was close to this phase."

Carpenter asked, "How close?"

"Let's just say that if I hadn't intervened, Lydia would have been killed by one of them."

"Lucas didn't put this in his report at the debriefing," Carpenter said.

Lucian smiled. "Would you?"

"Actually, yes I would," he replied.

"Lucas may have decided that TGC was shut down completely and the possibility of more creatures like this didn't exist."

"He still should have disclosed the information, no matter *what* he believed. You see what we're up against now? A blood battle between genetics research labs."

"No," Lucian said. "We're up against a lot worse. If what Brockton says is true, the enhancer bullets won't kill these assassins."

Carpenter studied Lucian closely. Carpenter weighted the information Lucian had just revealed. Carpenter's eyes narrowed for a moment. Lucian held a smug look on his face. A skeptical expression crossed Carpenter's face, but he remained silent.

Morton jumped to the bed and sat beside the duffle bag. "So you believe Typhis placed the city under curfew to keep an eye on your investigation?"

"Yes. Why?" Carpenter asked.

"He might have done so to keep people from finding more evidence that linked him to the Red Pawn Murders," Morton said.

Carpenter nodded. "That's true, too. What are you thinking?"

Morton smiled. "His warehouse burned down. What if there are hidden rooms beneath the warehouse that no one has found?"

"It's possible he might do that," Brockton said. "He sold GenTech to Grayson. These tissue cultures are possibly Typhis' research."

Lucian looked at Kat. "He may have sold them with the intent to steal them back and keep the money from the sale."

"Why do that?" Kat asked. "Why not just keep the tissue cultures? He didn't need to kill others."

"Knowledge is priceless," Morton said. "Killing the scientists with the ability to manufacture these cultures lessened the chance that Grayson will gain knowledge of them."

Kat sighed and looked at Carpenter. "Which should we do first? The brain-link for Kyle to Marissa is only possible for the next few hours. Beyond that, he can't do it and we might lose valuable information."

"Okay. You and Brockton take Kyle to the morgue," Carpenter replied.

"Morton and I will check out the warehouse," Lucian said.

Carpenter's face bore a smug smile when he looked at Lucian and said, "I'll accompany you and Morton."

Kat exchanged glances with Lucian. He nodded a slight agreement and shrugged, "You're free to examine the warehouse with us. With your experience, I'm sure you'll find things I'd miss."

Carpenter smiled. "That's why we work in teams."

Morton huffed. "I want to see how Kyle communicates with the dead."

"I will link what I see to you," Kyle said telepathically.

"Okay."

Chapter 52

Typhis rode the elevator to the basement of the municipal building. When the doors opened, the faint hall lighting hardly offered enough illumination for him to see the black tile floor. At first glance, he thought he was stepping off into a bottomless pit. Although his aged eyes favored the darkness, his stomach tensed at the thought of falling, but the floor held him and eased his false fear.

He thought of Trey and Simon, his sons, genetically enhanced, but his children all the same. His progeny of hope were dead. And now Trey's head had been stolen. Appalled that a sick soul treasured his loss, he resorted to hunting down the one responsible for the theft.

Typhis unlocked the fallout shelter door and slipped into an even darker room. Without blindly feeling the wall for the switch, he gently swiped his hand across a panel. The overhead lights glowed. He retrieved a pair of dark shades from his vest pocket and covered his eyes.

Dusty cobwebs hung in each corner of the ceiling. Cockroaches scurried across the floor and hid in narrow crevices. A large wooden door was centered in the opposing wall. He walked to the door and wiped a thin layer of dust off the brass doorknob.

Typhis slid a heavy brass key from his pocket and inserted it into the ancient lock. A simple twist clicked and broke the silence. He pulled the door toward him and the hinges wailed a long nerve-grinding creaking sound.

After Typhis unlocked the aged door, he returned the key to his pocket. The whine of the closing door triggered the overhead light mechanism. The black and white checkered tile floor brought to mind his favorite game.

Chess.

The fluorescent glow stung his eyes, but he continued down the quiet hall. His echoing footsteps wouldn't draw the attention of anyone. The majority of the people who knew this underground establishment existed were already dead.

He had not planned to return to this hidden area for another year, but the deaths of his beloved sons—Simon and Trey—made the trip necessary. His lifespan was ending. The drug remedies his cousin, Idris, had designed for him hadn't eliminated the sickness destroying his body. His only hope for longevity remained with the tissue cultures Gunter's lookalike had taken, and these too had been stolen.

Typhis longed for an heir to carry on his work and ambition. That hope hadn't exactly died with the deaths of Simon and Trey. Not if his new plan worked.

The hallway turned right. Large framed artwork from the previous century lined the walls. The faded beauty of their images hid beneath layers of dust and cobwebs. Uncounted wealth could have been attained from these rare pictures had they been kept in pristine condition.

Typhis made the turn and another row of sensory-activated lights brightened the hall. Less than twenty feet away stood an oak door. The image of Trey's dead face made his heart race. He paused and leaned against the wall to catch his breath. His lungs ached. A raspy, painful cough heaved from him deep inside his chest. The series of coughs continued until he thought he'd stop breathing. After the spell ended, he rose and wiped tears from his eyes. Perhaps his existence proved to be shorter than his physician had estimated.

He stared at the door. New hope resided on the other side.

Typhis pushed the door inward. Sitting on the floor with puzzles and games was a little girl. She placed the strange shaped cutouts into a puzzle frame while a female doctor timed her.

"Very good, Paula," she said. "You have set yourself a new record. You're *very* talented."

Paula forced a smile, in spite of her sad face. "When can I see Mommy?" she asked.

The doctor's eyes quickly shot to Typhis.

"Paula's doing well, Dr. Nicks?" he asked.

She smiled. "Superb."

"How about Paul?"

Dr. Nicks shook her head. "Not too well. He's not adjusting to their new home."

Typhis smiled down at Paula. "Play with your toys, dear," he said. "Dr. Nicks and I need to talk for a few minutes."

"When can I see Mommy?" she asked him directly.

"I'm afraid your mother isn't here, dear. We're taking care of you and your brother."

Paula's lip puckered. She slung puzzle pieces across the floor, folded her arms, and glared at him.

"She's a spirited one," Typhis said.

"Very."

He smiled. "I like that."

Nicks shook her head. "Her anger's getting worse."

Typhis motioned toward her office. "If we may," he said.

After she entered the office, he closed the door. "What positive results are you having?"

Nicks sat behind her desk. "With Paula? She's good with tests and puzzles, but the main problem is the absence of their mother. Paul doesn't want to play any games or cooperate with the testing. You took them from their mother way too early."

Typhis shook his head. "I don't have the luxury of years of waiting."

"Whatever your long term goals are, I'm not certain you'd be seeing the results you want anyway. The short term ones aren't working."

"They need a mother figure?"

She nodded. "Yes."

"They have you."

"No," she said. "That skews the results. As a psychiatrist, I strongly advise against your suggestion."

"Anna," Typhis said softly. "My sons are dead."

She nodded. "I know. I'm sorry for your loss. That's a horrible blow, but these children won't replace them. Not like you hope they will."

"Nurture them, Anna. You know what they need. You can do this."

Nicks sighed. "I could, yes. I know how to establish such a bond, but what you need is for that bond to be between you and them. *Not* me. Even if they allow you to get close to them, they'll never be what Simon and Trey were."

Typhis winced.

"Sorry to be blunt, sir, but you have to know the truth. Your sons were part of you, both genetically and emotionally. No matter how closely you become to these children, the results won't be the same."

"So will you do this?"

Anna stood and looked out the office window at Paula, who was still pouting. "I'll try, but if I don't see anything more positive in the next few weeks, I'll withdrawal from this project altogether."

Typhis took a deep breath. "I cannot ask any more than that of you. And what you're earning right now, consider it doubled from here on out."

"I appreciate that, sir, but the money isn't the issue. I'm not a parent, and some people simply aren't able to maintain a proper parental connection. I have book knowledge, but not personal, firsthand experience."

"I understand."

"I hope you do. My job is to view and measure their psychological growth from the outside. Interfering from the inside only changes what they will become and not necessarily in a good way."

"And the injections I sent you?"

"They aren't adapted enough for you to begin playing games with their genomes. I need to first get emotionally stabilized and make certain they are rational. You start injecting the canine binders into their gene pool, and it will be like trying to control a rabid wolf. You want them docile first."

Typhis frowned. "How long will that take?"

"There is no set timeframe on something like this. They're still grieving from being uprooted from their mother. Do you honestly expect them to just suddenly forget her?"

"So I made a premature decision on taking them this quickly. But if you strengthen a loving bond with them and replace what they miss from their mother, I believe they'll progress better."

Anna's eyes narrowed. "Love takes time. Something you said that you don't have much of."

"I know."

She smiled. "Do you? When have you really loved someone?"

"My sons. I loved them."

"Did you?"

Typhis' jaw tightened. "You're questioning my love for my own children?"

"Think about the situation. Did you have genuine love for them for their personal beings? Or did your affection lie more in what you could make them within your empire?"

"How dare you!"

"Easy, sir. It's something you should think about. Did they have the freedom to make choices or were those choices dictated by you?"

Typhis looked away and his shoulders slumped.

She didn't wait for an answer. His physical response was answer enough. "I'll do as you request with the twins. I cannot make guarantees. However, you should think about your judgments."

"You're right. I will."

"Would you like to see Paul before you leave?"

Typhis opened the door and said, "Sure."

Anna led him to the room on the other side of the playroom where Paula played with blocks. She opened the door. Paul lay on a cot in the fetal position, sucking his thumb.

"He's been like this for hours," she said.

Typhis walked to the cot and knelt beside the boy. He ran his hand through Paul's soft hair. The boy stared straight ahead and never blinked.

"It's okay, Paul," he said. "Anna is here. She wants to play with you."

Paul lay silent. His eyes didn't shift.

Typhis crouched lower and peered into Paul's eyes. The warmth of tears leaked from the old man's eyes. He whispered, "Son, everything will be okay. Come to me, and I'll make you invincible."

Chapter 53

The morgue was cold, dark. Kat shivered and hugged herself. Ahead of her Brockton pushed Kyle in the wheelchair. She hoped Kyle was able to gain access to Marissa Block's memories and that the information enabled them to prepare for what they would eventual face.

Brockton's information about the cell cultures disturbed her. These created tissues couldn't be destroyed easily.

TransGenCorp was a dead facility, but its genetic technological information had been divided and sent to other scientists and facilities that expanded the technology into more dangerous uses.

Some of these other corporations might not have revealed themselves either. At least when the experimentations were all encapsulated under one roof, the government and the FBI kept a tight, watchful eye over what was going on. But now, new enemies abounded and their exact locations and names were unknown.

The wheelchair rolled smoothly along the long, tiled hall. She expected the dark hall of the morgue to suddenly explode with lights. She wouldn't be surprised if men hired by Typhis attacked to prevent them from attaining the information they sought.

Kat rubbed her hands together to warm them. "Why's it so damn cold here?"

Brockton smiled. "To prevent the rapid decay of bodies."

"Were we supposed to meet the coroner?"

He glanced at his watch. "He should still be around here. He's probably waiting for us where Marissa's corpse is being kept."

"Todd's supposed to meet us, too."

Brockton slowed the wheelchair. "He probably knows the coroner."

The still air gave her more uneasiness.

"It's too quiet in here," she said.

"They don't want to wake the dead."

Kat forced a slight smile. "Funny."

"Well, they don't, but Kyle needs to link to one."

She hugged herself and rubbed her arms, trying to warm herself. When they neared the last room at the end of the hall, Brockton waited for her to open the door. Then he pushed Kyle through. Marissa Block's body lay beneath a sheet on a cold, metal table. The coroner wasn't in the room. No evidence indicated that anyone else was there.

After rolling the chair closer to the corpse, Brockton opened his bag. Kyle leaned forward.

Brockton nodded at Kat. "This should be a lot easier than the bathtub. At the table's height, at least Kyle has a direct reach for contact."

Kat walked to the head of the table and watched. Kyle placed his hands on Marissa's forehead. Veins swelled in his arms as he searched to reach her memories.

"Get him away from her," the coroner hissed, stepping out of the shadows. He pointed a gun at Kyle.

Kat turned and reached for her weapon.

"Don't," he said, turning the gun on her. "I may be a coroner, but trust me, I know how to use this. Now roll him away from her body."

"What are you doing?" Kat asked. "We have permission to do this."

He shook his head. "Not according to Typhis. He has demanded me to stop you."

"Where's Todd? He was to meet us here," Kat said.

The man smiled. "Todd sort of got sidetracked."

"Where *is* he?"

"I'm sure he's around here somewhere."

Kyle slid his hand toward Marissa's head and the coroner leveled the gun and pulled back the trigger.

Brockton stepped between the gun and Kyle with his hands raised. "Easy, sir. Just put the gun down. I'll back Kyle away."

The coroner shook his head. "I'm afraid it's not that easy. My orders are to kill you. Now, Agent Gaddis, carefully place your gun on the floor."

Kat obeyed. "You plan to kill all three of us? My FBI supervisor knows we're here. If he doesn't hear from us, he'll send help."

"That's the beauty of my job, ma'am. Incineration of your dead bodies and dumping the ashes into the river makes it damn near impossible for authorities to find you. Now, if you will, step away from Block's corpse, or I shoot Kyle where he sits."

JOE DROVE Lucas and Daniel to Desert Labs. The two detained deliverymen were tied to metal chairs in the parking lot.

Although the men hadn't been harmed, they were nervous. Lucas had the understanding that these men knew something bad was going to happen.

The name, Coyle, was stitched on the man's shirt.

Lucas eyed him with a fierce gaze. "Where's Lydia?"

Coyle's eyes shifted nervously. His lower lip trembled. "I'm sorry. I don't know anyone by that name."

Lucas backhanded him with enough force to sling the man's head hard to the left. Blood trickled from his mouth. The blow didn't draw a look of resentment, but one of submissive fear. He stared at Lucas' feet.

Daniel placed a hand on Lucas' shoulder. "He's probably telling the truth."

Lucas shook his head and balled his hands into tight fists.

Daniel stepped between Coyle and Lucas. "Where are you taking the incubation chamber?" Daniel asked.

Lucas pulled his gun and pressed it to the man's temple. "You'd best tell us."

Coyle swallowed hard and whispered, "Grayson Enterprises."

"Where is that?" Lucas asked.

"New York."

Lucas lowered the gun and looked at Daniel.

Daniel said, "We need an address. Where's your delivery order?"

"In the truck."

Joe hurried to the truck and returned with a metal clipboard. He handed it to Lucas.

Joe smiled. "We have the address now."

Lucas nodded. "Yes, but what do we do with them?"

"Listen," Coyle said. "Our orders were to disassemble and deliver the incubation chamber. Nothing else. We know nothing about this Lydia, so please let us go."

"Sorry," Lucas said. "No can do. At least we won't yet. I cannot risk you leaking information back to your boss."

"We won't contact them."

Joe said, "My brothers can watch them at our ranch for a few days. Until we find Lydia."

"That would be the best solution," Daniel said.

Lucas scratched his beard and thought. "Okay. You suppose we can use your friend's Learjet to get to New York?"

Daniel nodded. "Yes. I'm certain it won't be a problem for him."

"Then let's go get Lydia," Lucas said.

Chapter 54

Kyle focused a keen stare on the coroner. Brockton grabbed the handles of his wheelchair and pulled Kyle away from the table. With stealthy precision, Kyle crept into the coroner's mind.

"Put the gun down," Kyle commanded.

The man's hand shook. "What the hell are you doing?" he asked.

"Put the gun down," Kyle repeated. "Or die."

The man tried to regain a firm grip on the weapon, but he couldn't. The invisible force was too powerful.

———

A DEEP FURROWED FROWN APPEARED on Kyle's face. Slowly the man's wrist bent inward, in spite of the man's obvious struggle.

"Drop it," Kyle said inside the man's mind.

Although the words were soft, the power flow was harsh.

Sweat beaded across the man's face. He stared in horror at the turning gun. His trigger finger tightened. In seconds, the gun was pointed at his chest. He fought to turn the gun away.

Kyle's mind was too strong to fight.

Eyes wide. His face was pasty white. He did the only other thing possible. He opened his hand and let the gun drop to the floor.

Kat stooped and grabbed her gun. Her fingers tightened and she aimed at the coroner's head. "Hands behind your head," she said.

He obeyed and stared in absolute confusion. "How'd he do that?"

Kat reached into her back pocket and brought out handcuffs. "That's as much a mystery to me as it is to you. If you hadn't dropped the gun, you'd have been dead."

She cuffed his hands behind his back.

The coroner replied, "I'm dead anyway. He'll kill me for not carrying out his orders."

"Don't worry about Typhis. We're going after him. Now where's Todd?"

LUCIAN'S RIDE with Carpenter to the warehouse was more an interrogation than a discussion of procedure. Because Lucian had said too much, Carpenter automatically understood who he was. Lucian had to somehow change his mind. He created spontaneous stories of his fictional past to supersede the suspicions Carpenter held. He chose Jake as his alias, but a couple times, he seriously considered telling Carpenter who he really was. But he couldn't reveal that until after he fulfilled his promises to Kat and Lucas. In spite of every story and event Lucian told, he didn't think Carpenter was buying the charade.

"Kat places a lot of confidence in you," Carpenter said as he drove.

"She does with you, too, sir," Lucian replied.

"Not as much as she did. Not since Tyler's death."

"She lost a lot of trust after that."

Carpenter glanced at Lucian. He slowed the car to a stop about fifty yards from the warehouse. "At least she has someone to talk to about it."

"It's a sensitive subject. She seldom brings Tyler up."

Carpenter shoved his car door open. "Does she ever mention the clone?"

Lucian let Morton jump to the pavement before closing the door. "What clone?"

"She's never mentioned the clone to you?" he asked, pressing the door closed and propping his hands on the car roof.

Lucian shook his head. "No. Perhaps I should ask her?"

"I'm surprised she's not talked about him. We've been trying to find him for months."

Morton stared at Lucian and smiled.

Violet opened the rear driver-side door and Lucian shook his head. "You stay here. If you see anyone suspicious, hit the horn."

Carpenter nodded, although his determined eyes never left Lucian while he spoke. "Yes. It's safer for you to stay in the car."

She leaned against the door and folded her arms. Ocean smells mingled with the lingering scent of burnt lumber. The night sky hung thick with clouds, making everything darker. Even in the darkness, she was unable to hide her nervousness.

Morton smiled. "If I hear the horn, I can be here in seconds. Try not to worry."

Violet smiled and knelt to rub the cat's ears.

Morton shook his head. "There'll be time enough for that later." He pranced off to catch Lucian and Carpenter.

Plumes of smoke drifted from the caved-in warehouse. The thick smell of burnt wood fogged the air, making breathing difficult. Carpenter lifted the yellow police tape and allowed Lucian to cross first.

Morton paused at the charcoal cinders and perked his ears. When he was satisfied nothing moved within the rubble, he walked under the tape and took a different direction to investigate.

"Whatever accelerant they used was strong enough to wipe out most of the building," Carpenter said.

"Other than the tin roofing," Lucian replied.

Carpenter sighed. "I don't think there's enough left to evaluate what Typhis had been working on here."

"That's probably what they wanted," Lucian said.

"Total destruction."

"Not exactly," Morton called out. "Here's a trapdoor."

Carpenter and Lucian found Morton near the center of the building. Hinges and bolts from the incinerated storage crates littered the floor in piles of ashes. Charred, smoking beams formed a small lean-to shaped wooden skeleton.

"The door is metal," Morton said, wiping a thick layer of ash with his paw. The cat sighed. "And . . . it's locked."

Lucian leaned down, grabbed the handle, and pulled upward. "Sealed tight."

"Step aside," Carpenter said. He unfolded a leather pouch with lock picking tools.

"I guess the FBI teaches a lot of underhanded things," Lucian said.

Carpenter smiled. "No, but sometimes you learn useful skills along the way."

"Obviously."

Carpenter worked on the door, and Lucian scanned the parking lot for Violet. She remained beside the car.

Occasional gusts of wind brushed against the wooden remains and faint red embers glowed.

"There," Carpenter said. He pulled the handle and swung the door back. A ladder dropped down to the dark basement floor. He pulled out a flashlight, clicked it on, and started down. "Be careful. This is probably the only light we will have."

Lucian looked at Morton with yellow-tinted eyes. Morton's turned red. The cat said, "Light? Who needs light?"

Lucian laughed and started down the ladder after Carpenter.

After both men stepped away from the ladder, Morton dropped fifteen feet to the floor.

The flashlight scanned the room back and forth in a dizzying motion. Finally, Carpenter stopped the light on a large fluid-filled tank with glass walls.

"Shit," he said, stepping closer. "What the hell is this?"

Lucian placed his hands against the tank and shook his head. "Genetic failures. Dead experimental creatures too deformed to survive."

"And the stench?" Carpenter asked, placing his handkerchief over his nose and mouth.

"Formaldehyde," Morton replied.

"It doesn't bother you?" Carpenter asked Lucian.

"No."

"Hell, I don't see how scientists work with that shit. The smell gags me."

Morton jumped to a table to get a better view of the dead creatures in the tank. "It's a preservative. Unless you're in need of evaluating or dissecting a dead specimen that's stored in it, you don't need to smell it."

Carpenter coughed. "So someone's been here recently?"

The cat nodded. "I'd say so, but this tank wasn't opened. The smell's coming from another one nearby."

Lucian found the light switch and flipped it. "Lights are out."

"I'd say all power to this place is out due to the fire," Carpenter replied. "The power lines are probably melted beyond repair."

"Use your light so we can search for the open container. We might find where the scent is coming from."

Carpenter pointed the light at the large glass tank and said, "That might be difficult since there's not a breeze down here. The smell has permeated the entire room."

Morton stared at the strange misshapen creatures inside one of the containers filled with formaldehyde. Some of the creatures had two heads, missing appendages, deformed wings, or extra rows of teeth or fingers and toes. Scientific experiments weren't always successful. Seeing such deformities didn't surprise the cat. What bothered him the most was not knowing where the surviving creatures had gone. The possibility existed that Typhis had shipped them to other labs.

While Carpenter moved further into the room, Morton watched the bits of settlement move and spin in little whirlpools. He stared closer. Disturbing the bottom of the tank were little fishlike creatures that the formaldehyde didn't kill.

"Jake," Carpenter called out to Lucian. "Come here, quick."

Morton leapt to the floor and scampered to where Lucian had met up with Carpenter. A nude female body lay on a dissection table. Wet pools of formaldehyde and decaying, body fluids dripped from the table to the floor.

Morton stood near the table. Streams of drying fluids formed long lines that tracked back to an upright body-sized tank. "She was placed here recently," Morton said.

"I think you're right," Carpenter said. He brought the light up to the woman's face and gasped. "Dear God, no."

"What?" the cat asked.

Lucian picked the tabby up and set him at the head of the table. "It's Lydia," he said.

Morton stepped closer to see. He lowered his head and shut his eyes.

It was Lydia.

She was dead.

Chapter 55

Nancy flung her purse over her shoulder and locked her office door. When she turned around, Yvonne stood face to face with her. Nancy clamped her hand over her mouth to stop the rising scream in her throat once she recognized that it was Yvonne.

"Hi," Nancy said, taking in a deep breath. "You about scared me out of my skin."

"*Where* are you going?" she asked with a stern whisper.

"To a Broadway show with Alex. Why?"

Yvonne looked down the hall and pulled Nancy closer. "We have a problem."

"What?"

"Grayson."

Nancy appeared confused. "What about Grayson?"

"He doesn't want us to leave."

"What? I've not heard anything about this."

Yvonne frowned. "He's not requested that you to stay here overnight?"

"No."

"That's good. In that case, we need you to get a message to Kat. The phones are bugged."

Nancy's eyes widened. "Bugged?"

"Yes." She handed a note to the girl. "Call Kat when you get outside of the building and tell her Lydia is being held here."

"Lydia? Why?"

"We don't know. But I assure you, it's her."

Nancy nodded and crammed the paper into her pocket. "I'll call her once we get out of the parking lot."

Yvonne embraced her. "Be careful."

"I will."

Chapter 56

Kyle placed his hands on Marissa's head again and projected his mind into her memories. Jagged thoughts came and went. All he was interested in seeing were her last visuals before she died. That memory flickered in less than two seconds, giving him just a brief glimpse of the two men that had killed her. He recalled the image repeatedly, hoping for more clarity. After a dozen or more flashback bursts, their features made him question if he was viewing a hallucination.

Seeing the troubled expression on Kyle's face, Brockton asked, "What'd you see?"

"These men . . ." Kyle's eyes remained closed. His lulling voice rose just above a whisper. "Are the ones . . . Vanessa saw."

"Dead men?"

Kyle nodded. "That's one way . . . to describe them."

Brockton frowned. "They killed Dr. Block?"

Kyle's eyes never opened. He gave a slight tilt of his head and said, "She was in her office. Heard a disturbance outside. She turned on the laboratory lights. She was horrified by their appearance. Then they killed her."

Brockton patted Kyle's back. "Okay. That's all the information we need. Come back to me."

Kyle blinked. A trickle of sweat ran down the side of his face. His wide eyes were like a terrified rodent. Brockton didn't doubt Kyle had witnessed the same atrocities Vanessa had encountered in the alley.

Brockton pushed the wheelchair into the dark room. "We need to catch up to Kat. She might need our help getting Todd."

KAT KEPT a firm hand on the cuffed man's wrists while she pushed him ahead of her in the long corridor. Because he was a big man who could overpower her, she kept her free hand on the butt of her gun.

"What's your name?" she asked, pushing him forward.

"Not that it matters. But call me John."

"Well, John, where exactly did you put Todd?"

"Janitor closet."

"He'd best be unharmed."

John hung his head like a defeated child. His pudgy cheeks and pouting lips made him seem less threatening. "I didn't hurt him. I was told to stop you and Kyle from accessing Marissa's body."

"Killing us was part of the agreement?"

"Only if you didn't heed the warnings. Otherwise, you were free to leave."

Kat laughed softly. "You were almost a victim at your own hand."

"I know. That wasn't something I could have known about."

"Me, either."

"Typhis will kill me."

"I'm certain your prison cell won't be anywhere near his."

"It won't have to be. He can have me killed anywhere."

John stopped walking. His cold eyes pierced into hers. The innocence his face held vanished. "He's given a death order for you."

Kat swallowed hard. "What?"

He nodded. "Not by me. His orders are to find and kill you after curfew set in."

"Who received these orders?"

"Every guard Typhis controls. Most of the police force is looking for you."

"Keep moving," she said, squeezing his wrist.

The big man didn't take a step. He stared at her like a defiant child.

His shoulders tightened. His actions were a challenge. She pushed again, and he resisted.

Her cell phone rang. Nancy was on the other end.

"Yes?" she said.

"Yvonne asked me to call you once I got outside Grayson Enterprises."

"Why didn't she call me herself? Is something wrong?"

"Grayson isn't allowing her or my father to leave his facility."

"Why?"

"I don't know. Grayson Enterprises has Lydia. Yvonne said that she saw her unconscious on a gurney. They rolled her through and into the nurse station."

Kat cleared her throat. "They have Lydia?"

"That's what she told me."

"We'll be there soon."

"You'll never get past security. Alex and I had a difficult time leaving. Due to the murders, Grayson has heightened his security. I'm assuming that's why he doesn't want my father and Yvonne to leave. He doesn't seem sinister. I honestly think he has our best interests in mind."

"I don't know about that, but don't worry. We'll find a way inside."

Kat folded her cellphone. She slid it into her back pocket, and John shoved his weight against her, knocking her to the floor. With his hands cuffed behind his back he wasn't able to run fast, but he still managed to disappear further into the dark hall.

Disgusted, she brushed herself off and rose to her feet with her gun drawn. At this point, she didn't care whether John escaped or not. She wanted to find Todd. Preferably alive.

Kat understood Typhis. She had fully read his personality when she sat across from him. She knew his hatred for her brimmed because she didn't fear his authority. She never thought that her boldness would place a mark on her life. It had. Now returning to the streets of Newark meant she had to protect herself while seeking to arrest Typhis. Of course, had John not revealed this information to her, she'd be dead much quicker. She'd have ventured into the streets with a false sense of security, thinking any police officer was an ally rather than a foe. He had inadvertently given her a reason to become more cautious than she otherwise would have been.

She cautiously headed toward the end of the hallway, and the darkness became heavier and the air, colder. Fear choked her. Her tight hands held the gun. Sweat from her hands made the trigger slippery.

A scraping sound moved across the floor ahead of her. Kat leaned to the right and slid her back against the wall. Without light, she didn't want to fire haphazardly into the shadows. She wanted to be certain whom she'd shot at. Besides, there was a slight possibility that Todd might be tied up in the hall and not a closet.

She fought to see what hid where the shadows were invisible.

Using the wall to brace herself, she slid until a doorknob bumped against her hip. Keeping her gun aimed toward the hall, she turned the knob and pulled the door open.

Kat patted the wall for a light switch. When she found it, she turned on the light. A dim overhead bulb came to life. Todd was tied and gagged in the corner. Sweat coated his face.

The gag was soaked with saliva. She pulled it down so he could talk. He had chewed on the cloth for some time, apparently trying to rip it apart.

"Thanks, Kat woman," he said in a dry whisper. "I didn't think anyone would ever find me."

Kat struggled to untie the thick ropes around his hands and wrists. She loosened the ropes, and his eyes grew wide.

"Behind you," he whispered.

Kat turned, but not quick enough.

The impact of John's foot kicking into her ribs sent her against the wall. She shook her head to break the dizzying hold that staggered her. Coughing, she fought to breathe.

Todd pulled the loose ropes from his hands and pushed off the wall. John pulled back his foot to kick Kat a second time, but Todd landed a crushing blow to the man's jaw and then kneed him in the groin.

John bellowed a cry of despair and dropped to the floor on his side, writhing. Falling with his hands cuffed under his heavy weight dislocated both of his shoulders with two sickening pops. He wailed.

Todd struck him in the face again. "You damn bastard. It's one thing what you did to me, but you hurting her? I bet you feel all macho inside now, eh?"

Todd helped Kat to her feet. "Are you okay?"

Kat placed a hand against the wall to steady herself. "Yeah. I'm dizzy, but I'll survive."

Todd smeared the gag across the dirty floor and stepped over John's body. He leaned down to tie it around the man's mouth.

"Don't leave me here," John said.

Todd smiled. "Turnabout's not fair play for you?"

"Please."

Todd shrugged. Instead of gagging John with the filthy rag, he shoved the cloth into John's mouth when he opened it to protest.

"Don't worry, I'm sure someone will find you. Eventually," Todd said.

Todd looped his arm around Kat's, flipped off the light switch, and closed the door.

"You need to get to a hospital. You hit that wall pretty damn hard, Kat."

She shook her head. "No, I'll be fine. Kyle and Brockton are here. Let's find them."

Stepping from the dark hall where the light was bright, Todd rubbed his rope-burned wrists.

"Are you okay?" she asked.

He gave a solemn nod. "Nothing major. I think that bastard ethered me."

"Did you know him?"

Todd shook his head. "No, he introduced himself when I came to examine Dr. Block's body. When I pulled open her drawer, he forced a cloth over my nose and mouth. To be honest, I hope he rots in that closet."

"We still need you to do the autopsy."

"That's no problem," he said. He stopped in the hall and looked at her. "What exactly are you looking for?"

"I don't know. With her it may be nothing."

"Carpenter pulled a lot of strings to move her body here. There's something you're not telling me."

Kat smiled. "Nothing gets past you."

"Not if I can help it."

"We moved her body here, so an associate of mine could read her last memory imprints."

"Oh bullshit!" Todd said, shaking his head. He glanced at Kat and her face remained serious.

"I'm not kidding."

He frowned. "How?"

"It's hard to explain."

"Try."

"I don't know how he does it. But if he finds what we're looking for, we'll know who killed her."

Brockton stopped pushing the wheelchair at the far end of the hall.

"There they are. Maybe Brockton can explain it to you. Right now, I need to get this information to Carpenter."

Chapter 57

Morton sat beside Lydia's body and sulked.

"This will kill Lucas," Lucian said.

"That, or send him into a rage unlike anything any of us have ever seen," the cat said.

"Vengeance justified," Lucian replied.

Carpenter cocked an eyebrow as he looked at Lucian. "It's never justified."

"You've never lost someone so close and so dear?"

Carpenter looked away. "I have. You have to bury the rage."

Lucian shook his head and pointed at Lydia's body. "You cannot bury something like *this*. It will eat you alive and haunt your dreams forever."

Carpenter's narrow gaze bore at Lucian. "You're the clone, aren't you?"

Lucian laughed. "What? Why would you think that?"

"Your eyes. They changed." Carpenter pulled his gun and held it on him. "For a few seconds, they were a greenish yellow."

Lucian waved him off. "Easy, Carpenter. The room is dark. The only light we have is your damn flashlight, which is currently blinding me."

"I know what I saw."

"Do you?"

"Yes. You got away before, but you won't now."

Morton's angered eyes turned red. He peered straight at Carpenter. "Enough! We have issues that are more important at hand than whether he's the clone or not. Lydia, for one, and finding out who is responsible for this."

Carpenter lowered the gun and sighed. "You're right, Morton. I'm sorry . . . Jake, *if* that's your real name."

Lucian sighed. "I'm here to help, but damn."

Carpenter holstered his gun. "I'm sorry. I overreacted. The glow of the flashlight must have messed with my vision."

Morton closed his eyes and reached for Kyle through their mental link. "Lydia's dead."

Kyle didn't respond immediately, but when he finally answered, he said, "No. She's still alive."

"I'm sitting beside her corpse."

"Investigate closer. I still sense her. She's alive but nowhere near you."

Morton leapt to the floor. His eyes continued their crimson glow, which enabled him to see without light. He followed the wet trail of formaldehyde back to the tank. A brass plate was cemented to the base of the glass.

"TransGenCorp."

A rush of ecstatic relief made Morton tremble. "That's not Lydia. It's one of her long dead and preserved clones from TransGenCorp."

Carpenter brought the light to the lower part of the tank and read the plate. "I'll be damned. Why is her body on this table then?"

"Perhaps they want to find out exactly how Idris had made her," Morton replied.

"No, get away from her body!"

Carpenter swung the flashlight in the direction of the voice. The man held a tranquilizer gun.

"FBI," Carpenter said, reaching for his gun. "Put down your weapon."

The man's trigger finger tightened and fired. Lucian dove between the dart and Carpenter. He knocked Carpenter to the floor. The dart hit Lucian in the shoulder.

"Damn," Lucian said.

Carpenter rolled and came up with his gun drawn.

Morton lunged and leapt into the air. His sharp claws slashed the man's gun hand. The dart gun fell to the floor. The cat growled and climbed up the man's chest. Frantic to escape the sharp claws, the man fell backwards to the floor.

Morton pressed his claws into the soft flesh of the man's throat. "Give me a reason," he hissed.

Carpenter stepped over the man with the light and gun aimed at his frightened face. "Who are you?"

"Dr. Jensen. I work for Grayson Enterprises."

Morton's fiery eyes glared at the doctor.

"Why are you here?" Morton asked. "Did Grayson send you to steal Typhis' research?"

Jensen shook his head. "No. Grayson doesn't know I'm here. He's not behind this."

"Who is?"

Jensen looked at Morton's sharp teeth. He shuddered, closed his eyes, and said, "I'm here on my own behalf."

"Why?"

"Matthews has Lydia Ridale."

"Steven Matthews?"

"Yes. Grayson doesn't know that Matthews abducted her."

Lucian moaned.

"So why are you here?" Carpenter asked.

"I want to take this body and put it in place of Lydia's. By morning, if Matthews does what I think he will, Lydia will be placed inside an incubation chamber. If she is, she can never be removed or she'll die."

Carpenter frowned. "How'd you know Lydia had a clone here? You work for Grayson. This is Typhis' lab."

Jensen closed his eyes and released a sigh. "Steven Matthews worked for Typhis before. He speculated about Typhis moving TGC relics into this warehouse. I gambled that his assumption was correct."

Morton crouched closer to Jensen's face. "Even if you replaced Lydia with this clone, Matthews is smart enough to realize it's not her. The scent of formaldehyde is too strong. He'll smell it well before he gets to the body. And then there's the issue of her puffy skin and discoloration after she's left outside for a few hours."

"I realize that, but I'm desperate to save her."

Carpenter eased his gun back into its holster. "Why?"

"I don't agree with his technique or what he plans to do. I've done everything to stall this project, but by morning, there's no turning back."

"How'd you get a key?" Carpenter asked. "The steel door was locked when we arrived."

"It was unlocked. I locked the latch after I closed the door."

Morton sat on Jensen's chest. "How did you plan to carry her up the ladder? You don't look very strong."

Jensen shook his head and chuckled. "I discovered that problem after I removed her from the storage tank. I hoped there might be a door below the docks, but I haven't found one. They couldn't have brought all these tanks through the small trap door."

Carpenter nodded. "That's true."

"Since this won't work, can you help me rescue Lydia?"

Lucian pushed himself into a seated position and ran a hand through his hair. He rubbed his bearded chin. A few seconds later, he yanked the dart from his shoulder.

"Just don't go through with the incubation setup," Morton said.

"Matthews doesn't need me to finish the project. He knows how the chambers work. Even if I don't return, he can run the setup program without me."

"If you can get me inside," Morton said, looking at Carpenter. "I'll find a way to rescue her."

"I'll see if we can get the building plans for Grayson Enterprises."

Morton stepped off Jensen. Carpenter motioned the doctor to get up.

"Dr. Jensen, these other creatures in the tanks. The deformed ones. Is Matthews working on anything like this?"

"No. Just dead human resurrection."

Carpenter sighed. "I wonder if other labs are assembling these strange creatures?"

"Probably."

Morton licked his forepaw. "Jensen, what do you mean by 'dead human resurrection?'"

Jensen stood and brushed dirt from his clothes. "He's created a way for dead tissue to regenerate and . . . resurrect itself."

"Like a zombie?" Carpenter asked.

He nodded.

"That helps explain what the girl at La Vida Erotic saw. What else is he working on?"

"He seems a bit obsessed with some kind of rat experiment he's currently working on. But he won't tell me what it's all about."

Lucian rose to his feet and groaned loudly.

Jensen stared in disbelief. "You should've been out for hours."

Lucian shook his head and winced. "Damn. It feels like dynamite detonated inside my skull."

Carpenter's mouth opened to speak, but he chose to remain skeptically silent.

"What do we do with the clone body?" Morton asked.

"We put it back into the tank it came from," Carpenter said. "Then we back to the surface."

Jensen grabbed Carpenter by the sleeve and tugged him around. "You have to protect me from Matthews. He will kill me."

"We're going to arrest him," Carpenter said.

"I want protection. I'll even testify against him."

"Testify? For what?"

"I know far more about Matthews' corruption."

"More than this?"

Jensen nodded. "Yes."

"What else?"

"He's going to kill Typhis tonight."

"What?"

Jensen nodded nervously. "He is sending his agents to kill him."

"Matthews won't get far. Newark is under city-wide curfew."

"That doesn't matter. He's sending a machine to do it. Bullets cannot penetrate the titanium and steel. Even the glass shield is bulletproof."

"What kind of machine?" Lucian asked.

"A Cybergenetic Probe. I just finished hooking it up."

"What the hell is that?" Morton said.

"This is the prototype," Jensen said. "It's a turbo engine glider, equipped with laser rifles. The police won't be able to stop it. And to add more anguish to Typhis before Matthews kills him, the computerized machine has Trey's cryogenic head attached to the central control unit."

Carpenter folded his arms. "You mean this machine has a human head?"

"Yes."

"The brain still operates?"

Jensen frowned as he explained. "Not exactly like ours. Computerized synapses signal the brain's action, but the computer is what makes the commands, not Trey. The computer has the ability to animate the head's facial features. The head doesn't have any control, though."

"Then why use it?" Carpenter asked.

"Trey was one of Typhis' sons sent to kill Gunter," Jensen replied. "Matthews wanted me to attach it to the Probe to add to Typhis' mental trauma before he kills him. He wants to gloat over Typhis' misery. The machine is totally independent of the head. Matthews controls the machine from his office."

Lucian leaned against a Formica tabletop. "So basically Matthews is using the head like a trophy."

Jensen nodded. "Exactly. But the Probe isn't all he's sending."

Carpenter frowned. "What else?"

"About a dozen of his undead creations. They're alive, but they look like walking corpses."

"Like the ones that killed Dennis Schrader?"

"Yes. Typhis isn't his only target though."

Lucian massaged his temples. "What are you implying?"

"He's threatened to kill Grayson and Helmsby, too. He wants total control over genetic manipulation."

Glancing at his watch beneath the flashlight glow, Carpenter said, "When exactly will this attempted assassination take place?"

"I'd guess within the hour."

Carpenter pressed a contact number on his cell phone. "Kat, are you through at the morgue? Matthews is planning an assassination attempt on Typhis within the next hour. How close are you to the courthouse?"

"Several blocks away. Why?"

"You have to intercept him."

Lucian yelled, "Are you insane? She cannot go against that machine."

Carpenter nodded. "I know. You're right. Kat, you have to warn Typhis. His life's in danger."

"I can't," she replied.

Static cut off his phone. "Kat? Kat? You there?"

"What happened?" Morton asked.

"Dammit!" Carpenter said.

"What?" Lucian asked.

"Phone's been cut off."

"How?" Morton said.

Carpenter sighed. "I don't know. There's no signal."

Lucian turned on his phone and shook his head. "No signal, either."

"Jake," Carpenter said. "How fast can you get to the Newark Courthouse?"

"In minutes with the car," Lucian replied.

"I'll go," Morton said.

"No, Morton. We need to find a way to get you inside Grayson Enterprises undetected. Jake, you take Violet and the car. Warn Typhis. But be careful. With the city under curfew, police will shoot first, ask questions later."

"I might have to adopt that policy tonight myself."

Carpenter shook his head. "Try not to."

"What about Kat?" Morton asked.

He shrugged. "Right before I lost her, she said that she couldn't get to the courthouse."

Lucian ran to the ladder and started up.

"Jensen," Carpenter said. "I'm hopeful you drove here?"

"Yes. I parked a block over so I wouldn't draw any attention to myself."

"Good," he replied. "We'll take your car to Grayson Enterprises. Morton can find a tight spot to squeeze through and infiltrate the laboratories."

Morton's eyes narrowed. "Gutter crawling again? It's been a while."

AFTER CLIMBING through the trapdoor to the surface and stumbling through the charred remains to get to the street, Lucian noticed a black Jaguar slow and stop near Violet. She climbed in the passenger side without any resistance or hesitation.

"What the hell?" Lucian said.

Carpenter shook his head. "Don't worry about her right now. Find Kat while there's still time."

"No questioning that decision."

Lucian ran to their car while Carpenter followed Jensen to his.

CARPENTER CALLED headquarters from a street phone and wrote down a phone number.

He handed the phone to Jensen. "Call Grayson and warn him that his life is in danger."

Jensen nodded and dialed. "Mr. Grayson, this is Dr. Jensen."

"How'd you get this number?" Grayson asked.

"That's not important. You need to know that Matthews is plotting to kill you. Probably tonight."

"Where are you?" Grayson asked.

"On my way back to Grayson Enterprises with an FBI agent."

"Why?"

"They're going to arrest Matthews for conspiracy and murder."

"I don't need any outside help to take care of Matthews."

Grayson disconnected the call.

Jensen gave a nervous glance to Carpenter. "If you want to take Matthews alive, you'd best hurry."

"Why?"

"I think Grayson will kill him."

Chapter 58

Grayson fumed at the news Jensen had given him. How dare Matthews seek to kill him out of greed? No other reason existed for Matthews to murder his boss. Grayson had done everything to pamper Matthews to gain his employ, and Matthews offered this disrespect in return?

Opening his desk drawer, he removed a polished chrome 9mm. Although he never favored using handguns to solve his dilemmas, he didn't exclude the use of them, either. Most people feared him for his size alone, or because of his power and wealth and the possibility of what he could do to destroy an enemy through the media and public scrutiny. The gall of Matthews was bitter and needed to be eradicated.

Grayson snapped a bullet into the chamber, clicked on the safety, and put the gun inside his jacket pocket. He stood and smiled.

"You're a fool, Mr. Matthews," he seethed through clenched teeth. "You have no security in my building. None whatsoever."

When Matthews had hired a team to set all the security for his wing of the building, he never realized the men he had hired to do the job were actually employed by Grayson. Nothing in Grayson Enterprises was ever off-limits to Boyd Grayson. Nothing. Matthews' real problem was that no one had informed him of that information.

KAT TUCKED her phone in her back pocket.

"Who was that?" Todd asked.

"Carpenter," she replied.

"What does he want?"

"Urgent business. I have to go."

Todd placed his hand on her arm. "You can't go out there alone. It's too dangerous."

"I have no choice. You stay with Kyle and Dr. Brockton."

"Kat . . . "

Her eyes stared into his. "I have to. Brockton has his hands full with Kyle. He needs someone to keep an eye out in case Typhis sends more people."

"I'm a coroner, Kat."

"Yep, and I also know that you're a great shot with a 9mm. You don't leave home without one. Or your knife."

Todd smiled. "That's what happens when you grow up in the Bronx and want to stay alive."

"So," she said with an earnest smile. "Keep an eye on them, please."

"I will."

THE LEARJET LANDED in New York. Daniel, Lucas, and Joe hurried through the airport and found a car rental office. After they signed the rental agreement and were issued a car, they ran to the parking lot.

Lucas hurried into the driver's seat. Daniel climbed in the passenger side and typed Grayson Enterprises' address into the GPS mapping system. Joe sat in silence in the back seat.

"We're about twenty minutes away," Daniel said.

Lucas put the car into drive and headed out of the rental lot. "I just hope we're not twenty minutes too late."

"We'll be on time," Joe said.

HELMSBY SAT at the microscope with Yvonne at his side. "The DNA is highly modified, but in some ways, not too different from ours," he said.

Yvonne placed a hand on his shoulder and shook her head. "How can you do research right now?"

He shrugged. "How can I not? If I don't force myself to research these slides, I'll go out of my mind."

"Has Grayson ever told you how he obtained it?"

Helmsby shook his head. "No. I snooped a bit though, and as best I can tell, this sample was sent back from scientists working at his Deimos Life Station."

"I see why this intrigues you. I honestly don't blame you for jumping at this opportunity."

Helmsby smiled. "I appreciate your support, but I keep asking myself why they have Lydia here?"

"I don't know."

"The news stated that she was abducted."

"I know."

"Lucas will come once he finds out where she is. He'll tear this place apart until he find her."

"I don't blame him."

"I don't either." Helmsby removed a slide, marked data in tiny letters on the identification label, and said, "Have you tried to get through the nurse's station?"

"Not since they posted additional guards."

"I hate being held here against my will."

Yvonne sighed. "Nancy will contact Kat. If nothing else, the FBI will arrive and investigate."

"I hope so."

KAT LEFT the morgue with more uneasiness than she'd ever felt before. She had tried to tell Carpenter that she couldn't warn Typhis because the mayor had ordered a hit on her, but her phone had died.

She eased toward the parking lot with her gun drawn. Suddenly, she wondered if the Game of Pawns was reaching its final stage. Matthews had marked Typhis for death. Typhis wanted her dead. How many more players existed? Who else was a target?

If she attempted to save Typhis, she placed her life into deeper jeopardy, possibly sacrificing her life to save his. That wasn't a bargaining chip she'd ever play. For all practical reasoning, the old man simply wasn't worth it.

Instead, Kat hoped to discover and stop the assassin before he attempted the murder. Doing so placed her within the sites of unknown enemies.

Chapter 59

Morton crawled through the rusted airshaft. The old tunnels hadn't been used in more than a century. Most likely, the architects responsible for the renovation of Grayson Enterprises hadn't noticed these secret passageways. Newer air vents fastened beneath the rusted ones and concealed them. But even if the architects had noticed them, they wouldn't have feared the possibility of an intruder making his way through them. As tight and small as the vents were, no humans, not even a child, could fit through them. No one expected a cat to have the intellect to achieve such an invasion, either.

Morton smiled.

Water dripped and soaked his fur, but he had crawled through worse when he stalked the alleys in Pittsburgh. Rusty water wasn't deadly. The puddles of stagnant water collected and overflowed into small, meandering streams. He hurried along the shaft until he came to an old vent screen.

Morton peered through. Faint light beamed through the wire. He listened for the footsteps of possible guards or patrols.

Nothing.

The screen wouldn't be a problem after he reached the other side, but finding where they kept Lydia might not be so easy. Penetrating the building was easier for a cat than a human, but if she were inside a locked room, he'd have a harder time rescuing her.

From what Kyle indicated, he knew she was here but still unconscious. Morton could do a lot of things, but even he couldn't carry her body to safety. Although able to shift his form, he was limited to remain the same size and weight. There wasn't anyway to fight physics. And depending on how their security alarms worked, once he found her, he might have a few minutes to deactivate her I.V. but not enough time to wait for her to wake up.

Projecting his right front claws, he lengthened them into sharp, pick-like tools and sliced through the wire. Pushing his head through, he looked down the halls.

Silence.

Morton squeezed through the opening and shook his fur. Water droplets cascaded across the floor and walls. Moments later, a door opened further down the hall.

With narrowed eyes, the cat slinked near the corner of the next corridor and peered around. The small door plaque stated: **Research Laboratory**.

The door stood slightly ajar. Something struck the door from the other side. The door gap widened. Morton waited. His keen hearing didn't detect a man or woman's footsteps.

A few minutes passed and three rats scurried to the center of the hall-way. One tugged a small bag of Fritos with its teeth. The second carried a plastic straw in its mouth while the last opened a tiny novelty deck of cards.

The three rats gathered in a small circle. Just as they sat back on their haunches, a long, loud squeal emitted from inside the laboratory. A speed-ing, rolling can of Mountain Dew spun through the open door and headed straight for the other three. The rat riding the can tried to slow down its momentum, but failed. In panic, the three rats seated on the floor scurried out of the way. The can hit the wall, and its rider sat on the floor, dazed.

"Dammit, Fred!" The white rat with a gray stripe screamed. "Are you trying to kill us?"

Morton's eyebrows rose with surprise. *"Talking rats?"* he whispered.

"Sorry, Kip," Fred replied.

"Next time, Bandit brings the Dew," Kip said, grabbing the deck of cards and sitting back down. "That clear?"

"Yes."

"Okay, fine," Kip said. "Let's deal out the cards. I'd like to get a few hands out of the way before the next patrolling guard comes through. It's time I show you who the true *losers* are."

Kip shuffled the cards, and Morton crept around the corner, easing into the threshold of the nearest door without making his presence known. Listen and learn, he thought. He didn't need his curiosity to frighten them off, but he wanted to learn all he could about them.

The rat dealt the cards and paused to sniff the air. "You guys smell something?"

Fred sniffed the air and replied. "Wet fur?"

"Something like that."

"I don't see anything," Fred replied, looking around.

"You never do," said the white rat with red eyes.

Kip laughed. "Good one, Whitey."

Fred frowned and crossed his forelimbs.

Morton pushed himself tighter against the door to avoid being seen.

The rats sat in a circle with their hind legs and long tails supporting them. The white rat distributed the Fritos evenly.

"Ante up," Kip said. Each rat kicked a Fritos chip to the center of the circle.

The rat with the bandit mask held his cards and asked, "What's the game?"

"Sorry, Bandit. How about five card stud, Joker's wild?" Kip replied.

"Fine by me," Bandit said.

"Me, too," Fred exclaimed, placing his cards on the floor. "Read 'em and weep, boys. Four of a kind. Four eights."

Kip looked at the cards and frowned. "Fred, you idiot! That's two pair. Two threes and two eights! God, if they ever invent glasses for rats, I'm shoving you to the front of the line."

Fred shrugged. "Sorry."

"No problem. It's still a good hand, but not good enough."

Whitey placed three jacks down and swiped the chips for himself.

"Good hand, Whitey," Kip said. "But you and I need to talk about our running bet over the Miami Dolphins game this past Sunday. I still say they won, but I can't tell since you chose *that* particular part of the paper to smear your droppings."

Whitey rolled his eyes.

"I swear if I find out you did that to deliberately short me . . ."

Whitey flipped him off.

Kip put the cards down and flashed his teeth.

"That's enough, Kip," Bandit said. "Whitey just pay him."

"Like hell!"

"I saw the game score *before* you ruined the paper. The Dolphins won."

Whitey frowned and hissed, "Damn you."

Kip took the cards and sat back down. "Ten Fritos, Whitey. Settle the bet or leave the circle."

Whitey shoved ten chips over to Kip and mumbled under his breath.

Kip dealt a new hand, and Morton eased closer.

"Damn," Kip said. "There's that smell again. Stinkier though."

Morton's shadow swept over them.

The four rats flung their cards in the air and huddled together, looking up at Morton.

"Hell, who let the cat in?" Kip asked.

Morton smiled. "The door was open."

Whitey rubbed his eyes. "You talk, too?"

"Why does that surprise you?" he replied.

Kip shook his head. "I suppose it shouldn't, but I've not seen any cats in these laboratories."

"I'm not from these labs. I'm here to find someone."

"Who?"

"A woman named Lydia." Morton described her features and told them about her abduction.

The rats nodded in unison. "They have her. I believe she's the next hall over. But you'll never get in there."

"Why not?"

"You're too big."

"What does my size have to do with it?"

"Nurses at the center desk will see you."

"Then maybe you'll help me."

"Why would *we* want to help a cat?"

Morton frowned. "Because not helping me is helping them. They are your captors."

Kip smiled and folded his forelegs. "The scientist over us is a complete idiot. She has no knowledge of our abilities."

"She doesn't know you talk?"

"Nope. She also doesn't know we leave our cages every night, either."

"Obviously. How long have you been able to talk?"

Whitey scratched his head. "A few months now."

"Any idea how they achieved this?"

"High protein diets and some sort of DNA enhancer injections."

Morton asked, "And they're clueless?"

"Yep," Kip said. "They hold images in front of us and ask dumb questions. Of course, the rat maze is always the good one. It's kind of fun. I have the record time so far, and according to Becky, *I'm* a genius."

"Surely, they've noticed some changes."

"We just make blank stares into space, pretending nothing registers in our tiny brains. Fred is really good at it. Show him, Fred."

Fred tilted his head back and forth, peered straight ahead with his red eyes, and crinkled his nose while sniffing the air. Kip and the other two rats burst into laughter.

"Of course, it helps that he's nearly blind," Kip said.

Morton looked at Fred. "Is that true?"

Fred nodded.

"Help me rescue Lydia," Morton said. "And I'll get you out of here."

Kip shook his head. "We have everything we need right here. Food, water, and shelter. I'd add no threat of cats, but then you did show up."

"Threat? Do you consider me a threat?"

Kip stared at him for a moment and said, "In nature, cats are a danger for us. But you don't seem to want to hurt us, so, no I don't think you are."

"I'd only hurt you if you forced my, erm, paw."

"Are you implying that if we *don't* help you . . .?"

Morton's mouth spread into a thin grin.

"There's something else you might want to consider," Morton said.

"What?"

"Since they don't know you talk, you'll be considered a failed experiment. Failed experiments generally are killed. They'll do autopsies to examine your brains. Then they'll start fresh with new rats."

Kip's body shook. "I never thought about that."

"So you'll help?"

Kip nodded. "Yes."

Bandit said, "But what if we encounter guards?"

"I'll stop them," the cat replied.

"You?" Kip asked.

"Yes."

"How do you think you can do that?"

Morton's eyes glowed red. His mouth protruded. His teeth spread apart and longer fangs sprouted downward, filling the gaps. Bones in his head popped. His ears pointed. His paws swelled with sharper claws and he growled.

The rats trembled.

"I'll help," Bandit said.

"Me, too," Whitey added.

Kip said, "What exactly are you?"

"A shape-shifter, created by Dr. Helmsby."

Bandit's eyes widened. "*The* Dr. Helmsby?"

Morton nodded.

"He's a legend," Kip said.

"Some would say."

"He works here, too," Whitey said.

"I know. That's how we discovered Lydia was here."

"Why don't you get him to help?"

Morton sighed. "Grayson won't let him leave the facility and has his phones bugged."

Kip shook his head. "Grayson's not whom you should worry about. He's a great guy. It's Steven Matthews you should be concerned about. He's the one overseeing our project."

"That's why I should worry?"

"No. He works on worse things."

"Like what?" Morton asked.

"We'll have to show you."

"So you'll help?"

Kip bowed and said, "Oh mighty creation of Dr. Helmsby, we are at your service."

Morton rolled his eyes. "I'm having second thoughts now."

"Don't, I like to jest," Kip said. "We'll do all we can."

"I appreciate it."

Kip rubbed his forepaws together and with an embarrassed expression, he said, "I hate to ask, but do you happen to know where we might be able to get some cigarettes?"

Morton furrowed his brow. "Why?"

"Me and the guys are having like major nicotine fits."

"How could you be addicted to nicotine?"

"One of the scientists left his cigarettes and matches behind the other day, and well, we thought we'd give it a try. Talk about getting the heart pumping. The level of nicotine in those was probably too high for us, but what a buzz!"

"And they say curiosity kills cats." Morton shook his head. "It's a wonder your hearts didn't explode."

"They almost did, but not due to the nicotine," Kip replied.

"Why?"

"Bandit nearly set our bedding on fire. Luckily, we hadn't pissed for a while."

Morton shook his head.

"Tell me something," Kip said.

"What?"

"How can I get red eyes like yours? I mean Whitey's are cool, but I like yours better."

Morton opened his mouth to reply, but the elevator down the hall dinged.

"Damn," Kip said. "New patrols are early. Follow us, quick."

Morton rushed through the open lab door with the rats. They all turned and shoved their weight against the door. The lock clicked, and they hid in the darkness of the room.

Shadows of men stopped outside the door. They discussed the Fritos on the floor. One guard tested the doorknob and found it locked. After a few minutes, they headed down the hall to the next door.

"Where is Lydia?" Morton asked.

"Next hall over."

"Since I cannot get to her, this is what I need you to do."

SINCE FRED'S poor vision hampered aiding his rat-kin, he stayed behind with Morton. Kip and Bandit insisted that Whitey stay in the shadows, because his whiteness made him easily seen.

Following Morton's orders, they scampered along the darkest wall until they reached the hospital bed where Lydia lay. They gripped the sheet and clawed their way to her pillow. For a few minutes, they remained hidden under the loose end of the pillow.

When they were confident no nurse was in the room, they crawled out from hiding.

"Her wrists are strapped down," Kip said.

"Gnaw through the leather?" Bandit asked.

"You do that while I remove the I.V. from her arm; then I'll help you with the restraints."

Kip gnawed away the tape that fastened the I.V. needle to Lydia's wrist. With a gentle push, he slowly removed the needle and stuck the tip into the mattress to keep the flow going. He hoped the alarm on the machine didn't sound. He noticed a button to turn off the monitor. Using the plastic tubing like a rope, he pulled himself across to the machine.

Depending on the dosage of the sedative, it might be hours before she awakened. They weren't sure what Morton intended for them to do until then. Any nurse that came in to check would notice the needle not in her arm. They'd not only reinsert it, they'd scour the place until they found out who had removed it.

The thick leather was hard and difficult for them to chew through. Even with the two of them, the process would take at least an hour.

Chapter 60

Matthews locked his filing cabinet. He watched the sunset through his large, office window. He smiled. Newark's enacted curfew was the worst thing Typhis could have done. The mayor's rash decision had tilted the game board in Matthew's favor.

Matthews wasn't satisfied with taking out mere pawns. Pawns used efficiently made good distractions for the opposing, higher trump players, but weren't essentially powerful or necessary to win the game. Pawns were sacrificial. Getting past the pawns and removing the royal players wrought victory. He had succeeded at that and soon his enemy king, Typhis, would die. That left him to set things in order at Grayson Enterprises.

He opened a hidden door between two bookcases and headed downstairs. The Probe with Trey's head should be ready for assault. He needed to attend to another matter before commanding the Probe to find Typhis.

Matthews descended the spiral staircase. He thought about Lydia. He didn't know what action to take yet. Although he wanted to begin the cloning process immediately, he didn't like the thought the experiment died with her death. Premature decisions often failed. He detested failure.

Actually shipping her back to Desert Laboratories after the heat died down made more sense. However, long periods of sedation weren't safe. He didn't want to risk future gene mutations when her body was already near perfection. He needed to be able to duplicate that perfection continuously.

Matthews understood Lydia's one weakness. She could actually die. Her body could withstand a lot of brutal torture, but a point beyond self-repair existed. That's why he wanted to get those cultures from Gunter's twin. By combining Lydia's genetic code with regenerating tissues, he could eventually create an individual that could not die. Of course, the only thing he knew that killed the cells was fire at extreme temperatures.

The stairs ended three floors down from his office suite. Two sentries rested in chairs. Wires and tubes connected to their arms fed them intra-venous nutrients. Robbing Grayson's files, he had learned how to revive cryogenic tissues and organs. Eventual success came in how he had brought to life several corpses. Their deaths had deprived them of full memory capabilities, but all he needed was just enough motor skill func-tion for the simplest command—to kill.

Dennis Schrader had been their first mission. Without any question or remorse, they had followed their orders. Although that particular part of the assignment had been successful, they had made a mistake. They had left behind a witness.

Unhooking the I.V.s from the two sentries, Matthews laughed. He'd give a million dollars to have seen the looks on the FBI agents' faces when the woman told them what the men looked like. He didn't fear being sought by the FBI because such a testimony held no credibility with inves-tigators. They wanted cold, hard facts with as many details as possible. No one believed zombies existed, and after he mass-produced Lydia, he'd have no need for these men. They'd disappear as mysteriously as they had appeared.

Grayson set himself up to be an easier target. He was too trusting and too preoccupied with his space technology research to suspect he had hired a man dead set on killing him in order to take over his empire. Removing Grayson and Typhis granted Matthews greater power. Less competition meant greater market placement.

Not only did Lydia have a killer body, she also possessed such remark-able charisma that if he chose to capitalize on that added quality, he'd have a woman no man could ever resist. Placed properly, he'd have a genetic army of Jezebels mesmerizing rulers around the world to succumb to their demands, which were actually his own. None would be wiser.

Matthews stood before the two men and instructed them where to go and what to do. After they left, he ran up one flight of stairs and met with Dr. Wilks.

"How's the progress?" he asked.

Wilks nodded. "Set and ready."

"Where's Jensen?"

Wilks shrugged. "After he finished connecting Trey's head to the Probe, he said that he had some quick errands."

"Odd," Matthews said, looking at his watch. "At this hour?"

"I thought so, too."

"So these camera feeds work all right?"

Wilks nodded.

Matthews smiled. "I guess we're set to go. My six undead assassins are almost prepped. In less than a half hour, they'll hit the streets. Punch in the codes for the Probe."

Chapter 61

Kip stopped chewing the leather restraint and sat back. "My jaws are killing me."

Bandit nodded. "Mine, too."

"We're almost halfway through."

Lydia's right hand moved.

"So quickly? I think she's coming around," Bandit said.

"I hope so. It'd make things much easier."

CARPENTER SAT in the passenger seat and turned on his laptop while Jensen drove. He had been in the FBI for years and questioned hundreds of people in interviews. He had no doubt that Jake was actually the clone. The man had practically taunted that he was. However, proving the fact wasn't necessarily an easy factor.

Since Tyler's death, Kat had not been rational. She distanced herself from everyone she had been close to and formed her own investigation team. When he discovered she had taken a keen interest in Kyle, at first he thought it odd. But knowing her compassion, her action wasn't out of character. She would have sought to help Kyle anyway she could. And since

Brockton had worked at TGC, he was the logical choice to oversee Kyle's recovery.

But Jake, he didn't understand. If Kat needed another person to work as an investigator in her firm, she could have scoured hundreds of applications until she found one that stood out boldly. This wasn't the case.

Jake had stood beside her at Tyler's funeral, so Carpenter wondered how hasty a decision she had made to disregard the help of the FBI by quitting, only to hire someone she didn't really know. Since Lucas' clone still had not been accounted for, he speculated that Jake was the clone and the man who had killed the senators and many others. If so, he had to be brought to justice.

Kat's irrationality made her vulnerable. He sensed it, but he didn't understand why she had decided to harbor the clone to aid her in finding those responsible. Knowing as little as she did about him, how could she possibly trust him?

Carpenter feared she knew the clone would go to any means, including murder, to stop future genetic manufacturing. Perhaps that was why. He shook his head in disgust. He'd never allow illegal actions to bring people to justice.

Frustration raged inside him. He wanted to end the search for the clone, but he still needed more proof. The most outstanding fact that opposed his suspicion was seeing Jake at the funeral. He didn't look like Lucas at all. Not one bit. Plastic surgery took weeks, sometimes months, for the bruises and puffiness to fade away. That had only been two days.

Carpenter rubbed his eyes with the palms of his hands and then stared at the computer screen. He was too damn tired, but if everything fell into place, the Game of Pawns might end within the next few hours.

He had tried Kat's cell several times without success. With the enacted curfew, he wondered if Typhis had blocked all cell towers as well. He still awaited word from Jake about Kat.

Carpenter opened a file on Typhis and scanned through the contents. Midway down the page, he froze.

"How the hell did we miss this?" he asked.

A small paragraph listed Typhis' next of kin as Idris.

LUCAS DROVE AS FAST as he could through the New York City traffic.

"Do you sense Lydia now that we are closer?" Joe asked.

Lucas focused. "Yes. I think she's waking up. The place she's at doesn't seem as dark anymore."

Daniel frowned. "What are you talking about?"

"Soul links," Joe replied.

"Oh?"

Lucas nodded. "He thinks that my bond with Lydia is strong enough that we should be able to sense one another in our spirits. You probably can do that with Julia."

"Julia always seems to know where I'm at or what I'm thinking without me saying a word. So you're probably right or maybe she's psychic."

"I think when I see Lydia, I'll never stop hugging her," Lucas said.

GRAYSON ENTERPRISES

TWO PATROLS EXITED THE ELEVATOR. They stopped a few feet outside the door.

"Who are you?" one guard asked the two suited men standing midway down the hall. "Identify yourselves."

The two men turned and faced the patrols.

"What the hell?" the guard said, reaching for his gun.

Two shots fired before either guard prepared to fire. They dropped to the floor. Dead.

HELMSBY AND YVONNE sat in their makeshift bedroom. "Do you think Nancy got the message to Kat?"

"I think she will."

"Grayson seemed like a really great person when I met him. I understand his need for confidentiality in the realm of scientific discovery. I don't blame him at all for that. I went through similar ordeals before. That's what made Idris hate me."

Yvonne squeezed his hand. "Power does strange things to people, dear. They forget how other people feel inside because they've grown so cold that they lose compassion."

"I never lost my compassion."

"No," she replied. "But your obsession with science made you lose your connection to the ones who loved you the most."

Helmsby thought her statement over and said, "That's true. Daniel didn't speak to me for nearly three years. He blamed me for what happened in Pittsburgh. I guess I'm responsible for some of the bad things that occurred."

"How?"

"I knew the attacks were coming. I should have warned others."

"Why didn't you?"

Helmsby's face reddened. "My obsession with science controlled me."

She smiled. "You've outgrown that."

"Have I? We're trapped here because of my eagerness to work with alien DNA."

"The brink of such new discoveries would snare any devoted scientist if offered the same chance." Yvonne placed a hand on his arm. "Answer something for me."

"Anything."

"When Grayson told you that we had to stay here, did he sound genuinely concerned, or demanding?"

Helmsby cocked his head to the side and thought. "He didn't sound demanding, but he didn't want us to leave."

"So you felt somewhat trapped and threatened by his suggestion for us to stay?"

"Yes."

"With what all that has happened during the past six years I believe you simply overreacted to his statement."

He wrung his hands together. "I truly hope so. I don't like thinking I placed us all in danger again."

"I don't think you have."

"Then why bug the phones?"

"I don't know. I guess he has the right to make certain none of us break the confidentiality of his data. Information breaches are costly to a company."

Helmsby nodded. "That makes sense."

Chapter 62

Denton stood outside La Vida Erotica, waiting to get inside. Undercover, he hoped to find more information to shut down the corrupt strip club. He wore a ball cap turned backwards on his head and a leather jacket and denim jeans. The men standing ahead of him were dressed in similar attire.

Since the place crawled with lustful patrons, he didn't fear being identified in the crowd by any of the bouncers from earlier in the day.

Denton passed through the door with a quick show of his driver's license. Harder music played and a thick screen of smoke loomed above the tables. A DJ introduced the dancers as they stepped onto stage. Again, their empty stares bothered him. Their bodies swayed to the music but their minds seemed absent.

A chesty woman in a low cut shirt poured drinks. Her athletic arms were tanned and slender. She kept a constant smile.

Mick wasn't anywhere to be seen.

Denton eased to an empty barstool. The bartender smiled and shot him a quick wink. He smiled back.

"What will it be, handsome?" she asked.

"Light beer in a bottle."

She leaned over and opened a refrigerator, exposing her breasts to him. Popping the cap against the side of the bar, she slid the bottle to him.

"I've not seen you here before," she said. "What's your name?"

"Casey," he lied.

"Millie," she replied, extending her hand.

Denton politely squeezed her hand.

"What do you do?" she asked, wiping the bar.

He looked in the mirror behind her at the three girls dancing onstage. "I'm in between jobs right now."

She smiled, glanced over her shoulder, and turned back to him. "Well, enjoy the show."

Millie walked over to another customer while Denton berated himself under his breath. "She probably thinks I'm a pig just like the rest of the men here," he whispered.

As Denton thought about it, he realized Millie wasn't like the women onstage. She had a genuine personality. She was real. Well, *most* of her was real.

Rather than turn around on the barstool and watch the topless women, he hunched forward on the bar and held his beer between his hands. He stared at the bottle and sighed.

Tyler came to mind. They had gone to bars occasionally and even picked up women a couple of times. The last second of Tyler's life before the bullet lodged in his brain flashed through Denton's mind. Blood had sprayed across the car upholstery and Tyler fell lifeless against the steering wheel. The image of his friend's dead body haunted him. He couldn't shake the growing depression.

Millie returned and patted his hand. "You okay, Casey?" she asked.

"Yeah, fine."

"You look like you lost one of your best friends."

"I did. About six months ago."

Sadness came to her eyes. "I'm sorry."

Denton nodded. "Thanks. Just trying to remember our good times."

She slid another bottle to him. "On the house."

"Oh, no. I'm not here for sympathy."

"I know."

"How long have you worked for La Vida Erotica?" he asked.

"A couple months."

"You probably see a lot of strange occurrences here, don't you?"

"Where alcohol is served and women dance nude, you cannot prevent weirdness from following."

"I suppose that's true."

"Trust me, sweetie. I've seen about everything."

Denton smiled. "The girls certainly seem to be in a trance when they dance."

Millie nodded. "I've wondered about that myself. The best answer I've heard is they project their minds to another place to ignore the acts they perform these nude routines for cash. But I've also learned not to ask too many questions."

"Are any of those women your friends?"

"Me, no. They stick together like a flock of birds. Not to say I've not tried to befriend them. I have, but I don't believe I'm the type of company they're looking for."

Denton turned up his bottle.

"Are you hoping to make arrangements with any of them after the show?" she asked.

Denton quickly shook his head. "No. I don't pay for sex."

Millie smiled. "I wouldn't think you'd have to."

He blushed. "Thanks."

"You have a special lady in your life?"

"Not at the moment."

She looked at the clock. "I get off work in an hour, if you'd like to talk."

Denton smiled. "Sure. That'd be nice."

"You!" a man said, grabbing Denton by the arm and swinging him around on the stool.

"Mick!" Millie said. "What the hell are you doing?"

"He's a federal agent, Millie."

Her eyes widened. "Really? You are?"

"Yes," he replied.

"You bring a warrant tonight?" Mick asked.

Denton shook his head.

Mick's huge hands grabbed Denton's lapels and pulled him from the stool. He smiled. "That's what I wanted to hear."

"Mick!" Millie said. "Leave him be. He's not bothering anyone."

"He's spying."

"Spying for what? This is a strip club."

"Don't worry yourself over it. Tend the bar, and I'll take care of this."

Mick shoved Denton against the wall and pinned his arm against Denton's throat. With his free hand, Mick patted him for a gun.

"You came here without a weapon?" he asked.

Denton replied. "I'm not looking for trouble."

"You found it anyway."

Mick spun Denton toward the door that led behind the stage. He understood why. When he and Carpenter had inspected the halls and rooms, they couldn't hear the stage music out front. This meant that anyone watching the show would be unable to hear anything that happened backstage. A gun could fire and no one would be the wiser.

Mick shoved Denton into the dark hallway. "I told you to send Vanessa home."

"She doesn't belong here. She's not property."

"Some beg to differ."

"Who do you work for, Mick?"

"Want to meet him?"

Denton stopped walking and Mick shoved him harder. Denton turned and faced him, his hands balled into fists.

"Easy," Mick said, sliding brass knuckles onto his right hand.

Although Mick was small in stature, his speed wasn't something Denton expected. The swift rabbit punch struck and toppled him backwards. The metal across his wide hand jarred Denton's face. Denton reached for the wall to steady himself. Even without a mirror, he felt the instant bruise swell beneath his left eye.

"Mick, you realize the penalty for assaulting a federal agent?"

Mick laughed. "Assault? That's just the beginning. They won't even recognize you after I'm through."

"The agency knows I'm here."

Mick reared his fist to strike again, and a gun pressed firmly to the back of his head. The hammer cocked.

"Don't move, or you're dead."

Denton sighed. "Millie?"

She nodded. "I hope you at least brought cuffs."

Denton reached into his rear pocket and pulled them out. "That I did."

"You mind telling me what's going on?" she asked.

Denton tightened the cuffs until the metal bit into Mick's flesh.

"Dammit!" he cried out.

Denton steadied himself against the wall and touched the fiery bruise.

Millie lifted his hand and looked. "We should get some ice on that."

"In a few minutes. Whom do you work for?"

"I don't know his name," she replied.

"But you've met him?"

"Keep your mouth shut," Mick hissed at her.

Denton slammed Mick's head against the wall.

"A few times. But he seldom comes here. Why?"

"These women . . . the dancers . . . are clones."

"You're certain?"

"We have plenty of evidence. We're just trying to find out who is behind it all. Where is the owner's office?"

"Follow me," Millie said, walking past.

The flaring pain beneath Denton's eye pulsed, and in response, he applied extra pressure to Mick's cuffed wrists until tears leaked from the man's eyes. "You're both dead," he muttered.

"Save it for the court," Denton said.

Millie led them to the end of the hall. Between the two rooms where Denton and Carpenter had searched and found TGC evidence was a lever. When she pulled it, a rectangle section hidden in the wall opened.

Denton swung the door open and entered. Millie flipped on the light. Spider webs coated the old desk and were a telltale sign that no one used this office very often. He pulled out the wooden chair and seated himself. Opening the side drawers, he found envelopes stamped with Grayson Enterprises as the return address.

He sighed. "I never thought Grayson would be tied to this."

"Why?" Millie asked.

"Our suspect trail led in a different direction."

Behind them, a deep voice threatened. "Put your gun on the desk. Now."

Denton turned to look over his shoulder and a safety clicked off. Millie put her gun on the desk and stepped back.

"Keys to the handcuffs," he said.

Denton reached into his pocket and turned to hand them to the man. He froze. "You? You're the owner of La Vida Erotica?"

The older man nodded and puffed a thick cigar. He quickly unlocked Mick's handcuffs. The owner was obese and bald, dressed in an expensive gray striped suit. His evil eyes pierced a violence Denton had never seen before. The coldness within his black pupils revealed his ease of killing dozens of people without a second thought or any conscience.

Although Denton had never seen this man in person, he recognized him. He was the man who had killed Carpenter's wife and child. Slayton Arton.

Chapter 63

Kat stayed in the shadows as much as possible and avoided the sidewalks beneath streetlights whenever she could. Twice she had hidden behind shrubs when a police cruiser eased down the street.

The cold night air hung like a marble barrier that blocked any hope of getting a prayer through the atmosphere. The night chill and her fear hampered her breathing.

Although no visible threat manifested its presence, Kat kept her gun drawn with the safety off. To venture where death lingered meant being prepared at all times. The only thing that she knew was a hit was being made on Typhis. What she didn't know was how many were being sent or exactly what she was up against. What frightened her most was that she might get caught in the crossfire.

Neither side cared if she survived or not. And deep inside, she didn't really care if Typhis died. She knew he was evil. However, she needed to identify the people that wanted him dead. The information was more valuable than stopping them from assassinating the mayor.

However, while she dwelt on these thoughts, she realized something else. Knowing the type of person Typhis was prevented her from allowing someone else to kill him. She understood that the greater punishment was for Typhis to live behind bars. He'd stew over his failures and probably lose what little sanity he had left.

Another police cruiser turned onto the street and approached the area where she was hiding. The officer flashed the side beacon light along the shrubbery. She dove onto her stomach and flattened out on the cold ground. The light washed over her. She closed her eyes and held her breath.

The cruiser continued its slow pace, and she sighed at the miracle of not being seen. When the car reached the next intersection and turned left, she rose and darted across the street.

Kat almost screamed when flakes of concrete ripped from the sidewalk. The bullet had missed her by mere inches. She bolted into more shadows, and another bullet struck the brick wall above her head.

Squatting and turning to see where to fire, she saw no one. Her chest heaved as she ran down the alley. From out of nowhere, she heard footsteps coming fast behind her. She dug her feet hard and fast, trying to pull away from whatever pursued her.

Glancing back, she saw two men, *undead* men, coming after her. Their grim faces resembled death reapers. One lifted a gun and aimed; she turned left and dove over metal garbage cans. The gun never fired. When she rolled to gain footing, a cold clammy hand grabbed her wrist.

Kat screamed and swung the butt of the gun into the thing's face. Bone cracked like thick eggshells. Its head snapped back with a sickening thwack. The undead human dropped to the ground, writhing. She fired into its head. The body convulsed and stiffened.

Before she had a chance to recover from her shock, the second man reached for her. She was running before his icy fingers touched her. Firing behind her as she ran, one bullet ripped into its right shoulder. The impact jarred him ever so slightly. Realizing her counter assault, it emitted a harsh growl.

She gulped in the cold air. Her lungs ached, but she kept running. She knew the slightest hesitation meant death, or worse.

The alleyway ended at another street. Less than fifty yards and she could meander through parked cars or hide to catch her breath. She sprinted harder.

Kat neared the end of the alley, and with relief seemingly close, she felt her ambition waver when a police cruiser turned into the alley ahead of her. Blue and red lights flashed atop the car. Bright headlights blared, causing her to shield her eyes, but she didn't stop running.

The car doors opened, and two officers aimed their guns at her.

"Drop the gun and put your hands in the air," the driver demanded.

She didn't want to stop running. Not with the man pursuing her. If she continued moving, they'd gun her down without question.

Daring a glance over her shoulder, the undead man had stopped moving and shielded his face from the blinding headlights. He didn't seem to be a threat anymore.

"Put down the gun and identify yourself," the officer said.

Kat understood if she revealed her name, she was dead. Even if she gave a false name, they'd probably shoot her for disobeying curfew.

"Last warning," the officer said. "Put down your weapon."

The gun shook in her hand. She didn't want to relinquish the only protection she had.

The undead man fired his gun, not at her, but at the squad car. The right headlight shattered and went dark.

Kat dropped to the ground and rolled against the brick wall.

The officers fired at the undead man. He gnashed his teeth and rushed toward them.

Kat's body shuddered from fear, and she couldn't stop herself from crying. An engine roared from the direction she had come. A black car sped through the alley toward the police car.

Three-fourths of the way from the cruiser, the high-speeding car struck the undead man in the back and crushed him against the front of the police car.

Gunshots echoed in the alley. The police officers dropped to the pavement dead, victims of the undead man. The driver of the black car ran to her.

He helped her to her feet and embraced her. She sobbed against his chest and after a few minutes she dared to look into his face. With surprise, she said, "Lucian?"

He smiled.

"How'd you find me?"

"I gambled by hoping you'd stick to the streets closest to the coroner's lab."

She said nothing more for several minutes. She clung tightly to him. When she looked up, he placed a gentle hand to her cheek and smiled.

The warmth of his hand and his smile sent chills through her. Fresh tears formed in her eyes.

"This isn't over yet," he said.

"I know." Kat pulled back and wiped her eyes.

They walked to the front of the car. The undead man was still alive and trying to unpin his ripped and bloody body. His undead partner stood over one officer. Lucian shot the undead man in the back of the head. The genetic zombie staggered forward, slowly dropping to his knees. His dead limp body lay atop the officer.

The undead man pinned between the two vehicles snarled and struggled to free itself.

Stunned, Kat said, "How?"

"Welcome to the genetic revolution," he replied.

"I'm quite certain this isn't how I want our world to become."

The man looked viciously at Kat and growled. He hissed and gnashed his teeth like an injured animal. His eyes looked dead, but his body continued fighting to pry himself free and escape. Lucian finally fired a round into its brain.

"I'd like to say that put it out of its misery, but we both know that's not true," Lucian said.

Kat checked her gun clip. "Typhis has put a hit out on me."

"Carpenter knows I'm the clone."

Her eyes widened. "You told him?"

He shook his head. "He's an expert at solving mysteries."

"I warned you."

Lucian examined the body of the undead man. "We may run into a few more like this, but it's the machine we have to worry about the most."

Kat replied with a confused stare.

"Matthews built a machine to kill Typhis. It's bulletproof."

"How do we stop it?"

"I've not figured that out yet."

Lucian pulled the dead officers away from the cruiser. "Get in," he said. "This is the fastest way to get to the courthouse undetected."

Chapter 64

Morton eased from the shadows into Lydia's room. Fred and Whitey scurried to the bed and hid beside the locked wheels. Bandit and Kip sat on the bed massaging their tired jaws.

"What are you doing in here?" Kip asked.

"No nurses," Morton replied.

Bandit yawned. "She's waking up."

Morton leapt to the bed. The cuffs had another inch or more to be cut through. The cat lengthened his claws and slid them into the gnawed groove. With gentle saw-like motions, he finished cutting through the leather straps.

Kip shook his head in disbelief. "Where were you an hour ago?"

Morton cocked an eyebrow. "You said that I should wait. But the sore jaw should keep your tongue quiet for a while."

Whitey laughed.

Kip frowned. "Something wrong with my voice?"

"No," Morton said. "Just your constant wise cracks."

Kip huffed and pouted.

Lydia coughed.

Morton eased closer to her face.

Her eyes opened and after several blinks, she recognized him. She smiled. "Where am I?"

"Grayson Enterprises," Morton replied.

She frowned. "Where is that? Last I remember I was in Nevada."

"They moved you."

Lydia eased herself into a seated position and looked around the room. She swung her feet over the side of the bed. Noticing the paper-thin gown, she said, "I need better clothes."

Kip pointed toward the door at the opposite side of the room. "Locker rooms are that way."

She looked at Morton. She said, "Please tell me they're like you or these bastards gave me one hell of a medical treatment."

Morton nodded. "Yes. They're enhanced rodents."

"Rats," Kip asserted.

Lydia placed her feet onto the cold floor and tested her balance before heading toward the locker room. After a few steps, she became more surefooted.

"Have you heard from Lucas?" she asked.

"He should be on his way."

"This whole ordeal has probably sent him over the edge."

Morton nodded. "He was hospitalized for a day."

Lydia turned quickly and said, "Is he okay?"

"Anxiety attack or something like that." Morton figured he'd let Lucas give her the exact information. No sense distracting her mind further.

She opened a locker and found a nurse's scrubs. Tennis shoes set in the bottom of the locker. She dressed. "Who's behind my abduction?"

"According to the rats," Morton said, "Steven Matthews."

"Then we find him. He'll answer for what he did to me and the pain he has caused Lucas."

"Carpenter, Kat, and Lucian are looking for him. Daniel is with Lucas, so we should have Matthews cornered soon."

Lydia flashed a grim smile. "If I have my way, he won't get out of here alive."

TYPHIS REFILLED HIS BOURBON GLASS. The empty streets no longer held his interest. He thought of the twins. He wondered if killing their mother had been his biggest mistake. Perhaps he should have taken her with them and forced her to raise them his way.

Anna's words had cut Typhis deeply. He understood that these children could never replace Simon and Trey. He needed someone prepared to assume his position after he died. How had he become so blind? He had chanced his sons' lives one too many times to prove their worthiness and lost them. Paul and Paula could never fill their absence. Besides, time wasn't cooperating. These two children were too young to replace him and rule his empire.

GRAYSON EXITED the elevator and found two of his guards dead. Anger flared inside him. His arm and chest muscles swelled and bulged. He didn't want to use a gun on Matthews. He'd rather seek vengeance by using his hands.

After he examined the bodies, he knew Matthews hadn't killed these two guards. Both men had been shot through the heart with pinpoint accuracy. Their deaths were instant. No struggles. He didn't know how good a shot Matthews was, but he was certain the man wasn't a marksman. He didn't seem the type of person to carry a gun.

Grayson stood and listened. He might not want to use a gun on Matthews, but he might need it for whatever else lurked within his building.

MICK SWUNG a sharp uppercut into Denton's stomach. Denton folded over and dropped to the floor. After several deep breaths, he turned and vomited out of Millie's sight.

"Mick," she said firmly. "Stop."

He smiled at her. "Yours is coming soon, honey. I can be gentle, if you'd like."

Her eyes narrowed and she spat at him.

"Suit yourself." He hammered a bare fist into Denton's jaw. He collapsed. His cut and bruised lips bled.

"Enough," Slayton said. "We need him alive. Tie them up, and when he's caught his breath, I'll be back. He has a message to send Carpenter."

JENSEN PARKED the car outside Grayson Enterprises. Carpenter stepped out and headed to the glass doors. They were locked. No one stood on the inside.

Jensen met him at the door.

"You have a key?" Carpenter asked.

"No. The doors should be open."

"At this hour?"

"There's always a guard posted."

Carpenter peered through the tinted glass. "Not tonight."

DANIEL, Lucas, and Joe met Carpenter and Jensen at the door. Lucas tried the door.

"It's locked," Carpenter said.

"Lydia's in there?" Lucas asked.

Carpenter nodded. "As best we can tell."

"There has to be another way inside."

Jensen shook his head. "If it's locked, only Grayson can let us in."

"Where is he?" Daniel asked.

"Inside."

"Dammit!" Lucas said.

Carpenter placed a hand on Lucas' shoulder. "Morton's in there, too. He's looking for Lydia."

Lucas nodded, somewhat relieved. "He's never failed us before."

"If anyone can find her, Morton can," Daniel said.

"So we just wait?" Lucas asked.

"Not much more we can do," Jensen said. "The glass is bulletproof."

"Is Grayson that paranoid?"

Jensen smiled. "No, just very cautious."

Chapter 65

Denton leaned forward in a wooden chair with his wrists cuffed behind his back. When he regained consciousness, his painful injuries reminded him where he was. His one eye was swollen shut. Immediately, he looked around for Millie.

She sat in another chair, restrained in the same manner.

"You okay?" she asked.

Through his good eye, he stared at her. "I'm alive. That counts for something. He didn't hurt you in any way, did he?"

Millie shook her head. "No, that fat asshole made Mick cuff me and leave me alone."

"He's your boss?"

"I've never seen him before. Who is he?"

"Slayton Arton. He's tied to the mob." Denton frowned. "If Slayton's not your boss, who did you see?"

"A younger man. Very arrogant."

Footsteps approached in the hallway. A key turned in the lock and the wooden door opened.

Slayton stood in the door. "Good. You're awake. I believe you've taken someone who belongs to me."

"Vanessa?"

"Yes."

"It's a capital offense to propagate humans for monetary gains. Not to mention what you did to her sexually."

Millie's frightened eyes met Denton's with surprise. "What did he do?"

"He raped her and every dancer in La Vida Erotica."

Millie gagged but prevented herself from vomiting.

Slayton shook his head. "Rape is such a harsh word. I'd like to think more of it as breaking them in for their jobs. Someone has to teach them."

"You sick son-of-a-bitch," Denton said. "We're going to push to have you put to death for your crimes. These clones are nothing more than little children in grown bodies. You haven't the right to violate them like that."

"They belong to me. I can do whatever I desire. Since prostitution is legal, I don't have to muscle in on drug trafficking anymore."

"It's perverted," Millie said.

"Not really. People love sexual fantasies, and they're willing to pay for it."

"Your women aren't exactly willing recipients."

Slayton gave a narrow smile. "I've had no complaints."

"I suppose not," Denton said, his face burning red with anger. "They're programmed to do whatever you command them to do. Except for Vanessa. She told us what happened. She remembered, and she'll testify to that fact."

"Ahh, sweet Vanessa. So gentle. So timid. I doubt in court she'll be able to face me. Her word against mine and all. Hard to prove your case based on a young woman's vivid imagination."

"We found the crates from TransGenCorp in your basement."

Slayton shrugged. "So?"

"You received the clones from TGC?"

"Perhaps."

"Since the government shut them down, and once we do the same here, no one can replace these women. This type of business will cease to exist."

Slayton smiled. The threats were merely useless words to him. He said, "Other facilities operate under the same type of human manufacturing. What's it matter?"

"It violates every human ethic that exists."

Mick stepped around Slayton. He held a limp, lifeless form over his shoulder.

"I tell you what," Slayton said, taking Denton's cell phone. He unlocked the handcuffs. "You call Carpenter and tell him to send Vanessa to us, and we'll let you live."

"You know that's not going to happen," Denton said.

Mick tossed the dead woman to the floor in front of Denton and Millie. When her limp body rolled over, Millie screamed. Denton cringed. He recognized her face. It was Violet.

"Convince him, or you and your girlfriend are as dead as her."

"You know he won't give you anything. He'll come to kill you for what you did to his wife and baby."

Slayton appeared amused. "Watching him die sounds more entertaining. Go ahead and tell him I'm here."

"Glad to," Denton said, dialing the number.

WITH THE BLUE and red lights flashing as Lucian drove, they passed two other patrol cars and as he believed, the other officers never suspected anything.

"What exactly are we looking for?" Kat asked.

"A metal machine that hovers, and more of those undead men."

"Shouldn't we head straight to the courthouse? We can intercept this machine before it assassinates Typhis."

Lucian shrugged. "I suppose we could try that, but none of the patrol cars have stopped. They're all on patrol. If we park and wait, they'll suspect us."

"Then let's circle the courthouse."

"We'll head that direction."

When they slowed at a stop sign, the Probe zipped past. Another squad car pursued it. Lucian pulled in behind the car and followed. The radio informed more units of the pursuit and requested officers to block the next intersection.

Lucian pressed the accelerator until the car pushed seventy miles per hour. The Probe moved much faster than he had anticipated. The officers ahead of them were about to discover the other technological advancements this machine possessed.

Two patrol cars screeched to a halt and formed a roadblock. The Probe fired two laser blasts. The front tires on each car smoldered and expelled air. The front ends of the cars lowered. The officers stepped from their vehicles with their guns drawn.

Hover jets blasted and the Probe gained more speed, striking where the frontends of both cars met. The collision shoved the cars aside. The Probe never stalled, never faltered. The four officers opened fire, but their harmless bullets flicked off.

Kat stared in disbelief. "What the hell is it made of?"

"Titanium, steel, and bulletproof glass."

"How do we stop it?"

"Still pondering that."

"They didn't tell you how?"

"No."

"Damn."

"Yep."

A bright laser shot behind the Probe and sliced the driver side tire of the pursuing squad car. The police cruiser careened sharply to the left. Lucian swerved to the right. Sparks flew from beneath the spinning car. The cruiser slammed into the side of a parked car, the tank split open and gallons of fuel leaked out. Seconds later, the car was engulfed in flames.

Lucian didn't slow, but he was leery of coming too close to the Probe.

"We need to find a shortcut to the courthouse and cut it off. If we continue to follow, it will try to kill us. It's a war machine."

Kat typed in some commands to the map guide program. Seconds later, an alternate route appeared on the screen.

"Turn right up ahead."

The Probe went straight and they turned right. He sped down the street, and she pointed. "Make a left at that light."

He did.

"Three blocks ahead and we're there."

Lucian pressed harder on the accelerator.

HELMSBY AND YVONNE stood in his laboratory when the lights in the hallway went out.

"What happened to the outside lights?" he asked.

"I don't know."

The lab lights blared brightly. The absence of light on the outside made the inside of the window reflect like a mirror and prevented them from seeing out. On the reverse side of the glass, they were easily seen by anyone in the hallway.

The two undead guards stood in the shadowed hall. They raised their guns. A nurse left her station and approached. Seconds later, she was dead.

Their attention turned to Helmsby's lab again. In the brightness of the room he stood. They pointed their guns and aimed.

Chapter 66

Lydia rubbed Morton's head. "I'm thankful you came for me," she said.

Kip frowned and waved his forelegs in the air. "Sure, give the cat all the credit."

She smiled. "Sorry, of course, I'm thankful for all of you, too."

Lydia eased to the door and glanced out at the nursing station. She didn't see anyone in the darkness. Morton's eyes blazed red.

"Trouble in the hall," he said, running ahead of her.

Morton noticed the dead nurse and beyond her body, he saw the men with their guns trained on Helmsby. He growled and rows of sharper teeth lined his mouth.

Lydia was beside him and the men's attention suddenly turned toward them. Morton sprang forward in fast strides. The first man aimed, but Morton rolled and came up in the air with both forepaws extended. Razor-sharp claws sprouted outward.

The cat latched into the man's face, shoving the claws through his skull. The man toppled backwards. Lydia grabbed the second man's wrist and twisted. Bones snapped and the gun dropped to the floor.

The man snarled and hissed. She spun around behind him and grabbed his head. One sharp twist and his neck snapped. She dropped him to the floor, but he wasn't dead.

Even with a broken neck, he attempted to crawl toward his gun. She took the 9mm and fired a final headshot. His body became limp.

Morton tugged, but his claws were stuck in the other man's skull. He had managed to plunge his claws deep enough to kill him, but he couldn't pull them out. The rats cautiously scurried toward them.

Morton looked at Kip and shook his head. "Damn, this is so embarrassing."

Kip beamed back a smile but said nothing.

Morton struggled to pull his claws from the undead man's skull and finally yanked them free with a sickening wet sound.

Lydia took the other 9mm and tucked it behind her belt. She opened Helmsby's lab door and stepped inside.

"Lydia!" Helmsby said. "You escaped?"

"No help from you," she said with a harsh glare.

Yvonne stepped forward and said, "No, dear, we would have gotten you out if we could. We weren't allowed to go where they had you."

"How long have I been here?"

"Less than twenty-four hours. Honestly, we tried to find a way to get you. Nancy got a message to Kat. Help should be on the way."

Lydia's anger calmed. "Someone wants you dead," she said. "Morton and I just killed two men in the hall. Another ten seconds and they'd have succeeded in killing you."

Helmsby cupped his hands against the glass and peered through. The two dead men sprawled on the floor made him shudder.

"What should we do?" he asked Lydia.

"Turn out the lights and find a place to sit and hide."

Helmsby nodded.

"Any idea where I can find Steven Matthews?" she asked with an even smile.

"No."

"After I find him, I'll be back for you."

RIGHT AFTER CARPENTER picked the lock at the entrance of Grayson Enterprises, his cell phone rang.

"Hello?" he said. "What?"

Carpenter paled.

"You okay?" Lucas asked.

"I'll be okay," he said. "Go find Lydia."

"You want me to go with you?" Daniel asked.

"No. Stick together. Jensen knows the building. He can take you to Lydia. I have to make a quick trip."

Chapter 67

Dr. Wilks followed Matthews to Lydia's room. Her body wasn't there.

"It's not possible," Matthews said. "She was heavily sedated."

Wilks examined the I.V. pump. "She had help. The pump is off, and the needle is under her pillow."

"The restraints were locked."

"Look at the leather."

Matthews held up one chewed strap and exchanged glances with Wilks. "It looks like an animal chewed through this."

"I agree."

"How? The action was deliberate. No animal could . . . Dammit! Follow me."

Matthews stormed from Lydia's bed and headed for the animal lab. He scanned the cages. Four rats were missing.

"You think the rats escaped and freed her?" Wilks asked.

"The evidence is damn convincing, don't you think?"

"What motivation would they have?"

Matthews shrugged. "I have no idea. Rats? Hell, there'd be no motivation. But now I know the formula and injections worked. They're far more intelligent than we gave them credit for. Hell, they even played dumb to fool us."

"But if she's free . . . "

Matthews shook his head and then it dawned upon him. "Shit. She's coming after us."

"Tell her to get in line," Grayson said with his gun aimed at Wilks' chest.

TYPHIS RETURNED to the balcony with a glass of bourbon. Using an FM transmitter radio, he awaited information from the police. Nothing had come yet. He had hoped to hear the news of Kat's demise. She had to be in the city. He sensed her.

Since he hadn't heard back from the coroner, he believed the man had failed to kill Kat. However, if John had informed her of the death mark, Typhis had the feeling she'd come after him.

The icy wind flailed his withered body. The layers of clothing he wore didn't lessen its chill. An old man with a degenerating body couldn't battle the elements like a younger, healthier person. His mind pictured the wind as the hand of death wrapping around his tired, dying body. Until his new twins were enlisted and ready to replace him, he'd duel off death as long as he possibly could.

Sirens wailed in the streets. A pursuit. He smiled. Perhaps Kat's death was in process. He set down the bourbon and rubbed his hands together, hoping to warm them.

Flashing lights appeared in the distance. Ahead of them was a silver blur. He focused on the unusual object. Even when it came closer, he didn't have a clue what it was.

The wailing squad car silenced when the silver object fired countless blasts of light at it. Whatever the object was, its destination appeared to be him. His sanctuary suddenly seemed a prison. He dropped his glass of bourbon. Seconds later, the glass shattered on the sidewalk below.

Afraid to discover what approached the courthouse, Typhis also feared not knowing what was coming. He couldn't leave the balcony. The silver object was a hypnotic nemesis. His sudden fear swallowed his hope and arrogance.

LUCIAN PUT the cruiser in park outside the courthouse. He and Kat hurried to the door. They were shocked to find the door unlocked. The Probe could arrive at any time. Since they didn't know how to stop the machine, they had to find Typhis and warn him. As much as Kat hated the thought, it was her duty to protect him. They ran to the elevator and waited for the doors to open.

THE PROBE HOVERED on the sidewalk beneath Typhis' balcony. He studied it with sheer amazement. The engines roared and slowly the Probe ascended.

Typhis stepped back from the balcony edge. The machine hovered and slowly spun around to face him. His mouth gaped open. Tyler's pallid face forced Typhis to cry out in despair.

"No. God, no," he cried and dropped to his knees. "My son, I failed you. I'm sorry."

The Probe lowered onto the balcony floor and eased toward him. Mechanical levers operated Tyler's mouth, making it open and close. No audible words released in the motions. Streaks of dried blood from his eyes and ears lined his cheeks.

Regret brought the memories of his son begging for help and forgiveness the day Typhis had given the orders to cryogenically store Trey's head. In his madness, he had killed his own.

Tyler hadn't failed his father, he finally realized. It was the other way around. He had failed his son. Although he grieved over his sons, he hadn't understood Tyler's shock of losing his brother as being an emotion he had not been taught. Grief.

Typhis cried and continued apologizing. Agony broke his spirit.

THE ELEVATOR OPENED. Kat led Lucian to the office where she and Carpenter had questioned Typhis. The door stood ajar, so they entered the eerily cold room.

A scream of anguish wailed from the other end of the office. Lucian ran and pulled back the curtains. The sliding glass doors were open.

Typhis lay on his back with a hole burnt through his left shoulder. His wide eyes didn't blink. The Probe disappeared over the balcony edge and descended to the sidewalk below. The engines shut off. The Probe went silent.

"Why did it shut itself off?" Kat asked.

Lucian stooped to pick up a chess piece. He shook his head. A black King.

"It finished its assignment," Lucian said.

"The game is over?"

He shook his head. "No, we need to find the person who claims to be the red King."

Typhis' body suddenly heaved in a large gulp of air. He blinked and his eyes searched the balcony. They rested on Kat. His eyes indicated he had something to confess. They pleaded for her to come closer. She leaned down to hear him.

In a frail voice, he said, "The twins are in the basement. My pocket. Take the key. It unlocks the door. Tell Anna that I'm sorry. She won't protest you taking them."

Kat slid the heavy brass key from his jacket pocket. "This one?"

He nodded. "On my desk," he said. "The green button turns off the phone tower blockers. Press it."

His eyes became distant. His chest sank to breathe no more.

Lucian nudged Typhis but he didn't move. He checked for a pulse. Nothing. "He's dead."

"Don't get mad if I shed no tears," she replied.

"You want to dance? I'll dance with you."

She smiled. "No. Let's get those kids. No telling what mental damage they've suffered."

"They're young. Youth are resilient."

She shook her head. "Not always, Lucian."

"We can hope."

"I do."

Chapter 68

Grayson held the gun on Matthews. "Your loyalty has betrayed you."

Matthews frowned. "What are you implying?"

"You deny that you're going to kill me and Dr. Helmsby?"

"Oh. *That?*"

Grayson's huge hand tightened around the gun. "That."

Matthews shrugged. "Can't blame a man for having ambition."

"There's no ambition in dying."

"You can't say you're not possessed by greed."

Grayson smiled. "I don't need to kill to get what I desire."

"You're just pissed that I betrayed your trust."

Grayson laughed. "I've never trusted you. Not fully. You think your labs are coded to keep everyone else out? I have access to everything you operate here. I have an override code to your security panels. I'd be a fool otherwise."

"If you lacked trust, why'd you hire me?"

"I had hoped your intellect might enrich Grayson Enterprises. You stood to obtain great wealth under me."

Matthews gave a smug smile. "Greater wealth if I removed you."

"I think the situation has reversed."

Matthews laughed. "You're going to kill us?"

Grayson shrugged. "You created men and killed my guards. You hired

Dr. Wilks and kidnapped Lydia. It really doesn't matter if I kill you. There's a line of others waiting for that chance. I do have to commend you though."

"Why?"

"Those resurrected dead men. That's quite an accomplishment."

Matthews nodded.

"Too bad you chose not to share your ideas with me. We could have worked well together."

"Never. I resent you too much."

"I suppose our heads butt too much."

"They won't again."

Matthews grabbed Wilks from behind and wrapped his arm around his throat. Matthews pulled his gun to fire. Grayson pulled the trigger. The bullet struck Wilks in the chest. Grayson aimed again, but Matthews shoved the doctor at Grayson and ran.

Wilks gasped for air, clutching the fiery wound with both hands.

"Sorry, Wilks," Grayson said, stepping over his body. "You put your trust in the wrong man."

He peered around into the next room. Matthews wasn't there. Footsteps echoed up the stairwell. He shook his head in disgust.

"God help you if Lydia finds you before I do."

Grayson headed to the back of the room. Beside a bookcase, he pressed a small button that blended into the tile. A concealed elevator door opened. After he entered, he pushed the penthouse button to where Matthews' office was. Even in Matthews' elaborate design of his laboratory wing, he never knew about Grayson's hidden elevator.

JENSEN LED DANIEL, Lucas, and Joe to the elevator. They exited on the third floor.

"That's Dr. Helmsby's lab," Jensen said.

Daniel swung the door open. "Why are the lights out?"

"Daniel?" Helmsby said. "What are you doing here?"

"We're trying to find Lydia."

"She's gone after Matthews. She'll kill him if she finds him."

Lucas shook his head and grabbed Jensen's sleeve. "Where would he be?"

"Matthews has his own wing, and only he has access to the security codes."

"So there's the chance we can find her before she finds him?" Lucas asked.

"Unless he's left his laboratories, she won't be able to get to him."

"That's good," Lucas said. "Maybe we can prevent her from doing something she'll regret later."

***

CARPENTER ENTERED La Vida Erotica with his gun drawn. Two bouncers lay unconscious outside the main doors. He resorted to violence only when necessary and when the two men tried to manhandle him, he had no choice. He used the butt of his gun to sweet talk his way inside.

The loud music blared. The semi-nude women danced. They still possessed their hypnotic trances, and their slow, swaying dance moves mesmerized the onlookers. Carpenter eased toward the side stage curtain. Swift footsteps came from behind, and he turned to see another bouncer rushing at him. The man held an empty beer bottle and swung at Carpenter's head.

Carpenter ducked and swung a left jab into the man's gut. Air expelled from his mouth.

Carpenter struck the man's jaw with his second swing. The bouncer's head careened against the bar. He slumped between two barstools and didn't move.

He didn't fear the bodyguards. But if the information Denton had disclosed was true, he didn't want Slayton Arton slipping through his fingers again.

Carpenter clenched his jaw tightly. He remembered the mangled car the paramedics had pulled his pregnant wife out of. Tears welled and burned his eyes. The message of her death was a warning for him to back off. The lust for revenge, however, never died. Slayton may have had great power within his circle, but he had pissed off the wrong agent.

The garbage truck that ran the stop sign and collided with her compact car was no accident. Her routine had been the same for months, so he had no doubt that Slayton had planned for the truck to ram her vehicle and kill her at the appropriate time.

After beating Slayton unconscious, he had achieved some satisfaction, but he regretted not killing him. When Slayton dropped the charges, the press speculated his innocence and made Carpenter the villain. Then Slayton disappeared. Some thought he fled the country. Not Carpenter. He believed Slayton resided where he could watch and savor Carpenter's inner destruction.

Returning to his empty apartment each day and seeing the baby bed, changing table, and remembering all the dreams he and his wife had shared before her death, Carpenter failed to properly deal with his loss. He turned to heavy drinking to numb himself and to quiet his rage.

If Slayton was here, badge or no badge, Carpenter planned to tilt the justice scales the right direction this time.

The music faded after he passed through the side stage door. Several dancers stood at the stage entrance, waiting for their announced cue from the DJ. Their eyes never glanced toward him.

Carpenter kept his finger to the side of the trigger so he could access it quickly should someone advance from the shadows.

The musty corridor narrowed. The winding ropes for the curtains were tied near the wall. Stepping around the ropes, Carpenter heard Denton cry out down the hall. He hurried to reach him.

Carpenter never saw the man swing the mop stick until the stick was inches from his face. He brought up his right hand to block the blow and his gun spiraled across the floor. The pain in his forearm was instant.

His assailant charged and pivoted the end of the handle into Carpenter's stomach. Carpenter bent forward, grabbed the handle, and rolled. The handle split in half.

From the corner of his eye, he saw the bodyguard coming. Carpenter tightened his left hand around the crude wooden spear and drove it into the man's thigh. The man wailed. Carpenter shoved the sharp tip deeper and twisted. The bodyguard fell on his back, clutching his wound.

Carpenter found his 9mm and continued down the hallway. He rounded the corner. Mick slapped Denton's face. Blood leaked from his agent's mouth and nose. Anger swelled inside Carpenter. He raised the gun and fired.

The slug ripped a hole in the plaster wall near Mick's head. He turned and faced Carpenter with a stunned expression. Carpenter lowered the gun and aimed at Mick's head.

"Step away from my agent," Carpenter said.

Mick raised his hands in surrender.

"Uncuff them," he said.

Mick nodded.

The sound of gunfire echoed behind Carpenter. The heat of the bullet ripped through his shoulder and burned with such severe pain that he dropped his gun.

Carpenter clasped his shoulder and slumped against the wall. Warm, sticky blood coated his fingers. A hand shoved him to the floor between Denton and Millie.

Taking a deep breath, he rolled to see Slayton and Vincent standing right inside the door.

"It's been a long time," Slayton said.

Carpenter winced and shook his head. "Not long enough, I'm afraid."

***

GRAYSON EXITED the elevator and waited. He expected Matthews to arrive at his office in minutes. If Matthews planned to flee, he needed his files. The Red Pawn Murders weren't a mystery to Grayson anymore. Matthews was the prime suspect, and Grayson knew why. Matthews wanted the tissues from GenTech. Setting up a scandal with a line of murders made it easier to conceal the theft, but Matthews' greed had gotten the best of him. He had tried to take too much too quickly.

Footsteps stopped a floor down on the metal, spiral stairs. Grayson hid behind the office door. He smiled and waited.

***

LYDIA RETURNED to the room where she had been bound. Dr. Wilks lay dead. She paused when she recognized his face. He was the man at Desert Labs. She gritted her teeth. The bastard was already dead.

Morton looked up at her. "You know him?"

"He's the one responsible for bringing me here."

Kip pointed to the spiral stairs. "Matthews uses those stairs."

She headed for them.

"Wait," Kip said. "We might be able to help find him."

"How?" she asked.

"Place us above the ceiling tiles. He's either on the next floor or the one above. We can get there faster if you put us up there."

Lydia popped a tile upward. Scooping the rats two at a time, she placed them into the ceiling crawl space.

She looked at Morton. "And you?"

"*We* take the stairs."

Lydia nodded and ran for the stairs.

MATTHEWS STOPPED on the second floor of his laboratories. He had no idea where Lydia was, but she was loose in the building. From what Wilks had told him, she sought revenge religiously. When she found him, she'd kill him.

Before he escaped, he wanted to retrieve the data necessary to continue his undead projects. He listened for Grayson. Grayson had seen him take the stairs, and the determination in his eyes was enough for Matthews to take caution. Between Grayson and Lydia, he had little hope to escape alive. Of course, he had his gun, but his inexperience overshadowed any promise of taking them out before they killed him.

Bullets wouldn't stop Lydia. Wilks had mentioned that, too. The fact that she had killed four men at Desert Labs trying to escape brought him additional apprehension. She was dangerous, to say the least.

LUCAS and the others found Dr. Wilks' body just a few minutes after Lydia ascended the stairs. Daniel stood at the foot of the stairs when the gun fired a couple floors up.

"Hurry!" Lucas said, running past Daniel.

Chapter 69

Grayson's patience paid off. Matthews stepped into the threshold of his office. Grayson swung around and slammed his huge fist into Matthews' nose. He failed to see Matthews' gun. The gun fired, missing Grayson by an inch.

The impact of the punch lifted Matthews into the air. He plummeted backwards. His back hit the top metal stair. He cried out in pain and rolled down to the next floor. The gun fell through the rungs to the carpet below.

Grayson followed.

Matthews struggled to pull himself up. Blood gushed from his broken nose. When he came to his feet and turned to flee, Lydia stood face to face with him.

"I could kill you in an instant, Mr. Matthews," she said with a smile. "But where's the fun in that?"

The blood drained from Matthews' face. His eyes widened as he stared at the gun in her hand. Swallowing hard, he knew his life was over. Then, unexpectedly, she tossed the gun aside.

She struck him in the face before he noticed her hand move. He wiped blood from his nose and mouth and stared at it. She swung again. He pivoted off balance and dropped to the floor.

Matthews had never known pain. Always pampered by his wealthy parents, he had been given everything he ever wanted—the best clothes, the best private schools, and expensive cars. Not once had he ever been in a fight.

Breathing through his nose was impossible. Blood flowed down the back of his throat. He took deep breaths through his mouth and tasted blood. His lip pulsed with each heartbeat. The air stung the split skin. The room seemed to drift in and out. The pain in his back radiated with each gulp of air he inhaled. He blinked several times, hoping the room would quit spinning. On the floor, just inches away, lay his gun.

Matthews stretched his arm for the gun. Lydia grabbed his ankle and tugged him back.

"Get up!" Lydia said.

Matthews pulled himself into a seated position and slowly rose to his feet. She swung a sharp right into his ribs. He winced and fell to his knees.

"Kill him," Grayson said from behind her.

"Oh, I intend to," she seethed.

Matthews flung his hands before him and waved a weak surrender.

Lydia brought a solid roundhouse kick to the side of his head. He fell and rolled twice.

Beneath him, the cold gun pressed against his skin. Acting like he was trying to push himself to his feet, he positioned the gun in his hand. He swallowed hard, took a deep breath, and rolled to his side to aim at either Lydia or Grayson.

A squeal came from the ceiling. Kip dropped and landed on Matthews' head. He clamped his teeth down on Matthews' ear. Matthews fired a wild shot that struck the wall.

Morton leapt into the air and sliced the back of Matthews' hand, making him drop the gun. Lydia kicked the gun aside. She lifted Matthews and threw him across the desk. She grabbed the desk lamp and slammed it against the side of his head. He tried to shield his face with his arms but failed. He moaned in pain.

"Please don't," Matthews begged.

"You don't have a choice in what I do," Lydia said. "You're no longer in charge. I am. What I had to say didn't matter then, did it? You still wanted to proceed with your experiments. You wanted to use me as your prototype."

"I'm sorry," he said.

"You bastard. You're going to be very sorry."

Lucas entered the room with Daniel and Joe. "Lydia. It's over."

"Not until he's dead, it isn't."

"Lydia, please," Lucas said. "I understand your need for revenge."

She glared at him. "You understand *nothing*. I'm a laboratory project. I always will be. They'll never stop. Not unless I make examples of them. Others will come for me."

"Easy," Joe said with a gentle voice. "You're safe now. You're with family. We'll protect you. Come home with us."

Tears moistened her eyes. Her shoulders slumped. Lucas spread out his arms to her. She ran to him, and he embraced her. He whispered in her ear as she cried.

Morton sat at Daniel's feet and stared up at him. He tapped his forepaw to his chest. "Family reunions. They always get you right here."

Daniel stooped down and picked the cat up. He rubbed his head. "I've missed you."

Morton shook his head. "Not in front of them."

Daniel frowned. "Why? They know our bond."

"No, the rats. Not in front of them. Makes me look weak."

"What rats?"

Morton answered with a direct nod. The four rats sat a few feet away. Fred waved.

Daniel gave Morton a perplexed glance.

Morton smiled. "Oh, they're in need of a home. I kinda promised they could come home with me."

"Why?"

"Remember how I expressed I'd like some friends other than humans?"

Daniel nodded.

"By the way, they talk, too. Kip's a total smartass."

"Hey!" Kip said.

Grayson walked around the desk and pulled Matthews to his feet. He pinned Matthews' arms behind his back.

"I'll have the authorities here in a few minutes," Grayson said.

Chapter 70

Carpenter pressed a handkerchief into his bullet wound to stop the bleeding. The hole ached but not as badly as it had.

"Since you're not willing to give me Vanessa, I have a new request," Slayton said. "Send Lydia to me. Or I'll kill all of you."

Carpenter shook his head. "You'll kill us anyway."

Mick yanked out the handkerchief and shoved his thumb into the wound. Carpenter winced.

"I can torture you for a long time," Slayton smiled. "How about we start with Millie? Mick's wanted in her pants for months. Here's his chance. You all can watch. He likes to dish it out rough, too. Afterwards, if she's still conscious, Vincent will take his turn."

Mick unfastened his belt.

Carpenter saw the fear in Millie's wide eyes. Knowing what Lydia had done in self-defense at her farm and what she was capable of, provided she had been rescued by now, bringing her here was a nightmare Slayton would never suspect.

"I don't have a way to contact those who have Lydia," Carpenter said. "But a friend of mine could bring her here."

Slayton nodded. "Make the call."

Carpenter took his phone from Slayton. He dialed Kat's number.

"Hello?" Kat said.

"We have ourselves in a situation at La Vida Erotica."

"What happened?"

Carpenter took in a couple deep breaths. "Slayton's here."

"Oh, God."

"In exchange for our lives, he wants Lydia brought here. Otherwise, he's going to kill me, Denton, and Millie."

"Are you okay?" Kat asked.

"I took a round in the shoulder, but I'm holding together."

"I'll call Daniel to see if they've gotten Lydia free."

"Do that."

"Typhis is dead. We have the twins and are bringing them to head-quarters."

"Good. Send Lydia."

"I'm on it."

Carpenter ended the call and handed the phone back to Slayton. "She's on her way."

<hr>

"WHO WAS THAT?" Lucian asked.

"Carpenter. He's been shot."

"Seriously?"

"Slayton has them hostage and wants Lydia."

"Why?"

She shrugged. "Probably for the same purpose as Matthews. He must have something to do with the clone dancing prostitutes."

Lucian smiled. "I doubt he has a clue as to what Lydia is capable of doing."

"He will soon find out. I'm calling Daniel."

<hr>

DANIEL'S PHONE RANG. After he answered it, Kat explained the situation.

"Luke," he said after he disconnected the call. "We have a problem."

"What?"

Daniel told them what Kat had said.

Lydia's eyes narrowed. "I'll go."

"Wait," Lucas said. "We have just gotten you back."

"I don't care. If he's anything like Matthews, we stop him tonight, too."

Daniel looked at Grayson. "How far are we from La Vida Erotica?"

"At this hour? I'd say with the lack of traffic, you could be there in about fifteen minutes."

"Okay, we free Carpenter and the others."

Grayson smiled. "I'll keep an eye on Matthews until the authorities arrive."

"I'll stay, too," Joe said, giving Grayson a solemn, but stern glare.

KAT AND LUCIAN left the twins at the FBI headquarters and rushed to La Vida Erotica. Daniel and the others were already waiting outside.

Police cars parked along the street with their lights blaring, but none of the officers had attempted to enter. Kat motioned to the police captain. Captain Hawkins hurried to her.

"Carpenter, my supervisor, has been shot and is being held hostage by Slayton Arton. Two others are also hostage. My associates and I are going to rescue them."

"That's suicide."

Lucian shook his head. "We're experts in situations like this."

The Captain looked back at Kat. "What do you want us to do?"

"Get the dancers to safety. Keep them in custody. They're not criminals, but victims that we need to interview and help."

"And the patrons? What about them? If we make the dancers leave, we might have a riot."

Kat smiled. "Threaten to charge them with child porn."

"The dancers are underage?"

"In one sense, yes, you could say that. This place will be shut down for good after tonight."

Lydia stopped and stood beside Lucian. He said to her, "We should enter ahead of the others."

Lucas frowned. "Why?"

"She and I heal faster should we suffer any injuries. We can also move with stealth. It's our nature. Any accidental gunfire and Slayton is liable to kill Carpenter and the others."

A strange smile crossed Lydia's face. The look terrified Lucas. Her hunger and thirst for bloodshed hadn't ended. Could he ever reel her back from what she truly was?

Lucas started to say something but before he did, Lydia ran through the front door and headed for the side stage door. She paused at the door but saw no one.

She pushed the curtain aside and passed through. A bodyguard hidden in the shadows pressed a gun to the back of her head. Lucian grabbed the man's wrist, caught the trigger before it released, and snapped his arm. Before the man howled in pain, she turned and thrust a fist into his throat, crushing his windpipe. Lucian shoved the man onto a pile of sandbags.

They headed further down the dark corridor. Lucas followed from a distance. With all he had experienced in the past thirty-six hours, he feared that after getting her back, he might lose her to what Idris had created her to be.

From a side dark entrance hall, another bodyguard emerged. He crept up behind Lucas and placed a sharp knife to his throat.

"Straight ahead," the man said to Lydia. "Or he dies.'

Lucian turned with a frown, seething. He whispered to Lydia. "I can take him out."

"No," she said. "He'd slice Lucas' throat before you ever get close enough."

The man arched Lucas back and nodded. "Slayton is three more doors down on the left. Proceed or he dies."

Lydia turned, but Lucian ran ahead of her and vanished beyond the third door.

"If you do what your friend just did, he dies."

Lydia nodded and stopped outside the door. Carpenter was pinned between Mick and Vincent. Blood stained the lapel of his coat. His pale face indicated he was about to lose consciousness. His eyes were weak. Behind Carpenter, leaning against the wall, stood Slayton. He smiled when he saw her.

Lydia rested her hands on the front of the belt Joe had given her to keep her scrubs tighter. Without much movement, she loosened two small daggers behind her buckle.

She stepped into the room. She decided not to attack until Lucas was safe. The man from the hall entered behind her, but he kept the blade tightly against Lucas' throat.

Slayton walked to the center of the room. "I see Matthews failed with his part of our operation."

"What exactly was that?" Lydia asked. "Imprisoning me to make clones?"

He shrugged. "That was only a fraction of what we set out to accomplish."

"Matthews is in custody."

"Nothing a few million bucks thrown to the right judge can't fix."

Lydia glared at him. "I won't go with you."

"You'd sacrifice the life of your husband?" Slayton said, smiling at Lucas.

"No," Lucian said, coming into the room. He had assumed Lucas' face. "You have the wrong man. *I'm* her husband."

A puzzled expression crossed Slayton's face. The man holding Lucas loosened his grip. The knife lowered from his throat. Glancing back and forth between Lucas and Lucian, Carpenter's eyes also widened.

In the few seconds that the man holding Lucas dropped his guard, Lydia flung a knife, missing Lucas by inches. The blade sunk into his captor's throat.

Lucas pulled forward, rolled, and came to his feet with a gun he removed from his bootstrap. He fired and hit Vincent in the shoulder. Lydia's second knife pierced Mick's heart.

Slayton went for his gun, but Lydia planted a foot into his stomach, knocking the air from his lungs. Lucian sideswiped his feet, and the heavy man hit the floor hard. He gasped to breathe.

Lydia stood over him and aimed the gun at his head.

Slayton chuckled. "Go ahead."

Her eyes narrowed with hatred. "Don't tempt me."

"No!" Lucas and Carpenter shouted.

"Do it!" Slayton yelled.

Her hand shook. Her finger looped around the trigger and she tightened it.

"Don't," Lucas said. "Please."

Lydia's brow furrowed. "People like him shouldn't live," she replied.

"No, maybe not," Carpenter said. "But if you want to see him tortured, let him rot in prison. That's a worse punishment than death."

"With what he planned to do to me? And the threats he made on your lives? I cannot let that pass."

"You think it's easy for me?" Carpenter said weakly. "He killed my wife and unborn baby."

The statement jolted Lydia. "And you don't want him dead?"

"I do. In so many ways, I do. I came here to kill him, but I've sorted through it. I know the type of person he is. He wants luxury at the cost of others. Strip that away, and he's nothing. Place him in a cell without the luxuries he lusts for, and his life is nothing but misery. Pull that trigger, and it all ends. He wins."

Lydia closed her eyes and took a deep breath. Lucas eased the gun from her hand. She turned to him and shook her head. He wrapped his arms around her.

Lucian waited for their embrace to cease and extended his hand to Lucas. "Sorry, bro, about not keeping my promise. I had to resemble you again. Otherwise, they'd have killed you."

Lucas shook his hand firmly. "Thanks. Not just for that, but for everything you did to help Kat find Lydia."

"Never a problem."

"But if you don't mind?" Lucas said with a smile.

Lucian laughed. "Change back?"

"Yes, it's kind of strange looking at myself like this."

Lucian nodded reluctantly. "I understand."

The muscles in his face shifted until he became the face Carpenter knew as Jake's. When he stepped away from Lucas, he saw Violet's lifeless body. His stomach sank. He had failed to protect her.

Kat entered the room and knelt beside Carpenter. "Are you okay?"

"Yeah, the gunshot isn't that bad," he said. "Better for me is knowing that after all these years, Slayton will finally serve his time behind bars."

"The paramedics are on their way," she said.

"That's good. Help me up, please."

Kat helped him to his feet. Lucian came nearer, and Carpenter grabbed his arm. "You and I need to do some serious talking.

Chapter 71

One week later

"DO you think the twins will go to a good family?" Kat asked.

"I'm sure. They're beautiful children," Lucian replied.

She looked from the hotel balcony at the waves crashing on the Hawaiian shore.

"I'm sorry about Violet," she said.

"We tried to protect her."

"She may have been a scientist, but she was also tied to the wrong people. She worked for Slayton."

"I know. You were right."

"I didn't want to be right. I just wanted you to be happy and safe."

Lucian took her hand in his and turned her to face him. She stared at him with soft eyes. "Kat, I know you're still hurting inside, too."

"It's lessened."

"Some of it will always be there," he said. "But if you'll let me, I'll love the pain away."

He pulled her closer and kissed her. She wrapped her arms tightly around his neck and kissed his lips.

Passion burned between them, and he led her back inside their room while kissing her. They fumbled at one another's clothes and fell to the bed. She sighed and moaned as his tongue slid between her breasts and further down her stomach. Her hands grabbed fistfuls of the sheet as he explored between her thighs.

Kat cried out and fell limp, her insides trembling. He pulled himself above her and leaned down and kissed her lips. Her fingernails dug in his back.

After they made love, he held her and stared into her brown eyes. "Things will never be the same between us, you know?" he said.

"I don't want them to be," she replied.

"We're partners in everything now."

"I think I like that. I like that a lot."

CARPENTER SAT THROUGH SLAYTON AND MATTHEWS' trials. Both men received life in prison, but somehow to Carpenter that never seemed enough. For people to prey upon others and ruin their lives, there really wasn't any way to exact justice. The misery of prison isolation was far different than the misery of loss, rape, and murder. Some mind plagues never relaxed, never faded. Even though he ached from his loss, he had the satisfaction of knowing he had helped exact partial justice.

With Denton and Millie's testimonies, La Vida Erotica was shut down. The clones were sent for mental evaluations and treatments. The hope for successful rehabilitation appeared very good.

As for Lucas' clone, Carpenter knew his gut feeling had been right. Jake, or whatever his real name was, was the clone. Too many facts had slipped in conversation for him to deny who he really was. But when he changed to his rightful appearance of being Lucas' clone, Carpenter had all the proof he needed.

Thinking through all the corrupt things the clone had done, and what the clone had done to aid in ending this case, Carpenter decided, for once, to look the other way. After all, had he not intervened by looking like Lucas, they all might have died. If he were truly evil, he would have let them die, but he didn't.

Besides, others had given Carpenter a second chance when he had allowed his rage to rule his life. After recovering from his alcoholism, he found people who had forgiven him in spite of his humanity. Why couldn't he?

LYDIA SAT with Lucas on their front porch. She said, "You know I love you, but I don't know if I can control myself anymore."

"I love you, too. There's nothing for you to control. You were kidnapped and your life was threatened. That's why you had to kill."

She placed her hand to his face. "Luke, you don't understand. There's a reason why they wanted me. It's what I was created to do. It's in my blood, or my genes. I cannot help what I am. You can't take it out of me."

"We'll get ourselves out of the limelight for a few years. Let our sport reputations die down, and things will be better. People will forget about us. Joe and his brothers said that we could build a ranch house on their property."

"The urges remain."

"What urges?"

"To hunt and stalk and kill."

"We can do that during hunting season."

Lydia shook her head. "I'm a predator. The darkness is inside me. I cannot change."

Lucas embraced her. "We'll get through this. Maybe we should seek a psychiatrist."

"I don't think it would help. Besides, it would make me appear crazier. Even hypnosis won't change me."

Lucas sighed. "What do you propose to do?"

"I don't know what to do."

He looked into her eyes. "Give me six months? We disappear from the circuit and live off the land. We can see if that helps."

Lydia kissed him. "Six months. After that, we'll see."

"Hon, I don't want to be without you."

"You never should have had me in the first place, dear."

Lucas closed his eyes. "I love you and I need you."

"I can honestly say the same to you, but inside, I cannot explain what's tearing my mind apart. I'm like a ticking time bomb. I don't want to hurt you."

"I know you won't."

"How can you be so sure?"

"It's not in your nature."

"Neither of us fully understands what my nature is. I fear what happens when we do."

"I'm here for you, no matter what happens."

"I hope that's enough."

HELMSBY FINISHED PACKING his laboratory supplies. Grayson stepped into the room. "Nothing I can say to keep you employed with me?"

Helmsby offered a bleak smile. "I'm sorry, sir, but no. After all the incidents, I simply have to retire. I never imagined scientific technology belonged to so many madmen."

Grayson laughed. "The irrational pursuit of geniuses generally leads to insanity. I'm sorry you won't be working on this project."

"It's a once in a life opportunity. I know in my elder years I'll look back with deep regret."

"And Nancy?"

"She's heading overseas."

Grayson gave a solemn nod. "To Germany's space program?"

"Yes. I think she wants to be in a new environment altogether since she won't be working with me."

"I understand." Grayson extended his hand. "I wish you all the best, Dr. Helmsby."

"And you, sir," Helmsby said, squeezing his hand.

Chapter 72

Felicia sat at her tea table wearing a ball cap turned backwards. Cheese puffs were distributed around the table, as were teacups of grape Kool-aid. The rats and Morton sat around the table, all wearing bonnets with curly hair. Morton decided that if he had to wear one, the rest of them did as well.

"What's the game?" Kip asked.

"Texas Hold 'em," Felicia said, shuffling the cards.

Bandit nibbled a cheese ball. "These are much better than those Fritos."

"Agreed," Whitey said.

Morton whispered, "Just don't drink the Kool-aid."

Fred's eyebrows rose. "I *like* the Kool-aid."

Kip shook his head. "Not only are you blind, your taste buds are shot, too."

Felicia placed two cheese puffs in the center of the table. "Okay," she said. "Who's in?"

The rats and Morton shoved cheese puffs in and stared at their cards.

Daniel stood at the door with his arm draped across Julia's shoulder. He smiled. "Who'd have thought rats could teach a little girl how to play poker?"

"I never would have," she said, rubbing her pregnant belly. "Wonder what they'll teach our son?"

Daniel pulled her closer and kissed her.

"Time will tell," he replied. "Time will tell."

JOE TOOK a brush and wiped loose soil from the artifact. The white bone gleamed bright in the desert sun. His brothers dug small pits along the ridge near him.

Their only known danger was rattlesnakes that sought cooler places along the ridge during the heat of the day.

Joe brushed away more soil and discovered the bone wasn't a fragment. Carefully, he lifted. Dirt and pebbles broke away. He brushed again and pulled. A skull.

He marveled as he examined the skull closer. It wasn't human. It also wasn't an animal, either. The top of the skull had two large bulging bulbs. Beneath them were the overly large eye sockets. Of all the archeological items they had discovered, this was the most unusual. Whether he molded clay to flesh the skull or not, he knew he had found the ancient skull of an alien.

Joe called to his brothers. When they rushed to see what he had found, each told him to bury it. The ancients might consider it sacred. What was sacred must remain where it was laid.

He nodded, but when his brothers returned to their pits, he carefully placed the skull into the knapsack.

ACROSS THE DRY gulch stood a man. Through binoculars, he witnessed Joe's discovery. His eyebrows rose with intense excitement. He slung his rifle over his shoulder and headed for his Jeep. Such a find was worth millions, if not more. If he needed to kill to possess it, so be it.

Desert Labs was closed. Once he possessed the skull, he would purchase the labs and reopen them. He smiled. This wasn't called Death Valley for any other reason.

About the Author

Leonard D. Hilley II grew up a quiet, shy kid with an inquisitive mind. Learning to read at an early age, he fell in love with books. He read every book he could get his hands on and stacks of dark comics about ghosts, monsters, and creepy things that stalk the night.

Like a lot of boys, he caught beetles, wooly bears, butterflies, and had an ant farm. When he was ten, his interests in science increased even more after seeing a professor's insect collection. Soon he set out on his quest to build his own collection. He also learned to rear butterflies and moths to obtain perfect specimens. He learned botany, gardening, and set his goal to become an entomologist.

At eleven, he watched the original Star Wars on the big screen. His imagination soared. Soon after, he discovered Roger Zelazny's Chronicles of Amber. Six months later, he had written the first draft of a novel. A novel he later discarded, but the characters stuck with him. Years later, these characters came to life in Shawndirea, which Hilley intended to be a novella for Devils Den. The characters, however, refused to be ignored and took the opportunity to unveil Aetheaon in their first epic fantasy. Lady Squire: Dawn's Ascension was quick to follow.

Shawndirea was Hilley's farewell to butterfly collecting, and those who have read the novel understand why. He has taken Ray Bradbury's advice to heart: "Follow the characters." He does. He follows, listens, and take notes—often never knowing where they're going to take him, but he's never been disappointed in the results.

Hilley earned a B.S. in Biology and an MFA in Creative Writing to combine his love of science and writing.

Sci-fi Titles: Predators of Darkness: Aftermath, Beyond the Darkness, The Game of Pawns, Death's Valley, The Deimos Virus.

Epic Fantasy: Shawndirea (Aetheaon Chronicles: Book One), Lady Squire (Aetheaon Chronicles: Book Two), Frosthammer (Aetheaon Chronicles: Book Three), Shadowfae (Aetheaon Chronicles: Book Four), and Devils Den.

UF/PR: Succubus: Shadows of the Beast (Nocturnal Trinity Series: Book One), Raven (Nocturnal Trinity Series: Book Two), A Touch of the Familiar (Nocturnal Trinity Series: Book Three)

YA UF/Paranormal: Forrest Wollinsky Vampire Hunter; Forrest Wollinsky: Blood Mists of London; Forrest Wollinsky: Predestined Crossroads.